PENGUIN BOOKS

COMPANY OF LIARS

Karen Maitland lives in Lincolnshire and is the author of *The White Room*, which won an Authors' ClubBest First Novel Award.

COMPANY
OF LIARS

a novel of the plague

KAREN MAITLAND

PENGUIN BOOKS

PENGUIN BOOKS

Published by the Penguin Group
Penguin Books Ltd, 80 Strand, London WC2R ORL, England
Penguin Group (USA) Inc., 375 Hudson Street, New York, New York 10014, USA
Penguin Group (Canada), 90 Eglinton Avenue East, Suite 700, Toronto, Ontario, Canada M4P 2Y3
(a division of Pearson Penguin Canada Inc.)
Penguin Ireland, 25 St Stephen's Green, Dublin 2, Ireland
(a division of Penguin Books Ltd)
Penguin Group (Australia), 250 Camberwell Road, Camberwell, Victoria 3124, Australia
(a division of Pearson Australia Group Pty Ltd)
Penguin Books India Pvt Ltd, 11 Community Centre, Panchsheel Park, New Delhi – 110 017, India
Penguin Group (NZ), 67 Apollo Drive, Rosedale, North Shore 0632, New Zealand
(a division of Pearson New Zealand Ltd)
Penguin Books (South Africa) (Pty) Ltd, 24 Sturdee Avenue, Rosebank, Johannesburg 2196, South Africa

Penguin Books Ltd, Registered Offices: 80 Strand, London WC2R ORL, England

www.penguin.com

First published by Michael Joseph 2008
Published in Penguin Books 2009

1

Copyright © Karen Maitland, 2008
All rights reserved

The moral right of the author has been asserted

Typeset by Rowland Phototypesetting Ltd, Bury St Edmunds, Suffolk
Printed in England by Clays Ltd, St Ives plc

ISBN: 978-0-141-03191-0

www.greenpenguin.co.uk

The Footsteps of the
Company of Liars

① ⋈ Kilmington
② ß Thornfalcon
③ < The Cave
④ ⟩ Woolstone
⑤ ⟩ North Marston
⑥ ✗ Northampton
⑦ ⅄ The Chantry
⑧ N Gasthorpe
⑨ | The Hermit's Island

Scotland

Cheviot Hills

York

Lincoln · · The Wash

The Fens

England ⑨ ⑧

⑥

Wales ④ ⑤

· Gloucester

· Bristol London

Chedzoy ③

②

① Melcombe

The truth is often a terrible weapon of aggression.
It is possible to lie, and even to murder, for the truth.

Alfred Adler, psychiatrist

Wir haben die Lüge nötig . . . um zu leben.

We need lies . . . in order to live.

Friedrich Wilhelm Nietzsche, philosopher

Prologue

'So that's settled then, we bury her alive in the iron bridle. That'll keep her tongue still.' The innkeeper folded his arms, relieved that they had finally agreed on that much at least. 'Iron'll counter any curses she makes. Stop anything, iron will. One of the most powerful things you can get to work against evil, saving the host and holy water. 'Course, it'd be better if we had some of that and all, but we don't, not with things being the way they are. But iron'll do just as well.'

His wife snorted. 'Tell that to our neighbours. There's not a door or shutter in the village that's not covered with iron horseshoes, but we might as well have hung chicken feathers on doors for all the protection they've given us.'

Her husband glared at her. 'But if the bridle gags her then she'll not be able to utter any curses, will she? So, iron or not, it'll still work.'

'But suppose she doesn't die?' the potboy wailed. 'Suppose she claws her way out through the earth and comes for us in the dead of night?' He stared round nervously at the door as if he could already hear her scratching at it. 'Couldn't we drive an elder stake through her heart afore we bury her? Then we'd know for sure she's dead.'

'God's bones, boy! Are you going to volunteer to drive a

stake into her while she sits there watching you? Because I'm certainly not.'

The potboy shook his head vehemently and shrank lower on his stool, as if terrified someone was going to thrust a stake into his hands and make him do it.

With an exasperated sigh, the innkeeper surveyed the dozen or so men and women slumped on the benches of his gloomy ale room. Though it was still daylight outside, the shutters were fastened tight and the door bolted. Not that the bolts were necessary, force of habit really. It just felt safer to draw a bolt. But bolts would not stop her finding out what was being planned, and as for passing strangers bursting in, no one, unless he had a death wish, would approach within ten yards of a building whose doors and shutters were closed, however desperate they were for a drink or a bite to eat.

The innkeeper had every reason to be impatient. If they didn't get the matter settled soon, it would be too late to act before dark. To face her in daylight was bad enough, to try to kill her at night, with only a candle standing between you and her powers, was enough to turn the bravest man's bowels to water, and after twenty-three years of marriage the innkeeper had no illusions that he was a brave man.

The blacksmith's voice boomed out deep and resonant from the alcove where he squatted in his favourite seat, his broad buttocks spilling over the well-worn bench. 'Bridle her and bind her tight, cover her in a foot or so of earth, then once she's smothered to death, I'll drive an iron stake into her through the soil. That ought to do it.' He rubbed an itching flea bite on his back against the rough wall. 'I'll do it just as the moon rises; it'll impale her spirit in the grave. She'll not rise then.'

The tanner took a gulp of ale and wiped his mouth on

the back of his hand. 'But I've heard tell, the only sure way is to slice the head off with a gravedigger's spade – once she's good and dead, of course.'

'That's the way to kill a vampire, but she's not one of them, leastways, there's been no talk of that.' This from the old woman at the back. Old and frail now, she'd birthed most of the people in the village and seen them buried too.

'Who knows what she is or what she could turn into once she's dead? She's not natural, that's for sure.'

Several heads nodded in agreement with the tanner. That was about the only thing they were agreed upon. In all the hours of discussion no one had uttered her name, not even the potboy. Even he knew there are some things it is wiser not to name aloud.

'I'm still of a mind we should burn her,' the old woman said. 'There'd be no chance of her rising then.'

'But she's not a heretic,' the innkeeper protested. 'It would be better for all of us if she was. Heretics' souls fly straight to hell. God alone knows where her soul would fly, into the nearest living thing, I wouldn't wonder, be it man or beast, and then we'd be left with a monster ten times worse.'

'Father Talbot would know the words to send her soul to hell,' the old woman persisted stubbornly.

'Aye, he would, but he's dead, don't you remember? As is half the village and we'll all be joining them if we don't find a way to kill her first. And since there's not a single priest left within four days' ride of here, we must make shift to do it ourselves. We can't go on arguing how it's to be done. We must finish her today, before the sun goes down. We daren't risk leaving her alive another night.'

The blacksmith nodded. 'He's right. Every hour she's alive she grows stronger.'

The innkeeper heaved himself up off the bench in an

attempt to put paid to any further discussion. 'So then, we're all resolved,' he said firmly. 'She's to be buried alive in the bridle. Then once she's dead, William'll fix her in her grave with the iron stake. The only thing left to decide now is who's going to put the bridle on her.'

He looked hopefully around the room, but no one met his eyes.

1. The Midsummer Fair

They say that if you suddenly wake with a shudder, a ghost has walked over your grave. I woke with a shudder on that Midsummer's Day. And although I had no way of foreseeing the evil that day would bring to all of us, it was as if in that waking moment I felt the chill of it, glimpsed the shadow of it, as if something malevolent was hovering just out of sight.

It was dark when I woke, that blackest of hours before dawn when the candles have burnt out and the first rays of sun have not yet pierced the chinks in the shutters. But it wasn't the coldness of the hour that made me shiver. We were packed into the sleeping barn too snugly for anyone to feel a draught.

Every bed and every inch of floor was occupied by those who had poured into Kilmington for the Midsummer Fair. The air was fetid with sweat and the belches, farts and stinks from stomachs made sour by too much ale. Men and women grunted and snored on the creaking boards, groaning as here and there a restless sleeper, in the grip of a bad dream, elbowed his neighbours in the ribs.

I seldom dream, but that night I had dreamt and the dream was still with me when I woke. I had dreamt of the bleak Lowland hills they call the Cheviots, where England and Scotland crouch, battle-ready, staring each other down. I saw them as plainly as if I had been standing there, the rounded peaks and turbulent streams, the wild goats and the wind-tossed rooks, the Pele towers and the squat Bastle farmhouses. I knew them well. I had known that place from the day I first drew breath; it was the place I had once called home.

I had not dreamt of it for many years. I had never returned to it. I could never return. I knew that much on the day I walked away from it. And through all the years I have tried to put it from my mind and, mostly, I have succeeded. There's no point in hankering for a place where you cannot be. Anyway, what is home? The place where you were born? The place where you are still remembered? The memory of me will have long since rotted away. And even if there were any left alive who still remember, they would never forgive me, could never absolve me for what I have done. And on that Midsummer's Day, when I dreamt of those hills, I was about as far from home as it is possible to be.

I've travelled for many years, so many that I have long since ceased to count them. Besides, it's of no consequence. The sun rises in the east and sinks in the west and we told ourselves it always would. I should have known better than to believe that. I am, after all, a camelot, a peddler, a hawker of hopes and crossed fingers, of piecrust promises and gilded stories. And believe me, there are plenty who will buy such things. I sell faith in a bottle: the water of the Jordan drawn from the very spot where the dove descended, the bones of the innocents slaughtered in Bethlehem and the shards of the lamps carried by the wise virgins. I offer them skeins of Mary Magdalene's hair, redder than a young boy's blushes, and the white milk of the Virgin Mary in tiny ampoules no bigger than her nipples. I show them blackened fingers of St Joseph, palm leaves from the Promised Land and hair from the very ass that bore our blessed Lord into Jerusalem. And they believe me, they believe it all, for haven't I the scar to prove I've been all the way to the Holy Land to fight the heathen for these scraps?

You can't avoid my scar, purple and puckered as a hag's arsehole, spreading my nose half across my cheek. They sewed up the hole where my eye should have been and over the years the lid has shrunk and shrivelled into the socket, like the skin on a cold milk pudding. But I don't attempt to hide my face, for what better provenance can you want, what greater proof that every bone I sell is genuine, that every drop of blood splashed down upon the very stones of the Holy City itself? And I can tell them such stories – how I severed a Saracen's hand to wrest the strips of our Lord's swaddling clothes from his profaning grasp; how I had to slaughter five, nay a dozen, men, just to dip my flask in the Jordan. I charge extra for the stories, of course. I always charge.

We all have to make a living in this world and there are as many ways of getting by in this life as there are people in it. Compared to some, my trade might be considered respectable and it does no harm. You might say it even does good, for I sell hope and that's the most precious treasure of them all. Hope may be an illusion, but it's what keeps you from jumping in the river or swallowing hemlock. Hope is a beautiful lie and it requires talent to create it for others. And back then on that day when they say it first began, I truly believed that the creation of hope was the greatest of all the arts, the noblest of all the lies. I was wrong.

That day was counted a day of ill fortune by those who believe in such things. They like to have a day to fix it on, as if death can have an hour of birth or destruction a moment of conception. So they pinned it upon Midsummer's Day 1348; a date that everyone can remember. That was the day on which humans and beasts alike became the wager in a divine game. That was the cusp upon which the scales of heaven and hell swung free.

That particular Midsummer's Day was born shivering and sickly, wrapped in a dense mist of fine rain. Ghosts of cottages, trees and byres hovered in the frail grey light, as if at cockcrow they'd vanish. But the cock did not crow. It did not recognize that dawn. The birds were silent. All who met as they hurried to milking and tending of livestock called out cheerfully that the rain would not last long and then it would be as fine a Midsummer's Day as any yet seen, but you could see they were not convinced. The silence of the birds unnerved them. They knew that silence was a bad omen on this day of all days, though none dared say so.

But, as they predicted, the drizzle did finally dry up. A sliver of sun, wan and weak, shone fitfully between the heavy clouds. It had no warmth in it, but the villagers of Kilmington were not to be downcast by that small matter. Waves of laughter rolled across the Green. Bad omen or not, this was their holiday and even in the teeth of a gale they would have sworn they were enjoying themselves. Outlanders had poured in from neighbouring villages to sell and to buy, barter and haggle, settle old quarrels and start new ones. There were servants looking for masters, girls looking for husbands, widowers looking for good strong wives and thieves looking for any purse they could cut.

Beside the pond, a gutted pig turned on a great spit and the smoke of sweet roasting meat hung in the damp air, making the mouth water. A small boy cranked the spit slowly, kicking at the dogs that jumped and snapped at the carcass, but the poor brutes were driven to near frenzy by the smell and not even the spitting fire or the blows from a stout staff deterred them. The villagers cut juicy chunks from the sizzling loins, tearing at them with their teeth and licking the fat from greasy fingers. Even those whose teeth were long worn down to blackened stumps sucked greedily at wedges of fat and pork crackling as the juices ran down their chins. Such a rare extravagance of fresh meat was to be savoured down to the last succulent bone.

Small gangs of barefoot boys rushed through the gossiping adults, trying to distract the scarlet-clad jugglers and bring their clubs crashing to the ground. Lads and lasses made free, oblivious of the damp grass and the disapproving frowns of priest and clerk. Peddlers shouted their wares. Minstrels played upon fife and drum, and youngsters shouted loud enough to wake the demons in hell. It was the same every year. They made the most of their fair, for there was precious little else to make merry with for the rest of the year.

But even in the jostling, noisy crowd you could not fail to notice the child. It was her hair, not blonde but pure white, a silk-fine tumble of it like an old man's beard run wild, and beneath this snowcap, a face paler than a nun's thighs, white eyebrows, white lashes framing eyes translucent as a dawn sky. The fragile skin of her bony limbs glowed ice-blue against the nut-brown hides of the other market brats. But it wasn't just the absence of colour in her that drew my attention; it was the beating.

Nothing unusual in a child getting a thrashing; I'd probably seen half a dozen already that day – a switch across bare legs for a carelessly dropped basket of eggs, a tanned backside for running off without leave, a cuff around the ear for no good reason except that the brat was in the way. All of the young sinners trying to dodge the blows and yell loudly enough to satisfy the chastisers that the punishment had been fully appreciated, all, that is, except her. She didn't yell or struggle, but was as silent as if the blows to her back were inflicted with a feather instead of a belt, and this only seemed to infuriate the beater more. I thought he'd whip her senseless, but finally, defeated, he let her go. She stumbled a few yards away from him, unsteady but with her chin held high, though her legs almost gave way beneath her. Then she turned her head and looked at me as if she sensed me watching. Her pale blue eyes were as dry and clear as a summer's day, and around her mouth was the merest trace of a smile.

The beater was not the only one who'd been enraged by her silence. A fat, beringed merchant was shaking his fist at him, demanding recompense, almost purple in the face with rage. I couldn't hear what passed between them for the shouts and chatter of the small crowd that had gathered around them, but at last some deal seemed to be struck and the merchant allowed himself to be led off in the direction of the tavern, with the onlookers bringing up the rear. The beater doubtless intended to pacify the outraged man with a soporific quantity of strong wine. Clutching him ingratiatingly by the elbow with one hand, he didn't waste the opportunity to cuff the girl with the other as he passed her, a practised blow, delivered without apparently glancing in her direction. It sent her sprawling face down on the ground and wisely, this time, she stayed there until he was safely inside the tavern. Then she crawled into a narrow gap between a tree trunk and the wheels of a wagon and crouched there, arms wrapped around her knees, staring at me with wide, expressionless eyes like a cat watching from the hearth.

She looked about twelve years old, barefoot and dressed in a grubby white woollen shift, with a blood-red band about the neck that intensified the whiteness of her hair. She continued to stare, but not at my scar, at my good eye, with an intensity that was more imperious than curious. I turned away. Whatever had transpired had nothing to do with me. The girl had been punished for some crime, thieving probably, and doubtless deserved what she got, though she was obviously well hardened to it, since it had had so little effect on her. So there was no reason for me to say anything to her.

I pulled a pastry from my scrip, broke it in two and tossed half to her, then hunkered down with my back resting on the tree trunk to eat my share. I was hungry and it was a quiet spot to eat now that the crowd had moved on. And I couldn't have eaten and not offered the child a bite, now could I? I gazed out at the bustle of the fair, chewing slowly. The pastry was as dry as the devil's hoof, but the salt mutton inside was sweet enough and well herbed. The girl was holding her pastry in both fists as if she feared someone might snatch it from her. She said nothing, not even a thank you.

I took a swig of ale to wash the dry mouthful down. 'Do you have a name, girl?'

'Narigorm.'

'Well, Narigorm, if you're going to thieve from his sort you'll need to learn your trade better. You're fortunate he didn't send for the bailiff.'

'Wasn't thieving.' The words came out muffled from a well-stuffed mouth.

I shrugged and glanced sideways at her. She'd finished the pastry already and was licking her fingers with great concentration. I wondered when she'd last eaten. Given the man's mood, I doubted he was going to feed her again that day. But I half believed her about the stealing. A girl who stood out so vividly from the crowd was not likely to survive long as a pickpocket and it occurred to me that with her looks her father or her master, whichever the man was, might well have found a good living renting her out by the hour to men whose taste runs to young virgins. But she'd clearly upset the customer this time. Maybe she'd refused the merchant, or else he'd tried her and discovered he was not the first to come banging on her door. She'd learn ways to conceal that in time. More experienced women would teach her the trick of it, and she'd doubtless earn a good living when she mastered the art. She'd a fair few years ahead of her in the trade, more than most I reckoned, for even when the bloom of her youth was gone there would still be plenty who'd pay handsomely for a woman who looked so different from the rest.

'You want me to do it for you now, for the pastry?' Her voice was as emotionless as her gaze. 'We'll have to be quick before Master comes back, he'll not be best pleased if you don't pay in coins.'

Her small, cold hand tried to insinuate itself into mine. I put it back in her lap, gently but firmly, sad for her that she had already learned not to expect any gifts from life. Not even a crust comes free. Still, the younger you learn that lesson, the fewer disappointments you'll have.

'I'm past such things now, child. Much too old. Besides, it was only a bite of food. Take it and welcome. You're a pretty girl, Narigorm. You don't need to sell yourself so cheaply. Take a tip from an old camelot, the more people pay for something, the more they think it's worth.'

She frowned slightly and tilted her head, regarding me curiously. 'I know why you don't want me to read the runes for you. You don't want to know when you're going to die. Old men say they want to know, but they don't.' She rocked back and forth on her bottom like a toddler. 'I told the merchant he was going to lose all his money and his wife was going to run off and leave him. It's the truth, but he didn't like it. Master told him I was teasing and tried to make me give him a better fortune, but I wouldn't. I can't lie; if you lie you lose the gift. Morrigan destroys liars.'

So she was a diviner. A good trick if you can convince others of the truth of it. It's hard to tell with some of them if they believed in their own art or not. Was she convinced she had told the merchant the truth or had she taken a dislike to the fat toad and given him that ill fortune from devilment? If so, she'd paid for it and might well pay again if her master was forced to spend too much in the tavern appeasing him, but she probably thought it worth a hiding for the look on the merchant's face. I might have thought so too at her age. I chuckled.

'I *did* tell him the truth,' she hissed savagely. 'I'll tell yours, then you'll see.'

Startled by the malice in her voice, I glanced down, but her pale blue eyes were as wide and emotionless as before and I realized I was being foolish. Children hate to be laughed at. It was natural enough for her to be indignant if she thought she was doubted.

'I believe you, child, but I've no wish to have my fortune told. It's not that I doubt your skill,' I added quickly, 'but when you reach my age the future rushes towards you with too much haste as it is, without you running to meet it.'

I clambered slowly to my feet. I've no quarrel with any who make a living by divination, medicine or any other magic art they can use to con a few coins from people. Why should I? Don't I practise my art on the superstitious and the credulous? But I see no reason to part with my hard-earned money for such services. Besides, if you can read the future, you can read the past, for they are but ends of the same thread and I always take great care that no one should know anything of me except my present.

The shadows were lengthening on the ground. The breeze, never warm, now had a sharp edge to it. The pig was bones. Some people were returning home, but others, most none too steady on their feet, were drifting towards the forest to continue the celebrations now that the business of the fair was over. I tidied my old bones away in my pack. There would be no more customers today. I heaved it on to my back and followed the raggle-taggle crowd towards the trees. I guessed there'd be some good sack swilled down in the woods that night and rich meats too for those who still had stomach for them, which I had.

I said nothing more to the girl. I'd done my Christian duty, shared a bite with her, and that was the end of it. And there was something about the way she looked at me that unnerved me. I've got used to being stared at over the years. I hardly notice it now. No, it wasn't that she was staring at my scar that bothered me, it was rather that she was *not* looking at it; she was staring at me as if she were trying to see beyond it.

The men in front of me ambled down the track, stumbling over roots and stones. One sprawled on his hands and knees. I helped his friend haul him to his feet. He slapped me on the back and belched; his breath stank worse than a dragon's fart. There were going to be some sore heads in those parts come morning. As we steadied him until he could work out which foot to move first, I glanced behind me at the Green. Though I could not make out any faces at that distance, I could see a blur of white stark against all the browns, greens and scarlets around. She was standing on the edge of the grass, still watching me. I could feel her staring, trying to prise me open. I found myself suddenly furious with her. My anger was without cause, I knew that, for the poor child had done nothing to me at all, but I swear that if her master had come out of the tavern at that moment and given her another strapping, I would not have been sorry. Like him, I wanted her to cry. Tears are natural. Tears are human. Tears confine your curiosity to yourself.

So, you may ask, was that it? Was that the beginning? Was that what caused it all, half a pastry offered to a child with eyes of ice? Hardly a day of ill fortune for anyone except the fat merchant. You're right, if that had been all, it would have been nothing, but there was something else that happened on that day, several miles away, in a little town by the sea called Melcombe. Unconnected, you would have thought, yet those two events were to become as tightly woven as the warp and weft in a length of silk. Threads drawn from different directions, yet destined to become one. The warp thread in this cloth? That was the death of one man. We'll call him John, for I never knew his name. Someone must have known it, but they never admitted it and so he was buried without it.

John collapsed in the crowded market place. He was seen to stagger, clutching at the sides of a cart for support. Most thought him drunk, for he had the look of a sailor about him and, as everyone knows, sailors spend what time they have ashore supping liquor until their money runs out and they are forced back to sea again. John bent double, coughing and hacking his lungs out, until frothy spatters of blood sprayed from his mouth on to his hands and the wheels of the cart. Then he sank to his knees and keeled over.

The passers-by who went to his aid at once shrank back, gagging and clapping their hands over their noses. This stench was not the ordinary stink of an unwashed drunk, but so fetid it seemed to come from an opened tomb. Nevertheless, those with stronger stomachs did make shift to take him by the arms and turn him over, but he screamed so loudly with pain that they dropped him again, startled. The men stared at him, unwilling to risk touching him again, yet not knowing what to do to help.

The man who owned the cart prodded John with the toe of his shoe, trying to encourage him to crawl away, since he obviously didn't want to be lifted up. The carter wasn't a callous man, but he had to reach the next village by nightfall. He could smell rain on the wind and was anxious to be off before it fell again, turning the tracks into a quagmire. It was the devil's own job to drive that forest track once it got muddy and if you had to stop to shoulder the cart out of a rut, you were easy prey for any thief who fancied helping himself to your purse and your cart, leaving you as good as dead in a ditch. God knows there was no shortage of such scoundrels in the forest. He prodded John again, trying to make him roll out from under the cart. However anxious he was to leave, the carter could hardly drive over a sick man.

John, feeling the toe against him, seized the carter's leg and tried to hoist himself up on it. He lifted his sweating face, his eyes rolling back in his head as another wave of pain shuddered through his body, and it was then that the carter saw that John's face and arms were covered with livid blue-black spots. It was a sight to make any man flinch away, but the carter didn't comprehend what he was looking at. He didn't recognize the signs. Why should he? They had not been seen here before, not in this place, not in this land.

But someone recognized them; someone who had seen those telltale marks before. He was a merchant, well travelled beyond our shores, and he knew the signs only too well. For a moment he stood stupefied, as if he could not believe it could happen here. Then he grabbed the carter and croaked, '*Morte bleue*'. The small crowd that was gathering about them stared uncomprehendingly from the merchant to the writhing figure on the ground. The merchant pointed, his hand trembling. '*Morte bleue, morte bleue*', he yelled, his voice rising hysterically, then summoning up what few wits he still possessed, he screamed, 'He has the pestilence!'

The carter was right. That night it did rain. Not drizzling as it had done at dawn; that had only been the prologue. No, this time it poured. Hard, heavy drops striking leaves, earth, crops and thatches, turning paths into streams and fields into swamps. It rained as if it was the beginning of the flood and perhaps those who saw the first drops fall back in Noah's day thought, like us, that it signified nothing. Perhaps they too believed that by morning or the following day it would stop.

2. The Company

'Where have you come from, boy?'

It wasn't a friendly enquiry. The innkeeper stood in the doorway, bouncing a stout stick rhythmically against the palm of his hand. He was a big man, his muscular arms covered with black hair. He was not in his prime and his belly was too big to suggest he was nimble of foot, but then he didn't need to be. One crack from that stick and he would not be required to give chase to his opponents.

The lad facing him hesitated, his eyes fixed nervously on the bouncing stick. He took a step backwards and stumbled, hampered by his flamboyant travelling cloak. He was a slim youth, shorter than the innkeeper. He grasped the cloak tightly about him against the rain with a hand the colour of rosewood, long and softly elegant. A lute hung over his shoulder. No farmer's boy, this one.

'Answer me, boy, if you know what's good for you. Are you come from the south?'

The lad took another step back and swallowed, plainly uncertain whether yes or no was the right answer.

'Y . . . yes,' he finally ventured.

'He means he was born in the lands to the south,' I said, stepping as rapidly as I could between the raised cudgel and the shrinking boy. 'But he's not come from the south these many months. I myself saw him only last week at the Magdalene Fair at Chedzoy, that's up Bridgwater way. That's right, isn't it, boy?' I slid my foot across his and pressed hard.

The lad nodded vigorously. 'Yes, from Chedzoy, we came down from there.' He shivered miserably, the rain dripping from his hood.

The innkeeper looked him up and down suspiciously. 'You, Camelot, you'll swear you saw him there?'

'On the bones of St Peter.'

He looked back at the lad, then finally lowered his stick. 'Two pence for a room, penny for the barn. Hay's clean. Mind you keep it that way. Dogs sleep outside.'

There weren't many men in the inn at Thornfalcon that evening. A few travellers like myself and a handful of locals, but the rain was keeping many by their own hearths. The innkeeper was in as foul a mood as the weather. It was, after all, only the backend of July, and he counted on long, warm summer evenings to fill the benches in his courtyard. He bellowed and raged at his wife, who in turn slammed the ale down on the tables so that it slopped over, glowering at her customers as if they were to blame. Her sour face wasn't helping trade either. If a man wants bad-tempered company he can usually find it at his own hearth; he doesn't need to pay someone else for the privilege.

I saw the lad enter with an older man. He looked round and then, spotting me in the corner behind the fire, pointed me out to his companion. They both came across. The older man had to stoop to pass under the beams. He was olive-skinned like the boy, but whereas the lad was a slender, delicate-looking youth, the man had the broad, muscular frame of maturity, running a little to fat. The lines in the corners of his eyes had set and his dark hair was streaked with grey. He wasn't what you'd call handsome, but striking enough with his Roman nose and full mouth. He'd doubtless turned more than a few heads in his youth, probably still did. He gave a courtly bow and sat down heavily on the bench opposite.

'*Buona sera, signore*. I am Rodrigo. Your pardon for the intrusion, but I wanted to thank you. Jofre tells me that you spoke for him. We are in your debt, Camelot.'

'Jofre?'

He inclined his head towards the young man who stood respectfully at his side.

'My pupil.'

The young man gave a half bow in imitation of his master.

I nodded. 'You're welcome. It was just a word and words are freely given. But let me offer you one word more. I don't know where you really come from, and it's no concern of mine, but these days it's safest to say you've travelled from the north. These rumours make people cautious.'

The man laughed, a deep laugh that made his tired eyes dance. 'An innkeeper threatens his customers with a cudgel and that is cautious?'

'You said rumours, what rumours?' Jofre interrupted. He was plainly on easy terms with his master.

'From your lute and your garb, I took you to be minstrels. I'm surprised you've not heard the news on your travels. I thought all England knew by now.'

The master and pupil exchanged glances, but it was Rodrigo who answered, glancing around first to see if others were eavesdropping on the conversation.

'We have not long been on the road. We were both in the employ of a lord. But . . . but he is old and his son has taken over the running of his estates. He brought with him his own musicians and so now we try to make our fortune on the road. *È buono,*' he added with a forced cheerfulness, 'there is the whole world to see and many pretty girls as yet unbedded. Is that not right, Jofre?'

The lad, who was studying his hands with a miserable intensity, nodded briefly.

Rodrigo clapped him on the shoulder. 'A new start, is it not, *ragazzo?*'

Again the boy nodded and flushed a dull red, but did not raise his eyes.

A new start for which of them, I wondered. I guessed there was more to the story than Rodrigo had told. Perhaps the gaze of one or the other had strayed too close to a pretty girl in the lord's family; it's not unheard of. Bored women left too often alone are not averse to a dalliance with a good-looking minstrel.

'You said there were rumours,' Jofre reminded me, with a note of urgency in his voice.

'The great pestilence has finally reached our shores.'

Jofre's eyes widened in shock. 'But they said it could not reach this island.'

'They say before a battle that their king cannot be defeated, but they are usually wrong. It was brought on a ship from the isle of Guernsey, so they say, but who knows, they may be wrong about that too. But wherever it came from scarcely matters now; the point is it has arrived.'

'And it is spreading?' Rodrigo asked quietly.

'Along the south coast, but it will spread inland. Take my advice, travel north and stay well away from the ports.'

'They will close the ports, surely, as they did in Genoa?'

'To the south, maybe, but the merchants will not suffer

the ports to be closed on the east and west coasts, at least not until they see the dead lying in the streets. Too much money sails on the waves.'

A stifled sob made us both glance up. Jofre was standing, fists clenched, face blanched, his mouth working convulsively. Then he turned and barged blindly out of the inn, ignoring the furious curses of the innkeeper's wife as he rushed past her, knocking a dish out of her hands.

Rodrigo rose. 'Your pardon, Camelot, please excuse him. His mother – she was in Venice when the pestilence came there. There has been no word since.'

'But that doesn't necessarily mean the worst. How could she send a message in these times? True, the rumours say half have perished, but if that is so, then half have survived it. Why should she not be one of them?'

'So I tell him, but his heart tells him otherwise. He adores her. His father sent him away, but he did not want to leave her. Distance has translated a mortal woman into Holy Virgin in his memory. And because he worships her, so he is afraid he has lost her. I must find him. The young are impetuous. Who knows what they will do?'

He hurried out after the boy, pausing to speak to the innkeeper's wife whose temper had grown, if possible, even more savage since Jofre had spilled her dish. I couldn't hear what passed between them for the chatter of the other customers, but I could see her scowl melting to a reluctant smile and then to a deep, rosy blush. And when he bowed, kissed her hand and excused himself, she gazed at his retreating back with the cow eyes of a lovesick maid. Rodrigo had learned the art of courtly love well. I wondered how he dealt with jealous husbands. I guessed he was not quite so skilled at winning their admiration or he would not now find himself on the road.

I settled back to my ale, which was passable, and the pottage, which was not, but it was hot and filling and when you know what an empty belly feels like you learn to be more than grateful for that much. But I was not left to sit in peace for long. An unkempt man, who'd been warming his ample backside at the fire, slid on to the bench vacated by Rodrigo. I'd seen him in these parts before, but had never exchanged more than a gruff 'G'day' with him. He studied his tankard of ale in silence for a long time as if he expected to see something new and startling crawling out of it.

'They foreigners?' he asked suddenly without looking up.

'What makes you think that?'

'Look like foreigners, talk like 'em too.'

'How many foreigners have you heard talk?'

He scowled at me. 'Enough.'

I'd have been surprised if the man had encountered more than half a dozen in his life. He'd not have known an Icelander from a Moor by his looks, never mind his speech. Thornfalcon did not lie on the main merchants' road and the nearby priory contained only the relics of a local saint that few outside those parts would trouble to visit. The man's scowl settled more deeply into the grimy wrinkles of his face.

'You still ain't answered me. They foreigners?'

'English as you or me. Been minstrels in the court of some lord all their lives. You know what it's like, around the gentry all day, they start thinking themselves one of them. They dress in their cast-offs and before you know it they start talking like them too.'

The man gave a non-committal grunt. He'd almost certainly never heard a lord talk either, so that was a safe enough line.

'So long as they're not foreigners.' He hacked and spat on to the floor. 'Fecking foreigners. I'd have 'em run out of England, every man jack of 'em. And if they won't go . . .' He drew a thick stubby finger across his throat. 'Bringing their filthy diseases here.'

'The pestilence? I heard it was lads from Bristol who carried it aboard their ship.'

'Aye, 'cause they were mixing with fecking foreigners in Guernsey, that's why. If you go travelling to foreign parts, you deserve all you get.'

'Have you a family?'

He sighed. 'Five bairns, no, six it is now.'

'You'll be worried for them then, if the pestilence spreads.'

'The wife is, mithering about it morning and night. I keep telling her it won't spread. Told her I'd crack her one if she keeps going on about it. You have to, don't you, just to knock some sense into 'em.'

'Maybe she's right to be worried. They say it's already reached Southampton.'

'Aye, but it's only spreading along the coast, 'cause that's where the foreigners are, in the ports. Priest says it's a judgement on the foreigners, so it stands to reason it won't come here, 'cause we've no foreigners here.'

And that was pretty much what they all believed those first few weeks after the great pestilence crept in. Away from the south coast, life went on much as it had always done. You might have thought that people would panic, but the truth is they didn't believe it would touch them. They were suspicious of strangers, violent even, but still they assured themselves that pestilence was a foreign thing. Why, it even had a foreign name – *morte bleue*. How could any Englishman die of a sickness so plainly marked for foreigners?

Those towns along the south coast which had already

succumbed and were falling one after the other like wheat before the scythe were, if anything, proof of this, for ports, as everyone knew, were teeming with foreigners and it was those foreigners who were dying, proof positive that God had damned the other nations of the world in perpetuity. And if some Englishmen in those ports also died, well then, that was because they had been mixing with those same foreigners, sleeping with the foreign whores and boys. They deserved it. But England, true England, did not. Just as once they had been convinced it could not cross the Channel, now they convinced themselves it would stop at the ports, provided the foreigners were also stopped there.

The following morning the rain fell steadily as it had done the day before and the day before that. Rain drives men inside their own thoughts. No one looks at anyone else in the rain; they walk, heads bent, gaze fixed on the spinning puddles. I was out of the village, toiling along the track, before I noticed Rodrigo and Jofre; even then I probably would have walked right past them had the boy not been making a noise like a cow in labour as he retched repeatedly into a ditch.

Rodrigo was muttering something to Jofre, which sounded as if he was scolding him, but at the same time was soothingly rubbing his back.

I stayed on the other side of the road and drew my cloak across my nose and mouth. 'Is he sick?'

God's blood! I was the one who'd persuaded the inn-keeper to let them stay. If he had the pestilence . . .

Rodrigo glanced up sharply, then gave a tight-lipped smile. 'No, Camelot, it is not the sickness. His stomach is not used to the wine. It was rougher in the inn than he is accustomed to.'

The boy heaved again and groaned, holding his head, his eyes bloodshot and his face the colour of sour milk.

'Perhaps it's not the quality, but the quantity he's not accustomed to.'

Rodrigo grimaced, but didn't contradict. The boy continued to bend over the ditch, though his retching was dry now, unlike the rain.

'You are abroad early, Camelot. You have a long journey ahead of you?'

I hesitated. I don't like discussing my business with strangers. Start talking about where you are going and people start asking where you've come from. They want to know where you were born and where your home is, insisting you must have one somewhere. Some even think that if you have no roots you are to be pitied. That I chose to rip up those roots is something they could never understand.

But it was impossible to be rude to a man as courteous as Rodrigo.

'I'm making for St John Shorne's shrine at North Marston. There's money to be made there and it's well to the north of here and inland, far away from the ports.'

I knew it of old. It was a good place to sit out the autumn rains, the whole winter if need be. I was not so foolish as to think the pestilence would not creep inland, but it couldn't reach as far as North Marston, not before the winter frosts came. And, like all summer fevers, it would surely die out then. If you could just survive until the weather changed, by Christmas it would all be over, that's what they said, and even I was foolish enough to comfort myself with that thought.

'And you, where are you bound?' I asked Rodrigo. Like me, he also hesitated, as if reluctant to reveal the whole truth.

'We go to Maunsel Manor. It is only a few miles from here. We spent time there whenever our master visited the family. The mistress of the house always praised our playing. We will try for a place there.'

'It'll be a fruitless journey. I heard the household's gone to their summer estates. They'll not be back for weeks.'

Rodrigo looked beaten and helpless. I'd seen that expression before in those who've been in service all their lives and suddenly find themselves turned out. They've no more idea of how to survive than a lapdog abandoned in a forest.

'You'd be best making for a fair or better still a shrine. Fairs only run for a few days, a week at most, but a shrine never closes. Find one that's popular with the pilgrims and make friends with one of the innkeepers. The pilgrims always need entertaining in the evenings. Play a rousing battle song for the men and a love song for the women and you'll easily earn enough for a dry bed and a hot meal.'

There was a loud groan from Jofre.

'You may not feel like food now, my lad, but wait till that hangover wears off. You'll be groaning even harder once you feel the bite of hunger.'

Jofre glanced up long enough to glower at me before leaning against a tree, his eyes tightly closed.

'But other minstrels will already have found such inns, no?'

'I dare say they will, but he's a pretty lad. When he's washed and sober, that is,' I added, for he looked anything but pretty just then with his puffy face and tightly clenched jaw. 'If you can persuade him to flirt with the wealthy matrons instead of their daughters, you'll get your coins. You'll both stand out from the common rabble of minstrels. Merchants' wives fancy themselves as highborn ladies and they'll pay handsomely anyone who knows how to treat them as such. And who can say, you might be lucky enough to find yourselves another livery. Even the highborn make pilgrimages. They more than most, for they have more money to do it and more sins to atone for.'

'This shrine you are going to, you think we could get work there?'

I had a sinking feeling that I knew where this was leading and I cursed myself for ever having mentioned it.

'It's a good few weeks' walk from here. I'll have to work my way there via the fairs and markets along the way. You'll want to look for something closer.'

'I can't walk. I'm ill,' the boy whined.

'*I denti di Dio!* Whose fault is that?' Rodrigo snapped and Jofre looked as startled as if he'd been slapped.

Rodrigo also seemed surprised at his own sharpness for his next words were spoken soothingly, like a mother trying to coax a fretful child. 'You will feel better for walking and we cannot stay here. We need to earn money. Without food and shelter you will become ill.' He turned back to me, anxiety etched on his face. 'You know the way to this shrine? You could help us find work on the way?'

What could I do? Though I'd little doubt that Rodrigo was capable of holding his own in the subtle intrigue and politics of a court, to send them out alone into the blood and guts of the market place would have been like sending toddlers into a battlefield.

'You'd have to walk at my pace. I'm not as fast as I once was.'

Rodrigo glanced over at the listless boy. 'I think a slow pace would suit us well, Camelot.'

And so it was that the first members of our little company were drawn together, the first but by no means the last. On that wet morning, I thought I was doing them a kindness, saving them from learning the hard way how to survive on the roads. I thought I was sparing them the days of hungry bellies and the nights sleeping cold and friendless; I'd been there myself when I first started out and I knew the misery of it. But now I know it would have been kinder to have passed them by on the road than draw them into what was to come.

3. Zophiel

It's not every day you see a mermaid, though you hear tell of them often. Ask anyone in the fishing villages and they'll swear some old man in the village once caught a mermaid in his nets or fell overboard and was rescued by a maiden with hair that glistened like a shoal of silver fish in the moonlight and a tail that gleamed like opals under the stars. So when a magician says he has one in his tent, you can be sure there will be no shortage of people willing to hand over their pennies for a glimpse of a real live mermaid.

Not *live* exactly, for this one was dead. Dead, because they do die if they cannot return to the sea. They are half fish after all, and how long can a fish live out of water? A mermaid can live longer, but not for ever, not on land, at least that's what the magician explained.

The magician called himself Zophiel, 'God's spy'. The name fitted him almost too well. Spies have to be on their guard and he was guarded all right, you could tell that from the first time you heard him speak, careful, clever, you might say. He made no promises the crowd could dispute afterwards. If you promise a living beast and it's dead then word soon gets round. At best no one else will part with their money to see it, and at worst, well, there are no limits to what a drunken mob might do if they feel cheated. Afterwards I realized that Zophiel had not even claimed this to be a mermaid. 'One of the merpeople,' was all he'd said. Zophiel was clever all right, sharp as a flayer's knife.

The sun never seemed to rise at all in those dark days; it was as if we were living in some eternal twilight pressed down under the weight of the thick grey clouds and the heavy smoke of a thousand smouldering fires. Inside Zophiel's tent it was even darker, but cold, cloyingly cold. Not a place you'd want to linger in even to escape the rain. The tent was narrow, a kind of lean-to erected at the back of his wagon, room enough for three or four people to crowd in at a time. A viscous yellow light pooled out from a lantern illuminating the small cage balanced on the back of the wagon. The bars on the cage were not there to keep the creature in, it was in no state to run away, but to stop the customers breaking pieces off and carrying them away as they do from the relics at holy shrines. It's true that a mermaid is no saint, but neither is she of this world, so who knows what a fragment of mermaid might cure? The stench alone was enough to exorcize the most stubborn of demons.

The creature lay on its back in the cage on a nest of sea-smoothed pebbles, shells, dead crabs, sea urchins, star-fish and strands of dried seaweed. The smell of the seashore, of brine and fish, was powerful enough to convince any-one that this creature had its origins in the sea; powerful enough too to mask the fragrance of myrrh, incense, musk and aloes that lurked beneath it, unless you knew the smell of old.

Few in these times would have recognized that heady, bitter fragrance. It was a perfume I hadn't smelt for many years, but once you have smelt it, you never forget it. After all these years it still has the power to make the stomach tighten and tears well up in long-dry eyes. It is the smell of the embalmed corpses of knights returned from Acre. Returning as they swore they would, but not at the head of a retinue laden with treasure and pardoned of all past and future sins. No, these returned home in caskets, escorted by ghost-eyed brothers and emaciated servants, to be buried too young in the cold crypts beneath their families' crests. Myrrh does not come cheap. It is the rare perfume of a delicate craft. We learned many things from the Saracens, not least how to preserve our slaughtered dead. Had Zophiel acquired the art, or had he bought the creature from another? Whichever it was, someone had paid a pretty penny for her.

The mermaid, if maid it was, was no bigger than an infant. Its face was wizened, shrunken in on itself so that the eyes were mere slits, but slanted upwards at the corners. The head was covered with a fine straw-coloured fluff that stood up straight from the skin or perhaps the skin had shrunk away from the hair. Eyebrows and lashes were startlingly blonde against the tanned flesh, though it was hard to tell whether this was its natural colour or some artifice of the preservation of the body. The creature's chest was as smooth and sexless as a child's. The arms were human enough. One tiny fist grasped a hand-mirror of polished silver; the other was clenched around a doll carved from whalebone. The doll was in the form of a mermaid, the kind you might see among the grotesques on a church, with swollen hips, pendulous breasts and a long serpent's tail.

But what was below the waist of this little creature? Now that's what we'd really come to see. It did not have legs, certainly. Instead there was a single long piece of flesh that tapered down from the waist to two curious projections at the end, resembling the hind flippers of a seal. Like the rest of the body, the tail, if tail it could be called, was brown and wrinkled, but naked, devoid of either scales or fur.

'That's no mermaid,' sneered the man standing near me. 'That's a . . .' He trailed off, at a loss to find any name for the creature. He was sweating onions and the stench of his breath threatened to overpower even that of the creature's corpse.

'I heard,' his friend said, 'that some charlatans sew the body of a human to the tail of a fish to make it look like a mermaid.'

The sweating man peered closer. 'That's no fish's tail. It's not got scales.'

'It'll be a seal, then. They've joined a human babe to a seal.'

'It's got no fur neither,' he said impatiently 'and there's no join. If anyone could see a stitched-on tail, I could; after all, I've been stitching cloth since I were a babe myself.'

'So what is it, then?'

They asked the same question of Zophiel outside, loudly, with the aggression that comes from uncertainty.

Zophiel looked down his pale thin nose at them, as if the question had been asked by a simpleton. 'As I told you, it's one of the merpeople, a merchild.'

Onion-breath gave a mirthless guffaw as if he had been told such things many times before and didn't believe a word of it. 'So how come it's got no scales on its tail?' He glanced round at the small crowd with a smirk that said, answer that one, if you can. He was spurred on by many encouraging nods and winks. Townspeople are always eager to have a stranger confounded.

'You admit it has a tail, then?' Zophiel asked coolly.

The smile on Onion-breath's face waned. 'But not a scaly

tail, and it's got no hair on its head neither. I thought mermaids were supposed to have hair, yards of it.'

'Do you have any children, my friend?'

The man hesitated, uncertain where this line of argument was leading. 'I do, for my sins, three fine lads and a bonny little lass.'

'So, my friend, was your daughter born with hair?'

'When she were a mite she were as bald as her grandfather is now.'

'But she has a fine head of hair now, I wager.'

The man nodded.

'There you are then, her hair grew in. It's the same with merpeople. They are born as smooth and hairless as you or I, and the hair and scales grow in later.'

The man opened and closed his mouth, but seemed to have no answer.

Zophiel smiled, though the smile didn't reach his eyes. 'You're a wise man, my friend. People of lesser intelligence would not think to ask such questions and I'm not surprised that you didn't know the answer. Many of the greatest scholars in our land are ignorant of such things because merbabies are seldom seen, only the adults. The infants are kept hidden far below the waves in deep sea caves until they are old enough to swim to the surface. It's a rare thing to see one. Far more rare than seeing a mermaid, which is rare enough. Why, I doubt any merbabies have been seen for five hundred years, maybe more.'

There was a moment's hesitation as the crowd digested these momentous facts, then, as one, hands flew to purses, struggling to part with coins as fast as Zophiel could take them. Every man, woman and child who still had money to spend was desperate to part with their last penny to see this rarest of all rare creatures. Even old Onion-breath beamed as if he had personally discovered the merchild. Zophiel knew just how to work a crowd.

As it happens, we'd all been doing pretty well that day. The Bartholomew Fair was busier than usual. With markets closing along the south coast, the merchants were pushing inland. After all, as they said, life goes on. We all have to eat until we die. So the merchants were shouting one another hoarse and the crowd was just as excited. Wine and spices, salt and oil, dyes and cloth fairly flew off the stalls. 'Buy now,' the merchants urged, 'it may be months before we can get another shipment in. Stock up while you have the chance.' And they bought as if they were preparing for a siege.

I'd done all right too, sold half a dozen fragments of the bones of St Brigid, guaranteed to keep the cows in milk, and several ribs of St Ambrose to hang over the bee skeps to ensure that the combs would be bursting with honey come autumn. The farmers needed all the help they could get. The field beans were blackened with mildew and they'd be lucky to salvage enough to cover the bottom of a pot. The late hay crop had already been ruined by the rain and there was scarcely a sheaf of grain left standing. If it didn't stop raining soon, honey and cheese would be all anyone would have in their winter stores.

Prices were up, but that was to be expected. The buyers grumbled, but they bought anyway. No point saving a few pennies, if next week there'd be nothing to spend them on. Besides, if you had to pay more for a barrel of pickled pork, you charged more for your knives. Too bad for those who had nothing to sell, that was their problem.

Yes, all things considered it was a profitable fair for the merchants and peddlers, and Rodrigo and Jofre were doing well enough too, considering they had only been a month on the road. At night, in front of a warm hearth in the inns, satisfied with their day's shrewd bargaining and mellow from hot food and strong ale, people would pay generously for an evening's entertainment. And Rodrigo and Jofre had talent, more than I'd seen in many a year, though talent is not enough on the road and they still had much to learn.

They were used to playing to a lord's command. Lords and ladies know what they want. They can put a name to a song or demand you write a new one. They will even tell you what the subject of that song should be. But a crowd doesn't know what mood it's in, or if it does, it won't tell you. You have to be able to sense it. Is it in the mood for a love song or a rousing battle song, a story of daring adventure or a bawdy verse? Does the crowd want to sing along or sit and dream? It folds its arms and glowers as if to say, 'Go on, lad, amuse us, and God help you if you don't.'

But Rodrigo was anxious to learn. He could have spent his days dry and warm in the inns, for there was little point in attempting to play in the open market place in the rain, but he preferred to spend his time outside watching me work, trying to understand the rules of the new world in which he found himself.

'The trick,' I told him, 'is to know what a customer wants before they know themselves. Watch.

'Your daughter nearing her birth pangs, mistress? A dangerous time. You must be sick with worry. See this amulet. It has the names of the holy angels *Sanvi*, *Sansanvi* and *Semangelaf* engraved upon it. Demons will flee from the room the moment they catch sight of it. Expensive? Come now, mistress, what price would you put on the life of your daughter and grandchild? Thank you, mistress, and may she be delivered of a fine boy.'

As he watched me pocket the coins, Rodrigo shook

his head in disbelief. 'But how did you know her daughter was with child? Do you trade in fortunes as well as old bones?'

'You must keep your eyes open if you want to survive on the road. I saw her earlier buying horehound, cinnamon and pennyroyal from that woman over there. What would she use that combination for, except to ease birth pains? She's not pregnant herself and she's too well dressed to be a servant, so it was a safe guess that it was for her own daughter. Now, take that man walking towards us, what do you think he'll buy?'

I nodded towards a portly, sallow-skinned man wearing an outrageous confection of green and yellow on his head, clearly under the impression it was the last word in stylish hats. He constantly gazed around as he picked his way through the mud, beaming at anyone whom he perceived to be of a higher station than himself as if hoping to be recognized as one of them.

Rodrigo looked the man up and down. 'Now, that is the kind of man I do know. I have met many like him at my lord's court. He would only buy a relic if it came in a gold casket covered in jewels. You will never sell any of your wares to him.'

'You're certain of that, are you?'

'I would wager a tankard of mulled ale on it,' he grinned, slipping back a pace or two as the merchant approached, to give me space to work.

'Feeling a touch bilious, master? I can see you're suffering. You have a delicate constitution. Up all night with a bad stomach, I'll be bound. His Majesty the King suffers exactly the same trouble and I'm sure you know what he uses – wolf's dung. He wouldn't be without it. As luck would have it, I happen to have a packet here. And not ordinary wolf's dung, this is imported all the way from Russia, as used by the King himself. Would His Majesty use anything but the best? He always insists on Russian dung, for everyone knows they have the strongest wolves.'

The man waved his hand dismissively. 'I have no need of such stuff.' But his gaze lingered just a little too long on the packet for a man who was indifferent, and I knew I had a sale.

'My apologies, sir, but you're looking so pale. I can't bear to see any nobleman suffering unnecessarily, but no matter, I have a good customer in Gloucester, the sheriff there. Perhaps you know him. He's desperate for all I can bring him. With the foreign ships not putting to sea and demand higher than ever, he's stocking up –'

'I'll take it,' the man broke in hastily. Then, recovering his business sense, added, 'But you'll have to take rosewater for it. I have no money left. The price the merchant charged for this was extortionate.' He pulled out a flask. 'My wife insisted I bring her some back for her baking, but I'll tell her there was none to buy. It's good quality.' He pulled off the stopper and waved the flask in the air, allowing the smell to waft out.

Rosewater is no use to me. On the road, you need coins to buy food or goods that will keep long enough to sell at the next fair or the one after that. Rosewater, once unsealed, quickly loses its pungency or turns bad. I was about to refuse, when I heard a deep sigh next to me. Rodrigo had inched forward and was breathing in the sweet perfume. 'It is excellent.'

In three words Rodrigo had managed to destroy any bargaining power I had. The man sauntered away with his wolf's dung, confident that he had got the better of me.

I rounded on Rodrigo. 'Are you out to ruin me?'

He gave a sheepish grin. 'But I could not resist. I smell this and suddenly I am a little boy in Venice again. Always for Christmas children were given little figures of the Christ child made of *marzapane*. For days before the air was filled with the smell of almonds and rosewater and we could not wait to taste it. We tried to creep into the kitchens to steal just a little piece, but we never could.'

I shook my head. I'd never heard of it.

'It is a paste made from sugar, eggs and almonds and flavoured with rosewater. Very costly, that is why it was so special. I have not tasted such a thing since I left Venice. It is . . .' he kissed the tips of fingers, '*squisito*! To me it is the taste of Venice.'

Annoyed though I was, I couldn't help smiling at his ecstatic expression. 'You miss Venice very much?'

'Even more now that we live on the road.' He raised his eyes miserably to the heavy grey clouds. 'I never intended to stay away so long. When this pestilence is past I shall return to my homeland. Jofre too. I will take him back, no matter what his father says.'

The day we'd met in the inn, Rodrigo had me told that Jofre's father had sent him away. I'd thought nothing of the remark at the time; most boys are sent away to learn a trade or to serve in some great house. But most fathers would be overjoyed to see their sons again. Why would a father forbid his son's return?'

Rodrigo's gaze was still resting on the flask of rosewater as if it was a magic potion which had the power to carry him home. He smiled wistfully. '*Deo volente*, as soon as the curse of this sickness is lifted from us, I will go back to the place of my childhood.'

'But you can never return to that, Rodrigo. You can never again be what you were there. Just as a ewe rejects a lamb that has been separated from her, so your homeland will reject you as a stranger.'

He flinched. 'You would condemn me to be an exile all my life, Camelot?'

'We are exiles from the past. Besides, what do you have to return to? Or are the stories true that minstrels have a girl in every town?' I laughed, trying to dispel the melancholy that had settled on him. 'Have you left a trail of broken hearts behind you in Venice?'

'Have you not heard our songs? It is the poor minstrel's heart that is broken.' He smiled, pressing his hand dramatically to his chest and striking an exaggerated pose, like a lovesick swain in a mummers' play. But the light-hearted gesture didn't mask the shadow of pain I glimpsed in his eyes. That was real and deep.

'Here, you may as well take this,' I said, thrusting the flask of rosewater at him.

His eyes widened in surprise. 'But I cannot accept such a gift.'

'No use to me,' I said as gruffly as I could.

He grasped my shoulder. 'Thank you, thank you, my friend.'

'You've cost me a fortune,' I said severely, 'but don't think you can talk your way out of the wager.'

His mouth twitched. 'A fortune? Tell me truthfully, Camelot, how much did that Russian wolf's dung cost you, if it really was wolf's dung?'

'It was a mulled ale you wagered, wasn't it?' I slapped my tankard into his hand.

He bowed, and chuckling, squelched off through the rain in the direction of the tavern. Once his back was turned, I could not suppress a grin. My new apprentice was beginning to learn.

Jofre, though younger than Rodrigo, was finding his new life more difficult to adjust to, but unlike Rodrigo, he would accept advice from no one. Like most youths caught in that restless age between boy and man, he was moody and unpredictable. One minute he'd be in the thick of a crowd laughing and joking and the next skulking alone in a barn or on a riverbank.

But I believe he truly loved music, perhaps even more than Rodrigo. When Rodrigo gave him his daily lesson he would practise with great earnestness, studying Rodrigo's hands as if they were the hands of God. Sometimes Jofre would play for hours on end, while expressions of pain and joy, sorrow and passion beyond his years would pass across his eyes, like clouds blown by the wind. But then on other days, if he could not immediately master a difficult tune, he'd fly into a rage, throwing down his lute or pipes and storming off, not appearing again for several hours. He'd return eventually, swearing he'd never do it again, and quickly take up his lute. And as he played, the sharp reprimand Rodrigo had intended to deliver would be forgotten. And who can blame him, for when he was in the mood, Jofre's music could make you forgive him anything.

But although Jofre was kept busy in the evenings playing in the inns, for most of the day he had nothing to do, as the rain poured down relentlessly, except hang around in the taverns or the market place. Trouble was never far off. And at the Bartholomew Fair, it came in the guise of the great magician Zophiel, who, as Jofre soon discovered, had other tricks up his sleeve besides the mermaid.

By the third day of the fair, the flood of people waiting to see the creature had dried to a trickle. Those who wanted to see it had already done so, except for a few children who were still trying to sneak in under the tent flaps for free. But those who did manage to wriggle in were sadly disappointed for the merchild had been put away and Zophiel had taken up his place outside the tent in front of a low table. The crowd that now surrounded him was smaller and composed mainly of men and young lads. They pressed in tightly. But however closely they watched his hands, Zophiel was too quick for them.

It was the old three cups trick: carefully place the dried pea under the upturned cup in plain view of everyone and shuffle the cups around. Then get some poor fool to bet on which cup contains the pea. The bet seems a certainty except that, of course, the pea is never under the cup the gambler has put his money on. You'd think the trick had been around for so long that no one would be taken in by it any more, but there's always one who fancies himself sharper than the trickster.

Jofre, on this occasion at least, was not one of the gullible. He'd seen the trick performed by jesters and court entertainers too many times to be taken in by it and was amusing himself by telling the crowd how the sleight of hand was being performed. Most didn't believe him though, for however closely they watched, they couldn't catch Zophiel palming the pea and Zophiel was still able to take a fair few bets before he finally wearied of Jofre's commentary.

Packing away his cups, he informed the crowd that he would now show them a feat of magic. He sent a boy to a neighbouring stall to buy a hardboiled egg, which he carefully peeled in front of the crowd, who watched the action with surprising fascination considering they had themselves peeled hundreds of eggs. They continued to watch as Zophiel sat the peeled egg on top of the neck of a glass flask. The neck of the flask was far too narrow to admit the egg whole, but Zophiel told the crowd he could make the egg fall into the flask without touching the egg or crushing it. The crowd jeered, but it was a ritual jeer like booing the devil in a mummers' play. Most felt sure that something magical was about to happen, but you were supposed to show scepticism; it was part of the magician's game with his audience.

Zophiel turned his sharp green eyes upon Jofre. 'You, boy, you had a lot to say for yourself before. Do you think I can cause the egg to fall into the flask?'

Jofre hesitated. He looked at the plump glistening egg resting securely on the narrow neck of the flask. He knew as well as the rest of the crowd did that Zophiel would not have presented the challenge if he couldn't do it; the trouble was that Jofre could not see how it could be done.

The shadow of a smile began to play around Zophiel's mouth. 'Well now, you were swift enough to tell us all how the pea found its way under the cup, so tell us, boy, how will I make the egg enter the flask?'

Some of the other men who'd been irritated by Jofre's know-it-all comments began to grin and poke him in the back.

'Yes, lad, go on, tell us how he's going to do this one, if you're so smart.'

Jofre flushed. 'It can't be done,' he said defiantly, with a good deal more bravado than he apparently felt.

'Then perhaps you'd care to put a wager on it,' Zophiel said.

Jofre shook his head and tried to back out of the crowd, but the men behind him were having none of it.

'Put your money where your mouth is, lad, or are you all talk?'

Red-faced, Jofre fumbled for a coin and slapped it down. Zophiel raised one eyebrow. 'Is that the price of your conviction, boy?' He turned to the crowd. 'It looks as if our clever young friend is not that sure of himself after all.'

Jofre's head snapped up and, blazing with fury and humiliation, he threw a handful of coins down on the table. It was all he had and Zophiel seemed to know it.

He smiled. 'Well now, boy, shall we see if you are right?'

He lit a taper, removed the egg and dropped the burning taper inside the flask, quickly replacing the egg on the neck of the bottle, and stood well back. For a few long moments nothing happened. All gazed mesmerized as the taper burned inside the flask, then, in the same instant as the taper extinguished itself, there was a pop and the egg slid neatly through the neck of the flask, flopping undamaged on to the bottom.

I was thankful that Rodrigo was not with me to witness this. I couldn't bring myself to watch any more, but as I turned away something caught my eye, a child, standing a little way off in the shadow of a tree. The day was so dark and she was standing so still that I doubt I would even have noticed her there, but for the unnatural whiteness of her hair. I had seen that hair before. I recognized her at once. It was Narigorm, but she did not appear to have noticed me. All her attention was fixed on something else.

Her body was rigid with concentration. Only the index finger of her right hand moved as it repeatedly traced the outline of a tiny object she cradled in her other palm. She seemed to be muttering under her breath, her unblinking gaze fixed on something behind me. I turned to see what she was watching and realized she was staring at Zophiel, but when I turned back to look at her again, the shadow under the tree was empty. She had vanished.

*

The fair had been set to run for a week. It was in the charter and it had done so for as long as anyone could remember. But as things turned out that year, the fair came to an abrupt halt on the afternoon of that same day. A messenger had arrived, mud-splattered and sweating nearly as much as his horse. He demanded to see the town's elders and the bell tolled out, summoning them from every quarter of the town. Since most of them were in the middle of buying or selling at the time, they were not best pleased to be dragged to a meeting and the bell continued to toll for quite some time until the last of them had arrived, grumbling that this had better be important, or someone would be spending the rest of the fair in the town's gaol. By this time everyone had heard the bell and they knew something was afoot. No one was under any illusion that it would be good news. Business gave way to gossip and speculation – had the Scots or the French or even the Turks invaded? Was the King coming on a royal visit, bringing with him his whole court and half his army, all to be fed at the town's expense? 'May God bless and keep His Majesty – far away from us.' Or, more likely, had His Majesty imposed yet another tax? And what was there left to tax that he hadn't taxed already?

When the town's dignitaries finally crowded on to the balcony, the chatter and laughter died in people's throats. They looked grave and suddenly old. The crier had no need to ring his bell or even strain his voice. The news was delivered into shocked silence.

Pestilence had broken out in Bristol. To save itself, Gloucester had closed its gates. No one would be allowed in or out. The villages all along the river were following Gloucester's example. Whilst we had all been looking to the south, the pestilence had crept round on our western flank. It was spreading, spreading inland.

Afterwards, no one expressed surprise that Bristol had fallen to the pestilence. It was a port and sooner or later an infected ship would be bound to call there. Besides, it was a ship from Bristol that had brought the infection to these shores, so it was a kind of justice that their own town should be infected. But what stunned them was Gloucester closing itself off. A mighty town like that, dependent on its trade, walling itself up alive. So fearful of the pestilence, the people were willing to ruin themselves, starve even, rather than risk it entering their gates. Whoever remained inside the walls would be trapped there as surely as if they were in a dungeon, for however long it took for the pestilence to burn itself out. And anyone from Gloucester who had the misfortune to find themselves away from home and family when the gates were locked would have to take their chances alone on the outside. Gloucester was miles up river from Bristol. If the people of Gloucester feared the pestilence could spread that far, that fast, then just how quickly was it spreading?

Even before the town declared the fair was to be cut short, most of the travellers had already made up their minds to leave, to begin the big migration north and east. It was like watching a high wave forming out at sea. At first everyone had simply stood and looked, mesmerized, but now it started to roll towards them, they suddenly turned tail and ran for higher ground. Except that higher ground would not save them from this wave of destruction. There was no place that could; the only hope was to try to outrun it and pray that a miracle would happen and somehow it would be stopped before it swept them away.

Getting out of the town that night wasn't easy; the townspeople may have wanted us to leave and we to go, but there were only three gates out of the town. Merchants and peddlers had been arriving in a steady trickle for days before the fair, but now they were all trying to get out at once. Only a few who were desperate to get back to wives and families were taking roads leading south or west; the rest of us – wagons, carts, people, cattle, sheep, geese, pigs and horses – were squeezing and jostling through the one remaining gate. The roads, already waterlogged with all the rain, were becoming impassable as livestock and wagons churned up the mud, and every few yards the way was blocked by floundering carts and beasts.

Fortunately, I knew my way around those parts and, once we were clear of the gate, I led Rodrigo and Jofre off on a side path that connected to a parallel road which bypassed the town and so we were able to escape from the crowd. The road descended through a gorge. It was ancient, and though wide enough for carts, was seldom used any more. It had been dry once, but since winters had grown wetter, its low level meant that it flooded often, so the only people who used it were those on foot or horseback. No carter or herdsman would be foolish enough to attempt it unless the weather had been dry for weeks.

It had taken us so long to get out of the town that night was drawing in before we reached the road. We trudged along in silence, concentrating on keeping upright on the slippery track. Our clothes were soaked through and our boots were so heavy with mud, it felt as if we were wearing leg-irons. The rain drops beat down, drumming out their own psalms of contrition as if we were the condemned on the way to the gallows. We passed no one on the road and as darkness gathered around us, I hoped it would stay that way, for there are many kinds of traveller, human and worse, who stalk lonely roads after dark. And I had no desire to get acquainted with any of them.

Then, rounding a bend, we saw a solitary wagon ahead of us. It was stuck deep in a water-filled rut, listing heavily to one side. I recognized both the wagon and its owner immediately. Zophiel, the great magician, was up to his calves in glutinous mud, trying to hoist the wagon upright with his shoulder and push it forward at the same time, but the mud sucked on the wheel, pulling it down. The horse had long since given up trying to pull the wagon forward. It stood between the shafts, head down in the rain, trying to reach a solitary clump of grass that still remained upright in the mud. With Zophiel at the back of the wagon, there was no one to lead it forward, and none of his curses or threats was having the slightest effect on the beast.

Jofre's miserable expression melted into a grin of delight when he recognized the figure floundering in the mud. 'Serves him right,' he muttered.

Rodrigo, striding on ahead, didn't hear him and was not meant to either. I guessed Jofre, wisely, hadn't told Rodrigo about his wager with Zophiel.

Jofre nudged me. 'I say we lean on the wagon as we go by and push it down even further into the mud.'

'And I say it's better to help him. It puts him in our debt. You don't want to rush revenge, my lad; it always tastes sweeter if it's brewed slowly.'

But before we could draw level with the wagon a young man suddenly emerged from the shadows on the track ahead of us. Despite his preoccupation with the wagon, Zophiel sensed the movement and whirled around, whipping out a long thin dagger and jabbing it towards the young man's stomach. The man sprang back and held up his open hands in a gesture of surrender.

'No, please, I mean you no harm. It's my wife.'

Hands still raised, he gestured with his chin towards the

clump of trees from which he'd emerged. There was still just enough light to make out a woman sitting on the stump of a tree, her cloak wrapped tightly about her against the rain.

'My wife,' the young man began again. 'She can't walk any further tonight. She's pregnant.'

'So,' growled Zophiel, 'what are you telling me for? I didn't father her child.'

'I thought you might let her ride in your wagon. Not me, of course, I can walk. I don't mind walking, I'm used to it, but Adela, she –'

'Are you even more stupid than you appear? Does it look as if this wagon is going anywhere? Clear off.'

Zophiel walked around the wagon to his horse and began pulling on the halter, using his whip freely in a vain effort to get the poor beast to move forward. The boy followed him, keeping a safe distance from the whip.

'Please, she can't spend the night in the open in this rain. I'll help you lift the wheel out, if you'll –'

'You,' Zophiel spat, 'you couldn't lift the skin off a roast chicken.'

'But we could,' Rodrigo said, stepping forward.

The dagger was in Zophiel's hand again and he backed nervously up against the solid side of the wagon, his eyes darting all around, trying to see if there were any more of us hiding in the shadows. Jofre giggled. He was enjoying every minute of this.

Rodrigo gave his most courtly bow. 'The minstrel Rodrigo at your service, *signore*. My pupil, Jofre, and our companion, a camelot.'

Zophiel peered closely at us.

'You!' he said, as his gaze alighted on Jofre. He swiftly backed away, his dagger sweeping from side to side in front of him as if he were preparing to take us all on. 'If you think you're going to get the boy's money back, you are mistaken, my friend. He was –'

'Money?' Rodrigo looked puzzled.

Jofre was carefully studying his mud-caked boots.

'The price to see the merchild,' I explained quickly.

Rodrigo nodded, apparently satisfied, then turned back to Zophiel and held his hands up in imitation of the young man. 'Rest assured, *signore*, we have no intention of robbing you of your money. We were about to offer our help, one traveller to another, when this gentleman approached. But now he is here, between us we will soon get your wagon on the move.'

Zophiel continued to eye us suspiciously. 'And how much do you want for your help?'

I answered for him. 'These lads will shift the wagon, if you'll agree to give a ride to this man's wife.' I looked around. Rain was streaming down our faces. We were so wet and muddy that we might have been dragged out of a river. 'It's my guess that we're all in need of dry shelter tonight. There are no inns on this road, but I do know of a place that'll keep out the rain, if it's not already occupied.'

Zophiel glanced over to where, in the semi-darkness, we could just make out the smudge of the woman still huddled on the tree stump. 'If I put her on the wagon, it will weigh it down into the mud again. Besides,' he added petulantly, 'there's no room, the wagon's full.'

'Then let her ride where you sit. She can't weigh more than you. You walk and lead the horse. In the dark that would, in any case, be the safest course unless you want to end up overturned.'

'And why should I walk when a woman rides? If her

husband drags her on some fool journey on foot in her condition, he only has himself to blame.'

The wind was getting up and lashing the rain against our faces, burning the skin already raw from wet and cold.

'Come now, Zophiel,' I said. 'None of us would be on the road this night unless we were forced to be. Let's not waste any more time. We're all getting soaked to the skin and your wheels are settling deeper in the mud. It seems to me you have a simple choice: stay here all night in the rain with your wagon stuck fast and you prey to any cut-throat that comes along, or give the woman a ride and let us help you on your way. We'll all walk alongside you and put our shoulders to the wheel each time the wagon gets stuck, which it surely will in this mud with or without the woman. What do you say? If we help one another this night, we may all find a dry bed before dawn.'

4. Adela and Osmond

And so it was that the six of us found ourselves spending a night together, huddled round a fire in a cave listening to the river roaring over the boulders of its bed and the rain plashing down on the leaves of the trees. The cave was broad but low and shallow, like a fool's grin carved on the face of the rock. It was positioned about five or six feet up the cliff on the side of the gorge, but there were enough fallen boulders and ledges at the base to make it a comparatively easy climb even for me and the pregnant Adela. And it was unoccupied, as I hoped it would be, for even in daylight the cave was well concealed from the road behind a tangle of tall trees. In the dark it was impossible to see, unless you knew where to look for it, and it had even taken me a while to find it again.

The walls of the cave were smooth with long horizontal ridges as if a giant potter had run his fingertips along wet clay, and the floor sloped down towards the mouth, so that it was dry inside all year round. Years ago, a herdsman or hermit had built a low wall of rough stone across part of the entrance and over time dry vegetation and twigs had accumulated behind it, which provided good kindling for our fire. We soon had a fine blaze started and, within the wall's shelter, the fire burned true, with only the occasional plume of smoke billowing back into the cave.

We'd each thrown what we had into the pot – beans, onions, herbs and a few strips of salted pork – to make a pottage. It was hot and filling and a deal better than you'd find in any of the inns in those parts. With our bellies full and limbs at last warming up, we were all beginning to relax.

I set stones to heat on the edge of the fire. Hot stones wrapped in a bit of sacking make good comforters for the feet in the chill hours of the night. It was a trick I learned years ago and I guessed Adela would be glad of a little comfort later. Something told me that our pair of turtle doves were not accustomed to spending a night in a cave.

They say like seeks like and if that is true, then these two were made for each other. They were both blond with wide Saxon faces and eyes as blue and bright as speedwell flowers. Osmond was a broad, stocky lad, well fleshed, with a smooth, clear complexion that many a girl would envy. Adela too had the big bones of her Saxon ancestry, but unlike Osmond she was thin, her cheeks stood out sharply as if she had lately gone hungry for many weeks and there were dark circles around her eyes. Some women suffer such sickness through their early months of pregnancy that they can scarcely keep a morsel down, but if that was the cause of her emaciation, she had plainly recovered from it, for there was little wrong with her appetite that night.

She recovered a little after her meal and lay propped against some of the packs, resting, while Osmond fussed round her checking that she was warm enough, not tired, not in pain, not hungry, not thirsty, until even she laughingly begged him to rest. But that he could not do, and asked me again, though he had already done so a dozen times, if I thought there really were cut-throats or robbers living in this gorge.

That question hung heavy in Zophiel's mind also. We'd been forced to leave his wagon and horse at the base of the cliff and though we had covered the wagon well with branches and tethered his horse in the thick shrubbery where it could not be seen from the road, Zophiel would not rest until he had unloaded his boxes and stored them in the cave behind us. No one dared to enquire what the boxes contained; he was suspicious enough of us already, but whatever it was, it did not appear to be food, for although he contributed a generous quantity of dried beans to the pottage, he had to return to the wagon for them.

Jofre lay in the dark at the back of the cave wrapped in his cloak. Rodrigo had urged him to come closer to the fire and share its warmth with the rest of us, but he had made the excuse that he wanted to sleep, although I sensed he was still very much awake. I suspected he was faking sleep in order to avoid Zophiel, but it isn't easy to avoid someone when you're sharing a small cave with them.

Jofre had been as taut as a drawn bowstring ever since we'd pulled Zophiel's wagon out of the mud. I knew he was dreading Zophiel raising the subject of the wager again. I was as anxious as he was to prevent that particular word slipping out, for if Rodrigo found out just how much of their hard-earned money his pupil had lost, he'd be furious, and who could blame him? But if he tore a strip off the lad in front of everyone, Jofre was likely to storm off into the night, and if he didn't break his own neck in the dark, one of us would surely break ours if we had to go looking for him.

Up to then, Zophiel had been too preoccupied with his

boxes to concern himself with conversation, but now that everyone was settling in for the night, a diversion was called for, so I cast about for a subject that would lead us far away from wagers and magic tricks.

'Adela, is this your first baby? I thought so, judging by the way your poor husband is clucking round. Make the most of it now, come the second one and he'll be lying down with a headache while you do the fetching and carrying.'

Adela, blushing, glanced at Osmond, but said nothing.

I tried again. 'You'd best push it out early; his nerves won't stand a long confinement. When's it due?'

'Around Christmas or a little before,' she said shyly, glancing up at Osmond again.

He rubbed her hand and grimaced.

'That's four months yet. If she can't manage to walk now, what's she going to be like come December?' Zophiel said coldly, his gaze fixed on the darkness outside.

Osmond leaped to his wife's defence. 'She can walk. It was the crowd of people all leaving the town so quickly, they were jostling her and she grew faint. She's strong usually, aren't you, Adela? And besides, we'll have our own house somewhere long before her baby's due.'

Zophiel turned to look at Osmond. 'So you'll have your own house, will you, my young friend? You have property, do you? Money?' He inclined his head in a mocking bow. 'Do forgive me, my lord, I didn't realize I was travelling in the company of nobility.'

Osmond blushed furiously. 'I'll earn money.'

'Doing what exactly?' Osmond's earnestness seemed to amuse Zophiel. He glanced over at their packs. 'You're travelling light. So what are you, my friend, a merchant, a jester, a thief perhaps?'

Osmond's fists clenched and Adela's hand flew up to grab his shirt. He took a deep breath, evidently struggling to keep his reply civil.

'I, sir, am a painter, an artist employed to paint the pictures of saints and martyrs on church walls. The Nativity, the Crucifixion, the Last Judgment, I can do them all.'

Zophiel raised his eyebrows. 'Is that so? I've never heard of a married man in such employ, surely it's monks and lay brothers who undertake that holy task?'

Adela was biting her lip. She seemed on the point of saying something, but Osmond answered first.

'I paint those churches which are too far away from the abbeys and monasteries to be visited by the artists in holy orders. I paint the poor ones.'

'Then you will make a poor living.'

Osmond's fists clenched again. 'I can earn enough to –'

'What's that sound?' Jofre was leaning forward, staring beyond the fire, all pretence of sleep abandoned.

Zophiel was on his feet in an instant, staring out into the darkness beyond the cave. We listened, but heard nothing except for the crackling of the wood on the fire, and the thunder of water in the river below. After a few minutes, Zophiel shook his head and settled down by the fire once more, but his eyes darted restlessly around as he continued to peer out into the impenetrable blackness.

Rodrigo, with a glance at Osmond's still furious expression, broke the heavy silence that followed. 'And where will you go, Zophiel? You have plans?'

'I had planned to go to Bristol to find passage on a ship. I have business in Ireland.'

'You're too late,' Osmond said. 'If what they told us at the fair is right, you won't find any of the ports open anywhere between Bristol and Gloucester.' The knowledge that the great Zophiel's plans had been thwarted seemed to have cheered him up enormously.

Zophiel glared at him. 'Bristol and Gloucester are not the only ports in England, or did your schoolmaster neglect to teach you that? I assume of course that you did have some kind of rudimentary schooling, though perhaps your poor master gave up on the attempt, and who can blame him?'

Once again Adela had to grab Osmond's arm. She glanced over at us with a timid smile. 'Where will you all go now that they've closed the fair?'

'The three of us are travelling north to the shrine of St John Shorne,' Rodrigo told her before I could answer. 'I have not been there myself, but Camelot says there are many inns there, many pilgrims. It is a good place to find work and lodgings. A good place to stay until the pestilence has burned itself out. And they will not close a shrine.'

Osmond frowned. 'I thought I knew most of the saints of England, but I haven't heard of this St John.'

'That's because he is no saint,' Zophiel said, his gaze flicking momentarily from the mouth of the cave.

'It's true he's not actually been canonized,' I told them. 'Though don't say that too loudly at his shrine; the local clergy and villagers are apt to take violent offence. But he's only been dead these thirty years and the locals are so sure he will be recognized as a saint, they've given him the title already. And assayed saint or not, there's no question that his miracles draw in the crowds.'

'Miracles which have not been verified by the Holy Church,' Zophiel said.

I shrugged. 'Nevertheless the crowds believe in them and where there are crowds, there's money to be earned.'

'What kind of miracles?' Adela asked eagerly.

'He was the rector of the parish of North Marston, that's

where his shrine now stands, and there was a great drought there. Crops, animals and people were all suffering. They say Rector John struck the ground with his rod, just like Moses, and a wellspring opened up on that spot, which never failed and never froze. And since, when he was alive, Rector John is also said to have cured colds, fevers, melancholia and the toothache, and even revived those who died from drowning, people now flock to his well to be cured of those same maladies. After all, who hasn't suffered a fever or a toothache at some time?'

'And where exactly would people have drowned in North Marston, if there was no water?' Zophiel asked. 'Or perhaps they were so desperate to be cured of a runny nose that they fell into his miraculous well.'

He had a point. Zophiel was sharp, you had to admit that.

'I make no claims. I can only tell you what they say. Besides, most pilgrims come out of curiosity to see the boot. That's the miracle that really draws the crowds.'

Zophiel snorted. 'Ah yes, the famous boot. Proof, if any was needed, that the whole story is nothing but a sham to con money from the gullible.'

'But if people believe in it, then it will cure them. The art, Zophiel, is to sell a man what he believes in, then you're giving him the gift of hope. And hope itself is always genuine. It's only what it's placed in that can prove to be false.'

'Hope is for the weak, Camelot.'

'But what about the boot?' Adela interrupted, reddening as Zophiel turned to stare contemptuously at her.

'Apparently while he was exorcizing one poor man from the demon of gout, Rector John captured the devil himself inside the man's boot. Many old people in the village swear they actually saw the devil trapped in the boot, but he made himself as small as a beetle and crept out through one of the lace-holes and flew away. And now that same boot is on display beside his shrine. They say anyone who puts the boot on will feel their gout fly away with the devil out of the very same lace-hole. The crowds –'

'Listen!' Jofre called out again urgently.

We stiffened, motionless, straining to hear. And this time we heard the sound too. It was a long way off, but unmistakable, a howl, then another and another. Then nothing.

Rodrigo drew his cloak more tightly around him. 'Go back to sleep, *ragazzo*. It is only a dog.'

'That's no dog, that's a wolf's howl,' Zophiel said sharply.

Adela gasped and Osmond put his arms round her protectively. 'Don't joke; you're upsetting Adela.'

I shook my head. 'He's not jesting; it is a wolf. But it came from the other side of the hill, not the gorge. And even if it enters the gorge, the fire will keep it at bay.'

'If the wolf is a beast, yes,' said Zophiel, 'but if it's a human wolf then the fire will attract it towards us.' He was staring intently out of the mouth of the cave into the darkness beyond. He had rocked forward into a crouching position, his hand fumbling for the knife in his belt. 'There are bands of robbers and murderers who use the calls of wolves and owls to signal one another. Hills and gorges like this are infested with them.'

Osmond looked stricken. He seemed torn between rushing out of the cave to attack the cut-throat band single-handed and holding Adela so tightly in his arms that he was in danger of crushing her.

'That's a relief, Zophiel,' I said, trying to lighten the mood. 'For a moment I thought you were talking about werewolves, but if we're talking mere robbers and murderers, why, you four strapping lads are more than a match for them. Besides, as I said, the howl didn't come from the gorge, so they'll not see the fire, whatever they are.'

Zophiel, as we were all to discover in time, was not a man who tolerated his words being dismissed lightly. His eyes, when he turned to me, had narrowed and the mouth curled into that mocking smile I was beginning to know only too well.

'Werewolves, Camelot? Come now, you surely don't believe those tales told to frighten women and children. I didn't take you for a superstitious fool. Now, if young Osmond here had said such a thing . . .'

Young Osmond, his anxiety temporarily forgotten, looked as if he was about to do more than simply say something.

I feigned a look of surprise. 'I'm shocked, Zophiel. Has the Church not declared it heresy to deny the existence of werewolves? Are they not just as real as mermaids?' I touched my scar. 'How do you think I came by this?'

Adela opened her eyes wide. 'A werewolf did that?'

Rodrigo opened his mouth to say something, but I caught his eye and he contented himself with a knowing grin. Having gained their attention, I settled myself more comfortably and began my tale.

'Many years ago, when I was a child, I lived with my mother and father in a remote, thickly wooded valley on the border between Scotland and England. My father worked in the woods as a board-hewer, cutting trees to make joists and beams. He worked hard for a living and we got by well enough. But one day, as he was at his work, his axe head worked loose from the shaft and flew off, embedding itself in his foot. The cut was deep; it festered and in less than a week, he died. My mother struggled on, but it was a hard, cruel life for a woman alone and there was little food on the table.

'Then one summer's day, we found a stranger, a traveller, lying gravely wounded in the forest. We took him home and tended his wounds, not knowing whether he would live or die. For many days he tossed and turned in a fever, but eventually the fever broke and he began to recover. He was a handsome man, strong and tall, and my mother began to fall in love with him, so that when the time came that he proposed to her, she did not hesitate to say yes.

'I adored my stepfather. He was bold and brave and could run like the wind. And he was a good provider too, for once a month, when the moon was full enough for hunting, he would disappear into the forest before sunset and not return until dawn. When he did return he always had a good haul of birds and animals for the pot. Everyone remarked that he was an exceptionally skilled hunter, for he took with him neither dogs nor bow, but went out armed only with a knife. I wanted to become a hunter just like him and begged him to take me on his hunting trips, but he always refused, saying I was too young.

'Then farmers round about began to complain that a wolf had taken up residence in the valley. Lambs went missing and pigs were found with their throats torn out. A lone wolf was heard in the night howling at the full moon. The farmers knew that if they didn't kill the wolf, they wouldn't have an animal left alive come spring, so they decided to form a hunting party to track the wolf down. They invited my stepfather to join them for he was by far the best hunter, but he refused. He told them that he had neither heard nor seen a wolf in the forest and, in that, he spoke the truth.

'That night my stepfather set off alone as usual to hunt. Again I begged to go with him. He laughed, saying I was too slow to keep up with him. But I was determined to prove him wrong, so as the sun began to set, I slipped out of the cottage and followed my stepfather into the trees. I had to hurry to keep up with him. He didn't stop to lay traps or follow a trail, but kept bounding on with great loping strides, so that eventually I lost sight of him.

'By now it was dark and the moon was rising over the trees, and I realized there was nothing for it but to turn for home. But I'd not taken more than a few steps when I heard a sound which made my blood run cold. It was the cry of a wolf, and not just a cry, but a howl of pain as if the creature was in agony. I stood rooted to the spot. As the silver light of the moon shone full upon the forest floor, I saw it, the great shaggy head and yellow eyes of a wolf, except that this wolf was not crouched on all fours like a beast, it was standing upright like a man.

'I screamed in fear and the wolf turned. It bared its great white fangs and snarled. But as it sprang at me, there came the sounds of men crashing through the undergrowth and the barking of dogs. As it caught sight of the blazing torches, the wolf fled. The farmers and the dogs took off after it. The wolf easily outstripped them, but the dogs followed its trail and the farmers followed the dogs.

'But I knew where the wolf was going. When a creature is hunted it makes for its home. I reached our cottage before the farmers and their dogs, but not before the wolf. My mother lay on the floor, covered in blood, her throat torn out. The wolf was crouching over her. But as it turned to spring at me, I managed to roll under the bed where its snapping jaws couldn't reach me. In a fury, the wolf pawed at me and its huge claws caught my face, ripping it open.

'The farmers sent their dogs through the door to distract the wolf while they pulled me out through the tiny cottage window. But dogs are no match for a werewolf and no man would risk a bite from the creature, so they barricaded the werewolf in the cottage and burned it to the ground. The howls of the wolf rang through the forest and filled the valley, until at last it was consumed in the flames and howled no more.'

There was silence as I finished the story. No one moved. Adela's eyes were wide and Jofre's mouth was open.

Rodrigo suddenly gave a bellow of laughter, slapping me on the back. 'A good tale, Camelot, but did I not hear you swear to that merchant at the fair you left your eye in the Holy Land?'

'That my eye is lost is the truth, Rodrigo. And since it can no longer serve me by seeing, I may as well put it to good use to provide food for our bellies and a dry bed.'

Rodrigo shook his head, smiling, then he suddenly turned to Osmond. 'Speaking of shelter, I have been thinking. You and your wife should come with us to St John's shrine. You paint holy scenes. If the shrine is rich, perhaps they will need a painter. And, for Adela, it will be a good place to rest over winter while she has the child. You will find lodgings there and a midwife to help Adela when her time comes, will he not, Camelot?'

Osmond glanced at Adela and both beamed eagerly at me.

I could feel the smile freeze on my face and silently cursed Rodrigo. Did he think this was some sort of a pilgrimage? As if things weren't hard enough already, now he was making me responsible for getting a pregnant woman, who could barely walk, all the way to North Marston. I could not afford to be saddled with them too. I'd wager the skull of St Peter that our turtle doves had no more experience on the road than Rodrigo and Jofre. They would slow us down badly.

The pestilence was closing in from the south and west. I didn't have time to act as nursemaid to a pack of novices. Who did they think I was – Moses? But what could I do? I saw the hope in their faces and I could not bring myself to say no.

There were no more wolf howls; only the steady beat of rain on leaves and the rushing torrent of the river broke the silence of the darkness outside. My body was aching with tiredness, but my mind was too full of the journey which lay before us to allow me to sleep, so I offered to take first watch, and the others made themselves as comfortable as they could for the long night ahead.

Osmond unbuckled Adela's shoes, then peeled off her sodden and filthy hose, tenderly massaging her cold wet feet. The pointed red shoes were light and shapely, patterned with daisies formed by punched holes in the leather. They'd been fashioned for duties about the house or strolling in cloistered walkways, but they were useless for trailing through puddles or tramping along cart tracks. It was sheer stupidity to set out on the road in them. This journey they were bound on had not been well planned; maybe it had not been planned at all.

What would force a young couple like this on to the road in such haste? My throat suddenly grew dry. What if they had come from Bristol and had fled when the pestilence struck? What if the contagion already lay upon their clothes? I shook myself impatiently; I could not start jumping in fear every time I met a stranger, for everyone was a stranger on the road. There were not enough caves in England for us all to take to the hills and live like hermits. Besides, even hermits need someone to bring them food.

'Here.' I wrapped one of the hot stones in sacking and slid it towards Adela. 'Warm your feet on this.'

She smiled gratefully. 'You're kind. Thank you.'

I picked up her shoes and set them to dry near the fire. Cordwain leather, the finest, you could tell that simply by touch despite the mud on them. It was many years since I'd indulged in shoes that were not made for walking and I'd never have that luxury again. The skin on my feet had grown so hard and callused from all the miles I had tramped, they'd make a pair of leather shoes themselves.

Adela sat hunched, her arms wrapped around herself, her soft bare feet pressed tightly against the hot stone. She shivered. Her cloak was still too wet to wrap around her, but evidently neither of them had thought to bring anything else.

I sighed and tossed her my blanket. 'Wrap yourself in this before you catch your death.'

'But I can't take your blanket. You might catch a chill.'

It was not politeness that made her say it. Despite her exhaustion, her eyes were full of genuine concern. Doubtless at her young age she saw me as some old dotard who should be wrapped up and fed slops, but for all that I was touched – most would put their own comfort before that of an old man.

'It's best I don't get too warm if I'm to take first watch. At my great age I'm likely to nod off if I get comfortable. But you should try and get as much rest as you can. You'll need all your strength come morning.'

I hardly needed to urge her to sleep; her eyelids were already drooping with weariness.

'Why don't you take off your veil and make yourself comfortable? Your husband won't mind, I'm sure. You'll stick yourself with the pins if you fall asleep with that on.'

Her hand rapidly outlined the edges of the linen veil that framed her face, as if to reassure herself that it was still in place. It was pinned to a barbette beneath her chin, concealing all of her hair save for a flaxen wisp at the temple. It was a curiously old-fashioned style for such a beautiful young woman. These days you only saw old women still wearing the barbette, seeing no reason to forsake something they had worn all their lives. But most were only to glad to be free of such a chafing restraint.

'I can't . . . I don't need to take it off. I don't sleep lying down, because . . . of my baby. The bile rises if I lie flat,' she added hastily.

Osmond slipped his arm around her and she leaned back gratefully against his shoulder. Even if she didn't feel the pins, he would by morning; it took nearly a dozen to fasten a veil like that. But it seemed he would put up with anything to protect his new bride.

She was not used to sleeping among strangers, that much was plain. She'd had a sheltered upbringing, but neither shyness nor modesty was an asset on the road. Did she, did either of them have any idea what they were facing out there? Had I once really been as naïve as them? When you are in love and you are young, you think that nothing life can throw at you is insurmountable. You think that together you can overcome anything. I prayed they would never come to know how swiftly life can divide you.

The dancing orange flames cast huge grey shadows of us on to the wall of the cave, our every movement parodied in a grotesque form, like a mummers' play performed for our mockery. Our shadows poured into one another, so that monsters appeared with two shaggy heads. Humpbacked dragons curled in sleep and mermaids flicked their sinuous tails. Shadows are such insubstantial things, yet they are bigger than any of us.

Zophiel sat upright against his boxes, his head lolling

uncomfortably on his chest. He'd pay for that in the morning with a stiff neck, but I wasn't too sorry. Rodrigo lay stretched out, snoring, sleeping the untroubled sleep of the just. Adela and Osmond nestled against the wall of the cave, Adela's head snuggled against Osmond's shoulder as his arms cradled her.

Jofre was curled up in the back of the cave as he had been all evening, but he was not asleep. The firelight glittered in his open eyes. He was watching Osmond and Adela. He couldn't take his eyes off them. And suddenly it dawned on me why he'd been so quiet all evening. It was not just the fear that Zophiel might mention the wager; the poor boy was in love. Why do the young have to fall in love at first sight and fall so hard? Adela and Osmond were newly married; what did Jofre think could possibly come of it? But the eternal triangle is as old as man himself. You might even say that Adam, Eve and God were the first, and look where that led. And in all those centuries of lovers' knots, no good ever came of it. But it was useless to warn him that it would only lead to pain. The young can believe in werewolves and mermaids, but not that the old have ever been in love.

As I watched the still bodies of Adela and Osmond, Rodrigo and Jofre bathed in the soft red glow from the fire, I realized with a sudden rush of emptiness that I belonged to no one, and for the first time in many years, I felt terribly alone. I had thought that I wasn't afraid of death. I was old and I knew it was inevitable, but I had never given it a shape before. Now, as this terrible sickness rolled inexorably towards us, I glimpsed for the first time the form death might assume and felt the panic rising in my throat.

Zophiel was anxious to be off at first light. The gorge made him nervous; being away from his wagon made him nervous;

we made him nervous. I think he hoped that as soon as he was clear of the gorge, he could rid himself of all of us, especially Adela.

Adela seemed stronger after a night's sleep, but she was still pale and didn't look as if her new-found strength would hold out for long. But after Zophiel's jibes of the night before, she was determined to show that she could walk as well as the rest of us, and even Osmond seemed to want to prove his wife's stamina to Zophiel. But Rodrigo, gallant as ever, was having none of it. He insisted that if we were to pull and push the wagon filled with Zophiel's boxes out of every water-filled rut on the track, Zophiel should at least assist by leading his horse on foot and Adela should be allowed to ride and save her strength.

Zophiel, seeing no way out of the gorge without our help, acquiesced with ill grace, venting his spleen for the next mile or so by tormenting the morose Jofre. Having realized that Jofre had kept the wager from his master, Zophiel was amusing himself by constantly turning the conversation back to the point where he seemed about to reveal the secret, before deftly turning aside from it. Zophiel enjoyed the game of cat and mouse and he was a skilled practitioner.

But this time it was Rodrigo himself who created the diversion. He suddenly clapped his hand to his forehead.

'Camelot, I meant to tell you that a friend of yours, a child, was asking for you at the fair yesterday. I should have told you before, but all the commotion when we had to leave drove it from my head.'

I frowned. 'I don't know any children.'

'She said she knew you. She was a pretty child, unusual. Her hair, it was . . . like frost.'

I felt a chill as if cold, wet rags had been drawn over my skin. So Narigorm had been at the fair. I didn't know whether I was relieved or disturbed. I had begun to think that I had imagined seeing her. Then a thought struck me.

'Rodrigo, there were hundreds of people at the fair, how did she know that you knew me? Did you tell her?'

He shook his head, then shrugged. 'Maybe she saw us together. But she asked me to tell you she will be with you soon. That is good news, yes?'

'You didn't tell her where we were going, did you?' I said, struggling to keep the note of alarm out of my voice.

Again he shook his head. 'No, she did not ask.'

I breathed out heavily. I could see by the perplexed expression on Rodrigo's face that my reaction had not been what he expected and I couldn't explain my disquiet, not even to myself. Why would she send me such a message? Was she following me? No, that was a foolish thought. Now I really was imagining things; why on earth would a child want to follow an old man she'd barely met?

'Camelot, this child, is she –' Rodrigo began.

But his question was cut off by a sudden shriek which echoed through the gorge, freezing us in our tracks. There was no mistaking this sound; it was human and the human was in desperate trouble. The sound came from a little way ahead of us round the curve of the track, but our view was blocked by an outcrop of rock. As the shrieks continued, Rodrigo and Osmond pulled out their knives and sprinted down the track in the direction of the cries, closely followed by Jofre. But even as they ran, the screams stopped abruptly as if severed with an axe. Zophiel, Adela and I followed more slowly with the wagon, but as we cautiously rounded the bend we saw the others standing in the track, staring at something beyond.

Two men, their hoods drawn low over their heads, were bending over a third man lying in the mud. One of the hooded men was dragging a leather pack away from the prone body, the other rummaging clumsily through the dead man's clothes. The murder had not been subtle. The victim's head was a bloody mangle of hair, brain and bone. His face would have been unrecognizable even to his own mother. The blows had doubtless been inflicted by the heavy wooden clubs which still dangled on leather straps from the murderers' wrists. The robbers had not even troubled to drag him off the track into the undergrowth to do their work and now, far from running off in fear when they saw us approach, they continued to work over their prey, like feral dogs who cannot be scared away from their kill.

Osmond was the first to break the stunned silence; yelling, he started towards the men, waving his arms as if to drive off animals. The two robbers raised their heads. They threw back their hoods, but remained crouched over the bloody corpse.

'Going to stop us, young master?'

It was Osmond who stopped. The faces that leered up at him appeared at first to be grinning. But those were not smiles on their faces. Their lips, like their noses, were being eaten away. Patches of grey dead flesh covered their faces, like mould on rotting fruit. They were lepers.

They stood up and began to limp towards us, spinning the cudgels on their wrists as they no doubt had done before they struck the unfortunate wretch on the track.

'Going to lay hands on us, young master? Going to take us? I've got an idea – why don't you give us that fine wagon of yours? I'm tired of walking. I could do with a wagon to carry me. I'll bet you've some good food on that wagon, wine too. Come on then, hand it over, or do you want us to give you a great big kiss for it?'

They had nothing to lose. The Church had already

declared them dead to the world. What could the law do to them that was worse? Hang them? In their condition hanging might have been a blessing, if any man had dared, but they were right, who was going to lay hold of them to bring them to justice? Who would have the courage to seize those fingerless hands and bind them tight or put a noose round those scabby necks? Can you execute a dead man? We steal relics from the dead and now it seemed the dead were going to steal from us.

It was Rodrigo who threw the knife. It was a powerful throw from a muscular arm. The blade sank deep into the leper's chest. He screamed, staggering backwards from the impact, trying to wrench the knife out with the stumps of his fingerless hands. Then he tottered towards us, mouth open, arms stretched wide as if he would gather us all to the grave with him, before he crumpled lifeless into the mud. His companion had already turned tail and was scuttling into the trees. He did not look back to see his friend fall.

5. The Cripples' Wedding

The six of us were obliged to spend many more nights sleeping outdoors in the cold and wet. The encounter with the lepers in the gorge seemed to have convinced Zophiel that it was not safe to travel alone, especially with the roads and tracks as waterlogged as they were. And although I now know that Zophiel had a more pressing reason for travelling in our company, at the time I believed that, despite his contempt for St John and his miracles, even he could see the sense in making for his shrine and settling there until the worst was over and the ports were open again. I, for one, was thankful for that, for we needed his wagon for Adela. She was in no condition to trudge through the mud, wind and rain, mile after mile.

It had rained every day for the past three months and though summers had been bad these last few years, none of us could remember any as bad this.

'If rain on Midsummer's Day should fall, it will rain for seven weeks more,' Adela had recited cheerily at first, much to Zophiel's intense irritation.

But seven weeks had come and gone. St Swithin's Day and his forty days and forty nights of rain had also come and gone. And still it rained. Not even Adela had faith in her rhymes any more. There was nothing natural about this rain.

And with each day's downfall the mud grew deeper, the walking harder, our bellies emptier. The truth was, though none of us admitted as much, we had begun to depend on one another to survive. We shared all our food and ale which we bought with the little each of us earned from the villages we trundled through. We made makeshift shelters when we couldn't find an inn or a barn, and helped to gather fodder for the horse.

The mare, as we soon discovered, had been well named. Her coat had a fiery red-gold sheen to it and for that she had been named Xanthus, after the immortal talking horse given to Achilles. But in temperament she took after that more infamous beast of the same name, the man-eating mare of King Diomedes, except that our Xanthus was an even greater misanthrope, for unlike the king's horse who only devoured his enemies, she took delight in savaging friend as well as foe. She had a nasty habit of biting, without warning, anyone who got within range of her teeth, and for no good cause except that it amused her. So we quickly learned to judge the reach of her neck and to keep a safe distance, unless we had a firm grip on her bridle.

But Xanthus and the wagon she pulled became our ark, our covenant, the standard around which we rallied. We pulled them both out of ruts during the day and kept watch over them at night. The wagon carried our packs, our food, our ale; it even gave us shelter if we could find no other. All six of us now were headed towards the safety of St John's shrine to sit out the weather and the pestilence, and the thought of the dry beds that awaited us there, the easy money, the hot food and no more trudging in the mud and rain, was what kept us going when our bellies were aching and our feet so wet and numb we could have broken our toes off and sold them as relics.

And something else was spurring me on, though I did not confide it to any of them. Once I had led our little company to North Marston, I would be able to leave them there. They'd be safe. No more acting nursemaid or having to put up with Zophiel's tongue or Jofre's sulks. I'd only have myself to worry about. At North Marston they'd be able to fend for themselves and I could leave them behind with a clear conscience.

The need to reach the shrine was becoming more urgent by the day. Fear was creeping across the land. It rose silently, like the tide in a creek, a cold, grey fear that was seeping into everything. The country was full of the news that the pestilence had reached London. That shook even the most optimistic souls. True, London was a port; it was bound to succumb sooner or later, but it was not a southern port, it was not even a western port. It was on the east coast. The pestilence had crept up on three sides of the land and now it was reaching in to grasp the heart of England.

No one here had actually seen anyone sick with the pestilence; most people knew little of what it did to a man, but that only made them more fearful, for every headache, every cough, every touch of fever might be the beginning. How could you tell? To make matters worse, rumours were spreading that it wasn't just humans who fell to the pestilence; it was animals and birds too. Herds of pigs, sheep, cattle, even horses had sickened and died in the south. Stockmen left their animals at night well and hearty, and by morning when they woke there would not be a beast left standing in the flock.

'Maybe the flagellants will come,' said Rodrigo. 'I saw them once in Venice, marching from church to church. Men and women, naked to the waist save for their white hoods, flogging themselves bloody with metal-tipped whips. Now I hear there are whole armies of them right across Europe, screaming to one another to whip harder and pray louder.'

'And if they do come to England, will you join them?' I asked.

Rodrigo grimaced and bent his head in mock shame. 'You see before you an abject coward, Camelot. I do not relish pain, either giving or receiving it, even for the good of my soul. And you, Camelot? Will you don the white hood?'

My hand darted over the puckered surface of my scar. 'It seems to me that if God wants to punish his children, he is more than capable of wielding his own whip.'

The flagellants didn't come. The English are different. We don't have the passion of the other lands. It's not blood that runs in our veins, but rain. But though the English didn't throw themselves into an orgy of scourging, they found other ways to appease heaven and divert the wrath of God, and who's to say that the pain of that was not worse than a flogging for those who found themselves the victims of it?

It was not good weather for a wedding, not what a bride dreams of, but then nothing about this wedding was the stuff of romantic dreams. The day was bitterly cold as well as wet. A snide wind whipped through the streets, but the villagers of Woolstone were determined to throw themselves into the celebrations just the same and had dressed in their finery, which for the young girls meant their flimsiest and most revealing garments. Their mothers were rushing around arguing about where the garlands should be hung and how the food should be cooked, while their menfolk set up canopies, benches and trestles amongst the tombs and rolled barrels of ale across the graveyard, trampling even the new graves underfoot. It seemed that everyone had become so absorbed in the preparations they had entirely forgotten the reason for this collective madness. But if everyone around you is mad, then that becomes the new sanity, and who were we to complain? For where there is a wedding there is good food and drink, and plenty of it.

I'd heard of the custom of the cripples' wedding many years ago. Some say it dates back to the time before men were Christian. It is said that if you marry two cripples together in the graveyard at the community's expense it will turn away divine wrath and protect the village from whatever pestilence or sickness rages around it. For the charm to work, everyone in the village has to contribute something to the wedding. And in this village, everyone had been coerced into helping with the preparations whether they wanted to or not, for though Woolstone nestles beneath the hill of the White Horse, the villagers knew in their bones that their ancient nag could offer little protection against this new curse.

And when they discovered Rodrigo and Jofre in our company, they had taken it as a sign that this charade was already blessed by God, for had he not sent them two fine musicians just when they were needed? God's hand can be seen in any occurrence for those who are determined to find it there, but then again, so can the devil's.

The newly-weds sat under a canopy dressed simply in clean and serviceable clothes, but done up with chaplets of evergreens and garlanded with grain stalks, fruit and ribbons as if the villagers had been unable to make up their minds if this was a wedding or a harvest home. The wedding ring was fashioned from a scrap of tin, the loving cup was borrowed and the bride was barefoot, but many a young couple have started married life with less and thought it the most perfect wedding on earth, but then they were in love. This pair were not.

The bridegroom was probably no more than twenty, but his body was wasted away down one side. His left arm swung from the socket like a dead hare and his leg dragged uselessly behind him, so that he moved in a series of shuffling hops, leaning on a single crutch. His head was oversized like the head of a giant baby and though he tried to talk, twisting his mouth into contorted shapes, he could not make himself understood. He seemed bemused that everyone was smiling at him and shaking him by the hand. It must have been a bewildering change from the kicks and curses he normally received. He was stuffing food into his mouth and guzzling his ale as fast as he could, spilling it from the sides of his mouth in his haste as if he had never been offered so much food before and feared he never would be again.

The bride was not smiling. She sat motionless where she had been placed, her sightless eyes rolling from side to side. It was hard to tell her age. Years of near starvation had shrivelled her flesh and though some attempt had been made to comb out what remained of her hair, this did not conceal the crusted yellow sores on her scalp and face. The knuckles of her hands were shiny and swollen, the thin fingers twisted together against her palms, so that it would have been impossible to separate them.

She had quickly been abandoned by the village girls who had stood in as her attendants and now, their duty done, they had gone off to kiss and be kissed by their sweethearts. And, although she was surrounded by food, she made no attempt to eat or drink, as if she was well used to smelling the savour of food that was not hers to eat and ale that she could not afford to buy. I slid on to the bench beside the bride, tore a roasted goose leg from the carcass on the table and pressed the woman's cold, waxy hands to it. She half-turned her face towards me and nodded her thanks. At least the blind don't recoil at the sight of my scar. Pressing the goose leg between the knuckles of both hands, she slowly lifted it to her mouth, sniffing at it before biting into it. Unlike her new husband, she ate slowly, as if she had to make this pleasure last.

'You want to be careful, Camelot,' Zophiel drawled in my ear. 'They might choose you as the next groom.'

'Camelot is no cripple,' Rodrigo blazed angrily.

'You think not?' Zophiel reached over my shoulder to spear a succulent spicy mutton olive with the point of his knife. 'He's already carelessly mislaid one eye and doesn't appear to remember where. If he loses the other, he'll make a fine candidate, and with the pestilence spreading as fast as it is, they'll need every cripple they can find.'

'I'm counting on it, Zophiel,' I said quickly, seeing Rodrigo's fists clench. 'How else are old dotards like me going to grease their pikes?'

Zophiel laughed and wandered off in search of more food. I'd discovered that the best way to handle him was not to rise to his taunts. I wished Rodrigo would also realize that. I had an uneasy feeling there was going to be trouble between those two. The sooner we reached the shrine and we could all go our separate ways the better.

As the afternoon darkened into evening, the rain eased and the lanterns and torches were lit. Trestles and benches were moved aside for dancing. Rodrigo and Jofre played, joined by a handful of villagers on drums, whistles, reed-pipes, pots and pans. Jofre had been drinking steadily all evening, but if he played a few bad notes, they were buried under the screeches of the villagers' whistles and pipes.

Rodrigo was not used to having cooking pots thumped in time with his music, but he accepted it with good grace and tried to match his rhythm to their beat, which was rewarded with grins and cries of 'That's better, lad, you're getting it now.'

It was not easy dancing in the graveyard. The dancers tripped over humps and banged into wooden crosses and stone markers, but by now everyone was so merry on the free ale, cider and mead that they roared with laughter every time someone fell over. In the dark corners under the graveyard walls, couples made love, giggling and groaning, pumping up and down, only to roll exhausted off each other and fall asleep where they lay on the ground. Children created their own chaos. As drunk as their parents, they played mad games of chase, threw stones at swinging garlands or ganged up to torment some other poor child.

Zophiel was not dancing. He was still seated on the bench with his arm about the waist of a buxom village girl dressed in a bright yellow kirtle which was too light for the chill of the day. She shivered and, giggling, tried to wriggle under the folds of his cloak. She had that unsteady, bright-eyed look of someone not yet drunk, but well on the way to it. I'd never seen Zophiel with a woman before. I thought he despised them all, but it appeared he did have a use for some of them at least. I hoped for his sake that the girl was not betrothed or wed. Husbands and lovers don't appreciate their goods being pawed, especially by strangers and by travellers least of all.

Suddenly the girl yelped in pain and sprang away from him. A pinch too hard perhaps or a lock of her hair caught on the fastening of his cloak? She swore at him and, tossing her hair, flounced off to join friends on the other side of the graveyard, from where she threw furious glances back in his direction. Zophiel seemed quite unconcerned and made no attempt to go after her. He sat picking at the remains of a duck carcass and when he saw her looking across at him, he raised his tankard in a mocking salute.

The music stopped. A groan went up, but was quickly hushed as the miller clambered unsteadily up on to one of the benches.

'Good sirs.' He hiccuped, tried to bow and nearly toppled headfirst from the bench. Several men standing below pushed him back upright again. 'Good sirs 'n' ladies, the time has come to bed the happy couple, for as we all know, it is no true marriage until it's consum ... consum ... nimated ... until the groom's given her one.' The crowd roared with laughter. 'So let's not keep the happy pair waiting. Lead the bashful bridegroom to his lovely bride.'

'At your command, my lord,' sang out a voice from behind him, and a figure, nimble as a cat, sprang out from the shadows, wrapped in a dark hooded cloak. He bowed low, then threw off his cloak. Several people screamed as the flickering torchlight revealed that under the hood was not a man's face but a grinning white skull.

'Death at your service, good sirs.'

The figure capered before the crowd and the gasps gave way to drunken laughter. The dancing man was naked save for his skull mask. His body had been covered from head to toe in a thick black paste, over which someone had crudely painted white bones so that in the darkness he appeared as a living, cavorting skeleton. All at once the villagers struck up their instruments again, banging on pots and pans, blowing their whistles and pipes, and soon those who could still stand fell into step behind the prancing skeleton who began to lead them widdershins around the edge of the graveyard.

At the centre of this macabre procession was the groom, carried shoulder-high by a group of sturdy lads. He had been half stripped and was now dressed only in a shirt, his bare arse gleaming under the torchlight. The grey wrinkled skin of his withered leg contrasted oddly with the firm muscles of his sound leg, as if the limb of an ancient old man had been sewn on to the body of the youth. He was still grinning, but nervously now, as if he thought that the crowd might turn on him at any moment. I couldn't see the bride in the procession and I assumed that she had already been taken from the graveyard to some cottage where, in due course, the groom would also be carried to spend his wedding night, but there was to be no privacy for this consummation.

After circling the walls three times, the groom was carried back to the centre of the graveyard where they set him down on the ground on all fours like a dog. A straw-filled pallet had been set on top of a grave, pushed hard against the cross at one end which stood as the headboard for this bridal bed. The bride, dressed only in a long white shift, had already been laid on top of it, as if she was a corpse stretched out on her deathbed. Her sightless eyes were wide open and she was moving her head from side to side as if trying to hear what was afoot.

She didn't see the silvery clouds streaming like flood waters across the face of the moon or the flickering torches casting giant shadows on the graveyard walls, or the white glittering eyes of the circle of villagers looking down on her. She didn't see the figure of death lean over her, flicking water from his hyssop twigs as he parodied the blessing of the marriage bed. But she felt the drops fall on her naked face and feet and winced as if they were drops of boiling oil.

The groom, encouraged by playful kicks to his bare backside, crawled towards the prone woman until he was straddling her. Feeling him above her, she raised her hands to try to push him off, but the gesture was useless. Even a woman sound in limb would have been hard put to push his weight off her. She, with her twisted hands and wasted body, stood no chance.

One of the more sober village women took pity on her. 'There, there, lay still, my duck, and it'll soon be over,' she crooned, catching the bride's wrists and pinning them gently but firmly against the cross behind her head.

'Is that what she says to you?' one of the men called out to the woman's husband. The crowd roared with laughter.

'Go on, my son; give her all you've got. We're all counting on you, so see you make a good job of it.'

The bridegroom stared round, mouth hanging open, unable to believe that he was at last being given permission to do to a woman what had always been forbidden him. How many girls had he longed to do this to? Had he tried several times when he was younger and been repulsed? Perhaps he'd been given a sound thrashing into the bargain by the girls' brothers or his own father. Now everyone in the village was urging him to do it. This might be a dream; he might wake up soon.

After it was all over, the women helped the bride to a dark corner and pressed her hands round a beaker of hot spiced ale.

'There, there, my duck, at least you didn't have to look at him. Believe me, with a husband like mine, there's many a night when I wish I was blind.'

They left her crouching on the ground under the graveyard wall. She pressed her back hard against the sharp flinty stones as if pain was the only certainty she could trust in and then she wept. She wept silently, as she did everything; her eyes were sightless, but they could still make tears.

She could console herself with the wedding gifts from the village though – a few pots and pans, an armful of rushlights, some blankets and a pallet, hens and a cockerel, a bag or two of flour and a single-roomed hut which had once been used to store salt, so at least it was dry and had a good stout door. It was a palace compared to what she had owned up until that morning and since the whole community had pitched in she was better set up than many a village girl could expect to be when she wed.

So what if she had no choice in her bridegroom? In that, she was no different from any highborn lady in the land, even a merchant's daughter. For if land, trade or money is entailed, then marriage is simply a business transaction to be negotiated by the parents. Many a bride on her wedding night has passed from girl to woman with her eyes tightly shut and her teeth clenched, praying it will soon be over. No, all things considered, you could argue that the crippled bride had been treated no worse than any royal princess. But then, the flames of a fire are not made less painful by the knowledge that others are burning with you.

I had not yet given the bride a wedding gift myself. I took out of my scrip a little wisp of stiff coarse hair bound up with a white thread and placed it in her lap. She touched it tentatively, a puzzled expression on her face.

'A wedding gift for you, a relic. A few hairs from St Uncumber's beard. You know of St Uncumber?'

She slowly shook her head.

'Her real name was Wilgefortis. She was a princess of Portugal whose father tried to force her to marry the King of Sicily, but she'd taken a vow to remain a virgin, so she prayed that the Blessed Virgin would make her unattractive

83

to her betrothed and her prayers were answered with a beard that sprouted on her face. The King of Sicily withdrew in horror when he saw it and immediately called off the wedding. But the princess didn't have to live long with her beard, for her father, in a rage, had her crucified. Now women pray to her to be unencumbered from their husbands or any burden they bear. You could use this to pray for that too . . . if you wished.'

As I turned to go, she pressed her two hands tightly against the relic, the tears coursing once more down her hollow cheeks. A wisp of hair is not much to pin your hopes upon, but sometimes a wisp is all the hope you can give and it can be enough.

A woman standing near me settled herself back on to a bench and offered a flagon to her neighbour. 'If she doesn't get a bairn from this night's work, it won't be her husband's fault. Did you see him? He was in there quicker than a ferret down a rabbit hole.'

Her friend took a deep swig from the flagon. Cider trickled down her chin and she wiped it with the back of her hand. 'Never mind a bairn. I didn't part with a good cooking pot just to bring another useless cripple into this world. I want to know if it's done the trick and saved us from the pestilence.'

'If this doesn't, nothing will. That rune reader's been right about everything else. Her runes said the musicians would come to bless the wedding and it was her runes picked out the cripples to wed, so it's bound to work if the runes chose them.'

'Did you say a rune reader?' I blurted out before I could stop myself.

The two women stared at me, somewhat put out at having a stranger interrupt their gossip. Finally one said grudgingly:

'Aye, no one in the village could agree who they should choose as bride and groom, let's face it, it's not as if we've a shortage of cripples to pick from, so they asked the rune reader to cast the runes to find the lucky couple.'

'Is she here, the rune reader?'

The woman shook her head. 'If you want your fortune read, you're too late. She was a traveller same as you, just passing through, left a week or more ago.'

'Aye,' the other woman joined in. 'Queer thing she was. Those eyes of hers, give you the shivers just to look at them. It wouldn't surprise me if she was one of the faerie folk; she certainly had the gift.'

I did not ask more. I didn't want to know. There were many diviners working the roads, most of them fey. They deliberately try to look as if they might be descended from faerie folk; it impresses the customers, convinces them the diviner has second sight. There was no reason in the world why the rune reader who came through here should be Narigorm, and even if it was, why should she not have taken this road? Anyone with any sense was heading north. And if it was her, then it meant she was at least a week ahead of us. She was long gone. It was almost a relief to believe that. If she was ahead of us, she couldn't possibly be following me. Her message had been a simple greeting, nothing more, nothing more sinister than that.

I suddenly felt a great weariness. The revels were still continuing, but I'd had enough. The promise of a dry bed, after so many nights sleeping rough, was more tempting than ale or food. I began to pick my way through the drinkers towards the inn. Osmond had already taken Adela back there. He'd seemed troubled all evening. He had taken Adela to sit as far away from the bridal table as he could get, and several times I'd caught him studying her, looking down at her swollen belly with a deep and anxious frown. I began to fear that something was amiss with her. Perhaps she'd complained of pain, but if she had, she showed no signs of it now, eating with relish everything that was offered to her and laughing with the villagers around her. Osmond in contrast had hardly eaten a thing and as soon as the meal was ended, he had led Adela away, though she clearly would have liked to stay. Maybe he was jealous of other men speaking to her, but he'd never shown any sign of that before.

I couldn't see any of the others except for Zophiel who was talking low and earnestly to a big, square-headed youth. Whatever Zophiel said evidently didn't please the young man, for he broke away and strode across to the girl in the yellow kirtle who was now in the company of several lads and girls, laughing and drinking. He grabbed her arm, none too gently, and began to drag her away. The girl tried to wrest herself out of his grasp.

I glanced across at Zophiel. He had retreated to safety and was lounging against the wall, watching the proceedings with amusement. I wondered what exactly he had said to the girl's boyfriend or brother, whichever Square-head was, to make him so annoyed with her. Whatever it was, I was certain Zophiel had baited him deliberately. Perhaps Zophiel had not been as indifferent about the girl walking away as he had pretended to be.

Sensing trouble, a group of about a dozen lads moved nearer, watching with evident interest. I spotted Jofre among them. His face was flushed and he was laughing with two of the young men beside him and ignoring a baby-faced girl who was entwining her arms about him, trying in vain to get him to take notice of her. He swayed, pulled off balance by the weight of the girl hanging on his arm. It was hard to tell just how drunk he was from a distance, but he was not sober, that was certain.

Square-head was shouting at the girl in the yellow kirtle now and she was bawling back. She broke free from him and ran behind one of the other lads for protection, clinging on to him. Square-head drew back his fist and punched her protector hard on the nose. He staggered backwards, taking the girl down with him as he fell. All the lads standing around took this as their signal and entered the fray with a will. Fists and flagons flew through the air.

I heard a familiar roar above the screams and shouts.

'No, Jofre, your hands! *Faccia attenzione!*'

But it was too late; Jofre had pushed forward with the rest and was already lost among the flailing fists and kicking feet.

Bodies crashed down upon benches, tables were over-turned and pots came clattering to the ground. Suddenly the screams redoubled. A smashed lantern had sent a snake of flame slithering up the ribbons and dried grain stalks decorating one of the poles and set fire to the canopy. The fire took hold rapidly, sending orange flames leaping into the night. Fragments of blazing cloth and dry grain stalks floated up into the black sky, hovering menacingly over the thatches of the nearby cottages and wooden byres. The lads were too engrossed in the fight even to notice, but those villagers still sober enough to realize the danger came running over, trying to push the wrestling lads aside and pull the blazing canopy to the ground. Others flung the food from dishes and pots, using them to scoop water from the nearby horse trough to throw over the blaze.

The fire was finally doused. Fortunately, everything was so wet from the months of rain that the thatches on the cottages were not even scorched. The fight was extinguished too. Enough icy water had landed on the combatants to separate those who had not already been knocked out. One by one, the groaning lads were led or dragged away by scolding mothers, wives or girlfriends, their eyes and lips swelling rapidly. It was, you might say, a typical end to a wedding.

Jofre's exit was, if anything, more ignominious. He had thrown a couple of punches, but he was no street fighter. He'd done more damage to himself than his opponents and a vicious punch in his stomach finished him. Rodrigo found him winded and gasping, rolled in a ball, trying to protect his face from the trampling feet around him. His right hand was already purple and swelling. He would not be playing that night or for many nights to come.

6. St John Shorne's Shrine

In early October of that year, amid a cacophony of barking dogs and the blasting horns and raucous cheering of the pilgrims, we finally trundled into North Marston, the home of St John Shorne. We arrived on St Faith's Day, an auspicious day, even though that year there were few griddled Faith cakes on sale, for what little mildewed grain had been salvaged from the rain-sodden fields was already running out. We, like all the travellers arriving that day, gave thanks to St Faith, patron of pilgrims, for a safe conclusion to our journey. And, for once, even I lit a candle in sincere and heart-felt gratitude to her, for never was I more thankful to see a town. No more heaving the wagon out of water-filled ruts fifty times a day. No more trudging through mud and wading through puddles. No more sleeping in wet clothes. We would spend our nights warm and dry until the winter frosts came, bringing an end to the rain and with it, as everyone prayed fervently, an end to the pestilence.

But I, more than anyone, should have remembered that St Faith is also the patron saint of prisoners. I should have taken warning from that and kept on walking. We should never have entered that town.

The shrine of Johannes de Schorne, or John Shorne, as

local people call him, was even busier than I had anticipated. In those early months of the pestilence, shrines flourished. Pilgrimages to the continent were impossible, so those lesser saints in England, whose holy sites had been somewhat neglected in favour of the more fashionable shrines abroad, suddenly found the faithful and the not-so-faithful crowding to them. The waters of St John's well, which tasted strongly of iron, were sworn to be a guaranteed cure for colds and fevers, and though the pestilence was not a common cold, it was certainly a fever, so the crowds teeming around North Marston were more numerous than before. They drank the water to ward off the pestilence and took flasks of it away to drink in their sickbeds in case they did fall prey to it. I too stowed a few flasks in my pack. It always pays to restock whenever the opportunity arises.

The inns and taverns along the road and in the village itself had multiplied like loaves and fishes to feed and shelter the crowds of pilgrims who came to drink the waters of the holy well. The innkeepers had naturally raised their prices extortionately, but we managed to find warm beds in a shabby, but tolerably clean, inn. Zophiel was able to beat the surly innkeeper down a little in price, persuading him that we were there for the winter and that Rodrigo and Jofre would entertain his customers. Not that Zophiel was planning to spend the winter in North Marston, as I soon discovered.

The night after we arrived, I made my way to the Angel, a tavern favoured by the more experienced travellers, where you could still get fried brawn and sharp sauce for an honest price. In the dim mustard fug of the smoking rushlights, it was hard to make out any man's features and those who frequented that particular tavern preferred it that way. But you can't spend a month on the road walking behind a man without recognizing his shape, and I knew Zophiel at once, even though he had his back to me.

He was sitting at one of the corner tables, offering ale to the two men slouched opposite him. Not something Zophiel would do for a stranger, unless he wanted something. As it so happened, the bench behind Zophiel was empty.

One of the men was gesturing with his tankard. 'A ship? You'll be lucky to find one anywhere on the west, not till you get well to the north of here anyhow. Pestilence has spread right up the coast.'

'You're sure of that, my friend?' Zophiel sounded tense. 'There must be some small harbours that have escaped it.'

The man shrugged. 'Happen there is, but who's to say they won't have fallen by the time you reach them?'

His companion nodded. 'Even if you could find a ship putting in on that side, from what I've heard, the cost of passage is rising faster than the ports are closing. A man would have to be desperate to part with that kind of money.'

He and his friend exchanged knowing glances, obviously wondering just how desperate Zophiel was.

Zophiel nodded and rose abruptly. As he turned, he stumbled over a bone discarded in the rushes on the floor, and knocked into my table.

'My apologies,' he began, then jerked back. 'Camelot . . . what brings you here?'

'The same as you, I imagine, a decent meal and a little business.' I pushed my flagon of ale towards him. He hesitated before sitting down and pouring himself a measure.

'Knowing you, Camelot, I've no doubt you heard what we were discussing.' His long white fingers slithered round the hard brown leather of the tankard.

'That it's spreading up the west coast. I've heard others say as much, but we'll be safe enough here until the frosts come. We're well inland. But then, being inland is no advantage to a man who wants a ship, is it?' I watched his fingers tighten around the lip of the tankard. 'Is your business in Ireland so pressing? Worth risking your life for?'

'Life is a risk, Camelot. There is only one way to enter this world, but a million ways to leave it. Natural, accidental . . . deliberate.'

'And which would you choose, Zophiel?'

'I would choose the time and the place. The unexpected, that's what men fear most, not knowing where and when.'

'May St Barbara protect us from a sudden death.'

He laughed. 'Don't tell me, you just happen to have a scrap of her shift or a lock of her hair in your scrip.'

I spread my hands. 'Naturally, but even I wouldn't be foolish enough to attempt to sell them to you.'

He laughed again. 'You're no fool, Camelot. With your one eye I suspect you see more than most men do with two.' He drained his tankard in one, then set it down on the greasy table. He leaned forward, his hard green eyes fixed on mine. 'But a word of warning, my friend, don't try to see into my life or my business.'

'I've watched your conjuring tricks. It would take a faster eye than mine to detect something you wished to conceal.'

He smiled and pushed himself to his feet. 'For that, I shall buy you supper. You said the food was decent here, though that's hard to believe in such a midden, but I'll bow to your experience on this occasion.'

Zophiel could be surprisingly generous when the mood took him.

I watched him fight his way between the crowded tables in search of the serving girl. As usual, he'd deflected my questions neatly, but the urgency in his voice when he questioned the men told me that if it really was business that took him to Ireland, the stakes must be worth a king's ransom. And if it was not business, well then, if a man is willing to risk plunging into a flood, it is usually because he has a fire at his back.

But if what the men said was correct, Zophiel would need to entice many pilgrims to see his mermaid if he wanted to earn his fare to Ireland. Still, if there was any place left in England to make money, this was it. The crowds, having come all this way, were determined to make the most of their excursion and were in the mood to be entertained. Zophiel worked every waking hour exhibiting his mermaid and performing his conjuring tricks for those who queued waiting their turn at the well. And while there was no call for Osmond's skill as a painter of church walls, since every inch of the shrine and church had already been newly painted, he turned his hand to making toys for children, which were beginning to sell even better than the official tin emblems from the shrine, for he carved wooden boots from which little tar-black devils with red eyes and sharp horns could be made to pop up, to the delight of children and adults alike.

I had to be more circumspect around the shrine. I couldn't display my holy relics openly, for priests and pardoners don't welcome competition and the law is on their side and against the honest peddler. Church law forbids the selling of relics which have not been certified as genuine by Rome, though most clerics turn a blind eye to it. They know that those who buy from me can't afford the authenticated relics which change hands for a king's ransom. Besides, the ordinary people have more faith in my scar than in the seals and documents of Rome, for they know only too well that any document can be forged for a price. If a man wants a nail paring of St Walstan to protect his cattle or a woman wants a tooth of St Dympna to cure her child of the falling sickness, where will they come but to the likes of me?

So I found myself a sheltered spot on a bank under an ancient oak tree. It stood on the outskirts of the village, near the Boot Inn, well away from the shrine. The thick branches kept off the worst of the rain and the gnarled roots of the tree formed a natural seat, worn smooth and shiny by the hundreds of backsides of young and old who over the years had put them to that good use. Opposite was the village wash pool, a large tank fed by a small spring, covered over with a thatched roof supported by four pillars. It was a favourite meeting spot for the village women who came daily to gossip while they washed their clothes and hung them under the thatch to dry in the breeze that funnelled through the pillars.

The bank on which I sat ran alongside the main track through the village, a perfect vantage point to catch those entering and leaving North Marston. I displayed a few amulets and rings of amber, jacinth and sardonyx, known cures for deadly fevers, and for those who could not afford gemstones, genuine or otherwise, I sold spiders in walnut shells to hang round their necks. For, as I told them, even if you are armed with a flask of good St John Shorne's holy water, it does no harm to buy a little extra protection. A prudent man does not keep all his wealth in one purse, so a wise man does not put all his faith in one saint.

A few days after we arrived in North Marston I took my place as usual under the oak tree and Adela came to join me, occupying herself with repairing Osmond's hose which were full of rips and holes from weeks of ill-usage on the road. She was bored sitting alone in the sleeping barn of the inn day after day. Osmond had forbidden her to accompany him to the shrine where he sold his toys, for fear that she might catch some sickness from the crowds.

I could understand why he was afraid for her. She was beginning to recover her strength. Her face was filling out a little and was starting to brighten into that glow of vitality which pregnant women often exhibit. But she was by no means fully recovered yet. At least in North Marston she could rest and build up her strength, and when the baby came, she'd be safe in a warm inn, with plenty of goodwives around to help her through the birth. If Osmond's jack-in-boot toys continued to sell well, they might one day be able to rent a small cottage of their own. This was no bad place to raise a child. It would never be hard to find work around a shrine as popular as this one.

Adela looked up and smiled as she saw Rodrigo hurrying towards us, but he didn't stop. Instead he stormed straight past us towards the Boot Inn. Judging by the grim expression on his face, he was not going to the inn in search of ale. I hoped for Jofre's sake he was not inside.

Jofre was the only one of us who did not seem relieved to have reached North Marston. Though his hand was healing, it had still to regain its full dexterity. Rodrigo was torn between fear that the boy might have done permanent damage to his hand and fury that he had got into the fight at the Cripples' Wedding. If Jofre had admitted his stupidity, Rodrigo might have cooled down sooner, but young lads seldom admit they're in the wrong, especially when they've been humiliated, so he stubbornly stood his ground, claiming that he'd been an innocent bystander, unwillingly caught up in the fight and forced to defend himself. But unfortunately for him, Rodrigo had seen only too plainly what had taken place.

Rodrigo bought salves and oils, and twice a day massaged

them into the boy's hand, accompanied by long lectures on how his hands were his talent and his livelihood; how even minor injuries could result in permanent stiffness and how drunkenness could lead to just this kind of recklessness. Any repentance Jofre might have felt had quickly turned to sullen resentment and even I began to feel sorry for the lad.

'Ease up on the boy,' I told Rodrigo. 'What lad hasn't got into a foolish fight just to impress a girl? Did you ever stop to consider the consequences when you were his age?'

'He has too much talent to waste, Camelot. Jofre could be a great musician, the best, if only he would set his heart to it.'

'And if he doesn't want to be?'

'Music is his life. You only have to look at his face when he plays.'

'I can see it in yours, Rodrigo, but I'm not so sure about the boy's. He may have a great talent, but it doesn't seem to make him happy.'

Rodrigo had stared at the raindrops spinning across the puddles. 'Then he must learn to live without happiness.'

'As you have?' I asked him, but he did not answer.

Rodrigo stalked back to where we sat beneath the oak, scowling more morosely than before. He threw himself down on the thick carpet of last year's leaves at Adela's feet and took a great swig of ale from his flask before passing it to me, wiping his mouth with the back of his hand.

'*Il sangue di Dio!* I swear I shall flay Jofre alive when I catch up with him. I have searched every tavern and alehouse in the village and he is nowhere to be found.'

'And you need him now?' I asked.

'I need him to practise. He is my pupil, yet he thinks he has nothing left to learn. Did you hear his singing last night?'

'The people liked it.'

'The people would not know the difference between a well-sung tune and the yowling of an amorous tom-cat. It was . . .' Words seemed to fail him. He pounded his fist into his hand in exasperation. 'It was an abomination, an affront to the ears of God. To listen to him last night you would have thought he had learned nothing at all in the last five years. Yet the night before, he sang well. It was not perfect, but it was competent. If he can do it one night, why not the next?'

The boy had been more than competent the night before. He had sung like an angel, each note faultless and true, the clean, pure alto voice reaching so high to heaven that for once even the raucous drunks were silenced. He sang from the depths of his soul, any fool could hear that, and any fool could see why too. Adela and Osmond were in the inn that night and his every song was directed to the corner where they sat, Adela leaning upon Osmond, dreamily rubbing her belly and gazing into the firelight, her face, for once, serene and untroubled.

But they weren't there the following night. Adela had been tired and had retired early to the barn at the back of the inn and Osmond had gone to keep her company, keeping a watchful eye over her as he carved his wooden jack-in-boot toys. Jofre, forced by Rodrigo to stay in the inn and sing for the pilgrims, sulked throughout the entire evening, glancing up hopefully every time the door opened, only to sink into a worse temper as the evening wore on and there was no sign of his beloved.

Was it possible that Rodrigo had failed to notice Jofre's infatuation? Perhaps he was so used to the boy's sulks that he could not detect a difference. Still, I could hardly raise the matter then, not with Adela sitting beside me apparently equally ignorant of it.

Rodrigo's anger made him too restless to sit for long and he was soon off to resume his search, muttering another stream of threats under his breath.

Adela watched him stride away, mud splashing up round him. 'He won't really thrash the boy, will he?'

'He'll scold and threaten, but he won't do anything, more's the pity. Jofre will talk his way out of trouble as usual and Rodrigo will relent and forgive him.'

Adela's eyes opened wide. 'You think Rodrigo should beat him? But you always stand up for Jofre. I've often heard you tell Rodrigo not to lecture him so much.'

'Endless lectures only make the lad feel that he is permanently in disgrace, and as long as anyone remains in disgrace they know they are not forgiven. Punishment at least draws a line under the affair.'

Adela bit her lip. 'There are some things that can never be undone, no matter how severely you are punished. Punishment doesn't always bring forgiveness, Camelot.'

I looked at her quizzically.

She reddened slightly, adding hastily, 'But you said Rodrigo would forgive him.'

'He will and he does with all his heart, but Jofre doesn't feel forgiven, and more to the point he can't forgive himself.'

'For singing badly? It's only music. If he sings badly one night, where's the harm in that? It can easily be undone by singing better the next.'

'Don't let Rodrigo hear you say it's only music. He once told me that to squander the gift of music is worse than murder. "Music," he said, "is more precious than life itself for it lives on long after the composer is dust." But then he is from the Latin races and they are passionate about everything; they hang themselves over an ill-fitting shirt or throw themselves off a cliff for a pair of beautiful eyes. The only thing an Englishman gets passionate about is the merits of his ale or a pair of fighting cocks.'

Adela stared down at the pile of rotting leaves at her feet. The edges of her tightly pinned veil fell across her cheeks, masking her expression. 'Osmond feels as passionate about his painting. He once said that he could no more live without painting than he could without breathing, but he's had to give it up.' Her hand fluttered over her swollen belly.

'For you and the child?'

She nodded miserably.

'If painting is his life, then he must love you more than life itself.' I patted her hand. 'You're blessed with a good husband, Adela. Take it from me, most men would not give up a morning's hunting for their wives.'

But I was puzzled by her comment. I'd assumed that Osmond had been unable to find work as a painter, but that was not the same thing as giving up painting. Why should he have to give it up? He had told me he was twenty. He was of an age to be a journeyman of his craft by now, and if you were lucky enough in these times to have a trade, you'd apply yourself to it with a will if you'd a wife to support, unless . . . unless he could not produce his journeyman's papers. No law-abiding church, monastery or merchant would risk employing an artist without guild papers. Osmond had told Zophiel that night in the cave, he painted the poor churches. Maybe the truth was he painted for those who asked no questions.

Adela tugged at my sleeve. 'Camelot, look over there, that woman by the wash pool, she's been watching us for ages. I'm sure I've seen her before around the village. Do you know her?'

I glanced over. It was late in the afternoon and the wash pool was now deserted except for a lone woman standing behind one of the pillars which supported the roof. Adela was right; the woman was plainly staring in our direction. She was a small, slight woman of about thirty years, dressed in what I took to be a serving woman's gown, but one that had seen better days. I too had noticed her before on a number of occasions standing some distance away in a doorway or under the shelter of a porch, her gaze always appearing to be directed towards me even when I was in the midst of a crowd. I thought little of it; I'm used to people staring at my mutilated face. I'm well aware that even among the plain, the old and the ugly, I stand out as magnificently monstrous. But now to find her here, away from the crowds, staring at us again, was surely more than natural curiosity on her part.

'I think she's following me.'

Adela looked alarmed and began struggling to her feet. 'Do you think she's spying on you for those priests, trying to catch you selling relics?'

I tugged at her skirt. 'Sit, sit. She's no spy. Can't you see how nervous she looks? But I think it is high time I asked her what it is she seeks. Who knows, she may want to buy an amulet.'

Adela still looked apprehensive. 'Then why doesn't she simply come and speak to you? No one who lurks around in the shadows intends any good. You should take care, Camelot. She could be working as part of a gang, waiting for the chance to rob you.'

'You've been listening to Zophiel. He sees robber gangs lurking on every corner. Any cutpurse would seize an opportunity to steal if he happened to see a chance in passing, but no one would waste several days following a poor old camelot around when there are much richer pickings on offer in a place like this.'

I half expected the woman to run off as I approached, but she stood her ground until I had drawn close enough to talk to her.

'Did you want something from me, mistress? A charm, an amulet?' I lowered my voice. 'A relic?'

She glanced right and left as if seeking assurance we were not overheard. But when she spoke it was to the ground. 'Please, you must come with me.'

'Where must I come?'

'I was sent to fetch you. She said I'd know you by your . . .' Her words trailed off and she glanced rapidly up at my face, before lowering her gaze again.

'By my scar,' I finished for her.

She had a pale, thin face, sharp cheekbones framed by dark brown hair, tight curls of which were escaping from under the edges of her veil. Her dark blue eyes continually flickered nervously from side to side as if she had been long accustomed to being on her guard.

'And who is this woman who sent you? Why doesn't she come herself? Is she sick?'

The woman spat rapidly three times on the back of her two forefingers. 'It was not the pestilence and she's well again now. There's nothing to fear. But please, you must come. She'll be angry with me if I don't bring you.'

It was futile to question her further. Some lady had evidently sent her serving woman to find me; presumably she wanted to buy a relic, and judging by the agitated state of her maid, she was a lady who was well used to getting what she wanted. I despise mistresses who rule their servants with fear and I had half a mind to refuse, but then spoilt women are usually wealthy women and business is business after all.

'I'll come. Let me get my pack.'

Adela, still fearing a trap, refused to be left behind. She

either came, she said, or she would go to fetch Osmond and Rodrigo. The woman shrugged when this was put to her, as if such matters were beyond her control, and led us both up a maze of little lanes in the poorest quarter of the village.

In contrast to the prosperous cottages lined up in neat little rows around the church and shrine, this area was a nest of ill-assorted huts and lean-tos thrown up from bits of old wood, hurdles and sacking. You find such quarters in every big town, people scratching a living from the crumbs of others' prosperity, but it is not often seen in villages except those, like this one, with a well-visited shrine or a popular anchorite to bring in the pilgrims and the money. Foul puddles of mud and muck stagnated between the huts and the piles of rotting garbage. Half-naked children crawled around with the snuffling pigs, collecting dog dung in pails to sell to the tanners and fighting one another for the choicest pieces of shit. It was certainly not the quarter you'd expect to find a woman lodged who could afford to employ a servant.

Pleasance, as the woman reluctantly divulged was her name, moved rapidly, head down and hood drawn across her face, although whether that was to block out the stench or to conceal her identity was difficult to say. She was forced several times to wait for us to catch up with her. Adela clung to my arm, fearful of slipping in the mud in her condition and trying in vain to sidestep the worst of the rotting guts and slimy pools with which the track was paved. Several times I urged her to go back, but she gamely shook her head and gripping my arm more tightly pressed on.

This quarter of the village was divided by several deep open sewers which were full to overflowing with the rain. We perilously crossed one of them on a slippery plank and found ourselves picking our way by means of a series of randomly placed stones and odd bits of wood through a stretch of marshy wasteland. Here the huts were more widely spaced, dotted across a neglected expanse of sodden vegetation. Just as it seemed we were leaving the village entirely, Pleasance stopped outside a hut tucked into the shelter of some dripping trees and pulled aside a piece of heavy sacking which functioned as a door, motioning us to go in.

The hut was made from three sheep hurdles bound together with rope, with an assortment of broken planks nailed together to form a kind of roof which glistened green with slime. Rank vegetation grew waist-high around it and a cloud of winter gnats hung over it like a pillar of smoke. It was the sort of shelter a herdsman might erect as a temporary refuge in bad weather, but it was not the kind of place you'd choose to spend one night, let alone several, unless your purse was empty or you were in hiding. I could see the same thought had also struck Adela and she did not need to be prompted to stay outside and watch my back.

Despite the many gaps in the walls and roof, it was too dark inside to see the figure clearly at first. Then from out of the darkness came a child's voice.

'I told her you'd come, Camelot. I told her we had to wait for you.'

Her pale face turned up towards me and as my eyes adjusted to the darkness of the hut, I saw the glitter of her ice-blue eyes and the white mist of her hair. I felt the hairs on the back of my neck prickle and then an unreasoning rush of anger as if I had been tricked, lured into a place I should have had more sense than to enter. I fought my way out again through the sacking.

Pleasance and Adela were both waiting outside. Pleasance smiled for the first time, a sad, anxious little smile.

'Narigorm said you'd come,' she repeated hopefully as if that answered everything.

Adela brightened. 'You know this woman Narigorm, then? A kinswoman of yours?'

'She's not a woman. She's just a child and she is no relative of mine. I met her once and that briefly, several months ago.' I turned to Pleasance. 'She was working as a fortune-teller for a master then; is he hereabouts?'

Pleasance shook her head. 'She fell sick. Her master heard I was a healer so fetched me to tend her. But he slipped away in the middle of the night without paying me and leaving the child without anything except the clothes she stood up in and her runes. The woman who ran the inn threw her out. She said she was afraid of the sickness, but I think she knew we'd no money for lodgings. I cared for the child as best I could in the woods until she was well. We've worked a little since, her with her runes and me with my herbs, but when we came here . . .' She broke off with that now familiar shrug. 'A priest gave us till the compline bell to leave the bounds, or he said we'd be arrested for devilish practices.'

Did she mean the rune-casting or the herbs? Probably both, for either would be seen by the ever-jealous priests as rivals to their shrine's coffers.

'But Narigorm said you were coming. She said we would travel with you, so we hid here until you –'

'She cannot travel with me!'

The words burst out more vehemently than I had meant them to. The eyes of both women opened wide in surprise.

It was Adela who broke the silence. 'But why ever not? There are enough of us travelling together for two more to make little difference. We can't leave a child or this woman in such a place. Besides, I'd love a child for company and Osmond loves children too.'

'You're not travelling on until after your child is born, remember. You don't want to have your baby on the road in the middle of winter, do you? Anyway, why would you want to leave at all? You've got a warm dry bed here and Osmond is earning good money. You'd be hard put to find better. But these two have been ordered to go. If they're found here in defiance of the Church it will mean a whipping or worse. They should leave at once, today.'

It was a well-reasoned argument, a practical argument. It was the best thing for the two of them to leave right away, for their own safety. Pleasance stared at the ground, her shoulders sagging.

'Come now, Pleasance, there are other villages where your skills will be welcomed, you and the child both. You will earn enough to eat well.'

'She said we would travel with you,' Pleasance repeated dully, as if it was a prayer learned by rote.

Adela had slipped inside the hut and when she emerged she was leading the child by the hand. Narigorm looked, if possible, even more transparent. Her white woollen shift was nearly black with grime and dirt, but her hair stood out whiter than ever against the dark trees. She lowered her chin and innocently raised her eyes up to Adela. She did not have to speak, that look was enough.

'She's an angel,' said Adela. 'We can't send this child out on the road alone.'

'Plenty of children her age have to fend for themselves and she won't be alone. She has Pleasance with her. We can't afford to leave yet and they must go at once.'

Narigorm turned her unblinking stare upon me. 'You'll

have to leave too, I saw it in the runes, you'll be gone by the next new moon.'

Pleasance raised her head sharply. 'That's the day after tomorrow.'

'And the runes never lie,' said Narigorm. She took a step closer to me and hissed, 'This time you'll see.'

7. The Prophecy

Narigorm was right, of course, and before the new moon rose as sharp as death's scythe on the land, our company was once again on the road. I knew I couldn't blame the child; how could she have brought it about? She merely spoke what she read in the runes. Could she help it if the runes foretold ill fortune? Yet for all that, I did blame her. I felt that somehow, though I could not tell how, she was the instigator as well as the messenger.

But if truth be told I need have looked no further than human nature for the cause of our misfortune. When Adela and I returned to the inn that evening there was already trouble brewing. A delegation of tin emblers had gone to the shrine officials to protest about the jack-in-boot toys. People were buying those instead of the official tin emblems which were sanctified and blessed by the clergy at the shrine. The priest in charge of the shrine had taken matters into his own hands and arbitrarily ruled that, since the jack-in-boot toys were fashioned after the legend of John Shorne, Osmond should pay a levy to the shrine amounting to half the price of every toy he sold, as payment for the use of their legend and their saint. This was double what the tin emblers paid to the clergy to buy their concession and

Osmond, his stubborn Saxon blood rising in his veins, swore he would rather smash every toy himself than hand over one penny. The priest shrugged: Osmond could either smash the toys or pay up; it made no difference to him – either way his problem with the emblers was solved.

Though it was clear that Osmond would have to turn his hand to other work if we remained, things might still have been well had it not been for Jofre. The following night when he and Rodrigo were playing in the inn, three men burst in and before anyone could stop them, they were bundling Jofre out of the door. By the time we got outside, two big men had him pinned against the wall of the inn and a third, a small, ferret-faced man, was tickling his knife against Jofre's throat as he struggled in vain.

Rodrigo roared like a bull and rushed towards him, but Ferret-face did not flinch. He thrust the point of his knife up under the boy's chin until a tiny trickle of blood oozed out. Jofre gasped and instantly stopped struggling, not daring to move a muscle for fear the blade might sink deeper.

'Stay back – one step closer and he's had it.'

Even in his fury Rodrigo could see the man was not bluffing. He took a step back, holding up his hands, palms open.

'I take it you're the boy's master?'

Rodrigo nodded. 'What is it . . . what do you want from him?'

'Want?' Ferret-face gave a high-pitched giggle. 'I want my money, that's what I want. Your apprentice laid a wager on the fighting cocks. Thought he was man enough to play with the big boys, but then surprise, surprise, when he lost, he suddenly found his purse was empty. "Must have been robbed," he said. Really upset he was at not being able to pay up, so me, being a soft-hearted man,' and again he let out his mirthless little giggle, 'I said to him, I said, "That's a shame, lad. You can't trust anyone these days, terrible lot of villains about. Tell you what I'll do, my lad," I said, "I'll give you two days to come up with the money." That's the kind of generous man, I am, aren't I, boys? Too soft-hearted for my own good, aren't I? The boys here are always telling me so.'

The two henchmen holding Jofre by the wrists grinned broadly and ground Jofre's arms harder into the rough stone wall of the inn.

'Our young friend here was supposed to bring me the money at noon today, only he didn't show up. So now my lads here are going to break his fingers, one by one, nice and slowly. See if he can play his lute so well then.'

Jofre had turned deathly pale; he was begging and pleading incoherently, which seemed to amuse Ferret-face all the more. Rodrigo had to be forcibly restrained from knocking him to the ground, but finally managed to get a grip on his anger and in a voice that was barely above a whisper, he asked how much Jofre owed. It was a princely sum even by Jofre's standards. The sum owed, as Ferret-face patiently explained, was naturally higher than the original wager because he had been forced to wait for his money.

'Let's call it interest – my interest in getting my money.' He giggled again.

There was no question of not paying it. Rodrigo and I pooled the contents of our purses, but it was not enough, and the henchmen looked on the point of carrying out their master's threat when Zophiel stepped forward and handed over the remaining money, saying savagely to Jofre, 'You owe me, boy.'

The men left, Ferret-face clearly pleased with himself, but his two henchmen growling like frustrated wolfhounds who have been called to heel before the kill. As soon as they were out of sight, the innkeeper stepped out of the shadows.

'Right, I want you lot gone at first light. Those lads are trouble wherever they go; they come looking for their money and if they don't get it, they start smashing the place up. This is a respectable inn for decent folk and I'll not have that lowlife coming in here again.'

'But they've no reason to be back,' I said. 'They got their money.'

'This time,' said the innkeeper darkly, 'but what happens next time when your lad here lays another wager he can't pay? Besides, it looks to me as if you three got your purses cleaned out. How are you going to pay for your board? And word is that your friend's been upsetting the emblers with those toys of his. I don't need aggravation from them. They're good customers of mine. It's all very well for you, you're just passing through, but some of us have got to live here. So I want you all out before there's any more trouble. And I'll thank you to take that fish with you too,' he added, turning to Zophiel. 'Stinks the place out.'

'That, you ignorant oaf, is not a fish, it's a mermaid,' Zophiel said furiously. 'It's an extremely rare and valuable creature and the only one you are ever likely to see in this rancid pigsty you call an inn.'

'What I say is, if it stinks like a fish, it is a fish. And this may not be the smartest inn in the village, but as long as I own it, I say who sleeps in it. So if you and your company of vagabonds are not on the road by sunrise, I'll be breaking more than just a few fingers. And don't even think of trying to get lodgings elsewhere in these parts. Once word gets out, you'll not be welcome anywhere. I'll see to that.'

So with the blessings of the innkeeper ringing in our ears

we left the inn the following morning, as the cold, grey dawn oozed across the sodden fields. All our hopes of a safe dry haven had come to nothing. Osmond was blaming himself, distraught at the thought of taking Adela out on the road again, and Zophiel was blaming Jofre. I too was furious with the boy. Any hope I had of leaving the company behind and travelling northward alone was gone. But there was little point in getting angry with Jofre. Blame cannot undo the deed. And I couldn't just abandon them on the road, could I? So there was nothing for it but to take them with me.

I was saddled with a pregnant woman and a bunch of novices. We had no money. It was the worst possible weather in which to travel and the pestilence was rapidly closing in on three sides. It could not get any worse. Misery was written on every face as once more we hunched our shoulders against the chilling rain.

But there is no cloud so black that a glimmer of sun does not shine through it and I consoled myself with the thought that our hasty departure from North Marston meant that at least Narigorm would not be travelling with us. By the time Pleasance had searched for us and discovered we'd gone, we'd already be hours ahead on the road.

I tried my best to cheer the others. 'There are other shrines north of here: St Robert's at Knaresborough and many shrines at York. If we could reach those, we'd be safe. They're well inland. They won't close their gates. Adela can have her child in comfort and you'll all earn good money there, better even than at North Marston.'

Rodrigo and Osmond nodded gratefully, but I knew that Zophiel would not be so easily swayed. I had to keep him with us. Adela was stronger, but her belly was swelling by the day and her strength would not last if she had to walk far in this mud. She'd never reach York on foot, and neither would the rest of us if we had to slow our pace to hers, especially if we had to carry our food and packs.

I could see the agony of choice written across Zophiel's face. He desperately wanted to turn towards the coast and any chance of a ship, but between him and a port lay the ravaging monster that was the pestilence. For the first time since we met, I pitied the man, for whatever was driving him was merciless.

I took a deep breath. 'Zophiel, you must see it would be madness to turn west from here. If you go west now you will be walking straight into it. We have to keep as far from the coasts as we can until we are further north. Then you can turn west with some chance of finding a port still open.'

Zophiel studied me carefully before he spoke. 'Do you really believe that you can outstrip it?'

'At least if we travel north we will be walking away from it, not running to meet it. If we can just keep clear of the places it has struck for a few more weeks until the winter freeze sets in, then the pestilence will die out and you can go to any port you please.'

Adela clutched at my arm. 'It will die out when the frosts come, won't it?'

I tried to sound convincing. 'Fevers always rage in the heat and foul air of summer, but come the winter frosts, they all die away.'

Zophiel gave a hollow laugh. 'I have to admire your optimism, Camelot, but there is just one trifling point you seem to have overlooked. There has been no summer's heat this year. There has, in fact, been no summer and still the pestilence rages.'

Adela shook her head. 'But everyone says it's the rain itself that spawns this pestilence, just as it spawns the biting flies and the midges.' Her youthful eyes shone with conviction. 'The frost kills pernicious flies and stinging creatures; I know it will stop this.'

'Just as you *knew* it would only rain for forty days and forty nights, Adela. Perhaps you have a rhyme for this as well? Do share it with us.'

Adela flinched and Osmond, slipping his arm around her, led her away from us, glowering over his shoulder at Zophiel, though I noticed that he didn't rise to his wife's defence. But I, for one, was glad to let Zophiel have his little triumph. It was a small price to pay if we had succeeded in persuading him to come with us.

We fell into our accustomed places beside the wagon and trudged on, leaving the last of the cottages behind until we were once more among the trees. Then, as we rounded the corner of the road, I saw two figures standing at the crossroads. My stomach lurched. There was no mistaking the unnatural whiteness of that hair. Narigorm and Pleasance were patiently waiting by the side of the road, as if they were expecting us.

Adela's face brightened a little as she saw the child and she waved eagerly to her. 'Look, Osmond, that's the little girl I told you about. Didn't I say she was a little poppet? Have you ever seen a child who looked so angelic?'

Osmond smiled and Rodrigo beamed fondly, like an indulgent uncle, as we drew closer to the waiting figures.

Only Zophiel seemed to find the sight of Narigorm as unwelcome as I did. 'As if we didn't have enough liabilities already.' He stared pointedly at Jofre who flushed a dull red. 'Now I suppose I'm expected to allow that freakish little brat to ride on my wagon as well. What next, a performing bear?'

Adela suddenly turned back to me, an awestruck look on face. 'Camelot, don't you remember, she said that we'd have to leave today and that she'd travel with us. She really does have the gift.'

But before I could answer, Xanthus suddenly jerked up her head and shied. Her nostrils flared, her eyes rolled back and she reared up, trying, in her panic, to pull the wagon off the road. It took the combined strength of both Zophiel and Rodrigo to hold her head and bring her to a stop.

Zophiel glanced apprehensively into the trees. 'She smells danger, a wild boar perhaps or fresh blood. Horses hate the smell of blood. Get the brat on the wagon quickly if you must bring her. I've no wish to loiter here any longer than I have to.'

So in the end there was no debate. There was nothing I could do. Narigorm and Pleasance had joined our company and no one had time to think about it, for Xanthus continued to be agitated for the rest of that day and Zophiel could not calm her. She fought us all the way along the road as though whatever she had sensed was keeping pace with us. Perhaps she did smell death on the air that day, but the stench of death did not come from the forest.

8. Swan-boy

The storyteller leaned forward. 'In the morning, the servants found the baby's cradle empty and the queen asleep in her bed with blood smeared on her lips. But when the king begged her to explain what had happened to his infant son, his wife remained silent and not one word would she utter, not even to defend her innocence.'

There was a sizeable crowd gathered around the storyteller: children squatting on the ground in front of him and adults leaning against the wall of the church, their baskets and bales at their feet, buying and selling halted until the tale was finished. Even the glances of the town whores were drawn the storyteller's way though he was not a well-built young man. His boots were old and worn through, his clothes brown and threadbare, indistinguishable from the garb of those who crowded round to listen to him, except, that is, for the purple cloak fastened crossways over his shoulder covering his shirt and left arm.

You don't often see purple, not at a market. Generally only the nobility wear it, for only the nobility can afford to, and you don't get many of them coming to the back of beyond to buy a scrawny goose or a second-hand butter churn. But this was no royal cloak, not silk nor satin and not lined with fur nor trimmed with gold thread. It was, like his breeches, worn and stained, made of coarse, homespun wool, oily and thick enough to keep off all but the heaviest rain. A serviceable cloak for a life on the road, made by a doting mother's hand no doubt. But what on earth had possessed the good woman to waste money on purple dye for it? Did she think her son a king-in-waiting? There's many a mother fondly believes that, just as there's many a son believes their mother is a virgin, but not even Mary was besotted enough to dress her carpenter's brat in purple.

'And so the queen was condemned to death by fire, but even when the sentence was pronounced still she would not speak, not one word would she utter, not even to save her life. And all through the days and nights that she sat in her cell she continued to spin and sew the nettles to make the six shirts.'

The children shuffled nearer on their bottoms, eyes wide. The adults too leaned in closer. Death by fire. That was something they all knew about, even those who hadn't seen it, hadn't smelt the stench that hangs round a town for days, hadn't heard the screams that echo night after night through your dreams; even those who had not witnessed a burning had heard tell of it and shuddered. They knew the queen would not keep silent when the flames touched her, not even a saint is that strong. They held their breath.

'Seven full years had passed since the queen made the vow to release her enchanted brothers and turn them from swans into men again. And true to her vow, not one word had passed her lips in all that time; not a single sound had escaped her. The queen continued to work night and day sewing the shirts. Until, on the morning of her execution, all the nettle shirts were completed, all that is except for the shirt for the youngest brother which still wanted the left sleeve.'

He seemed too young to be a storyteller, an occupation usually reserved for those with at least a full beard. But he was holding the crowd better than many an older man. He wasn't handsome, his face too narrow and angular, nose too long, chin too small, as if his features had all grown at different rates. Plumped out with age and softened with a beard, in time they might come together into some sort of order, but that scarcely mattered for what held the crowd was not his face but his eyes. They were dark, almost black, so that it was impossible to distinguish the pupil from the iris. His gaze brushed across the faces of the listeners from infants to crones, holding each person in turn for a fraction of a second, and their eyes followed his without a backward glance.

'The queen was led out to the place of execution. She was bound by the waist to the stake and the six nettle shirts were thrust into her arms to be burned with her. The faggots of wood were piled up around her bare feet and the executioner lit the flaming torch. The priest stepped forward to urge her to confess the murder of her baby, so that her soul, at least, might be saved from the fires everlasting, but not one word would she utter, not even to save her own soul. Weeping with grief, for he still loved her dearly, the king had no option but to give the sign. The executioner raised the flaming torch and thrust it into the faggots at her feet.'

The storyteller raised his right arm high as if he held a torch in it and suddenly thrust his fist towards the knot of children at his feet. They gasped and jumped, delighted by terror. He lifted his hand again, pointing at the sky.

'But in that moment there was the sound of singing wings

in the sky overhead. Six white swans flew out of the dawn towards the queen.'

The audience looked up to where he pointed, as if they expected to see the swans flying towards them.

'As the swans glided down they beat out the fire with the force of their broad white wings. And as they alighted the queen threw the nettle shirts over them and at once their feathers fell away and each swan was transformed into a man again. All were restored to their human form, all, that is, except the youngest brother, for his shirt still wanted the left sleeve. And when he regained his human form, his left arm remained as the wing of a swan.'

At that the storyteller threw back his purple cloak and there was a gasp from the crowd so deep that for an instant everyone seemed in two minds whether to turn and run or push towards him. From under the cloak the storyteller withdrew his left arm, except that it wasn't an arm, it was the pure white wing of a swan.

The wing unfolded, stretched, as if it had been held bound for a long time, then rose and fell in a steady beat. The air hummed with its power and the breeze lifted the children's hair and made them blink. Then the wing folded itself against his body and lay at rest, tucked back inside the cloak.

The adults shook themselves slightly, as if they knew they were dreaming, for they couldn't possibly have seen what they thought they'd seen. The storyteller resumed his tale as if nothing had happened.

'As soon as the spell was broken and her brothers had regained their human form the queen was able to speak. She told the king how the witch, his wicked stepmother, had enchanted her brothers –'

'Is it real?' a small boy blurted out, unable to contain himself any longer.

The storyteller's wing unfolded and gave a single beat before furling itself again inside the cloak. The children shrieked in a mixture of wonder and horror.

'Were you really turned into a swan?'

'How else could I have a swan's wing in place of an arm?'

'But couldn't the king make the witch give you back your arm?'

'Once a spell is broken, what is left of it can never be undone, especially if the witch who cast the spell is dead. And she was dead. She was burnt to ashes in the fire she meant for the queen and her ashes blew away on the wind and were scattered over the four corners of the earth.'

'And what happened then?'

'The king and queen had six sons and six daughters and ruled their kingdom with justice and mercy. As for the swan-brothers, they lived in the palace and became great knights, riding out to do battle for the king and queen. They went to distant lands on brave quests to slay dragons and rescue maidens and they found beautiful princesses to marry and they all lived happily ever after.'

The coins fell thick and fast; even though people didn't have much to spare, the crowd appreciated someone who put effort into the telling. The children crowded up close to the storyteller, daring one another to touch that wing to see if it was truly alive, but one by one their parents grabbed them and hurried their protesting offspring away.

'Come on now, girl, enough stories, there's work to be done before dark.'

'Back to the cart now, boy, your father'll be needing a hand with the loading.'

'Let the storyteller rest now, his throat must be parched.'

But nobody offered the storyteller a drink to ease his throat. It was not his throat that concerned them.

Storytellers are always suspect. They are exotic strangers, swallows who stay only for the heady days of sunshine. Where they go after that is a mystery. They're welcomed for the tales that will be told again through dark winter evenings. They have an honoured place by the fire, but like any guest who knows his welcome depends on not outstaying it, they are expected to move on quickly. They don't belong. You wouldn't want your daughter to marry one, in case your grandchildren turned out as fey as the creatures they tell stories about. Could you really trust someone who is in the habit of conversing with sorcerers or who freely utters the names of those who must not be named?

And this particular storyteller was more suspect than most. You don't want to go mixing with someone who admits they've been enchanted by a witch; the curse might be catching. It could break out again at any time, especially when it's not been fully lifted. And besides, as the priests would say, each after his own kind, that's the rule. No half-breeds. No animal-men. If it died, what would you do with it, bury it like a Christian or hang it up like game? A swan-boy, what kind of a creature is that? Not one you'd want your children to mix with, that's for certain. You could read the distrust in their faces as they hurried their children away.

The storyteller gathered up his coins with one hand and deftly slid them into his purse, pulling the leather drawstring tight with sharp white teeth.

'Did you marry a beautiful princess?'

He looked round, startled. One little girl had sneaked back and was shyly tugging at his cloak. A small, scruffy dog leaned against her bare leg. The storyteller reached down and stroked the dog's ears and it looked up at him with eyes as big and brown as the little girl's. Then he crouched down so that he could look directly into her earnest little face and smiled.

'Princesses don't marry knights who only have one arm. What use would a one-armed knight be? He couldn't defend her honour or champion her cause. He couldn't slay dragons for her. A swan-boy can't hold a sword and shield or pull a bow. No, no, little one, the swan-boy lived on in the palace for a while and everyone was kind to him, the queen especially, for she felt guilty that she had not been able to finish the shirt. There were servants to cut up his meat for him, and servants to dress him and servants to wash him. He wanted for nothing, except a purpose. Finally, when he could no longer bear the kindness of the servants or the sadness he saw in the queen's eyes each time she looked at him, he set off to seek his fortune, like all princes must.'

'If I was a princess, I'd marry you.'

'Thank you, little one. But one day you'll find a handsome prince who will take you to live in a castle with golden turrets and dress you in rainbows and give you the moon to play ball with and the stars to spangle your hair.'

The child giggled. 'You can't play ball with the moon.'

'You can do anything, princess, if you want it enough. Now you'd best run along or your mother will start fretting for you and it would never do to make your mother worry.'

'Mam's always worried. She worries about everything.'

'They always do, princess.' The storyteller turned her round and sent her off with a pat on her rump and she skipped away as blithely as only a princess can, the little dog following faithfully at her heels.

A snide wind whipped rain against our faces and hands. Those who had stalls with covered roofs were braving it outside in the open, blowing on numb, rag-covered fingers to try to get the feeling back into them. A few braziers had been lit, but they spluttered and spat, coughing out a thick phlegm of smoke but no heat. The market square in Northampton, and every road leading to it, were ankle-deep in stinking mud. They'd thrown down armfuls of rushes, straw and bracken to try to make passable walkways, but it was a losing battle. As fast as they threw it down, it was trampled into the mud, which swallowed it up as if it had no bottom.

There'd been a hanging earlier in the day. Two poor devils strung up for sheep-stealing, thrashed as they slowly choked to death on the end of a rope in front of a jeering crowd. The corpses would hang in the market place until close of business as a warning to others. Now a fine mist of rain washed them, dripping from their swollen purple faces as the ropes creaked in the wind. They say rain blesses a corpse. They'd need a blessing in death, for they'd found little mercy in life.

Osmond came to stand near me. From the hook on his staff dangled a tangle of wooden dolls and carved knights mounted on horseback. He'd been working long into the night on the toys whenever we stopped to make camp. He tried as hard as any man could to provide for Adela and in all the time we'd been on the road, I'd never seen him idle. He rubbed his hands and spread them over the smoking brazier to catch the little warmth which rose from it. I'd never noticed it before, but the last joint of his little finger was missing. It was not a great price to pay for such a skill, however. I'd known many a woodcarver lose more than one finger before they mastered the craft.

He glanced up at the hanging corpses before turning rapidly away, crossing himself and shaking his head. 'Hanging's a cruel death, Camelot. I can understand a man coming to the noose for committing murder in a passion; that's only too easy. But what kind of man would risk hanging for a sheep?'

'If your wife or children were starving, you might be driven to it. A parent will risk anything to save their child, even death. It's a passion that grips you from the moment you hold your first child in your arms and it never goes away. You'll feel it when you hold your own baby.'

'Will I?' He turned to me, his face strained with anxiety. 'What if I hold my child and I don't feel anything? What if I can't love it or, worse than that, what if I can't even stand to be near it?'

I was startled by the panic in his voice. 'But you love Adela. Why should you not love your child?'

He chewed agitatedly at his thumbnail before answering, 'If the child is born cursed like that cripple at the wedding . . .'

'Come now,' I said soothingly. 'Why should your child be cursed? And besides, in the end, whatever he is like, you'll love him, because he is your child. You'll see more and more of Adela in your baby's face with every passing day. If you love him for no other reason, you will love him for that.'

He shivered in the rain, drawing his cloak tighter around him. 'That's what I am most afraid of, Camelot. I am afraid of what I shall see in its face.'

'Osmond?' I laid my hand on his arm.

He gave a wan smile. 'Take no notice, Camelot. I'm just worried for Adela, the birth, everything. I'll feel better when we reach York and we have a roof over our heads.' He took a deep breath and glanced up at the corpses again. 'And standing here, chewing the cud, won't get us to York. I must sell some of these toys, otherwise I'll have to start sheep-stealing myself soon, if I don't make some money.'

He was right. Despite the weather, all of us were desperately trying to earn what little money we could. This was the first market we had found open since we left North Marston nearly two weeks ago, and God alone knew if we would find another. We needed to buy food. Travelling cold and wet is bad enough, but no one can travel long when they are hungry. An aching belly drives you to work more smartly than any master's curses. So believe me, we were all working hard that day.

'This book, master? You're obviously a man of great education and discernment for this is no ordinary book, as you can see. It once belonged to a Jew. Very rare. Impossible to come by since the Jews were driven out. People would pay a fortune to get their hands on a Jewish book. With this book and the right words you can make a clay golem and bring it to life. Think of it, master, a giant with the strength of fifty men to do your bidding and crush your enemies.

'Does it work? Does it work, he asks me? Tell me this, would the King have banished the Jews from England if they had not had such dangerous powers? I tell you, it was only because he seized all their possessions first that he was able to do it at all. If they'd still had their books, there'd not have been a Christian soul left alive in this realm.

'The spell to make the golem live? I couldn't bring myself to tell you, master, such potent words, such malefic phrases. Golems conjured up with such words can turn and rend you into pieces if you can't command them. If you lose control for an instant . . . well, look at me if you want proof of their strength, just a flick of its finger and my eye was gone. I tell you, I barely escaped with my life. If you should come to any harm, I'd never forgive myself. If I could be sure that you could command it . . .

'Now you come to mention it, master, that purse does seem to have a certain weight of authority.'

The merchant departed, the book, well wrapped, tucked under his arm, and the parchment with the spell on it hastily stuffed in the concealed money belt hidden deep inside his clothes. He seemed to stride out with a new confidence as if he already felt invincible.

'So now it is a golem you have to thank for the loss of your eye, is it, Camelot? And I thought it was a werewolf or was it a Saracen?' drawled Zophiel. 'I can hardly keep up.'

He was leaning against the back of his wagon, watching Adela and Pleasance stowing away the food they had bought for the company. 'You'd better hope he doesn't try that spell until the market is over. He's not going to be a happy man when he discovers it won't work.'

'You've tried it then?'

'Me use anything that had been touched by a Jew? I'd rather cut off my own hand. Their books are full of sorcery, any fool knows that. If I'd known you'd such a book in your pack . . .'

'So you do believe their books can conjure golems then, Zophiel.'

Zophiel scowled. 'One day you'll go too far and someone will cut out that lying tongue of yours, old man . . . Clear off, you little brat! Don't you dare try that one on me.'

I glanced up just in time to see Zophiel aim a cuff at the head of a young lad who had come limping up, palm outstretched for alms. The beggar ducked nimbly out of arm's reach with an alacrity that was surprising from one with such a marked limp. The lad, though about twelve years old, was stark naked, and his body, limbs and face were caked in mud and covered with streaks of dried blood and livid purple bruises. He slipped round the side of the wagon to try his luck with Adela.

'Please, mistress, for pity's sake help me.'

Adela, who had not seen him approach, gave a startled little cry.

'You poor boy, whatever's happened to you?'

'Set upon by thieves on the road . . . beat me. Took my clothes. Everything. They killed my father. Would have done for me too, but . . .' He broke off and began to wail piteously.

Adela hastened to put her arm round the lad, her face full of concern. 'There, there, you're safe now. We'll help you. We'll . . .'

'We will do no such thing,' Zophiel cut in.

Adela looked up, horrified. 'But you heard what he said, Zophiel, he's been robbed, his father killed. We have to help him.'

Zophiel gave his mirthless laugh, 'I know you're a woman, Adela, but even you can't be that codwitted. The lad's avering, can't you tell? It's the oldest trick in the book. They strip themselves, leave their clothes concealed somewhere and then come into town pretending to have been robbed, in the hope of finding some muttonhead like you to take pity on them and give money or clothes they can sell.'

The lad began to wail again, grabbing hold of Adela as if she was his mother, and blubbing out yet more details of his story. Adela wrapped her arms tightly about him, cradling his head to her chest. 'But look at him, Zophiel. He's covered in blood.'

Zophiel snorted. 'He'll have got it from butcher's row. Puddles of it there, isn't that right, boy?'

'How can you be so cruel?' Adela was almost in tears herself now. 'You're wrong. Anyone can see he's in pain.'

'Wrong, am I?' Zophiel suddenly strode forward and

before Adela could stop him, he had grabbed the boy by the neck and was marching him away.

'What are you doing? Leave him alone.' Adela tried to follow, but clutched at her swollen belly and sank back, breathless, against the wheel of the wagon.

Zophiel didn't answer. He dragged the lad towards the horse trough. The boy, who could see plain enough what was coming, was wriggling and fighting with all his strength to get out of Zophiel's grasp. His cries had turned to curses, but Zophiel took no notice. He picked up the boy and threw him into the horse trough, ducking him under the icy water. The boy thrashed helplessly. Zophiel pulled his head up by the hair long enough for him to take a gulp of air and then shoved him under again. It took two or three more duckings under the water before Zophiel was satisfied and finally hauled him out of the trough. Then he marched him, dripping and shivering, back towards Adela. The fight had gone out of the lad and although Zophiel still held him in a vice-like grip, he no longer put up any resistance.

The water had done its job. Most of the blood had been washed off the boy's body and what remained was now trickling down his legs as the water dripped off him. Apart from the odd bruise any boy might have collected through normal living, there were no signs of any wounds or injuries. Adela looked away.

Zophiel, still gripping the lad firmly, looked smugly triumphant. 'I've cured him. It's a miracle, isn't it, boy?'

The boy cursed richly and got his head cuffed.

'Come, boy, where's your gratitude? That's no way to thank me.'

This time the lad didn't risk a reply, but glowered as if he would dearly like to kill Zophiel.

'At least he's had the sense not to try the sickness trick.

They used to roll themselves in nettles to give themselves a rash and stick on fake boils with maggots crawling in them to try to get alms from the worshippers on the church steps. You daren't try that trick any more, do you, boy, not now the pestilence is raging?'

The lad looked mutinous, but didn't answer.

'But he must be in need to go to those lengths to beg,' Pleasance said softly.

'He's just too idle to work; besides, he enjoys tricking people, don't you, boy? Avering's a good game, laughing at the fools who deserve to be parted from their purses. Well, maybe you're right, boy, they do, but I'm not one of them, and you try that trick on me again and I'll give you bruises that won't wash off. Now clear off.'

In one swift movement Zophiel spun the boy round and landed a good kick on his backside which sent him sprawling in the mud. He scrambled up and clutching his backside was off like a startled hare. Only when he reached a good safe distance did he pause to make obscene gestures in our direction, yelling curses until he was scarlet in the face, before he ran off into the crowd.

As I turned away, I caught sight of Narigorm. The crowds had thinned now and most of the stallholders were packing up to go, but she was crouching on the ground in the corner of the market place. A young girl, her hair covered with a married woman's fret and fillet, stood awkwardly in front of her, while the girl's mother handed Narigorm a coin. Narigorm tucked it away and drew three concentric circles in the dirt. She fumbled at the neck of her shift and pulled out a small leather pouch which hung round her neck on a thong. She tipped the contents over the circles. Lozenges of wood tumbled out. Women paused in their shopping, peering at the slashed patterns on the pieces of wood, which were as meaningless to them as the Latin words in the church bible. Like them I drew closer, intrigued. I had not seen Narigorm work the runes before.

She began rocking back and forth, whispering something under her breath, as her hand hovered over the runes like a bird of prey. Then she selected one of the runes and held it up. It resembled two triangles on their sides, facing each other, their points touching.

'*Daeg*. It means day. Something is about to begin. Something is about to change and grow. *Daeg* stands for one. There is one to come before it can begin.'

'Something about to grow and someone to come,' beamed the girl's mother. 'There, I told you, my angel, you're going to have a baby.'

But Narigorm was not looking at the young girl as she spoke her words; she was looking past her and staring straight at me.

Zophiel did not let Adela forget the episode of the averer in a hurry. He treated the company in the inn that night to a lively retelling of the story of how Adela had been taken in, and amid laughter and jokes the men agreed how easy it was to dupe a woman. Even Osmond did not rise to his wife's defence, but patted her arm affectionately and told her what a kind-hearted, silly little goose she was, though I suspected he knew as little of the tricks of avering as she did. This last was too much for Adela and, with a tight little smile, she took herself off to bed, her cheeks flushed and her hands clenched.

Osmond half-rose to follow her and probably would have done had Zophiel not met his eyes and grinned.

'That's right, you'd better go running after her and apologize, boy.' He turned to the grinning faces. 'He daren't say boo to that little goose. If he does there's no plucking her for a week. Isn't that right, boy? Come to think of it, I've yet to see you share her bed.'

'Keeps you on short rations, does she, m'lad?' said another man. 'You don't want to stand for that, not with a new bride. Wives are like dogs, lad, got to show them who's master from the first otherwise they'll be snarling and snapping any time they please and you'll never get the leash on them.'

'I heard that, Tom,' said a mature, buxom woman, gathering up the empty platters from the table behind him. 'You wait till I tell your Ann, she'll soon show you who's wearing the leash. She'll be tethering you by your balls, if I know Ann.'

The man grinned sheepishly and reached across to slide his hand up her skirt. 'Ah, but you won't tell, will you, my sweet, because I wouldn't be much use to you if I was damaged goods, now would I?'

The banter and laughter continued. Adela was forgotten by all but Osmond who made another attempt to slip out, but this time it was Jofre who restrained him, putting out a hand to grasp his arm.

'She'll be all right. Please stay.'

He looked up into Osmond's face, his hand still resting on his arm. Something in the pleading tone of his voice or the expression in his eyes seemed to startle Osmond. For a moment neither of them moved. Then Pleasance, scraping the last of her pottage into her mouth, stood up.

'Jofre's right. Best you leave her for a while. You've said enough for one evening. I'll sit with her.'

Osmond nodded gratefully. 'Perhaps that would be better. Tell her I didn't mean . . .'

'She doesn't need upsetting in her condition,' Pleasance

scolded. 'Women take things harder when they're with child. But who listens to me?'

Osmond flushed, but before he could reply, Pleasance had turned away and was making her way towards the door, muttering, 'Men, they never think before they open their mouths. Brains of a donkey.'

As she pulled the door open, someone burst in from outside. Thrown off balance by the unexpected opening of the door, the man staggered into the room, grabbing at Pleasance's shoulder to stop himself sprawling headlong into the rushes.

'Steady there, Giles,' the landlord called out. 'No need to flatten my customers. You that desperate for drink?'

'They've raised the hue and cry.'

Most of the occupants of the room pushed back their tankards and trenchers and scrambled to their feet. A hue and cry was not a summons you could ignore.

'What's to do, Giles? Robbery, a killing?'

'How many of them?'

'Which way did they go?'

The men crowded round Giles, fastening cloaks and pulling up hoods against the rain outside.

Giles looked as grim as a man can. 'Little lass found dead, Odo the flesher's youngest. Didn't come home by nightfall. Not like her to stay out past suppertime, so her mam got a few of the neighbours to go looking. Her dog showed where she was. Her body was hidden behind some bales of wool in the warehouse down by the river. Well hidden she was too, we'd have not found her for days if it hadn't been for her dog barking.'

The men's expressions became as grim as Giles's.

'No chance the little lass got trapped by accident, suffocated maybe?' one asked.

'You'd not ask that if you'd seen her neck. Purple marks clear as day. It was no accident, not unless she strangled herself.'

An angry buzz filled the room.

'What kind of bastard would do that to a little child?'

Giles shook his head. 'I dunno, but they reckon she was last seen talking to that storyteller. We'll start with him.'

'If he's got aught to do with this, queens and witches won't be the only thing burning on a fire. I'll tie him to a spit and grill the scum myself. Come on, lads, I fancy a slice of roast swan.'

9. Vampires and Jews

It was already mid-morning and we had still not left the town of Northampton. We were not the only ones to be late on the road: since first light, a steady stream of carts and wagons had been trying to make their way to the town gates. But the gates were still firmly locked and now the streets and alleys of the town were jammed solid with carts, wagons, horses, oxen, dogs, sheep, geese, people on foot and people with handcarts, all trying to leave and all getting nowhere. The bleary-eyed drivers cursed those in front, though precious little good it did for no one could move forward or back. Their wives yelled at their children, trying in vain to prevent them from wandering off. And the local housewives and traders shouted at the travellers, as they tried to squeeze past the wagons with their baskets and loads, anxious to be about their own business.

Everyone was wet, tired and irritable. It had been the early hours of the morning before we got to our beds and when we finally did, we were constantly woken by drunken revellers and gangs of men storming in and out of barns and outbuildings, searching for the storyteller. They stabbed at piles of hay with pitchforks and swept every dark corner with their blazing torches until the women screamed they'd set the whole town afire if they didn't stop waving them about. No one in the town could have slept through the shouting and banging, but for all their noise, the only miscreants they flushed out were a few unfortunate couples who fled the scene half-clad or naked, surprised in their lovemaking by a pitchfork jabbed in their backsides or a light shone on to them in the corner of some dark alley.

As for the storyteller, he was nowhere to be found. He'd probably slipped out of town long before the gates were shut for the night. The gatekeeper couldn't recall seeing him leave, but since he couldn't recall seeing him arrive either, not much store could be set by that. As the poor man protested, there had been throngs of travellers arriving and departing; how could he be expected to notice one among so many? And besides, no one could tell him for certain if the storyteller was on foot or travelling on horseback and if he was alone or in company.

With their only lead vanished, no one knew what do next except inform the sheriff and coroner in the hope that one or other might dispatch soldiers to nearby towns and villages in case the storyteller turned up there. For if he did, he'd certainly be easy to identify, assuming, of course, that the swan's wing was real and not as fake as an averer's boil.

Some of the townspeople were all for keeping the gates locked until the murderer was discovered for, they said, the killer might not be the storyteller after all, but one of the other outlanders come for the market. However, wiser heads reasoned that all those extra mouths would be a considerable drain on the town's resources of food and ale, and the way the pestilence was spreading, they'd need every last scrap of food for themselves. Besides, what about the other children in the town? If there was a child-killer on the loose did they really want him to be trapped with their children? Better to risk letting the murderer walk free than have him strike again in their town. If he moved elsewhere and killed again, well, that wasn't their problem, at least their children would be safe. 'And who knows,' they said cheerfully, 'if we send him out on to the road, he might catch the pestilence and that would solve the problem once and for all.' And while they argued back and forth, the gates remained shut.

Like everyone else, we had been packed and ready since first light. Zophiel had insisted on moving out early and had Xanthus harnessed between the shafts of the wagon before dawn. We had pulled out into Fishmongers Row and taken our place in the queue before anyone realized they were not going to open the gates, by which time other wagons had pulled up behind us and it was impossible to return to the inn.

Zophiel was not in the best of humour. He had sat up all night defending his wagon. A few brave souls had demanded to search it. They were searching all the wagons and carts for the fugitive, but Zophiel was having none of it. He was not going to have his delicate mermaid destroyed by those clumsy oafs. Pulling out his dagger, he threatened that the first man who laid a hand on his wagon would have it cut off. Whether it was this threat or the stream of Latin curses that followed which dissuaded the men was hard to say, but it takes a brave man or a foolish one to risk a curse from a magician and the men were not that brave or foolish.

Despite his victory, Zophiel was worried that all the wagons might be searched again at the gates. A mob of half-drunken men with no authority he could handle, but soldiers with the sheriff's backing could not be denied and soldiers did not have a reputation for being great respecters of other people's property.

The others in the party, though they didn't have mermaids

to worry about, were in no better humour. Adela, white from lack of sleep, had retched into the gutter several times that morning, sickened by the stench of smoked fish and rotting fish guts in the alley in which we were stuck. Zophiel had coldly told her to be grateful we were not stuck in Tanners Row, and when Pleasance suggested that she might take Adela back on foot to wait in the inn, Zophiel had told them that once the gates opened and the carts started moving, he'd have no choice but to set off immediately with the other carts and it would be up to them to catch up. Given his mood, he'd have likely whipped Xanthus to a gallop once he was clear of the town, and the women knew it. Adela dared not risk leaving the wagon.

Pleasance helped her to settle next to Narigorm on the driver's seat of the wagon, solicitously tucking sacking around her shoulders and more across her knees to protect her from the cold and wet. For all that I still had an uneasy feeling about Narigorm travelling with us, there was no denying Pleasance was proving a godsend to Adela.

Pleasance slipped off the wagon and squeezed round to where I stood. As usual she addressed the puddles, though by now I realized it was not my scar that made her avert her eyes; she kept face turned aside whenever she spoke to anyone, as if she hoped that if she did not look at them, they could not see her.

'I'm going to the apothecary to fetch some syrup of balm and mint for Adela. It will settle her stomach, but I have none left in my pack.'

'But Zophiel said –'

She nodded impatiently. 'If I miss you, I can walk fast enough to catch up with you on the road.'

'You're a kind soul, Pleasance. I'll try to make Zophiel wait as soon as we are clear of the town.'

She raised her hand in front of her face, as if warding off the compliment. 'It is a mitz . . . an obligation. I'm a healer, it is what I do.' She pulled her cloak tightly around her. 'I must go.'

There was something so final about the way she said *go* that it alarmed me. I caught her arm as she turned. 'You are coming back, aren't you, Pleasance?'

She recoiled from the touch and glanced swiftly up at me, before staring hard at the metal rim of the cart wheel. 'I will stay with you as long as I can, but sometimes . . . sometimes you have to leave. You must never become so attached to places or people that it hurts you to say goodbye.'

I nodded. 'Now you are talking like a seasoned traveller.'

I had made that same resolution once. I'd promised myself I would never again suffer such pain as I'd felt that day I'd left my home. But it is easier said than done. Attachment creeps up on you before you can raise your guard.

As I watched Pleasance disappear among the throng of people, I wondered what hurt had brought about her own resolution. I had a feeling there was more behind her words than simply a traveller's itch to move on. But I hoped she'd stay with Adela long enough to bring her through her labour. Pleasance knew just how to massage her back to relieve the ache and which herbs to brew to ease the swelling of her ankles. She'd know how to ease the pain of labour and staunch the bleeding. Pleasance had a skill with herbs that went far beyond those few potions which every woman is taught to brew. Wherever she had acquired that knowledge it was not as a serving wench or villein.

The rain splashed down, stirring a witches' brew of blood, guts and fish eyes in the puddles around the wagon. House-wives, blaming all outlanders for the murder, tipped slops from the upstairs casements, taking malicious pleasure in the bellows of rage from below. The fishmongers cursed as they tried to squeeze baskets of fish through the narrow spaces between the shops and the wagons and we cursed back as they tried to elbow us out of the way. But it made no difference, we were stuck there and so were they.

Jofre, restless and impatient, was drumming out a rhythm on the wagon which was becoming annoying even to Rodrigo. To distract him, Rodrigo suggested that they go ahead to the gate to see if there was any news. If the gates opened while they were there, they would wait and join us as we passed through.

Rodrigo glanced at Osmond who was tightening the ropes on the wagon, which he had already tested a dozen times. Osmond's lips were drawn as tight as the ropes. He had apologized for calling Adela a goose the night before. Adela in turn had protested it was all her fault and she *was* a goose, but both were avoiding each other's eyes. Adela was still hurt for all that she denied it, and Osmond knew it, but did not know how to make amends.

Rodrigo looked over at the wretched Adela and then back at the equally miserable Osmond. 'Come with us, Osmond. It is better than kicking your heels here.'

Jofre turned, his smile radiant. 'Yes, come on. We'll make those old fools open the gate.'

Osmond hesitated. 'I should stay with Adela. She's not well.'

'She's never well,' snarled Zophiel. 'If she were a chicken, I'd wring her neck and put the dumb creature out of her misery.'

Osmond wheeled round, his fists clenched, but Rodrigo laid a restraining hand on his shoulder.

'Have a care, Zophiel,' Rodrigo said. 'It is not wise to

threaten to strangle a woman when they are still hunting the murderer of a strangled girl. What you speak in jest, others might take in earnest.'

Two patches of angry red appeared on Zophiel's cheeks and his eyes blazed.

'You go, Osmond,' Adela broke in quickly.

Osmond turned away without looking at her and followed Rodrigo, squeezing between the wagons and the fish-mongers' slabs. Jofre brought up the rear.

'Frenzy, filth and lust.' Narigorm, curled up like a little white rat in the well at the front of the wagon, stared at their retreating backs.

Pleasance glanced down at her. 'Did you say something, little one?'

Narigorm chanted in a sing-song voice, '*Troll runes I cut and cut three more. Frenzy, filth and lust.*' Then she smiled, a cold little triumphant smile. 'I cast *thurisaz*, the troll rune, last night. Twists everything that follows it, the troll rune does. Turns the runes to the dark side of meaning. But I couldn't tell who the runes were for, not last night.'

Adela, looking decidedly queasy, rapidly crossed herself. 'Please don't sing like that, Narigorm. It frightens me. It sounds like a curse and I know you wouldn't want to ... You were tired last night. I expect the runes fell like that by accident, because you weren't able to concentrate after ...' she hesitated, 'after all that nasty talk of the storyteller and that poor child.'

I expected Narigorm to fly into a rage. She usually did if anyone questioned the truth of her reading. But when I looked at her she was still smiling as if nothing anyone said could wipe that look of satisfaction off her face.

'Oh no, Adela, the runes can never fall by accident. They

spoke the truth about someone and it wasn't the storyteller, but I know who it was now. I know.'

Finally, sense prevailed and the gates were opened. It took a long time for all the traffic to squeeze out of the town, and Pleasance had returned long before the wagon was able to move, but once we were on the open road we all took in great gulps of clean air and began to relax. The wagons had not been searched again. The townspeople, having decided to let us go, could not wait to get rid of us.

Xanthus was being surprisingly docile. She had hardly tried to bite anyone in the town, well, not seriously anyway, though many people had pushed past her. She'd not kicked out or reared even in the crush and now on the open road she was ambling along, occasionally snatching at mouthfuls of sodden grass, but allowing herself to be pulled on with only an irritated shake of her head.

The road wended its way through the trees, gradually ascending, with painful slowness, to the top of the hill. Xanthus pulled with more will than usual, but the laden wagon, long incline and thick mud were more than a match for the horse and we all had to lend a hand at pushing the wagon except Adela, who clung fearfully to her seat as Xanthus's hooves slipped in the mud. The wagon felt even heavier than usual thanks to Adela and Pleasance having loaded it up with as much food and ale as they could cram on board between Zophiel's boxes, and despite the chill of the rain we were all sweating by the time we reached the top. There we paused to catch our breath and pass round a skin of ale. The trees were thick and tall, obscuring the view, but as the branches swayed in the wind we glimpsed the occasional silver flash of what appeared to be a lake in the valley below.

The rain dripped from the leaves and trickled in little rivulets round the stones on the track ahead. The leaves had turned to gold, bronze and copper on the trees and had begun to fall, lying in thick slippery drifts on the track. It was going to be even harder going down than up. But if what we were glimpsing was a large lake, with luck there'd be a few villages dotted about the edges, which was a cheering prospect, for by the time we got down there, we'd all be in need of a good fire and a hot meal.

It was a hazardous business getting the wagon down the hill. Zophiel had tied sacking over Xanthus's hooves to help her to grip in the mud, but the laden wagon kept slewing sideways on the slippery track, threatening to pull the horse down with it. Zophiel and I held Xanthus's head to keep her calm, while Jofre, Osmond and Rodrigo walked alongside the wagon, using their shoulders and thick poles to block the wheels whenever it seemed in danger of slipping.

Dusk was gathering quickly under the heavy canopy of the trees and we were so intent on keeping ourselves and the wagon upright that at first we didn't notice the dull roar above the constant rustling of the wind in the trees. Then as we rounded the bend the noise hit us as if a thousand knights were galloping past in a full battle charge. Zophiel pulled Xanthus up so sharply that for the first time that day she reared and tried to back in the shafts, rolling her eyes in fright. I knew just how she felt.

The glints of silver we had glimpsed below were not from any lake. The valley was flooded. Just a few yards ahead of us, the track had been swallowed up by a rushing torrent of thick brown water. Whole trees tumbled past like twigs thrown into a stream by a giant's child. Something blue, a piece of cloth maybe or a woman's kirtle, surfaced briefly, then was whisked out of sight and snatched away by the flood. Other half-familiar objects bobbed up, only to be sucked under again before we could comprehend what they were. As far as we could see through the rain and dusk of that evening, there was nothing solid left between us and the distant hills, only the rage of water.

You might think that with all those weeks and months of rain, England would have drowned weeks before. In Noah's day it took just forty days to wipe the face of the earth clean. And in my lifetime, which though long does not yet match the nine hundred and fifty years of Noah's life, I've seen rivers burst their banks and villages swept away after just a few hours of violent rains on to dry land. But the rain which had fallen since Midsummer's Day was neither violent nor sudden; it was steady and continuous as if the sky was a cracked bowl that was slowly leaking, dripping its contents down on to the earth below. And the earth soaked the water up, like a thick trencher of bread soaks up the juices of the meat. Rivers were swollen and dangerously fast, ditches full, water meadows turned to shallow lakes, but still it rained and still the land continued to absorb it. There comes a point, though, when even a trencher of stale bread can soak up no more. The land had taken all it could.

There was no way of knowing if the water was still rising, but we could not afford to take the chance. We couldn't risk making camp beside those flood waters. Late though it was, there was nothing for it but to turn and make our way slowly and achingly back up the hill again. Our way north was now well and truly barred. Our only hope was to slip sideways and try to work our way round by higher ground, or trust that the flood waters would eventually recede, but as long as it continued to rain there seemed little hope of that happening. Even if it did, the road and any bridges that crossed the rivers would be washed away, making it impossible to move the wagon by that route.

'East or west, Camelot?'

We stood at the crossroads. Rodrigo, Jofre and Osmond all favoured west, for whereas the road east appeared level and straight for as far as we could see, the road west climbed still higher and they were in favour of any direction that took them up away from the valleys. Adela shyly backed her husband.

But Zophiel, much to my surprise, wanted to go east. 'The news in Northampton was that the pestilence has only reached as far as London on the east side and we are well to the north of that. Towns may have closed on the west, but they'll still be open to the east.'

Osmond eyed him suspiciously. 'By towns, do you mean ports? You're not still hoping to find a ship, are you? Is that why you want to drag us all east? What is this business you have in Ireland anyway? The Irish won't have any more money than the English to waste on mermaids, not if they're cursed with this same rain.'

'Do you have the faintest understanding of what the pestilence is, Osmond? It is a sentence of death, and not a merciful one. Do you want to watch your wife screaming in agony as she dies? Because that is what will happen if we go west.'

Adela covered her face in her hands. I glanced at Jofre. He was trembling and looked as if he was about to be sick. I knew he was thinking of his mother.

Osmond took an angry pace towards Zophiel, but I pushed between them and held up my hands.

'Zophiel may lack tact, but what he says about the pestilence is right; we stand more chance of outstripping it on the eastern side. And besides, the flood waters were flowing west. We'll walk straight into them again if we take the track west. I'm forced to agree with Zophiel, east is safest course on both counts, just until we can find another road north to the shrines at York and Knaresborough. Pleasance, what do you say?'

By way of an answer, Pleasance pointed at Narigorm who crouched on her haunches in the centre of the crossroads. Three runes lay in front of her. Her hand hovered briefly above them, then she scooped them up and thrust them back into her pouch.

'We go east,' she said simply, as if she was a queen ordering her troops to march.

'Do you hear that, Adela?' Zophiel said. 'The runes direct us east.'

Though Zophiel had hitherto dismissed Narigorm's readings, like my relics, as nothing more than chicanery to fleece the gullible of their money, he was not above using them to support his argument when they worked in his favour.

'And I think we can take it that Pleasance will go wherever her little mistress commands. So since there are eight of us, we are evenly split. Therefore we –'

'There are nine,' Narigorm cut in, her tone as matter of fact as before. 'We are complete. There are nine, so now we go east.'

Zophiel looked slightly taken aback by this interruption, then laughed. 'I take it the child counts Xanthus as one of us. Well, why not, since she has to pull us whichever way we go.' He let go of the horse's head and taking a step back, gave her a mocking bow. 'Xanthus, you shall decide. Which way?'

The horse, as if she understood what was being asked of

her, stepped sideways and began to turn the wagon on to the eastern path.

'You don't know what you're gabbing about, you great lummox.' The old man scowled at his son and shuffled closer to the fire, crouching on the edge of the low wooden stool.

Old Walter and his son Abel had been welcoming enough, sharing their hearth with us, glad of the food that we offered them in exchange. Theirs was a simple cottage, but warm and dry, with a thin wattle partition dividing the family's living quarters from the warm, steaming bodies of their cattle who shared the dwelling. A ladder led to a platform up in the rafters where the hay was stored and the women and children had once slept. The old man's wife was long dead and his daughters were married and gone to their husbands' families, so son and father were all that remained and, like a long-married couple, they got along by bickering. It was an old and comforting habit, and even the presence of strangers did not change it.

'Vampires aren't spreading the pestilence,' Old Walter continued. 'For vampires to go around biting everyone, there'd have to be as many vampires as there are midges and if there were swarms of bloody great vampires flying round the towns and villages, someone would have seen them by now. It's not vampires, it's Jews, everyone knows that. They're in league with the Saracens, the Jews, always have been. The Lionheart said as much when he was king. They want to murder us all. They're poisoning the wells. You get a whole street of people fall sick on one night, stands to reason it's got to be the water from their well that poisoned them.'

Abel glared back at him. He wore the same habitual frown

as his father. 'Well, that just proves you're talking out of your arse as usual, you old pisspot, because there aren't any Jews in England. Not been for nigh on sixty years since the King's grandfather banished them. I bet you've never even seen a Jew, you old fool.'

Zophiel's drawl broke in on the argument. 'Actually, your father may well have seen a Jew or two in his time.'

'There, see, I told you.' The old man triumphantly slapped his thigh. 'He's been around, haven't you, sir? He knows a thing or two.'

Abel flushed, furious at being contradicted. 'Aye, well, he may have seen Jews in France or some such place, but you've not been further than our field strips in your life. If you've seen them, they must've been lurking in the ditch along with the boggarts and goblins you always reckon you've seen on your way home from the ale house.'

Zophiel smiled his cold, humourless smile. 'The ditches and gutters are certainly where they deserve to be, but I'm afraid they are far too cunning for that. King Edward, though he did well to banish them, made a grave mistake by not killing the vermin outright. A dead Jew is visible, but I fear a living one is not, and they have a way of wriggling in among the God-fearing Christians, like mice in a tithe barn, and breeding there until the time comes for them to strike. They didn't all flee England; some chose to convert and stay. But their conversions were false, for how can a Christ-killer who's damned before birth ever become a true Christian? They practised their religion in secret, spitting on the host and making a mockery of the sacraments.'

The young man was still anxious to defend himself. 'That's as may be, but so what if a few did remain? Those who are still alive must be older than this old fool and he's so old he can't even piss straight, never mind brew a deadly poison and put it down a well without anyone seeing. There's no proof they've poisoned anybody.'

Zophiel looked triumphant. 'Ah, but there is, my young friend; many a Jew in France has been brought to trial and found guilty of causing the pestilence by poisoning the wells. They've freely admitted their guilt under torture and –'

'The Archbishop of Canterbury would claim his own mother was a black cockerel and he was in league with the devil if the question was put to him under torture, as would we all,' I said.

But Zophiel continued as if I had not spoken. 'And have been justly executed for their heinous crimes. So, if the pestilence is proved to be their doing in France, how can the same malady have a different cause in England? No, the cause is plain enough, but here it will be harder to root them out and bring them to the bonfires. We must all be vigilant and on our guard for any who might be hiding amongst us.'

Adela, looking thoroughly alarmed, shrank against Osmond and buried her face in his shoulder. The gesture pleased him, for it seemed to signal that the quarrel of the night before was finally forgotten. He seized the opportunity to show her he was on her side.

'As usual, Zophiel, you've succeeded in upsetting Adela. When will you learn to keep your malicious thoughts to yourself?'

Zophiel looked anything but repentant. 'I merely point out the facts. If you have married a woman whose mind is so weak that she has to be constantly shielded from reality, that's your problem, but you really cannot expect the rest of us to tiptoe around her pretending that the clouds are made of cream, in case we upset her. Or is she afraid that someone might take her for a Jew?'

At that, even old Walter looked startled. 'She's no Jew.

Jews have got dark hair and hooked noses. I've seen them in the paintings on the church walls. Shifty-looking creatures they are, you'd spot them a mile off. She's a lovely lass, look at her, fair as our Lord himself.'

Adela smiled wanly at him as he leaned towards her, giving her a big lecherous wink, but she was still visibly trembling and Osmond, as usual, seemed torn between comforting her and wanting to punch Zophiel.

I tried to put an end to the bickering. 'Pleasance, have you some of that poppy syrup that you gave Adela before, the potion that helps her to sleep?'

But Pleasance didn't appear to have heard me. She was staring wide-eyed at Zophiel, looking as terrified as Adela. I heaved myself up and on the pretext of handing Pleasance her pack, drew her away from the fire.

'Take no notice, Pleasance. There are neither Jews nor vampires lurking here. People are frightened. They can't fight a miasma, so they create an enemy to fight. It makes them feel less helpless. Though in Zophiel's case, I don't think he believes a word of it; he just says it because he enjoys an argument. Why don't you find Adela that poppy syrup, see if we can't calm her down a bit before Osmond takes it into his head to start a fist-fight with Zophiel?'

Pleasance gave a weak smile and bent over her pack, but her hands were trembling as she struggled to undo the leather fastenings. She pushed the pack away and fled to the door.

'I left the syrup in the wagon,' she mumbled, and ran out of the door without even pausing to shut it behind her.

Narigorm stared after her, a curious expression on her face, as if she had just remembered something. Then she folded her arms and began rocking on her bottom, like a small child hugging a great secret.

'Born in a barn, was she?' Abel grumbled, getting up to close the door, but before he reached it we heard a scream outside the cottage. Snatching up a stout staff, Abel bounded through the door, followed closely by Rodrigo and more slowly by Osmond who had first to prise Adela's hand from his arm.

There was the sound of a scuffle and a cry of, 'Oh, no, you don't, my lad.' Then Abel and Rodrigo returned, dragging a struggling figure between them, immobilized by a cloak which had been wound tightly over his head and arms. Osmond followed hard on their heels, his arm supporting Pleasance, who was clearly shaken. Abel slammed the door and swung the heavy brace across it before turning to face the figure under the cloak, still firmly in the grip of Rodrigo.

'Now, my lad, let's be having a look at you.' He stepped forward to pull the cloak away, but I knew who it was before the face was unmasked. There was no mistaking the purple of that cloak.

10. Cygnus

'So we've caught a murderer,' Zophiel said triumphantly. 'You'll hang, boy, or worse, when the sheriff gets hold of you, and he will, make no mistake about that, for there'll be a price on your head which will come in very handy for us all in these hard times.'

'If anyone's going to claim the bounty for him, it'll be me and him.' Abel indicated Rodrigo with a jerk of his head. 'We're the ones who caught him. You sat on your arse by the fire, too scared to come outside in case there was any real fighting.' Abel had not forgiven Zophiel for contradicting him.

'I'm no murderer,' the swan-boy interrupted desperately. 'I never touched that child. I never laid eyes on her again after I spoke to her in the market place.'

'So if you are as innocent as you claim, why run away?' Zophiel said, ignoring Abel.

'Be fair, Zophiel,' I said. 'Running away is no proof of guilt. You saw that mob; their blood was up. Do you think they'd have taken him off for a fair trial? By the time they'd handed him over to the sheriff there wouldn't have been a lot left of him to hang, guilty or innocent. If I'd been in his shoes, I'd have run too.'

The swan-boy nodded vigorously. 'He's right. I was scared, and with good reason. I think I may have seen the man who killed the child and he knows I saw him. I think it was him who said he'd seen me with the child to cover his own tracks.'

'We all saw you with the child,' Zophiel snapped. 'As did half the town.'

'No, you don't understand. I saw a man leaving that warehouse about the time the little girl went missing. He was looking up and down the street as if he wanted to make sure it was empty. I was standing in a doorway sheltering from the rain. He wouldn't have seen me at first. I only noticed him because there was a little dog jumping up at him, barking. He kicked it away really viciously. That made me angry. I thought the dog looked familiar, but it wasn't until after the child was found I realized . . . I had no reason to think at the time . . .'

'Then why not tell your story to the authorities?' Zophiel demanded. 'You saw his face, I take it. You could describe him.'

'I saw his face all right; he walked past the door where I was standing. He saw me too when he drew level and looked none too happy about it either.'

'Then I repeat my question.'

'Because I saw something else, an emblem on his cloak. If it was his cloak, he was Master of the Guild of Cordwainers. Do you think the townspeople would take the word of an itinerant storyteller against a fellow townsman, especially one who's the master of such a wealthy guild?'

Zophiel raised one eyebrow. 'And do you think that we are more gullible than the townspeople, that we'd believe such a fanciful tale, where they would not? How convenient that you just happened to be hanging around, watching the very warehouse where the child was murdered.'

'But I did see the cordwainer there.'

'*If* you saw him, I dare say he had gone there to inspect a consignment of leather. What could be more natural at market time? He had a perfectly legitimate reason for being in a warehouse, unlike a vagabond storyteller who could only have been there with nefarious intent. At the very least, you obviously intended to steal. Did the child see you stealing and threaten to tell? Is that why you killed her? Or did you lure the child to the warehouse in order to rape her and murder her?'

'The child was strangled, Zophiel,' I reminded him. 'Hard to do that with a wing.'

'He has a hand also. It's easy enough for a man to throttle a small child with just one hand. The fingers on his hand will be stronger than most, for he has to do everything with that one hand.'

'Can he fly?' Old Walter suddenly blurted out from his place at the fireside. He'd been rubbing his eyes and staring at the storyteller's wing ever since the cloak was pulled off, as he if thought that what he was seeing was an illusion brought on by drink.

''Course he can't, you daft old pisspot. How do you expect him to fly with only one wing?' his son snapped, as if winged men regularly made an appearance in his house.

'These folks said he got out of the town when all the gates were closed. So maybe he flew out.'

Zophiel addressed himself to the swan-boy. 'He has a point; how exactly did you get out?'

'I stowed away . . . on your wagon.'

'You did what?' Zophiel screamed. All the colour seemed

to drain from his face. He seized the swan-boy by the front of his shirt, almost lifting him off his feet.

'If you've damaged anything, boy, I'll string you up myself.'

He pushed the boy aside, who fell heavily to the floor, and rushed to the door, cursing as he swung aside the heavy brace. Rodrigo helped the storyteller to his feet, gripping his shoulder firmly but gently, in case he should make a bolt for the open door, but he made no move to escape.

'Zophiel lives in fear of someone damaging his mermaid and his other precious boxes, though God alone knows what he has in there that is so precious,' I said by way of explanation, for Abel and his father were staring at the open door as if they thought Zophiel had gone mad.

The storyteller took a breath as if he was about to say something, but seemed to think better of it and quickly closed his mouth again.

'I hope for your sake nothing is damaged, lad,' I continued, 'otherwise you'll wish you were back with that mob. What do they call you anyway?'

'Cygnus.'

'Well then, Cygnus, there's a scraping of beans left in that pot, so you may as well settle down and eat. Whatever's to be done with you, can't be done till morning. No sense in going hungry while there's food to be eaten. This is going to be a long night for us all.'

The door was barred once more and we all settled down around the fire on the beaten earth floor, hunkered down on pieces of old sacking or logs, for the cottager only had a small bench and a single stool to his name. We were packed as tight as eels in a barrel, but grateful for our full bellies and the soporific heat of the spitting fire.

After careful inspection, Zophiel had been forced to admit that nothing in the wagon had been damaged, but his anger had, if anything, increased. He had unwittingly given shelter to a fugitive by refusing to allow his wagon to be searched and he took that as an insult to his pride. He was determined not to be made a fool of twice and was all for lashing the prisoner to one of the wagon wheels to spend the night outside in the rain, but the rest of us stopped him. Our hosts had no objections to the boy being housed in the cottage; in fact they seemed positively to welcome the idea, fascinated as they were by him. So Zophiel, unable to punish the boy as he would have liked, took to goading him instead.

'Tell us the truth, boy,' he said, 'and don't try your swan-prince or cordwainer tales on us – we are not a bunch of children. That is a false wing, is it not, a trick to get a few more pennies from the townsfolk than they'd pay you for a good tale? I imagine you managed to convince many fools that it's real, but don't you try to take me for a fool as well.'

Cygnus glanced nervously round the group. 'It's a long story.'

'We're not going anywhere and neither are you, boy,' Zophiel said grimly.

Adela smiled at Cygnus encouragingly and with a scared glance at Zophiel, he addressed himself to her.

'I was born with one good arm and one . . . one that was not an arm. It was a stump just a few inches long, with six tiny projections from it spread out in a line at its base, like the buds of pinion feathers. It was as well that my mother gave birth alone for if a goodwife had been present and had seen what my mother had birthed she'd have never allowed me to draw my first breath. My mother said she's known many do that, for they know a crippled child brings nothing but trouble to a family.'

Zophiel snapped, 'Only God can say if a child should live or die. Such women should be brought to a gallows. If I had my way no woman would be permitted to attend a birth.' He glared across at Pleasance who shrank further into her corner.

'They're not heartless women,' Cygnus protested. 'They don't want a child to live in suffering or its mother to be blamed. I've seen mothers hounded from the village or worse still tried as witches, accused of fornicating with a demon. There's no mercy shown to either mother or child then; baby and mother hanged together.'

'And such women should be tried as witches, for how else would such a monster be conceived? Not through them lying with their God-given husbands, that's for sure,' Zophiel snapped.

'You just said a baby was innocent. But now you want to hang the baby with its mother,' Adela said, her face flushed, though whether from indignation or the heat of the stuffy room was hard to tell.

'I said nothing of innocence, Adela.' Zophiel's tone, as ever, grew quieter and colder as others become more heated. 'What I said was that God would decide if the brat lived or died. If the mother is guilty, then the child is a demon and must die. Surely not even you would be foolish enough to plead for a demon to be spared the gallows, however seemingly innocent its form? But if the mother is not guilty her trial will prove her so. God will protect the innocent and save them from death.'

'Like he saves them from the pestilence?' Jofre said savagely.

There was an uncomfortable silence. Osmond crossed

himself. No one looked at anyone else. It was the question that was in everyone's mind, the one question no one could bring themselves to answer.

I nudged Cygnus with my staff. 'You were telling us about your birth. How is it that your mother gave birth alone with no one to attend her?'

There was a collective release of breath as if we had all momentarily looked over the edge of a cliff and had now drawn back to safer ground.

'My mother,' his eyes flicked nervously in the direction of Zophiel, 'my mother knew that I would be special.'

Zophiel snorted. 'How did she know? Did an angel appear to her?'

Cygnus seemed to wilt under his sarcastic tongue. 'Not an angel,' he muttered.

'A dream, then,' Adela suggested eagerly.

'She saw . . . she thought that a swan came to her, by night. The night before she was married . . .'

'I've heard that if you see something frightening you can often give birth to a mon . . .' Adela corrected herself hastily, 'to an unusual child. There was a woman in our town that was frightened by a bear when she was carrying and when the baby was born it was covered from head to foot in thick black hair.'

'I didn't mean my mother was frightened by a swan, she –'

Zophiel was staring at him, comprehension dawning and horror with it. Zophiel was hostile enough to the boy already without believing that he was the product of some bestial encounter between a bird and virgin. That would be all Zophiel needed to pronounce him guilty – a beast who murders little children. What else would be born from such a union?

I leaped in quickly. 'So because of the strange *dream* she had, your mother thought you would be special? Is that why she chose to give birth alone?'

Cygnus grimaced. 'She knew I would be different, but she wanted me. She always told me that.'

I glanced at Osmond; his expression was strained. I guessed he was not thinking of Cygnus, but of his own unborn child.

'It is a wonderful thing to grow up knowing you are wanted,' I said, and for the first time that evening Cygnus smiled, staring into the middle of the fire as if he could see his mother's face gazing lovingly back at him from the flames. Finally, after a long pause, he resumed his tale.

'On the night I was born, my mother's husband lay sleeping in the bed beside her. When the pains came upon her, my mother betrayed them to no one. Without a word she rose and left the cottage. It was a clear night, still and cold, the ground covered in frost that sparkled blue in the moonlight. My mother slipped silently between the shadows of silver birches, until she reached the dark waters of the lake. There, among the rushes, she made a nest for herself. She was alone, yet not lonely, for watching over her was the Swan that swims upon the River of Heaven some call the Milky Way. And so beneath the Swan stars I was born. And for that constellation I was named. She wrapped me in down to keep me warm and sang to me as the silver waters of the lake lapped softly at her feet.

'When at dawn she returned to the cottage, my mother's husband took one look at me and said I was a useless mouth to feed. He said my mother should take me back to the lake and drown me. But my mother kept me safe from him. He stayed for a few months, but as soon as I began to try to crawl, as soon as my stump could no longer be concealed beneath swaddling bands, he left to set up home with an alewife at the other end of the village. We saw him most days, but he chose not to see us.

'My mother worked. She worked as hard as ten women. She was a dairymaid by day and at night she spun wool and wove cloth to sell. She was so accustomed to spinning and weaving she could do it in the dark. The little light that filtered in from the torches in the yard was all she needed, so we didn't waste rushlights. And every night as she spun, she sang me to sleep with songs of the lake.

'For as long as she could, she kept me by her side and away from the other children. When I began to walk she kept me tethered to a post inside the byre, so that I wouldn't stray outside, but eventually I learned to untie myself even with my one hand. I started to explore and found other children. It wasn't long before I realized that I wasn't like them. Even had I not worked that out for myself, they wasted no time in telling me. One day my mother found me in a corner of the byre, beating my little stump with a stick and sobbing. It was then that she told me the story of my wonderful birth and explained that my little buds would soon sprout feathers and grow into a beautiful white wing, just like a swan's.

'I was delighted that I was to grow a wing of shining feathers, that to me seemed better than any arm and I couldn't wait to tell the other children. But when I told them, they just laughed and teased me all the more. From then on, they grabbed hold of me every day, pulling up my shirt to see if my feathers had grown yet and mocking and kicking me when they saw my stump was as bare as ever. But when I ran home crying to my mother she said, have faith, little swan, the feathers will come, if you want them enough, they will come. But however hard I wished for feathers, the skin remained pink and naked, like a newborn rat's.

'I used to set myself tests. If I see seven magpies today, then in the morning the wing will have begun to grow. If I eat only herbs for a week . . . if it rains for three days, if . . . if . . . And every day, when there was no sign of feathers, the children laughed more and I cried harder. At last my mother could bear it no longer. She went to the lake where she had birthed me and begged the swans for some of their feathers for their little brother and out of them she made me a wing and fastened it to my stump so that I could see what I would become. She said, if I could feel it, then I would believe it and have faith enough in it to make it happen. And so I did, for once I began to wear the wing, I knew what it felt like to have a wing. And so my buds sprouted into feathers and my stump grew into a wing, just as she said it would.'

Adela clapped her hands in delight. 'So it really did grow in the end. When did it happen?'

'When I became so accustomed to my wing that I believed it was my wing, then I found that it was. There was my wing as if it had always been, just as my arm has always been my arm.'

'But didn't the other children torment you more when you had a wing?' Jofre asked. 'Because you were . . .' he hesitated, 'different from them.'

'I was proud to be different from them. I had something they never could. I was not an ordinary boy.'

'And you could bear that? Bear to be different?' Jofre leaned forward, a strange urgency in his voice 'You weren't . . . ashamed?'

Cygnus smiled and for an answer unfurled his wing, beating it in the air, sending the smoke from the fire billowing round the room, until Abel snapped, 'Stop that, you'll have us ablaze.'

'A pretty trick,' Zophiel said. 'But you can't fly, so what use is one wing?'

Adela turned angrily. 'Leave him alone, can't you? Why do you have to spoil everything? The wing is beautiful. May I touch it?'

He nodded, and Adela reached out and stroked it as gently as she would have done if it had been the wing of some tiny fragile creature, shivering with delight as she did so. Osmond grabbed her by the wrist and pulled her back.

'Remember your own child,' he said sharply.

I glanced at Cygnus and saw a momentary look of pain pass across his face. It was Adela herself who had said that a pregnant woman who looked upon a bear gave birth to a monster. I'd seen men shield their pregnant wives from the sight of me before. Jofre was right; it is a fearful thing to be different.

Cygnus suddenly yelped in pain. Looking down, I saw that Narigorm had wriggled forward to his side and was sitting there holding a long white feather in her hand. Cygnus stretched out his wing and we could all plainly see the gap where a single feather had been pulled out.

Adela frowned. 'That was cruel, Narigorm, you mustn't pull feathers out from a living creature. You've hurt him.'

Cygnus reached down and stroked Narigorm's soft white hair. 'She didn't mean to, I'm sure. Children are often rough without meaning to be, like kittens at play.'

Narigorm gazed innocently at him. 'Another will soon grow in its place, won't it, Cygnus? It does on real swans. When one falls out a new one grows in its place. When your feather grows back that'll prove your wing is real, won't it?'

She turned and looked across at Zophiel. He stared at her for a moment, then suddenly he laughed.

Come first light we were again on the road, leaving old Walter and his son Abel with enough to argue about for many a long winter's evening whenever they recalled their night spent in our strange company. Although Abel had told Zophiel, the night before, that he had a claim on any bounty that might be offered for capturing the fugitive, in the cold light of dawn he seemed reluctant to pursue the matter. The only way of claiming a reward was to take Cygnus back to Northampton and hand him over to the authorities, but Abel, it transpired, didn't hold with towns – nasty, crowded places, full of thieves and cutpurses, and with things being as they were with the pestilence and such, nothing would induce him to set foot in one until the fever was past.

Old Walter didn't hold with towns or authorities either for, as he said, 'There's many an innocent man goes to do their duty and help them-as-is-in-charge only to find himself arrested for having broken some law he knew nowt about.' He coughed and spat copiously on the floor. 'Miller in the village fished a bloated corpse out of his mill pond where the river had carried it. Raised the hue and cry and sent for the coroner, all right and proper, but the coroner was that many days in coming the miller had to bury the corpse. The stench was making his wife and young 'uns sick and was starting to get into the flour. He'd have had no customers left if he hadn't buried the rotting body. And when the coroner did finally shift his arse and bother to turn up, instead of thanking the miller for doing his duty, the coroner recorded him in his Roll for not preserving the body and the miller was fined a tidy sum when he came before the justices. That's what you get for doing your duty. He should have buried the body quietly, soon as he fished it out, and said nowt about it. If you ask me, the coroner delayed coming on purpose, just so he could raise some fines.' Old Walter coughed and spat again. 'Lesson to us all, that is; let sleeping dogs lie; don't go bothering them unless they come bothering you.'

And so Cygnus's fate was placed firmly in our hands. None of our company, except for Zophiel, wanted to return to the town we'd left the day before. And even Zophiel was eventually forced to agree that returning was not a good idea, after Rodrigo pointed out that some of the towns-people might well remember that he had refused to let them search his wagon. Zophiel could find himself on trial for aiding and abetting the escape of a wanted man, a crime which carried no less of a penalty than that of the murder itself. Zophiel could not deny the truth of what Rodrigo said, but it did nothing to sweeten his temper.

Cygnus continued to protest his innocence, but his guilt or innocence, as Osmond said, was irrelevant; the point was he was a fugitive, wanted for a capital offence, and if we let him loose and he was caught, they'd force him to tell them how he'd escaped. Once that was known, they'd certainly come after us. It was just possible that the justices might believe we had unwittingly carried him out of town, but if they learned that we had apprehended him and then let him go, that was something no court would pardon. The only safe course was to take Cygnus with us and hand him over when we came across a bailiff or a King's man who could take him off our hands.

Cygnus looked terrified, his eyes darting in mute appeal around the company. He finally turned to me, fear and desperation straining every inch of his frame.

'You said yourself, Camelot, that I couldn't have strangled

the child with just one hand. Let me go and I promise they'll not catch me, and if they do I'll not breathe one word about you or your company. I swear it on my mother's life.'

'If it were just me, I wouldn't hesitate,' I told him. 'But there are the others to consider, a pregnant woman . . . the child . . .' I didn't add that despite his best resolution, he might do or say anything before his trial was ended. I'd seen stronger men than him broken, and he was no warrior.

He wilted, all the fight suddenly going out of him, and stared hopelessly at a water-filled rut at his feet. 'I'd not endanger them. Forgive me.'

Rodrigo, his expression grim, patted his shoulder. 'You will get a fair trial, *ragazzo*. We will see to that.'

Zophiel insisted that Cygnus should be tethered to the back of the wagon and forced to walk behind it like a prisoner; in that way there could be no doubting our intent if any of those searching for him caught up with us on the road. If he walked freely with us then he would be seen as one of our company and we would all surely be arrested as his accomplices. Adela protested bitterly, but the rest of us saw the sense in it, though I suspected that Zophiel had suggested it as much to punish the boy as to safeguard ourselves. Zophiel bound his good arm behind his back and tethered him waist and neck to the wagon, in such a way that if the boy tried to move his hand to free it, it would only tighten the rope about his neck.

'If he slips in the mud and is dragged behind the wagon, that rope will break his neck,' Rodrigo growled angrily, pushing Zophiel aside and working the knots loose.

'He told us himself how he learned to undo his mother's rope with one hand when he was a small child. I intend to ensure he can't escape from these bonds.'

'You think he is going to escape with the eight of us watching him?' Rodrigo retied Cygnus to the back of the wagon, but by his wrist only. 'Take a man prisoner, this I will do, but I will not murder him.'

Zophiel, still glowering, took his customary place by Xanthus, jerking her head savagely forward as he grasped her bridle, an action she repaid by taking a step sideways and treading down hard on his foot. Zophiel howled and cursed her roundly as he clung to the wagon, massaging his bruised foot, while Xanthus calmly resumed nibbling the grass as if nothing had happened. I was beginning to like that horse.

We were to spend several days on the road before we slept under a roof again. It was not a well-trodden track and the only other travellers we saw were local people passing with wood for their fires or moving their livestock from field to byre and back again. When anyone approached us on the road we drew our cloaks across our noses and mouths, searching their faces anxiously for any sign of sickness, as they did ours, but we saw only hunger in their eyes. They stared at us from a dull curiosity, sometimes returning our greetings, most often not. Who could blame them? Start talking to a company of strangers on the road and the next thing you know you'll find yourself having to offer them hospitality at your fireside. By the looks of them, most were having a hard time filling their own bellies, never mind someone else's.

The crops were ruined. You didn't need to be a farmer to see that. There's a stink that rotting roots give off that hangs over the countryside for miles around. There was no hope of salvaging grain or beans and while herbs flourish in the rain, they do not fill bellies in the cold of winter. Even autumn fruit needs a little sun to ripen.

We were more fortunate than the cottagers. We at least had been able to buy some dried beans, salted mutton and dried fish at Northampton, though a year ago I'd have called any merchant a rogue and a swindler who had charged such extortionate prices, but when food is scarce those that have it can name their price. The stores would not last long, however, with so many in our company, so whenever we came across a patch of sorrel or a hazelnut tree on common land we halted and gathered what we could to stretch out our provisions for the day.

Hunting for game was far too risky in those early months. Even to be caught with a bow or a deer trap was dangerous; no one wants to lose his ears or his hands, but birds fly free and Osmond, it turned out, was a fair mark with the sling-shot and Jofre was learning fast. As dusk drew in, the birds would wing their way towards their roosts in the bare branches of the trees and as we set up camp for the night, Osmond and Jofre would set off to see what they could bring down. They'd return an hour or so later with a handful of assorted birds, mostly starlings, blackbirds and pigeons, but once a brace of woodcock. There was little meat upon them, especially the starlings, but they added welcome flavour to the pot and even a mouthful of meat can seem like a feast when you are cold and hungry.

Narigorm was always hungry. Though she received a share of food equal to any of the adults in the company, her appetite was never satisfied. She took to setting tiny snares among the trees at night for small foraging animals. She would listen for the squeal in the darkness that told her something had been caught, then swiftly follow the sound. After a long time, too long, we would hear the squeals die away and she would return holding some limp creature carefully in both hands. Sometimes it would be edible, a squirrel or a hedgehog. Often it was a shrew or a weasel that had to be thrown away. But always it would be dead.

Osmond offered to go with her to show her how to dispatch the creatures more swiftly, but she stubbornly refused, saying she knew how to kill them. And although the prolonged shrieks of the little animals made us all uncomfortable, especially Adela, as Zophiel said, the child had to learn and she should not be discouraged from helping to find food. He was right, we needed every scrap we could get.

We were permanently wet and cold, and spending the nights camping in the woods meant that we woke stiff and still tired after a fitful night's sleep. But the cold was not the only thing disturbing my sleep. Several times I had woken convinced I had heard a howl in the night. It was too faint at first for me to be sure I'd heard it at all, and I might have dismissed it as no more than the wind in the trees, except that I saw Zophiel sitting up, tense in the darkness, as if he too was straining to listen. I told myself it was just the baying of a distant farm dog, but as the nights passed, the howl grew stronger and more distinct. It wasn't the howl of a dog. I'd have sworn it was a wolf, except that I knew it couldn't be a wolf, not in those parts. Your mind plays strange tricks when you are weary.

And Cygnus was more exhausted than any of us. Being tied to a wagon, splattered with mud from the wheels and unable to pick your own course through the ruts and puddles, would sap even the strongest man. You must constantly match your stride to the pace of the wagon. One slip and you find yourself being dragged along the ground. Rodrigo usually walked at the back of the wagon with him, trying to cheer him up with tales of courtly life. As Cygnus began to tire, Rodrigo would wrap his arm around the lad, holding him upright as he stumbled. Often he would call a halt on the pretext of needing to adjust the rags he had wrapped around Cygnus's wrist where it rubbed raw against the rope, taking his time, until Cygnus had recovered his breath enough to walk on. When we stopped to make camp for the night Zophiel insisted that Cygnus should be bound to a tree or the wheel of the cart, so his nights were even more uncomfortable than ours, but one of us always managed to slacken his bonds a little while Zophiel was occupied with his boxes, so that Cygnus could at least change his position once in a while.

But for all the misery Cygnus had to endure, he was still managing to keep more cheerful than Jofre. Whether it was Rodrigo's attention to Cygnus, stultifying boredom or simply being wet and cold that made Jofre increasingly morose was hard to tell, but only the evening hunt for birds seem to lift his mood and then for no more than an hour or two. Jofre was aglow after these hunts, his faced flushed, his eyes dancing with excitement. I suppose it was the most amusement he got all day, hard for a young man used to life in a lord's service where his days were filled with music, sport and the intrigue of gossip. But once we were all hunkered down around the fire, a black depression seemed to settle on Jofre, like flies on a corpse, and for the rest of the evening he would sit staring listlessly into the flames or else watch Adela and Osmond as they dozed together.

Jofre couldn't even practise on his instruments for the rain would have ruined them. Rodrigo tried to insist that he practise his singing, but Jofre always had some excuse, which inevitably generated a long lecture from Rodrigo and that only increased the lad's defiance. Zophiel didn't help, openly sneering at Rodrigo for not being able to control his pupil, saying that any master worthy of the name would take a stick to the boy and that would soon make him sing out, but neither Zophiel's sneers, Rodrigo's nagging nor Adela's coaxing had any good effect on Jofre. With his cheeks burning, he'd storm off to the shelter of a tree, well away from the company, with a flagon of ale or cider grasped tightly in his hand. It was always empty come morning and Jofre's mood would be blacker than ever.

One morning, after such a night, we all woke stiff, wet and cold, groaning as we stirred ourselves to break camp and move out. Jofre, as penance, had been told to remove the hobble from Xanthus and harness her to the wagon. It was a job he hated at the best of times and Xanthus was being more refractory than usual that morning. She had discovered an unusually juicy patch of grass, and having found such a feast she was not going to give it up without a fight. She continued to nibble rapidly at the grass as Jofre crept up and quietly caught her halter. She didn't try to resist and, flushed with success, Jofre foolishly turned his back as he led her to the wagon. That was the moment Xanthus had been waiting for; she suddenly jerked her head, sending him sprawling face down, and followed it up with a swift and painful nip to his calf, before calmly resuming her meal as if he was of no more significance than a troublesome fly. It was such a deft move that even the normally sympathetic Adela couldn't help laughing, but Jofre didn't see the funny side of it. He was writhing around on the grass massaging his leg, moaning that he probably wouldn't be able to walk for the rest of the day.

In the end it took the combined efforts of Zophiel, Rodrigo, Osmond and a good switch to get Xanthus as far as the wagon, and then they had to try to back her between the shafts. Dragged away from her meal, Xanthus was in no mood to cooperate. Free from the hobble and now able to buck, rear and kick as well as bite, she soon had the three of them sweating despite the coldness of the morning. As Zophiel paused to wipe his face, he suddenly held up his hand for silence. We all stopped. The sound of distant hooves and voices carried from the track just beyond the trees. Rodrigo put his hand on Jofre's shoulder.

'Go and look, *ragazzo*. But stay hidden,' he whispered.

Jofre, his injury forgotten, darted off. None of us moved. A group of riders on this remote track might mean trouble. Best not draw attention to ourselves till we could be sure what nature of men were out there.

Jofre was back in no time at all. 'Soldiers,' he whispered. 'Five of them. Travelling light, no packhorses.'

'From which direction?' Zophiel asked.

'The same as we've come from.'

Zophiel glanced over to where Cygnus crouched still tethered to the tree. 'So they are on the trail of our little game bird.' He smiled maliciously. 'It seems your time is up, my friend.'

'No,' Adela whispered hoarsely. She waddled over to Cygnus as if she intended to hide him behind her skirts. 'You can't hand him over. I won't let you.'

'And how are you going to stop me? A single shout will be enough to attract their attention,' Zophiel said, but he took care to keep his voice as low as hers.

The hooves came closer, a steady trot, men with a purpose. Were they really searching for Cygnus? We had our staves and knives; we could have put up a fight. But even if it was only one soldier, if he was acting for the King's peace, only a man with nothing left to lose would dare to put up any kind of resistance. Spending a lifetime as an outlaw on the run with a price on your head and every man's hand against you is not something to be undertaken lightly.

The others were all standing motionless, hardly daring to breathe. Cygnus crouched on the ground, a look of abject fear on his face. He began desperately pulling at the rope which tied him to the tree, but Zophiel had done his work too well. The beat of the hooves grew closer until they seemed to be right at the place where we had driven the wagon off the track and into the trees. Would they see the tracks and, if they did, would they stop to investigate? All eyes were fastened upon Zophiel, waiting. All he had to do was call out now and it would be over. Adela's hands were grasped tight in front of her, her lips moving silently as if she was praying, but whether to God or Zophiel I could not say.

The hoofbeats passed us, moving away. They had not seen the tracks. But still we waited. If we could hear them, they could hear us. Zophiel could still call out to them. He took a step forward. Osmond made as if to stop him, but Rodrigo held him back. Rodrigo knew, as did we all, that any attempt at restraint would only make Zophiel shout out, and it would be enough to bring the soldiers back, so we stood immobilized, listening as the sounds of the hooves died away to nothing. The rain pattered down and the wind whistled through the bare branches of the trees and above that – silence.

Zophiel turned to survey us, apparently deriving great amusement from our frozen attitudes. 'An interesting diversion. Now, if you have all rested sufficiently, shall we attempt once more to get this recalcitrant beast between the shafts?'

As he broke the silence, everyone seemed to remember they had been holding their breath and let it out in a great collective sigh. Adela turned to Zophiel and opened her mouth as if she was about to say something, but I caught her eye and shook my head. Sometimes, of men like Zophiel, it is better not to ask why and just be thankful. Perhaps I had misjudged him and there was a vein of compassion buried deep inside him after all.

No one spoke as we set about the tasks of clearing our camp. Ropes were tightened, the ashes from the long-dead fire scattered, and Xanthus, having made her point, graciously allowed herself to be harnessed to the wagon.

Finally, when we were all ready to depart, Zophiel strolled across to the tree where Cygnus was still tethered. Cygnus smiled weakly up at him, still white-faced.

'Th . . . thank you,' he stammered.

'Of course, we could simply leave you here for the soldiers to find on their return. That would save us all a lot of trouble. With luck you might starve to death and save the good citizens of England the expense of hanging you.'

'But I thought –' said Cygnus, his voice trembling.

'You thought because I didn't call out to the soldiers that I've changed my mind about handing you in,' Zophiel laughed. 'Oh no, my young friend, I've no intention of handing you over to soldiers unless I am forced to it. On a road like this without witnesses they'd doubtless claim they'd captured you themselves and, as our wise friend Rodrigo reminded me, they might arrest us too on the grounds that we were sheltering you. Why take one prisoner when you can just as easily take nine and earn yourself extra favours with your officers? No, I intend to hand you to a bailiff in person and in front of as many witnesses as I can find so that there shall be no mistake.'

Cygnus, still shaking, was once more led to the back of the wagon and the others turned away, busying themselves with their packs, unwilling to meet his eyes.

'Narigorm, come quickly, we're ready to go,' Pleasance called out, heaving her pack on to the wagon. Narigorm, crouching a little way off, had her head bent over the ground and did not appear to have heard.

'I'll fetch her,' I said. 'You finish stowing your pack.'

Narigorm was squatting on the roots of a tree, playing with her runes. They were scattered across a patch of cleared earth in which she had drawn three concentric circles. She looked up as she sensed me approaching and scooped up the runes, rubbing out the circles with her hands as she did so, but not before I saw something else lying in them – a long white feather and a small seashell, which the fishermen call a mermaid's fan. She quickly gathered these up as well and stuffed them in her pouch along with the runes, before standing up.

'Narigorm, were you –?'

'Camelot! Narigorm! Come on. We're moving out,' Adela called from her perch on the front of the wagon.

Narigorm darted forward and I followed more slowly, glancing back at the half-obliterated circles in the earth. Had Narigorm been playing with her runes when the soldiers were passing? Could she have . . . ? No, Zophiel was not acting under compulsion. His decision not to attract the soldiers' attention was conscious and, I had to admit, logical. But all the same, I couldn't help wondering if Narigorm had any other little keepsakes in that bag of hers.

11. All Souls' Night

We were to spend another wet and cold night camping among the trees, but on the day after, things began to look up. Trees gave way to cultivated land once more and we passed several lay brothers working the field strips, wading calf-deep through the sticky mud and looking as miserable as if they were performing a bare-foot pilgrimage of penance. Pools of water had collected along the furrows. There would be no harrowing until it had drained away, and since the rain was still falling, there seemed little chance of that before Christmas.

But it was evident we were now on monastery land, and where there is a monastery, there is a pilgrims' hall with dry beds, food, fire and company to while away the long winter evenings. We all began to brighten at the prospect and picked up our feet to get there the sooner. Even Xanthus seemed to have caught our excitement and quickened her pace without being urged to.

Then as we rounded a corner Rodrigo suddenly called for us to stop. He caught up with Zophiel and pulled the horse's head, turning horse and wagon into the shelter of a little coppice.

We all peered anxiously around – more soldiers? But Rodrigo beckoned us close.

'What are we to do with him?' Rodrigo asked, gesturing at the mud-splattered storyteller slumped against the back of the wagon. 'If we take him into the monastery tied to the wagon, they will know at once he is a wanted man.'

'So?' said Zophiel. 'He is.'

'But we are a week's journey now from the town. What if they have not heard of the crime?'

'Rodrigo is right,' Adela said eagerly. 'If news hasn't spread this far, then we could take Cygnus in with us as a companion and a free man. After all, you all said we were only keeping him bound to protect ourselves in case he was being pursued.'

Zophiel shook his head. 'You are forgetting the soldiers. They must have passed this way and they will certainly have made enquiries for him at the monastery.'

'Maybe they were on other business,' Rodrigo said.

'And maybe they were not. Do you propose to wager our freedom on guessing the mission of a soldier? Now we know where Jofre learned his recklessness. Gamble if you must, Rodrigo, but with coins, not our liberty.'

Rodrigo's eyes blazed and he took a step forward.

I broke in quickly. 'There's only one way to find out. You all remain here and I'll go in alone as a single traveller and make discreet enquiries about the soldiers, find out if there has been any news from the town. If they know nothing at the monastery, then you can enter with Cygnus, provided he keeps that wing well hidden and that cloak concealed, for its colour is too distinctive. Jofre or Osmond could lend him a shirt with two sleeves and a cote-hardie. With his wing bound tightly to his body underneath, it will look as if the boy has lost an arm. There's nothing remarkable about a lad with a missing limb seeking alms in a monastery. No one will remember him.'

'And if they have heard about the murder?' Zophiel asked.

'Then we must wait here until dark and try to slip past the monastery at night. There'll be too many about during the day for us to pass by unnoticed.'

'Are you seriously suggesting I should give up a warm bed and a hot meal to protect that creature?' said Zophiel.

'No, Zophiel, I know you better than that, but you might forego the warm bed for the fugitive's bounty. If Cygnus is forced to it, he might choose to seek sanctuary in the monastery church and then your prize will have escaped you.'

Zophiel snorted. 'Abjure the realm, be an exile for the rest of his life, that's if he made it to a port without being killed. I hardly think our little bird has the stomach to stand knee-deep in water for weeks on end, begging for a boat to take him. No ship's captain would take a man who can neither work his passage nor buy it, unless they took him to sell as a freak to a wealthy man who can afford to collect strange animals for his cages.'

'He might prefer even that slim chance of life to the certainty of death. Men will cling to the faintest shadow of a hope to escape death.'

Monasteries are hives of news and gossip. The lives of the monks and lay brothers are as monotonous as the liturgy, so they must glean what excitement they can from the travellers who pass through their doors. I've yet to meet a monk who's reluctant to stop for a gossip and I soon learned all I needed.

The soldiers had indeed stopped at the monastery, but not to search for the fugitive storyteller. One of the soldier's mounts had cast a shoe and the monastery blacksmith was summoned to fit a new one, while the soldiers seized the opportunity to demand ale and meat before riding on. The news they brought was from London and it was the worst. Two hundred a day were dying in that city from the pestilence alone. The churchyards could no longer contain them. Mass graves had been dug in the poorest quarters of the city. The old monk shuddered and crossed himself, his voice dropping to a low whisper as if he feared the evil of his own words. 'The ground, they say, is not consecrated; imagine that, those poor souls.'

'To whom do the soldiers carry this terrible news?' I was curious. It seemed unlikely that they had been sent out simply to spread alarm in the country at large.

The old monk looked up in surprise. 'It was not *that* news they were charged to carry. One of the soldiers told me what was afoot in London, but only because I asked him. I have kin there, you see, my brother and his family. Nieces and nephews, perhaps by now, even great-nieces and nephews, God save them. I know we should renounce all thoughts of kin when we enter the order, but still, one cannot help . . .' He spread his hands wide in a gesture of helplessness.

'And the soldiers?' I prompted.

'Ah yes, the soldiers, they go to summon one of the King's noble lords. A Knight of the Garter has fallen to the pestilence and must be replaced, for the King must have twenty-four Garter Knights to attend him at Windsor – he insists on it for the Christmas feasting.'

'The King is going ahead with the Christmas revels, despite the news from London?'

'Windsor is not London. The court continues as usual and the King will have his new round table and his knights of chivalry.'

'Perhaps he thinks the Garter Knights will protect him from the pestilence as well as give him victory in France.'

The old monk peered at me as if he wasn't sure if I was mocking him. 'The knights are sworn to St George; he will protect them from the arrows that fly from heaven as well as those which fly from the King's enemies.'

'But you said one had already fallen?'

The old monk wagged his finger at me. 'Even the King, God save him, cannot read men's hearts. It may be that the knight was not worthy or he betrayed his oath. This pestilence is God's scourge by which he cleanses his temple of licentiousness and lust. We must all pray to be spared, pray to the holy and blessed St Benedict to have mercy. You have not forgotten it is All Souls' Eve. There will be special services tonight for those in purgatory. You will join us, brother, will you not? If those poor Londoners are to be laid to rest in unconsecrated ground, their souls will need all our prayers.'

If the soldiers had no interest in the fugitive, neither did the handful of other travellers who were spending the night in the guest hall. The talk was of rain, flooding, pestilence and their own personal hardships, which brought them back to the rain again. So, after we had ensured that Cygnus's wing was bound tightly beneath his clothes, and with a warning not to play the storyteller in case someone's memory was jogged, Cygnus and the rest of our company came wet, cold and hungry into the hall.

With few in the guest hall, we had our pick of the beds. At least in a monastery you can be reasonably certain that the beds will be clean and not lousy. The ale was good too, though the meal was meagre – thick soup and a small portion of bread; no meat, of course, for it was fast day. The wind had got up and the rain was lashing against the thick walls, so most of the company were content to spend the afternoon dozing around the great fire in the pilgrims' hall.

As Adela settled herself with her sewing, she and Osmond exchanged a conspiratorial smile and nod, which sent Osmond rummaging in his pack. He straightened up, holding something behind his back, and beckoned to Narigorm. With a flourish, he triumphantly produced a wooden doll and held it out to the child. It had a daintily carved wooden nose and ears, painted eyes, a smiling mouth, rosy cheeks and brown sheep's wool for hair. Even the limbs were jointed and moved. It was a pretty little thing.

'Adela thought you must get rather lonely, because you don't have any children to play with, so I've made you your very own baby to nurse.'

Adela beamed. 'And I have some scraps of cloth, so you can come and sit by me and I'll show you how to make a cap for your baby's head to keep her warm, just like I'm making for mine.'

Narigorm, her hands firmly clasped behind her back, stared blankly at them both.

'She's yours, little one, take her,' Adela said encouragingly. 'You can rock her and dress her and pretend she's a real baby. It'll be good practice for you for when my baby's born, because you're going to help me look after my baby, aren't you?'

Narigorm finally took the doll and examined it carefully, running her fingers across the doll's eyes and pressing them hard against its painted mouth. Then she looked up again at Adela. 'I will practise for your baby. I'll take care of them both, you'll see.'

Adela and Osmond smiled at each other like fond parents,

well pleased with the success of their gift. But Narigorm wasn't smiling.

Cygnus and Zophiel had slipped out separately immediately after the meal and when I awoke from the first comfortable nap I'd had in weeks, I found they had still not returned and Jofre had left as well. Still, he was young and full of energy; he'd doubtless gone off to find more amusing company, if that is possible in a monastery, but Cygnus's absence was more worrying. Had he decided to seek sanctuary after all? Surely not; Zophiel was right, no one would take that way out unless they were cornered. Besides, I'd not heard the sanctuary bell ringing. More likely he'd decided to slip out and run for it while Zophiel was not around to stop him. I wouldn't blame the lad if he had.

But I had an appointment of my own to keep. I stepped outside. The day, never bright under the thick grey rain clouds, was darkening as evening hurried on. I wrapped my cloak tightly around me against the wind and rain and hurried across the courtyard towards the stables. A cobbled slope led down from the courtyard into a long underground chamber with a high vaulted ceiling. One side was divided by wooden partitions into stalls for the horses, with wooden platforms above for the grooms to sleep on. Oats, hay and straw were stacked on raised platforms on the other side, though there seemed to be precious little of any, considering winter had barely begun. If the winter turned icy as well as wet, animals would starve as well as people, for there were not enough stores for either. Perhaps it was the living we should be praying for, not the dead. At least the dead had no more need of food.

That afternoon there were only a few horses tethered in the stalls, tugging contentedly at their fodder, blissfully unaware of what the future might hold, but otherwise the stables appeared deserted. At the far end was a huge store chamber stacked with barrels and kegs. The only light filtered down from two grated holes in the floor above, but there was enough for me to see the man I sought there.

The lay brother who worked in the laundry had exceeded my expectations. At best I had hoped for a couple of worn-out monks' habits, maybe three at the most, but he had managed to bring half a dozen. They were patched, threadbare and stained, just what I was looking for. The longer the robe appears to have been worn the more valuable it is, and as for stains, if there's blood on it or what appears to be blood, so much the better. It was best not to enquire whether the monks' old habits had really been discarded or if some would simply be marked 'missing' in the laundry lists, but the lay brother would doubtless ensure that one way or another he would not be called to account for them. He seemed well content with his half of the bargain – a few coins and half a dozen bottles of St John Shorne's water. It was as well I'd stocked up in North Marston.

He slipped out of the stables by his own staircase while I ambled back past the lines of stalls, feeling thoroughly content with the day: a good deal struck, a belly full of hot food and the prospect of a warm and comfortable night's sleep to come. Things were looking up for once.

'Camelot?'

I jumped as a figure emerged from the shadows behind one of the tethered horses. Such frights are not good at my time of life. I leaned against the partition, heart thumping a little.

'Sorry. I didn't mean to startle you,' Cygnus said, grinning sheepishly like a child that has been caught out in a prank.

'I wondered where you'd got to, Cygnus.'

'I thought I'd best keep out of the way of the other travellers, just in case one of them should happen . . .' He trailed off, looking miserable. 'Anyway, I thought I may as well make myself useful. You've fed me for a week and I've done nothing to earn my keep. Poor old Xanthus needed a good wash down. Get the mud off her coat. Horses take a chill if their coats are matted; they can't keep warm. Hooves rot too if you don't clean them.'

As if to confirm this Xanthus gave a low whinny and nudged Cygnus gently. He smiled and resumed wiping her down.

'Didn't Zophiel see to his horse when he stabled her?'

'He fed her, but he was in a hurry to get back to his cart. Said he needed to check if the boxes had shifted. But never mind Zophiel,' he added impatiently. 'What were you and that lay brother up to, Camelot? Are you hoping to sell those old monks' habits to the poor? They won't fetch much, hardly worth the trouble of carrying them, I should think.'

'Not to the poor, Cygnus, to the rich. Anyone poor enough to need to dress in these rags would not have the money to buy them.'

'But the rich wouldn't be seen dead in such old things.'

'Ah, but that's where you're wrong, my lad, the rich would only be seen dead in them.'

He shook his head in bewilderment.

'The rich with guilty consciences buy monks' robes to be buried in, then when the devil comes to carry their souls to hell for all their wickedness, he passes over them for he sees not a rich sinner, but a poor, pious monk. If the monk who wore it was holy enough, then the odour of sanctity will be in his robes and may shorten the sinner's time in purgatory or even open the doors of heaven itself. Smell these.' I thrust a particularly rank robe under Cygnus's long nose.

He recoiled at the stench.

I laughed. 'The angels will smell the holiness on this one long before he ascends the ladder and will fling wide the gates. They'll not want to stop and question him too long, for they'll be too busy drawing him water for a bath.'

'Do they think the angels and the devil can be so easily fooled by such tricks?'

'If a man can be fooled himself he takes everyone else for a fool too, even the devil himself. And if it comforts their last hours and their grieving families, who are we to grudge them that? Every man, rich or poor, needs hope in his last hours and every widow needs solace in her grief.'

'But surely that's why they pay for chantry prayers and masses, so they can shorten their days in purgatory by prayer.'

'Ah, but that is not enough to reassure them. The rich have learned to mistrust their fellow men. In their experience loyalty can only be secured by two things: money and fear. When a rich man is dead he can no longer command by fear, and what if the money runs out or those paid to pray grow negligent? Better to wear your salvation than depend on others for it.' I thrust the last of the robes into my pack.

'I still can't believe the rich will buy these rags.'

I chuckled. 'You'll see in time, my lad, that's if you stay with us, of course.'

Anxiety returned to his face. 'Narigorm said that Zophiel won't hand me over to the bailiff,' he said uncertainly.

'Did he tell her so?'

He frowned as if trying to remember her words. 'I don't think she said as much, but he must have done. She seemed so certain.'

The image of the runes, the feather and the seashell flashed across my mind. Was she reading the future or was she trying to create it?

Cygnus bit his lip, peering anxiously at me, trying to find some kind of reassurance in my face. 'Why? Don't you think she's right?'

'Let's hope so.' Then, seeing the flash of fear again in his face, I added hastily, 'I doubt anyone is looking for you any more. The message would have reached here by now if they were. People have more pressing concerns. With things being what they are, they won't have the men to spare to go scouring the countryside looking for a fugitive.'

It was better that he should believe that than worry himself to death. If they did arrest him, there would be time enough for him to worry about his fate then.

I grasped his arm. 'Don't be tempted to run from here, lad. You can't return to your old profession, at least not until you know for certain they're no longer looking for you, and life is hard out there for anyone on the road just now. You'd end up begging for a living and that's no living at all. At least, with us, you'll eat when we eat, and who knows, if you make yourself useful enough with that horse, Zophiel might see you're more use to him as a groom than a bounty.'

Cygnus nodded. 'I won't run, Camelot. I meant it when I said I wouldn't endanger Adela or little Narigorm. I don't believe that anyone who brings harm to a child can ever be forgiven; that's why I could never have done such a dreadful thing to that little girl. If I had a child, I would wrap her so tightly she would never know a moment's pain or fear.' Tears shone in his eyes, and he fiercely brushed them away.

I remembered that passion only too well. When I first held my baby son and saw the blueness of the sky concentrated in those big eyes, his soft little mouth open in wonderment, his fragile little fingers curling tightly around mine, trusting that I could protect him from anything in the world, I knew I would give my life to defend my son from harm. I could never have foreseen how that promise would be put to the test, but I meant it then and I have not for a single day of my life regretted keeping it. Cygnus didn't weep for a lost child, though, he wept for the child he knew he would never have. It's not just princesses who refuse to marry swan-boys.

He suddenly blurted out, 'Zophiel was right when he said, "What use is one wing?" That was my mother's grief. I saw it every day in her eyes, that look of pity and guilt when she watched me, like the way you might look at an animal that you have maimed without meaning to. I think she'd hoped that I would be born with two wings or with two hands. I don't think she would have minded which it was, but I was born neither bird nor man. She had faith, you see, but not enough for two wings, not enough to believe that a wing would grow in place of a good right hand. That's why I left in the end.'

'Like the swan-brother in the story?' I asked gently.

'That part of the swan-prince is true. I left because I couldn't bear to see the guilt in her eyes, because I was the cause. And I left because I didn't want to be cared for, like a crippled bird.'

'We leave as much to get away from where we are, as to find something we seek.'

'You too?' He glanced up at my empty eye socket.

'Believe me,' I said, 'I know what it is to be looked at with pity. I had my reasons to leave. I know why you left, but I'm curious about what you seek.'

'My other wing, of course. Do you think I want to go through life with one arm and one wing?'

'Maybe not, but why not an arm in place of the wing? If you had two arms you would be wholly a man.'

'You think two arms make you a man?'

'Do two wings make you a bird?'

He smiled sadly. 'With two wings you can fly.'

All Souls' Night is a time when all good Christian folk are either safely abed with the covers pulled tightly over their heads or piously in church sheltering under the saints and their prayers. For they say that it is the night when, between sunset and sunrise, the gates of purgatory are flung open, the dead creep forth as toads or cats, owls or bats to torment those who have forgotten or neglected them.

On All Souls' Night, when I was a child, people used to leave garlands, food and ale on the graves of their relatives to convince them that they were not neglected. But the dead were not fooled by one day's show of remembrance; they came anyway, creeping into houses, scratching at walls, rattling at shutters. We children curled up together in our beds, pretending to one another that we feared nothing, but quaking under our covers as we listened to every creak and groan, every screech and howl of that long night, thankful for the comfort of the warm and living bodies of our siblings pressed tightly beside us. But adults must face their ghosts and we, like the rest of the travellers in the monastery guest hall, braved the cold night to join the monks in their prayers for their dead and ours, and for the dead who belonged to no one.

'*Convertere, anima mea, in requiem tuam* . . . Turn, O my soul, into thy rest . . .'

Beside me, Rodrigo sighed and crossed himself, mouthing the words with the monks, settling into the old familiar service as a dog settles down by a warm fire. Cygnus, his long sharp nose prominently silhouetted in the candlelight, stared fixedly at the floor, as if he feared to meet the eyes of either the living or the dead. Adela, her arm around Narigorm's shoulder, gazed down at her then up at Osmond, as if they were already a family. Would they take Narigorm in, when they finally found a place to settle, I wondered. They both seemed fond of the child, and already treated her as a niece if not a daughter, but would that change when their own baby was born? I suspected Narigorm would not take kindly to being displaced in their affections.

In front of us, Zophiel, his back rigid, stared straight ahead. It was hard to know if he prayed or not. And if he prayed for the dead, whom did he name? A wife? A child? I had never asked if he had such in his life. It was hard to imagine him being civil to any woman long enough to ask her to wed him, but perhaps in his youth he had been a different man, a kind and gentle man, with romance in his soul. And maybe it was a faithless wife who had soured him against her kind. Or maybe not. I don't think any man could change that much. Thinking of women, I realized that Pleasance was nowhere to be seen in the church. I was surprised by her absence; I would have taken her to be a devout woman. Jofre's absence, on the other hand, was no surprise.

The church was unusually dark that night, to remind those present of the darkness of the grave that awaits us all. An open empty coffin had been set upon the bier and placed before the rood screen, a candle at each corner, ready and waiting for the next corpse. And there would be one, if not today, then tomorrow. Death is the only certainty in life, it reminded us.

Every inch of the church walls and pillars had been painted with scenes from the Bible and the lives of the saints. By day the reds and blues, greens and gold of the paintings glowed more vibrant than a newly stitched tapestry. But the candles for this service had been carefully placed to illuminate, not the gold of the saints' haloes or the full round breasts of the Virgin, but the red flames which leaped between the teeth of the mouth of hell, where sinners held up their arms, beseeching in vain for mercy, while the two-faced demons prodded them down. Prayers were too late for those condemned to hell, but not for those in purgatory. As the walls taught us, they might yet be released.

Beneath the painting there were offerings left by the faithful – jewelled necklaces, pins, brooches and rings, silver crucifixes and jars containing costly spices – bargains struck between the faithful and the Church, goods to barter for the prayers of St Odilo who had insisted that all the Cluny monks should devote one day a year to pray for the dead in purgatory in addition to their regular prayers for the departed.

The monks in procession halted before the painting. In the gloom of the church, they were faceless under their deep hoods.

'Quia eripuit animam meam de morte . . . For he has delivered my soul from death . . .'

Would God deliver the monks? Would he spare the monasteries? If the rumours were true, he had not spared the priests. But if pestilence also crept into the monasteries, who would be left to pray for the dead? And what of those who lay unshriven and unnamed in mass graves – would they ever be released from purgatory, if there was no one left to name them?

The monks filed out of the church, two by two, fat candles in their hands shielded by caps of horn against the wind which burst into the church as soon as the great

187

door was opened. We followed in a solemn procession, like mourners after a coffin. The service was not yet over; there were the corpses of the monks buried in the orchard grave-yard to be blessed and sprinkled with holy water.

Outside it was cold and dark. The rain had eased, but the wind had strengthened to make up for it. It tore at our clothes and bent the branches of the yews until they moaned like those souls in purgatory. We stood in a huddle under the bare branches of the fruit trees, trying to shelter behind one another from the biting wet wind, as the monks pro-cessed from grave to grave, stopping to flick water from the hyssop on each one. But little of the holy water reached the mounds for it was snatched away by the wind as soon as it was flung.

'*Dirige, Domine, Deus meus, in conspectu tuo viam meam . . .* Direct, O Lord, my God, my way in your sight . . .'

A high-pitched giggle suddenly erupted from the far side of the graveyard. The monks faltered in their chanting and turned in the direction of the sound. We all strained our ears to listen, but could hear nothing except for the groaning trees and the howling wind. The monks resumed their chant-ing, but then another shriek rang out. There was no ignoring this.

The prior stepped forward, raising his candle, and called out in a voice that was none too steady, 'Who's there? Come out and show yourselves, whoever you are.'

But the candle flame did not penetrate more than a few feet into the darkness.

'Come out, I say. I command you in the name of . . .'

But he got no further for three dark figures rose up out of the ground and lurched forward.

Several people in the crowd screamed and tried to scramble over the wall of the graveyard. Even the monks backed away, crossing themselves, but the prior was made of sterner stuff. He stood his ground and, thrusting his crucifix out before him, gabbled, '*Libera nos a malo.* Deliver us from evil,' over and over again as the figures stumbled towards him.

Then, as the candlelight caught them, we saw what the creatures were; they were human and very much alive. Two of them I did not recognize, but I could tell from their garb that one was a young novice, the other a slightly older lay brother. There was no mistaking the third; it was Jofre. And he, like his two companions, was as drunk as a lord. He let go of his new friends and, stumbling to the nearest grave, raised his flagon. He made an exaggerated bow.

'Here, Broth ... Brother Bones, you don't want water, do you? Had ... had quite enough of that already. Have some wine, my good man.' He dribbled some wine on to the grave. 'That'll put hairs on your chest, no, wait ... you don't have a chest,' he giggled. 'And here's some for all your little w ... worms and maggots.'

He tipped the remains of his flagon on to the grave. Then he swayed sideways, tripped over the mound and fell straight into the arms of the prior, on whose portly chest he vomited, copiously.

12. Retribution

We were fortunate that they did not put us out of their gates that night, though it was not mercy which spared us a night on the road, but the determination of the prior and novice master to keep Jofre within their walls long enough to discover every detail of the outrage. It was plain that they would get no sense out of any of the three lads until they had sobered up and only a night's sleep would bring about that transformation.

The monks dragged the lay brother and novice off to spend a less than comfortable night on the hard, cold boards of the penitents' cells where they would be locked up until their real punishment was determined. But they allowed us to carry Jofre to the stables to spend the night on the floor in the straw where he could do least damage if he vomited again. Rodrigo, almost white with fury, shouted and railed at him all the way. Cygnus, the only person at that moment who seemed to feel any sympathy for the boy, tried to persuade Rodrigo to take himself off to bed, telling him that he would keep an eye on Jofre and see that he didn't choke in the night.

Zophiel turned on him furiously. 'Let him choke; it would do us all a favour. Don't you realize that he's wrecked any chance of us passing through here unnoticed? Anyone who comes looking for you now is bound to find you; they'll remember us for years thanks to him. That lout is a liability to us all. This is the second time he has lost us our lodgings, for the monastery certainly won't be extending their hospitality to us after tomorrow.'

Rodrigo looked stricken, as though he had only just realized what the night's events might mean for Cygnus.

'Cygnus, I do not know how to apologize to you . . . to all of you.' He grabbed the comatose Jofre by the shoulders and shook him. '*I denti di Dio!* Why do you do this? You swore to me after –'

'You're wasting your breath,' Zophiel said impatiently. 'Cygnus is right for once; let him sleep it off and deal with him tomorrow when he's sober. But when you do, Rodrigo, make sure you deliver a lesson he won't forget. He has gone too far this time and you can't go on ignoring it. As his master, you're responsible for him. If he continues to behave like this, he'll find himself stretching a rope before long and if he does end up on the gallows, you will be to blame.'

The following morning Jofre was roused none too gently from his stable stall at first light. He looked pale and complained of a headache and feeling queasy, but he was not suffering nearly as much as Zophiel would have liked, nor as much as his two puffy-eyed drinking companions who, unlike Jofre, were not used to an excess of wine. They were dragged out of their cells holding their heads and wincing at the slightest sound.

The story, when it was finally wrung out of the three of them, did not exonerate any as the innocent party. It seemed that Jofre had got into conversation with the young lay brother and a couple of novices. Which of them proposed the game of dice was never determined, they all blamed one another, but dice was played. Since the novices had nothing to bet against Jofre's money, they'd appropriated some wine from the stores in lieu of a stake. Only a small quantity at first, nothing that would be missed, and certainly not enough to get them drunk. But what they did drink was enough to loosen their inhibitions and it wasn't long before the gambling stakes increased and more wine was stolen and consumed. On hearing the monastery bell rung for the All Souls' service, one of the two novices, who had drunk rather less than his companions, wisely withdrew from the game, and taking advantage of the darkened church, slipped into the service by a side door to join the back of the procession, hoping his earlier absence would go unnoticed. But the others continued drinking and playing, too inebriated by this time to heed the warning of the bell.

After they had questioned the mutinous Jofre, the prior and novice master withdrew to seek out the second of the two novices who had not yet been apprehended and was doubtless on his knees somewhere praying more earnestly than he had ever done in his life that his identity would not be revealed. We for our part set about packing up to leave.

In all probability the lay brother would be locked up in the penitents' cell and made to suffer for a week or so before being kicked out of the monastery. He would undoubtedly bear the hardest punishment in the long run, for work and shelter were hard to find. As for the novices, they would be likely to face a month or more of severe penances and would consider themselves fortunate if they were permitted to eat anything but hard bread for weeks; certainly they'd tasted their last drop of wine for a good while.

It was fortunate for Jofre that the prior wanted to keep the disgraceful incident as quiet as possible and deal with it privately behind closed doors, for he knew it did not reflect well on the discipline of the monastery and both prior and novice master might be called to account, a situation they wanted to avoid at all costs. Had it not been for that, Jofre could well have found himself facing the Church courts on a serious charge and the penalties would have been grim indeed. As it was, the prior was content to leave the matter of Jofre's discipline to his master Rodrigo.

But if Rodrigo intended to blister Jofre's ears with a lecture, he was obviously saving his words until we were well away from the monastery. For unlike the night before, he remained tight-lipped and silent, despite Jofre's anxious glances in his direction and, like Jofre, the rest of us waited for the explosion which we knew must surely come.

It was a silent, grim-faced party that followed Xanthus and the wagon back out on to the road once more. Not even Zophiel suggested that Cygnus should be tied to the back of the wagon now. There was no point in pretending he was our prisoner any more. As before, once we were clear of the monastery lands, the road was nigh on deserted. The rain had settled in again, a fine mizzle, and the only sounds were trundling wagon wheels and the raucous cries of the rooks wheeling in the grey skies above as they mobbed a heron who flapped heavily too near their roosts. The thought of another night sleeping out in the open was depressing us all.

The river in front of us was swollen, brimming to the top of the banks after all the rain, but at least it hadn't flooded, though it threatened to at any time. Where the river crossed the road the banks had been widened out and the bottom raised with large flat stones to form a ford. But it was hard to tell if the ford was passable for the fast-flowing water was muddy and full of swirling brown leaves and twigs carried down from higher up the stream. To one side of the ford, a stone humpback bridge had been built, wide enough for people and horses, but not for the wagon.

Zophiel handed Xanthus's bridle rein to Osmond and prodded his long stave into the ford to test the depth. 'Faster and deeper than I'd like, but we've little choice. We've not passed another track wide enough for a wagon since well before the monastery. We must either cross the river here or retrace our steps a good many miles. And,' he added, glaring at Jofre, 'thanks to our young friend, we will hardly be welcome at the monastery if we are forced to return that way. So we will have to cross.'

Jofre glowered at the ground.

'Two people will have to wade out in front of Xanthus, spaced as far apart as the wagon wheels, then they can warn in time if any of the ford stones have been washed away. It had better be someone who can swim. Cygnus?'

Cygnus shook his head. 'I never learned.'

Zophiel swung his stave on to the wagon, almost hitting Cygnus on the head, so that he was forced to flinch away. 'A swan that can't fly or swim. What exactly can you do, boy?'

'I'll do it,' said Osmond. 'I was always in and out of the river when I was a lad, wasn't I, Adela?' She looked at him sharply and Osmond suddenly flushed as if he had said something he shouldn't.

'I will go too,' said Rodrigo quietly. They were the first words he had spoken all day. 'I am taller and heavier than Camelot. The river will not find it so easy to knock me over.'

I grinned. 'Thank you, Rodrigo, for your tact in not saying what you really meant, that you are younger than me.'

Rodrigo made a courtly bow, but he didn't chuckle as he normally would have; this business of Jofre was clearly preying on his mind. The sooner he tackled the boy and cleared the air, the better for everyone.

Narigorm scrambled down from her little nest in the well at the front of the wagon as Zophiel went to check that his boxes were secured, but Adela had to wait until Osmond could help her down. Her swollen belly was making the manoeuvre more difficult by the day.

'I swear that if the wagon was swept away, Zophiel would let us drown and save his boxes,' Osmond muttered. 'I'd give anything to know what he's got in them. Cygnus, didn't you see what it was when you were hiding in the wagon?'

Cygnus, with a curious expression on his face, began, 'I did see . . .'

But he broke off abruptly as Zophiel reappeared from round the back of the wagon. Cygnus hastily turned away and made for the bridge. The rest of us followed, except for Adela who was begging Osmond to be careful. He assured her that he'd be across the river before she was and with an embarrassed grin at Rodrigo, took a tentative step into the fast-flowing stream, shuddering as the icy water crept slowly up his legs.

I'll say this for Xanthus, she could rear and buck with the best of them when she was in a bad temper, but faced with real danger she was as steady as a rock, and though she hesitated on the edge of the water, she plodded her way across as Zophiel led her forward. Perhaps the familiar shapes of Rodrigo and Osmond walking ahead of her helped to keep her calm as the muddy water swirled about her.

Rodrigo and Osmond had almost reached the other side when a cry rang out from behind us on the bridge and almost at the same instant from Osmond. We spun round to see a young lad with his arm around Adela's breasts and a knife at her throat. An older man stood on the bank holding a long, murderous-looking pike under Osmond's chin, the sharp point digging into his throat. As we stared, a woman and a girl appeared on the far side of the bridge, blocking our way across. They too were armed with knives. They were a wiry-looking family, scrawny but tough, like those who have known many times of hunger but have survived and become the stronger for it. Filthy and ragged they may have been, but these were no cringing beggars. There was a look of malice in their faces, even in that of the young girl, which told you at once they would have no hesitation in using their weapons if they were so minded.

'Pay the toll if you want to use this crossing.' The man's legs were bare, but the rest of him was encased in some kind of dark, mildewed leather and he wore a round leather cap on his head. His skin was as leathery as his clothes, so weathered and crinkled by sun, wind and snow that it was hard to tell flesh from garments.

'Is this the way you collect tolls, at knife point? Does your master know of this?' demanded Zophiel. 'Who owns this crossing anyway?'

'I own it. I live under the bridge, so I own it and I say who crosses and who don't. I'm master here.'

'You think so?' Rodrigo jerked his stave up out of the water, knocking the pike away from Osmond's throat, and in one fluid movement he struck his stave down hard across the man's knuckles. Old Leatherskin gave a yell, dropped the pike and fell backwards on to the bank. In the same moment Osmond, staggering backwards as the pike blade grazed his throat, lost his footing on the slippery river bottom, slid off the ford stones and sank into the deeper part of the river. He surfaced, gasping, and struggled to regain his footing, but the current was too strong. Rodrigo tried to grab him, but he was too late. Osmond was swept downstream, his stave still clutched in his hand, and without a sound he disappeared from sight round the bend of the river. Adela screamed.

Rodrigo hesitated only for a moment, then, using his stave as a vaulting pole, he leaped for the bank just as Leatherskin was reaching again for the pike. But Rodrigo's stave had done its work; the man's hands were still numb from the blow and Rodrigo was able to wrench the pike from him and turn it against him, pinning him down on the grass with the pike's lethal point aimed straight at his heart.

Faced with all the commotion inches from her face, Xanthus, not unreasonably, began to rear and tried to back away. As she pushed, the back wheel of the wagon slipped off the edge of the ford and the wagon lurched sideways. It teetered perilously back and forth, the current threatening at any moment to sweep Zophiel, Xanthus and the wagon into the river. Zophiel took a wild gamble. Grabbing her bridle firmly, he brought his whip down hard on Xanthus's hindquarters. She skipped forward and bolted for the bank, dragging the wagon the last few feet safely to the water's edge.

As soon as Zophiel reached the bank he swiftly hitched the horse's reins to the branch of a tree and ran over to where Leatherskin lay pinned down by his own pike. Zophiel hauled him to his feet, twisting Leatherskin's arm behind him.

'Now, my friend, what were you saying about a toll?'

Leatherskin, though clearly shaken, had not lost his fighting spirit.

'You may have bested me, but he's still got the girl,' he said with a malicious grin, nodding towards the opposite bank. The boy had pulled Adela back off the bridge on to the bank and had her kneeling on the ground in front of him, his knife pressed against her throat, like a ewe about to be slaughtered. Adela was sobbing wildly, calling out for Osmond.

The boy looked over the river at his father and then up at us on the bridge. He grinned, showing several missing teeth. 'Don't you try and come near me,' he warned. 'I'll cut her throat afore you get within a yard of her.'

Zophiel, not to be outdone, thrust Leatherskin down on his knees. 'Tell your brat that if he doesn't let her go immediately, we'll run you through.' And to prove he was quite capable of carrying out his threat, Zophiel jerked the man's arm up behind his back until he squealed with pain.

'If . . . if you kill me, he'll kill her. So I reckon it's stalemate. But see here,' he added, in a wheedling tone, 'all we want is to make a living same as you. We look after the ford, keep it clear for folks like you, so it's only right and proper you give us a few pennies for our trouble.'

'Who granted you the licence to collect tolls here?' Zophiel demanded.

Rodrigo broke in. '*I denti di Dio*, Zophiel! What does it matter if he has a licence or not? That boy has a knife to Adela's throat —'

'Watch out behind you, son!' the woman yelled from the far bank, but the boy turned his head too late. Osmond's stave cracked down upon his skull and he fell senseless to the ground, the knife rolling harmlessly away. Then Osmond was lifting Adela to her feet and pressing her to his dripping wet shirt. Blood was oozing from the pike cut on his throat. They clung to each other desperately as if they had both feared the other dead.

The boy's mother cried out and tried to push her way through over the bridge to reach her unconscious son, but Cygnus and Pleasance held her back. Cygnus firmly grasped her knife arm, trying to keep the dangerously waving blade away from his face. So frantic was she to get to her son that she put up no resistance when I pulled the knife from her hand. The girl, meanwhile, had run back to hide under the bridge from whence came the shrill, echoing cries of a baby.

Zophiel turned his attention to Leatherskin once more, his eyebrows raised in that triumphant way of his. 'Did you say stalemate? I think, my friend, you'll find it's checkmate.'

Leatherskin struggled to put on his most ingratiating smile. 'It was only a little joke. He'd never have harmed her, but you can't be too careful. We get all kinds trying to cross the bridge. They'd rob a poor man blind if we didn't put on a show of strength and that's all it was, a show. Wouldn't dream of harming you good folk.'

'Don't give me that,' Zophiel spat. 'Collecting illegal tolls. Threatening travellers. How many others have you robbed? You'll swing for this, you and your whole family.' He gave Leatherskin's arm another sharp twist.

The little man squealed and a flicker of satisfaction crossed Zophiel's face.

'Your lad crac . . . cracked my boy's skull,' Leatherskin gasped. 'If he's dead, I'll not be the only one for the noose.'

Zophiel made no reply, but slightly relaxed his grip on the man's arm.

Leatherskin looked up at him, a cunning smile on his face. 'Come now, we neither of us want to go involving the justices, do we? We can both do each other a bit of good. You'll be looking for a place to sleep tonight, somewhere warm where you can dry off. But there's no inn for two days' walking, so it looks like you'll be sleeping rough, unless . . .' He paused in mock thought. 'I just might know of somewhere you can sleep warm tonight. What do you say? Worth a penny or two, that, I reckon.'

'What are you suggesting, that we spend the night like rats crouched under the bridge with you?' Zophiel sneered.

'Oh no, my great lord,' Leatherskin replied with equal sarcasm. 'Our little bridge would be too humble for the likes of you. No, I'm talking about an inn. Leastways, it was.'

'I thought you said there was no inn in these parts.'

'There isn't. Like I say, it *was* an inn. A widow woman took it over after her husband died. Did all right too, until those bloodsuckers at the monastery told her she couldn't sell her own brew any more, had to sell what the monks sold her at the prices they chose. Ruined her it did. I reckon they wanted her out, but she refused to budge, said she wouldn't give 'em the satisfaction.'

'So if the inn is closed, what good's that to us?'

'You're so sharp you'll cut yourself. I'm coming to that. She doesn't sell ale no more, nor meals. I doubt she's got enough food for herself these days, no one has around here except for those bleeding monks.' He spat. 'They still do all right for themselves, no matter the rest of us starve. Still, that won't worry folks like you. I dare say you carry plenty of food and ale of your own.' He stole a covetous glance at the wagon. 'But the sleeping barn at the inn is still standing. 'Course, she's not allowed to call herself an innkeeper any more, nor hang a sign, but she'll let you bed down in the barn for a few pennies and a share of your supper. She's a sour old skinflint, but who can blame her after what they did? Come on, what do you say? Want to know where it is? You'll not find it without I tell you where to look.'

He nodded across at the far bank towards the shivering, wet Osmond. Adela had stopped crying, but was still clinging to him, plainly shaken, her face white.

'Looks as if they could do with a night in the dry. Not

good for a lass in her condition to be sleeping rough, if she's not accustomed to it.'

'How do we know you're not sending us into a den of thieves and cut-throats just like yourself?'

Leatherskin put on an injured air. 'There's me trying to do a good turn and help folks . . .'

In the end, after Leatherskin had sworn on his mother's grave, his children's lives and upon the tears of the Virgin which I produced from my pack that the place was safe, and Zophiel had threatened to come back and personally cut him into little pieces if it wasn't, Zophiel finally handed over the small sum Leatherskin demanded for his directions. The coins disappeared inside Leatherskin's tunic so fast that even Zophiel, who was practised in sleight of hand, could not have bettered him.

That done, Leatherskin looked around the company and added slyly, 'The old inn's a good place to hide out too, if you were trying to shake someone off. Ride right on by, they would, and never see it.'

He gulped as Zophiel grabbed him by the throat again. 'If you're after money to keep your mouth shut, my friend, you're wasting your time. We're law-abiding people. We fear no pursuers.'

Leatherskin struggled out of Zophiel's grip, massaging his throat. 'I'm only saying if you were . . . Folks come looking for people, ask me if I've seen owt.' He shrugged. 'Sometimes I have, sometimes I haven't.'

Zophiel hesitated and his eyes narrowed. Then he laughed and tossed another small coin to Leatherskin. 'For your barefaced impudence, my friend.'

Pleasance bandaged both Osmond's neck and the boy's head, after rubbing a foul-smelling green ointment on both their wounds. She wasn't helped in her task by the boy's mother who sat cradling her groaning son, alternately cursing Osmond and blessing Pleasance with equal vehemence. I pitied the woman, robber though she may have been and worse. She and her brood were forced to nest like birds under the bridge on a little platform fashioned from old bits of wood. They slept among the flotsam and jetsam they'd salvaged from the river. But the river is a capricious master; without warning it can take back all it gives and more besides.

We finally set off on the road again. Looking back, I saw old Leatherskin kicking his son back on to his feet, cursing him for a fool, while his wife, in turn, belaboured Leatherskin about the ears, more than outdoing him with her curses. Their daughter, the only one who seemed to notice our departure, stared vacantly after us from under the bridge, indifferent to the cries of the wailing infant clutched in her arms.

Leatherskin was right, we wouldn't have found the old place without his directions. The track was almost overgrown with weeds and without a sign to guide the traveller, no one would have known it was there. Leatherskin was also right about the widow. She was indeed as sour as he had predicted, but the sleeping barn at least had a roof and door, even if it had not been used for years except by a few moth-eaten chickens.

The widow was as scrawny as her fowls. Her cheeks were sunken and she had dark hollows around her eyes as if she had eaten little but herbs for months, but for all that she was a feisty gammer, ready to defend her property with a pitchfork in one hand and a dog-whip in the other. A couple of huge, hungry-looking dogs ran round the wagon, growling and barking. Only the crack of Zophiel's whip and our staves discouraged them from sinking their teeth into us.

We could hardly blame the widow for her suspicions. The sudden appearance of a wagon and nine strangers must have been an alarming sight, and it took a long time to convince her that all we wanted was a dry place to bed down for the night. Finally the coins tossed to her as a mark of good faith and the promise of a share in our supper won her over and she grudgingly called off the dogs – not, however, before she had tested each coin thoroughly by biting them with her few remaining blackened teeth.

The old bedding in the barn was mildewed, stinking and verminous. There was no sleeping on that, so we gathered it up and threw it outside into the overgrown yard. But the wooden bed bases were sound enough and, though hard, better than sleeping on a damp floor, and the partitions between them at least kept some of the draughts out. Zophiel unloaded his precious boxes and stacked them neatly in the corner of the barn, as far from the door as possible.

That done, while Cygnus went off to gather fodder for Xanthus, the rest of the company set about making preparations for supper in the big fireplace of the old ale room. It was the only stone fireplace remaining where a fire could be safely lit without fear of a spark catching the old wooden buildings around. We had promised the old woman a feast and since none of us had eaten that day, we were all looking forward to a good hot meal.

The ale room was in a worse state than the sleeping barn. The tables and benches that remained were piled high with a ragbag of broken and worn-out objects that the old widow had hoarded. Cracked pots, cooking vessels long burnt through, scraps of leather that might have come from old harnesses, rags and rope were all heaped together with sacks and empty kegs. In the corner was the widow's truckle bed heaped with assorted coverings and old clothes, which was presently occupied by a tortoiseshell cat that hissed balefully at our entrance and dug its claws into the coverings, defying us to remove it.

'People come stealing things,' the widow said by way of explanation. 'I keep all my belongings where I can keep an eye on them. They want me out, you know. But I'll not budge.'

She meant it. The air in the room was fetid, stinking of wet dog and cat piss, for the shutters on the windows were nailed shut and the heavy door was bolted. Two square props lay ready either side of it.

Osmond took Narigorm to search for more fuel for the fire while Adela and Pleasance set about preparing the food, after repeatedly reassuring the old widow that we had our own beans and mutton, so had no designs on her chickens.

'Stop fussing, woman,' Zophiel said. 'What would we want with your lice-ridden birds? You'd have to boil those fowls for a month to be able to get your teeth into them.'

That set her off again, this time a long tirade about the quality of her chickens. Having lived alone for so long with no one to complain to, she seemed determined to make up for it now by keeping up a continuous stream of grumbling. Between the prior, the novice master, Zophiel and Leatherskin, I'd already had to listen to enough sourness in one day to pickle a barrel of pork. So I left the old widow moaning to Adela and slipped off to the barn, intending to take a little nap before supper. You know what they say about too many cooks.

As you get older, you find you can't sleep much at night, but perversely you can fall asleep in the daytime quicker than a pot boils and this had been a particularly long and wearisome day. But I was not the only one who needed a nap. Jofre already lay curled up on one of the wooden sleeping platforms, his cloak over his face, snoring like a pig in mud. The excesses of the night before had clearly caught up with him. Doubtless he was also trying to avoid Rodrigo and thought the barn as good a place as any to lie low for a while until Rodrigo's temper had cooled.

Above the beds was a long wide hayloft, reached by a rickety ladder, which had once been used for storing food and fodder. There, as I hoped, I found a pile of old sacks and a little of last year's hay. The hay was blackened and stank of mice, but it was softer for my old bones than the hard wooden boards and Jofre's snores were not quite so loud up there. So I shook out the hay to ensure no mice still nested in it, covered it with the old sacks and settled myself down in the corner of the hayloft, prepared to follow Jofre's example.

I'd just begun to doze off when the barn door below me opened and Rodrigo strode in, carrying a lantern. He hung it carefully on the wall hook and swung the heavy beam across the door so that none could follow him. He walked across to the bed where Jofre lay snoring and stood looking down at him. I sighed; there was going to be no nap for either of us. Judging by Rodrigo's determined stance, the lecture that had been threatening all day was about to break over Jofre. Since I did not want to have to listen to it, there was nothing for it but to leave them to it and join the others outside. I began to heave myself up, then stopped as I glimpsed what Rodrigo grasped in his hand.

He bent down and pulled the cloak from Jofre. Jofre, his eyes still closed, muttered something, groped for the cloak and tried to turn over, but Rodrigo was not going to let him sleep.

'Get up.'

Jofre eyes flew open, then all in one movement he had sprung to his feet and was backing away from Rodrigo into the gloom of the barn. It was easy to see what had alarmed him, for Rodrigo was holding a whip in his hand, the kind you'd use to school a dog.

Boy and master faced each other, tense and unmoving. Rodrigo's face was grim and determined.

'I do not want to do this, Jofre, God knows I do not. But I cannot stand aside and watch you destroy yourself. You have such talent. I will not let you throw it away. Zophiel is right, that you behave like this is my fault. I am responsible for you.' He shook his head as if he knew the words were again falling on deaf ears. 'I have tried talking to you, but you will not listen. There are many who said I should have done this a long time ago.' He swallowed hard and then in as stern a voice as he could summon said, 'Take down your breeches, *ragazzo*.'

Jofre stood motionless, apparently unable to believe his ears.

'You heard me, take them down.' Rodrigo turned abruptly and seated himself on the low wooden bed, one leg stretched out.

So he was finally going to do it. But it was not to be a whipping on the back as a servant, felon or martyr might receive, which allows the dignity of stoicism and defiance. This was to be a child's chastisement, a humiliation. That was not wise. Much as I knew that Jofre deserved a whipping, it should not be done like this. No good could come of it.

'Please,' Jofre begged, 'this is the last time, I swear on –'

'No,' Rodrigo roared, 'I will not listen to any more of your promises. Do as you are told, *ragazzo*, or I swear I will take you outside and thrash you in front of the entire company which, God knows, you deserve.'

Jofre, scarlet in face, struggled to undo the knot in the drawstring around his waist, but his hands were trembling so hard that it seemed to take him an age. At last his breeches dropped to the floor. He stood, head hanging, as if he knew this time there was no escape and when Rodrigo beckoned, he stumbled towards him without looking at him and bent over his master's leg. Rodrigo held him down firmly by the back of the neck and pulled up his shirt with his whip hand.

The young man's buttocks gleamed round and firm in the lamplight, the pale brown skin stretched tight and flawless, so smooth that it made you long to reach out and stroke it. But for the nervous tightening of the muscles under the skin, they looked as if they belonged to the statue of a god. Rodrigo hesitated as if he could not bear to mar something so perfect. I think even then he might have relented had Jofre not whined, 'No, please, I promise I'll . . .'

That sealed his fate. Rodrigo's knuckles whitened around the handle of the whip.

'It will not work this time, Jofre,' he said softly.

The whip descended and Jofre jerked violently, but only a gasp escaped him. A dark and rapidly swelling welt appeared across the trembling backside. The whip rose and fell again and again. The muscles in Rodrigo's arm were hard as iron from years of playing and the master beat his apprentice with a musician's precision. He whipped him grimly, slowly and thoroughly, pausing just long enough between the strokes to allow the pain of each one to register. Jofre was biting his own hand to stop himself from screaming out. But now that he had begun it, Rodrigo seemed determined that the thrashing would not be quickly forgotten. Blood glistened in the light of the lantern, but he not did waver.

Jofre was sobbing, a noisy, scalding gush of tears, too fierce for its cause to be merely physical pain. 'I'm sorry,

I'm sorry.' For once, it seemed to come from the heart, not the lips.

As if the words had broken the spell he was under, Rodrigo suddenly flung the whip away and caught the boy in his arms, cradling him fiercely and rocking him to and fro. Jofre sobbed uncontrollably, as if a dam had broken inside him and the pain and shame of his soul were bursting out.

'Why do you do it, *ragazzo*?' Rodrigo murmured. 'You have so much beauty, so much life ahead of you.'

'I'm so . . . so afraid. Can't . . . stop it. I've tried, but . . . but I can't. I can't.'

'I know it, I know.'

The hand that had grimly wielded the whip stroked down the boy's arched neck, down his back tracing the curves and hollows, and gently over the bruised and bleeding flesh. A shudder convulsed Jofre's body. Rodrigo bent to kiss the back of his neck where tiny curls of chestnut hair clung drenched in sweat, and Jofre lifted his tear-stained face. He kissed Rodrigo on the lips, hesitatingly at first, then passionately, almost angrily. Rodrigo leaned back on the hard boards of the bed and Jofre wriggled until he was lying on top of him, fumbling at the older man's crotch. It was the master's turn to lie still as Jofre rubbed his groin against him, covering his face and neck with fierce hot kisses. Only Rodrigo's hands moved as he tenderly caressed the boy's back, like a mother soothing a distraught child.

As Jofre reached a climax, arching and groaning, his breath coming in short rhythmic gasps, Rodrigo clasped him tightly to him, containing Jofre's passion against his own body, as if he could hold him safe against his own self-destruction.

Jofre gave a single loud cry, rolled off and fell asleep

almost instantly. He lay on his belly, sprawled on the boards, one arm thrown above his head, his shirt pulled up, his back glistening with perspiration. The guttering yellow light from the lantern flickered across the curls plastered to his wet forehead, throwing the muscles of his body into sharp relief. His face was flushed and beaded with sweat, but relaxed and unfurrowed. His lips, slightly parted, held all the innocence of a sleeping angel, an angel not yet fallen from heaven.

Rodrigo leaned on one elbow, watching him sleeping, as if trying to memorize every detail of the young man's beauty. Then he got to his feet, gathered up Jofre's discarded cloak and covered him with it. He picked up the whip from the corner where he had flung it and walked wearily to the door. He turned and stood for a moment, looking back at the sleeping form. And by the soft yellow light of the lantern, I saw that tears were streaming silently down his face.

13. Pleasance's Tale

We heard the wolf again that night. We all heard it, and this time I couldn't dismiss it as a bad dream brought on by fatigue. We had decided to eat our meal where it had been cooked in the old inn, even though it was crammed with the old widow's rubbish. Osmond grumbled that despite the sleeping barn being cold and draughty, it would be better to eat in there where we had at least had room to bend our elbows, but I persuaded him otherwise. It would be wrong to hurt the old woman's feelings by refusing her hospitality, I said, and besides, Adela needed to stay warm at least until she had a good meal inside her. I was anxious to keep them out of the barn as long as possible for Jofre's sake.

In truth, hospitality was not a word the widow seemed over familiar with. She fussed around as we made spaces to sit, agitated lest we touch anything. She pushed crocks under tables and stacked kegs still higher on the teetering piles, warning us that she knew exactly what was in the room and not to get any ideas. I think it was only the irresistible aroma of hot food rising up from the cooking fire that made her tolerate us at all. Even the dogs seemed disposed to make friends with us, drooling round our legs and whining as the pot began to bubble and the sweet smell of mutton rose up from its depths. Finally, after what felt like hours, for we were nearly as ravenous as the dogs, Pleasance and Adela pronounced the supper ready and asked Narigorm to round up Zophiel, Cygnus and Jofre and tell them to come and eat.

'Not Jofre,' Rodrigo said quickly.

Adela frowned. 'I know he is in disgrace, Rodrigo, but he must eat. The poor boy has had nothing since yesterday.'

'Jofre's sleeping,' I broke in quickly. 'He's not feeling well. Too much wine. But you're right, Adela, he does need to eat. Narigorm, you fetch Zophiel and Cygnus while I take Jofre some mutton. Run along now,' I added, for she was staring at me with those ice-blue, disbelieving eyes of hers. 'The sooner you find them, the sooner you'll eat.'

Zophiel, had he been there, would undoubtedly have said that the boy deserved to go hungry, but I knew Jofre had been punished enough for one evening. No one should have to suffer the pangs of hunger through a long cold night, when there is food to be eaten. I collected a bowl of mutton and some flat bread which Pleasance had baked in the embers of the fire and set off towards the barn.

Rodrigo caught up with me just before I reached it. 'Jofre . . . I . . .'

'I know, Rodrigo. I saw you go into the barn with a whip. I guessed what you used it for.' I could not tell him I had witnessed it.

Rodrigo grimaced. 'I had to do it, Camelot. You understand?'

'What you did was nothing compared to what would have happened to the boy if the prior had taken action. With luck it might have brought him to his senses.'

'If it does not, I do not know what else I can do.'

There was nothing I could say to that. But I guessed that neither master nor pupil was yet ready to face each other.

'Go get some food, Rodrigo, I'll see to the boy.'

He gripped my shoulder. 'Once again we are in your debt, Camelot.'

Jofre was still sleeping when I went in. He was lying curled up on his side, his cloak pulled up to his chin. But when I put the bowl and bread down beside him he jerked awake with a groan and tried to prop himself up, wincing and clutching his backside.

'I thought you'd rather eat in here tonight. I don't suppose you feel much like sitting down at a table just now.'

In an instant Jofre was wide awake.

'I suppose he's told everyone,' he said angrily. 'Zophiel too?'

'He's told no one. I happened to see Rodrigo come in here. And I can tell by the way you're wincing you took a beating. I'll try to keep the others out of here as long as I can, but you'd better make the most of tonight's rest. If Zophiel hears you groaning, he won't need to be told, so you'd best think of a good excuse or learn to hide your discomfort till you heal. It's my betting it'll be a good few days before you're sitting or walking comfortably again.'

Jofre's fists clenched. 'It's all that bastard Zophiel's fault. Rodrigo would never have done it if Zophiel hadn't told him to. He'd no right to treat me like that, like a . . . a child.'

'Rodrigo would never have beaten you if you hadn't given him cause. You're fortunate; many masters would have done far worse for much less and you know it.'

'I suppose you want me to say I deserved it,' he said sullenly.

I shrugged. 'What you say doesn't matter, lad, the question is, has it cured you?'

'I won't be sitting down to a game of dice today, if that's what you mean.'

'I dare say that was the idea, but when the strips are healed?'

For a moment he glared furiously at me, then his shoulders sagged and the truculence suddenly seemed to drain out of him. He stared down at the floor.

'I can't help it, Camelot. Rodrigo is the greatest musician there is and the greatest teacher. I don't mean to hurt him. It's not his fault I behave as I do and that bastard Zophiel has no right to tell him he's a lousy master. It's me. It's my fault. I'm stupid and useless.'

'You're neither of those. Rodrigo believes you have a great talent, greater even than his, that's why he pushes you. I know it is hard when you are young, but –'

'Why does everyone say "When you are young", as if things are going to change when I grow up and become a man? I am already a man, Camelot, though you all treat me like a child. You don't understand; there are some things I cannot help, some things which are never going to change. I don't want to be what I am, but I can't stop it.'

But although I couldn't tell him, I understood only too well. I had been blind not to see it before. That evening in the barn I had realized for the first time what was buried inside Jofre and it was something he both feared and despised. He loathed himself, loathed his own nature. I almost believed that Jofre wanted to be punished for what he carried inside himself. Perhaps that's why he had deliberately done those things that would anger Rodrigo the most. I wondered if Rodrigo had sensed that all along.

But Jofre spoke the truth when he did not answer my question, for we both knew that even if Rodrigo flogged every inch of skin from his body, it would not cure him.

The only cure for his misery was to learn to embrace his own nature and he could only do that when he found someone who could give him the kind of love he both despised and craved. Until that happened, no punishment that God or man could devise would be able to stop him destroying himself. Like Rodrigo, I too left the barn on the verge of tears.

I'd not gone more than a few paces when I ran into Narigorm. She was leaning against the side of barn, a malevolent smile playing on her face. Her attention was fixed on two figures struggling against the wall. It was an unequal match. Zophiel had Cygnus pinned to the wall by his throat in a way that looked far from friendly.

'You're lying, boy, I know you are. You were about to say something to Osmond at the bridge this afternoon. Don't deny it. I heard you. But whatever you think you saw, you keep your mouth shut, do you understand me, freak? If I catch you –'

'Problem, Zophiel?'

Zophiel looked round at the sound of my voice and immediately dropped his hand. Cygnus took a big gulp of breath. He looked scared, as well he might.

'Didn't Narigorm tell you, supper is ready? You'd best come at once unless you want to find your supper in those dogs, for I doubt we can hold them off much longer.'

It was pointless asking Narigorm why she hadn't delivered the message. I wondered just how long she'd been standing there beside the barn and what else she might have overheard.

We were all too hungry to talk while we ate, which was just as well. The simple act of eating can cover many kinds of silences and that night several of us round the table had reason to be grateful for that. As the pot emptied and our bellies filled, the eating slowed and finally the dogs, who had been whining and scratching at the door, were allowed in to devour what was left. This they did in several huge gulps as if fearing that if they didn't swallow it fast it would be snatched from their mouths. Finally, when the pot had been scraped clean and even they were convinced there was no more, they lay down and closed their eyes to dream it all again.

We were dozing in the mellow contentment that comes from a good meal when we heard the howl. The dogs' heads came up; they too had heard something, but they soon settled again. We relaxed too, thinking that what we had heard was nothing more than the wind wailing like a banshee as it tore through the trees and ramshackle buildings. But the howl came again, louder and longer. This time there was no mistake.

Zophiel and the dogs leaped up at the same time. The dogs ran growling to the door, the hair bristling between their shoulder blades. Zophiel hovered in the centre of the room.

'You heard it? You all heard it? Camelot, was that a wolf or a dog?'

'It sounded like a wolf.'

The old widow crossed herself. 'Saints and all the angels preserve us!'

Though the door was shut, Zophiel made a grab for one of the props to push it up against the door, but Rodrigo too was on his feet.

'No, wait. I have to fetch Jofre. He is alone in the barn.'

'The barn!' Zophiel's hand froze on the prop. He swayed as if his head wanted to rush out of the door, but his legs were refusing to carry it. I knew he was not concerned for Jofre, but his precious boxes.

I tried to calm them both. 'If it is a wolf, it is only one. The barn door is shut and so is this. Jofre will be fine as long as he doesn't open the door and he's not that foolish.'

'That's as maybe,' the old widow said, 'but I've not heard of a wolf in these parts since I was a girl. If there's one there's bound to be more. Always run in packs, they do.'

Zophiel's face had paled. 'You're sure you've not heard a wolf until tonight?'

The old woman pulled a face, 'I may be old, but I'm not deaf. I tell you, there's been no wolf in these parts for years. Hungry they are, like the rest of us. It's driving them out of the forests. You prop those doors, before we all get eaten alive.'

Cygnus stumbled towards the door. 'Xanthus! She's tethered in the old stable, but the walls are half tumbled-down; she may as well be staked out for them.'

Zophiel moved swiftly in front of him and opened the door wide. In an instant the two dogs had bounded out. Cygnus made to follow, but Zophiel grabbed the back of the boy's shirt, flung him back into the room and slammed the door shut.

The old widow tottered to her feet. 'My boys,' she screeched, clawing ineffectually at Zophiel as he bolted the door. 'My boys'll be torn to pieces.'

We could hear their excited barking fading as they ran off into the darkness. Pleasance got up and, putting her arms round the widow, gently led her back to her bench.

'Hush, now. It was only a lone wolf. If there were more, we'd have heard them answering the call. It was probably old or sick, driven out by the pack. The smell of the dogs alone will be enough to drive it off. They won't need to fight it.'

She looked up and smiled reassuringly at Cygnus who sat

rubbing a bruise, the second he had received from Zophiel in as many hours.

'Don't fret, Cygnus, the poor old beast won't attack any animal as big as a horse, not without its pack. The chickens are much easier prey, if it should come this way.'

I thought of the little family huddled under their bridge with no doors to keep wolves out and I prayed she was right.

Zophiel rounded on Pleasance. 'So you know about wolves, do you? Perhaps we should send you out there and see which it prefers, chicken or human.'

Pleasance's cheeks flushed and she looked down at her lap, trying as she usually did to blend unnoticed into the background.

'Or maybe,' Zophiel continued, 'I should have let young Cygnus go out there after all, seeing as he is half-fowl.'

Having cowed Pleasance into silence again, Zophiel might well have continued venting his spleen on Cygnus, a game he much preferred, had not Narigorm suddenly piped up, 'Pleasance isn't afraid of wolves.'

Zophiel turned to stare at Narigorm, who was sitting cross-legged on the widow's truckle bed behind us. 'Then she is either more foolish than she looks or she has never encountered one.'

'Oh, but she has,' said Narigorm. 'Tell them, Pleasance. Tell them the story you told me.'

Pleasance shook her head and tried to retreat further into her corner. But Narigorm persisted. 'She was midwife to a wolf once, weren't you, Pleasance?'

'Midwife to a wolf!' Adela's face lit up with excitement. 'How is that possible?'

'It was nothing.'

'Come now, Pleasance,' said Zophiel. 'Don't be modest,

midwife to a wolf, that's hardly nothing. Now that we know this much, you must satisfy our curiosity. Besides, it would be ungracious to our hostess not to repay her exceptional hospitality with a story. Camelot has already favoured us with his wolf story; yours can hardly be more fanciful.'

His tone was again cold and calm as if nothing had happened, but he remained standing, his head inclined to the door, listening to the distant barking of the dogs.

'Please, Pleasance,' Adela begged. 'We won't let you rest until you do.'

Pleasance gave a wan smile and with obvious reluctance began her tale.

'Once, many years ago, I served my neighbours as a midwife, delivering their little ones and helping the mothers through their time of travail. One day a neighbour of mine was nearing her time and I went to fetch some herbs to brew a draught that would ease her birth pangs.'

Adela reached out and squeezed Pleasance's hand, smiling warmly. 'I am so thankful you will deliver my baby. I was so frightened thinking of it before. I am such a coward when it comes to pain, but now that I know you will be there to help –'

'It is against God's will that the pain of birth should be eased,' Zophiel broke in coldly. 'Birth pain is woman's punishment for succumbing to temptation. God ordains that she should suffer pain for the good of her soul.' He glared at Adela as if hoping that she would suffer all the torments of hell during her labour.

'You'd soon change your tune if you had to give birth,' I told him. 'Now, let Pleasance tell her story in peace; you were the one who asked to hear it.'

I thought of Jofre lying in the barn and wondered if pain would indeed redeem his soul. Pain certainly changes the sufferer, but I'd never seen anyone change for the better because of it.

Pleasance hesitated, glancing at Zophiel.

'Get on with it, woman,' he snapped, turning his head once more towards the door, listening to the sounds outside.

Nervously Pleasance resumed her tale. 'It had been a long winter and when I went to my stores I found that my stock of pennyroyal was exhausted. It was not yet sprouting in my herb garden for I lived high up on a hill where spring comes late. So I went down into the valley where the plants have more shelter and leaves come earlier. Pennyroyal grows best along the banks of streams and rivers, so I found a stream and followed its course into the forest. But no matter how hard I looked, I could not find a single sprig of that plant.

'I grew hungry and settled down in a sheltered spot to eat a hunk of bread, but as I ate I felt a prickling on the back of my neck and knew that I was not alone. Looking up, I saw a huge she-wolf drinking at the stream not a few feet away from me. Her belly was swollen with cubs. She was a beautiful creature, with a thick glossy pelt and powerful shoulders. At first I was terrified, and then she lifted her head and looked at me with big amber eyes, like flame, and as I looked into those eyes the fear left me and I saw she was just a mother, hungry and thirsty. I threw her the remains of my bread and she caught it deftly in her sharp white teeth. I stayed motionless until she had disappeared, then I stood up. That's when I saw it, right where the wolf had been standing, a thick clump of pennyroyal in full leaf.

'A week passed and then one night there was a knocking at my door. At first I thought it was my neighbour's husband come to tell me her pains had started, but when I opened the door I found a stranger standing there. He was a tall man, wild of hair and eye, but not unhandsome.

'"Goodwife, bring your herbs and come quickly," he said. "The birth pains are upon my wife and there is no one who can help her."

'It was a bitterly cold night, frost already sparkled on the ground in the moonlight, not the night you want to leave your warm fireside, but when a child comes, he comes. So I gathered those herbs and ointments I thought I might need and followed the man out into the night. Soon we had walked past all the cottages and out of the village into the valley beyond. The man led and I followed, tracking the tall dark figure by the light of the moon. It was then, as moonlight flooded the path, I noticed that he left no footprints in the frost, nor shadow on the ground. I was afraid, but I said nothing.

'Finally we came to a narrow gap between two rocks. The man motioned me to enter, but I hesitated for the gap looked little more than a crevice in the rock. And as I stood there I heard a loud, booming voice call out from inside, "Enter, goodwife, and do your work."

'I stooped down and squeezed through the gap and all at once found myself standing in a huge cavern. Then I saw a sight which made my heart stop. For the cavern was full of *sheidim* dancing and laughing and howling like wolves around a huge fire whose flames leaped up red and blue.'

'What are *sheidim*?' Adela asked.

For a moment Pleasance seemed startled by the question and hesitated, then her voice dropped to a whisper. 'They are demons.'

'I've never heard that word before.'

Rodrigo broke in quickly, 'Maybe it is not used where you come from. I have found every village has a different word for such things. Is that not so, Pleasance?'

He was staring at her with a curiously troubled expression

on his face. His gaze momentarily darted to Zophiel, but he was still apparently intent on the sounds outside. An odd look passed between Rodrigo and Pleasance which I could not interpret and she suddenly looked scared.

Rodrigo squeezed her hand and smiled reassuringly. 'Go on with the story. The *demon* . . .'

I noticed that Pleasance's hands were trembling as she took up the tale again.

'The . . . the demon who had called out to me spoke again. "Goodwife, do your work. If you bring forth a boy, you may ask for anything you want, but if you bring forth a girl, you will wish that you had never been born."

'At his words the *sheid* . . . the demons howled with laughter and I shook so much I could hardly hold my pack. The demons pulled aside a curtain and there in the corner I saw the she-wolf that I had fed at the stream. She was snarling, but when I looked into her amber eyes I saw a woman suffering in labour.

'She spoke, a low, throaty sound which I had to strain to hear. "Goodwife, you gave me food, so I shall give you this – take care not to eat or drink anything in this place, however hungry or thirsty you become, for if you do you will become one of us."

'I did what I could for her, but the labour was long. I do not know how many hours I was in the cavern, but I worked and said nothing. From time to time one of the demons would bring plates of food and goblets of blood-red wine to sustain me, but I remembered the warning and ate and drank nothing though I was faint with hunger and my throat was parched from the stifling heat of the fire.

'Finally, the she-wolf gave birth to a single cub, a male, and the demons howled with delight. Shimmering flames of black and silver shot up from the fire and the ground trembled under the stamping feet of the demons as they linked arms and danced round it. The demon who had called out to me called for me again and asked me what I wanted as payment for my work. I refused to take anything, saying that to deliver a child is a blessing, no matter what that child may turn out to be. The Holy One himself blesses those who perform a blessing; no other payment is needed.

'But the demon said that I must take something, else they would be in debt to a human and that could never be, for then they would be bound to the human until the debt was paid. I in turn had no wish to be bound to a demon, so I looked around for the thing of least value I could take. The floor of the cavern was covered with stones, so I picked up a stone and said I would take this as payment for the debt. No sooner had I said those words than I found myself outside the cave and standing alone on the edge of my village, staring up into the frosty night sky. It was as if no time at all had passed, yet I felt as though I had been in the cave for days.

'As I turned for home I felt something hard in my hand. It was the stone I had picked up. I was about to toss it away when the moonlight fell on it and I saw that it was shining. I took it home to examine it more closely. I swear that when I picked it up it was just an ordinary stone, but when I looked at it again I saw this.'

Pleasance reached inside her kirtle and pulled out a thick leather thong which hung about her neck, on the end of which was a large round piece of amber, fiery as a wolf's eye.

'So you see,' she said, 'the wolves will not harm me. It is their sign.'

Zophiel, from the door, began a slow mocking clap.

Pleasance flushed and quickly dropped the amber back inside her kirtle.

'I confess, my dear Pleasance, I was wrong. I thought the camelot's tale was far-fetched, but I have to say you have outdone even Camelot. Tell us, my dear Pleasance, do you honestly imagine that God would bless a woman who brings a demon into the world? To give succour to a demon is damnation to your soul.'

'I think what Pleasance meant,' I said, 'was that it is a good deed which is blessed regardless of the merit of the person for whom the deed is performed. There'd be no good deeds performed in this world at all if they were only performed for the sinless, isn't that so, Pleasance?'

She raised her head just briefly enough to give me a weak smile and then lowered it again, as if she would have gladly crawled back into the cave of demons again rather than answer Zophiel.

Zophiel turned on me as I hoped he would. 'A fascinating idea, Camelot. So, if a demon appeared to you and –'

He broke off as for the third time the wolf's howl rang through the inn. It was closer this time, still a way off, but much closer. We fell silent, listening for another howl, aware of the crackling of the fire and the rasping breathing of the old widow. Outside the wind dashed rain against the walls, whining like a dog pleading to come in. The fire burned low and the rushes burned still lower, finally sputtering out in a thin, stinking trail of smoke, but no one stirred themselves to light new ones. We sat stupefied in the hot, stuffy room, staring into the embers of the fire. Zophiel alone was alert, his head bent close to the door, waiting for another howl. He was tense and agitated, much as he had been that night in the cave. I wondered if he too had his own wolf story. If he did, it was one that had unnerved him far more than those we had told.

It was only when we heard the dogs scratching and barking at the door that the rest of us stirred out of our lethargy. Zophiel made no move to open the door, but the widow pushed him aside and unfastened it. Her boys bounded in, pausing only to shake themselves vigorously in the centre of the room, liberally spraying us all with mud, water and blood. The widow wailed, clapping her hand to her gummy mouth, until she realized that the blood was not that of the dogs. Though they were both soaked and covered in mud, there was no sign of any wounds on them. But they both held something furry and bleeding in their mouths which they laid happily in the old woman's lap, clearly expecting praise. Adela covered her eyes and shuddered.

'What is it? Is it the wolf?'

The old widow laughed, the first time she had done so since we arrived.

'Saints preserve us. It'd be a pretty miserable runt of a wolf if it were. It's a hare. My boys have been hunting and caught me a hare for my breakfast. There's my clever boys!'

She held aloft the two ripped halves of hare in triumph, like an executioner displaying a severed head for the crowd, while the dogs leaped up at her to catch the drops of blood that dripped from the gory remains.

We left the old woman to the skinning of her hare and made our way back to the barn. She hardly seemed to notice us leaving. She was too busy rubbing the dogs dry and telling them over and over what good boys they were.

Rain was lashing down outside and though we hurried to the barn, we still got thoroughly drenched. There was no sign of Jofre when we entered and I saw an expression of panic cross Rodrigo's face as he caught sight of the empty bed. Looking around, I noticed that the ladder to the hay-loft was not where I had left it, and glancing up, I saw it had been pulled up into the loft. I tugged his sleeve and silently pointed. As he directed the light of the lantern upwards I could just make out Jofre's form curled up on the pile of hay that I had earlier earmarked for myself. He was asleep or pretending to be. Perhaps he too had heard the wolf and had climbed up into the loft just in case it found its way in or, more likely, he wanted to make sure he spent the night alone where he could nurse his stripes unobserved. I didn't grudge him the hay. His need was greater than mine for a soft place to lie that night, and even with the hay under him I doubted he was going to get a comfortable night's sleep.

Zophiel rushed to check his boxes as soon as the barn door was safely barred behind us. Thankfully, for all our sakes, they were intact and undisturbed, or so we concluded from his relieved expression, for he said nothing. He stripped off his wet clothes as rapidly as he could, slipping naked and shivering under his blanket on the bed-boards closest to his boxes, but I noticed that for all his haste, he did not neglect to slide his long knife under the covers where it would lie ready if it should be needed.

Narigorm sat in the corner of one of the beds, her knees pulled up to her chin and her skinny white arms wrapped tightly around her legs. In the dim light from the lantern, her hair glowed like a fall of new snow. She was watching Cygnus as he struggled with one hand to peel the wet hose from his goose-pimpled legs. Her doll lay beside her.

Cygnus caught sight of it and chuckled. 'What have you done to your poor baby, Narigorm? I hope you don't intend to treat your children that way when you become a mother.'

I followed his gaze. Narigorm had swaddled her doll in

strips of cloth, as Adela had taught her, except that the swaddling bands had been wound not only the length of the doll's body, but up over the face, so it now looked more like a corpse prepared for burial than a swaddled baby. The same thought seemed to have struck Cygnus for he suddenly looked serious and lowered his voice.

'I know you're only playing, Narigorm, but uncover the doll's face now, there's a good girl. If Adela sees it, it might upset her in her condition.'

Narigorm tilted her head to one side. 'Why do you still keep your wing tied down?' she said, in a clear, piping voice.

'Camelot said I should, in case my wing was remembered.'

'But there's no one to see it here except us.'

Adela, her attention attracted by Narigorm's raised voice, glanced over. 'She's right. It must be uncomfortable bound so tightly like that. Don't you get cramp in it?'

'A little, but I don't mind. It's safer to keep it bound. Safer for all of us if I do.'

Adela waddled towards him in her shift, reaching out her hands to the bindings. 'At least let me take it off for you tonight, so you can stretch it. We can rebind it in the morning if you want.'

'Maybe the feather's regrown,' said Narigorm. 'You said it would.'

Cygnus smiled. 'Maybe. It has been itching.'

He submitted to Adela's deft fingers as she unwound the bindings. Then, as soon as she had peeled the bindings off, he sighed with relief and stretched out the great white wing. We saw at once that there was still a gap where Narigorm had pulled out the feather. But as he lifted his wing, three more long feathers fell from it. They spiralled slowly round and round until they lay starkly white against the beaten earth of the floor. Cygnus stared at the feathers, aghast.

Without lifting her gaze from the feathers on the ground, Narigorm began slowly and deliberately to wind another strip of cloth across her doll's face.

14. The Glassblower

Even after all that I have witnessed, I can still remember the day we first heard those bells. Many of the villages and towns are one now in my memory, but not this one. You never forget that sound, like your first kiss or the birth of your first child, or your first encounter with death.

It was early December, the feast of St Barbara to be exact. In my line of work, you have to remember these things. In the days leading up to a saint's feast day a fragment from that saint is worth twice what it is at any other time of the year. And the demand for relics grew ever greater, so desperate were people for hope.

The rains still fell, the water continued to rise in hollows and lakes. There were no flash floods in this part of the country for there were no steep-sided hills or rocky valleys to funnel the water. Much of the land was flat and marshy, with numerous streams and ditches to carry the rain away. But the forests, meadows and marshes absorbed the rain until the ground oozed water like a weeping sore. Ditches overflowed, streams became rivers and ponds became lakes. Those whose homes lay low down in the hollows watched helplessly as the water rose higher and higher until it crept up to the thresholds of their byres and cottages.

We had to retrace our footsteps several times, returning to a crossroads and trying a different route as we encountered tracks washed out and rivers impassable. Although at every opportunity I tried to turn our company once again towards the north and the safety of the shrines at York, the way was constantly barred. We were herded along by the water snarling at our heels, forced upwards on to the higher tracks, no longer in command of our own direction.

Up till then we had passed few travellers on the road. Save for villagers walking between home and fields, the tracks had been almost deserted, as they usually are in winter. But now, several times a day, we passed huddles of wet, starving families trudging along, women and children carrying bundles on their backs, men harnessed by ropes to small carts which they struggled to drag through the thick mud. The carts were piled high with bits of old furniture and cooking pots. They carried all they could salvage from their sodden cottages, though where they were going to find another home was impossible to say. Most likely they'd spend the winter on the roadside, burning their precious furniture to keep warm.

The bodies of those too weak and hungry to walk lay dead beside the tracks. For food which had been scarce for months was daily growing harder to find and those who had it were charging a king's ransom for a handful of mildewed grain or some fragments of weevily dried fish that once they would not have thought fit for pigs.

Once, half-submerged in a sodden field, we saw the statue of St Florian, his millstone tied around his neck. Since their saint was unable to protect them from the rains, the parishioners had stripped his statue of his scarlet cloak and golden halo, beaten him and cast him out to face the elements. Many of the cottagers were no longer begging

God for mercy, they were angry with him. They felt betrayed, and with good reason.

We kept travelling, eking our way through the days with the birds we caught for the pot and whatever we could find to buy in the villages with the few coins we earned. Pleasance, Narigorm and I were now the only ones in our company who had earned any money for several weeks, for no one had money to waste on music or mermaids. But though the villagers' purses were as empty as our own, they would still somehow manage to find a coin so that Pleasance could tend the suppurating sores on their feet, or barter a necklace with me for a relic which might change their luck. They could also find a coin to have the runes read for them, even if it meant going hungry for another day. Strange how desperate people are to know the future, even if they know they cannot change it. We each crave our little fragment of St Barbara – may she preserve us from an unexpected death.

And so it was that on St Barbara's Day we found ourselves on another nameless track, making for another nameless village in which to spend the night. The track led over a treeless plateau of short, springy grass. Xanthus kept turning her head sideways away from the wind, much to Zophiel's irritation as she dragged the cart continually to one side. But I didn't blame the poor creature; the wind stung our faces like a wet rag flicked hard against bare skin. Then in the distance we heard the bells. We didn't take any notice at first, for all we could hear were snatches of ringing carried on the wind. The village lay in the fold of the plateau. It was not a deep valley, but the curve of the slope as we approached concealed all but the wooden steeple of the church and the smoke of the hearth fires.

As we drew close the sound reached us more clearly. It

was not the single sonorous tolling of a bell that signified a death, nor the regular pattern of the church bells calling the faithful to mass, but a random jumble of noise, as if those who were ringing no longer cared if the bells tolled in unison or not. There were other sounds too, hollow, metallic sounds as if people were striking iron pots with metal bars.

Zophiel pulled on Xanthus's bridle and we all stopped, looking at one another for answers.

'Are those warning bells?' Adela called out from her perch in the front of the wagon. 'What if it's a fire?'

'Have some sense, woman,' retorted Zophiel. 'How likely is it to be a fire after all this rain?'

Adela's belly was now so swollen with child that it took the combined efforts of both Rodrigo and Osmond to get her on to the wagon and just as long for them both to heave her off again. This, together with her increasingly frequent need to dismount to pass water, was doing nothing to temper Zophiel's antagonism towards her.

'They could be raising the hue and cry,' Osmond suggested. 'Perhaps there's been a murder.'

None of us could help glancing over at Cygnus, who bit his lip. Over the weeks even Zophiel had ceased to treat Cygnus as a fugitive, though we were still careful not to let his wing be seen in the villages, nor let him work as a storyteller just in case someone's memory should be jogged. But the rest of the time it was easy to forget he might still have a price on his head.

'It doesn't sound like a watchman's alarm,' I said. 'The watchman's bell sounds just long enough to summon help and in the daytime how long could it take to assemble some men? Perhaps this is some local custom celebrating St Barbara. Maybe the noise signifies the lightning and thunder which struck her executioner down. If it's a feast, there'll be food, and they may be in need of Rodrigo and Jofre to play for their dancing.'

Rodrigo chuckled. 'If that is the best they can do for music, then they need us.' He slapped Zophiel on the back. 'Come, a feast, I like the sound of that. Warm fire, good food, maybe even some wine, what do you say, Zophiel?'

I couldn't help smiling at Rodrigo's grin. The others, faces brightened too and we set our shoulders to the wagon with a will to get it rolling again.

The track sloped gently upwards, continuing to hide the village from view, but as soon as we reached the top of the curve, we not only saw it, we smelt it. Every street and village in England has its own smell. You can sniff out the butchers' streets and the fishmongers' alleys, the tanners, the dyers and the woodworkers with your eyes shut, and for those living there, however foul the stench, it is the familiar smell of home. But this rotten-eggs stink was not the smell of home in this or any other town. It was the choking stench of burning sulphur.

Across the field strips a thick pall of smoke rose up from a patch of common land. A haywain was pulled up there and a group of four or five men were busy lifting sacks from it. A large hole had been dug in the field and fires built all round it. Thick smoke from the smouldering wood and wet leaves rolled out across the land and the men appeared and disappeared, like ghosts, as the wind gusted it across them. For one sickening moment it looked as if the men had no faces; then I realized each wore a sack over his head with slits cut it in for eyes, the sacking tucked well down into their shirts.

At that distance and with all the smoke, it was hard to make out what they were doing. They worked swiftly, moving back and forth from the haywain to the pit. At first

I thought they were moving sacks of grain, then the bile rose up in my throat as I realized the sacks contained not grain, but bodies. They carried the bodies over to the pit, swung them and threw them down inside. It took two men to carry each adult body, but then I saw one man with two small sacks in his hands swinging like dead rabbits as he walked, and I knew they must be little children. He tossed those in on top of the rest.

I turned to look again at the village. The ringing of bells and the clanging of metal continued unabated. Most of the smoke was coming not from hearth fires in the cottages, but from small braziers in the streets which sent up billows of thick yellow smoke into the darkening sky. A man walked rapidly down the street. He too had his face covered and held a burning torch up in front of him though it wasn't yet dark enough to need such a light to see by. As he passed a shuttered cottage, the light from his torch illuminated the door just long enough to show that a mark had been daubed on it. It was a black cross.

The others in the company simply stared at the scene before them without a word. I hurried to Zophiel's side. 'We'd best get moving. Go as rapidly as you can, till we're clear of the village.'

But he didn't move. He stood, staring at the field of smoke and the ghost figures moving around in the heart of it. 'So this is it then. It has overtaken us.'

Jofre crouched down by the wheels of the wagon and retched. Rodrigo wordlessly crouched down beside him, his hand automatically rubbing the boy's back as I had seen him do that day I first saw them on the road.

Adela wrapped her arms around her swollen belly and began rocking back and forth, sobbing uncontrollably with the dry animal wail of a woman keening for her children, as if the bodies being thrown into the pits were her own loved ones. Osmond clambered up on the wagon and tried to take her in his arms, but she struggled from him, beating her fists against his chest, screaming at him to get away from her as though he had the contagion himself.

I could see despair setting in on everyone's faces and felt it clutching at my own heart. 'Come on now, let's get moving, get away from this stinking smoke.'

'Where, Camelot, where exactly are we to go now?' Zophiel demanded. 'The pestilence is in front of us and behind us. There is nowhere left to go. Osmond, if you don't stop your stupid wife screaming, I will.' He whirled round on Narigorm. 'You, girl, you're supposed to be the soothsayer. Your runes led us here. You got us into this mess. Suppose you tell us where to go now. Up? Shall we all grow wings like Cygnus and fly up, because that is the only place left to go?'

Any other child would have shrunk from his anger, but Narigorm did not. She looked him squarely in the face, meeting his eyes unblinkingly. 'East,' she said simply. 'I told you already, we will go east.'

For a moment I wondered if she actually understood what she was witnessing, that the sacks being thrown into the pit contained human bodies, but Narigorm was no ordinary child. Something in those pale, expressionless eyes chilled me more than anything I was witnessing.

'No, not east, north,' I blurted out. 'We must go north. If the pestilence is in the east and west we have to go north, it is the only way clear now.'

'Don't be a damn fool, Camelot,' Zophiel shouted. 'The road north lies straight through that village.'

Pleasance put a protective arm about Narigorm. 'If the runes say go east we should go. Just because the pestilence has come here doesn't mean that it will touch every village. We have to go somewhere. We can't stay here. Better to go on than back.'

Though I didn't want to admit it, I knew she was right. At this moment in time there were only two choices, east or west, and we could not retrace our steps.

Zophiel had obviously reached the same conclusion for he gave a curt nod.

I swallowed hard. 'But then we must turn north at the next clear road, that will be the only safe thing to do.'

Narigorm watched Zophiel walk back to Xanthus, then she slid her cold little hand into mine just as she had done at the Midsummer Fair, and whispered, 'You won't ever reach York, Camelot. We're going east, you'll see.'

We skirted the village as rapidly as mud and rain would allow. Xanthus seemed as anxious as the rest of us to put the village behind us and pulled the wagon with an energy I had not seen in her for weeks. She kept rolling her eyes and pricking her ears as if she felt something was pursuing her. They say horses can smell death, but perhaps it was just the smoke which bothered her.

The way grew more hazardous as darkness fell. We were in another stretch of forest which made the track seem darker still, but no one suggested stopping to make camp for the night. The sound of the bells haunted our steps long after we were out of sight of the houses, gradually growing fainter, masked by the roar of the wind in the canopy of trees. When, thankfully, we could no longer hear them, we finally halted long enough to light the lanterns on the wagon and walked alongside it, each of us with a hand on the wagon, tightly grasping the wet wood. It was a sensible precaution on the dark muddy track, but it was not fear of slipping that made us hold tight to the wagon, it was that more than ever it seemed like the only home we had, the only certainty we could grasp.

We began to catch glimpses of red glowing fires between the trees and brighter yellow dots of what looked like lanterns. We looked at one another fearfully, but there was no stink of sulphur here, only the sweet, wholesome smell of wood smoke. We rounded a bend and found ourselves beside a long, low open-sided building, set in a wide clearing. The building was evidently a workshop of sorts for there were two furnaces inside, with fire trenches beneath. Each had a pair of great bellows operated by treadles. Obviously whatever they made here required great heat. A third furnace, this one shaped like a bread oven, had no door and it was glowing red-hot inside. A number of trestles stood about with long metal tubes resting on them, great long iron pincers and wooden boards charred black. Tubs of water stood by each trestle.

Two young apprentices lay curled up asleep on the floor of the building, but four or five more were scurrying around outside in the clearing, tending fires over which stood big iron pots belching clouds of steam into the night. There were more furnaces dotted about the clearing, which was so thoroughly cleared and trampled that not even a blade of grass survived. Towering piles of logs were stacked at one end of the clearing and near them were a number of smaller huts. The place smelt of burning beech wood, a pure, clean smell after the cloying, sulphurous stink we had left behind.

As Zophiel halted the wagon, a man in his early twenties came round the back of the building and started slightly as he saw us. The apprentices too caught sight of us at the same time and stopped their work. He waved a hand at them.

'Back to work, lads. If that potash isn't ready by first light, the master'll have my guts for garters, and if he has mine, you can be sure I'll have yours.'

He hurried towards us, stopping a little way off.

'Where are you from, good sirs?'

Zophiel pointed back in the direction we'd come, then, seeing the look of panic on the man's face, said, 'We know the village has the pestilence, but don't worry, my friend, we gave it a wide berth and we have no sick among us. And you, my friend, any sickness here?'

The journeyman did not get a chance to answer.

A deep voice boomed out of the shadows. 'We are all well, the Blessed Virgin be praised.'

A grey-haired man, face and arms covered with burn scars, stepped out of the shadows. 'I am Michael, master glassmaker.' He bowed. 'This man is my journeyman, Hugh. Though I should say he is the master now, for he has the skill that my old fingers have forgotten. Still, that is how it should be, no?'

I recognized his accent at once and so did Rodrigo.

'*È un fratello veneziano?*' he asked eagerly.

'*Sì, sì.*'

Both men, beaming from ear to ear, threw their arms wide and fell into a big bear hug as if they were long-lost brothers. They began introducing everyone in sight, pausing only to hug and slap each other on the back again.

Finally Master Michael threw his arms wide as if he would embrace all of us at the same time. 'Come, come, we must eat and drink. You spend the night here. I cannot give you a soft bed, but a warm one I can give you.' He laughed, gesturing to all the fires. 'Hugh,' he said turning to the journeyman, 'make our guests welcome. It is not every day I meet two of my countrymen, so let us eat while we can.

Tonight we enjoy ourselves, but tomorrow we work, so do not let the boys neglect those fires, *si*?'

The apprentices realized that the coming of the strangers had put their master in an exceptionally good mood and that extra food might be forthcoming, so they hurried to help us to set up camp. They stabled Xanthus in a lean-to with their two oxen which were used for pulling their own wagon to market and dragging logs from the forest. Cygnus was, for once, relieved of the duty of having to find fodder for the horse, and one of the boys slipped her an apple, which won him the eternal gratitude of both Xanthus and Cygnus.

Michael was a good master, the boys confided in whispers, strict but kind, apt to fly into rages if a boy was careless, but quick to cool down and above all he was fair. I could understand his rages; lose concentration when throwing a clay pot and usually only the pot is spoiled, but get careless with a rod of molten glass and man could be burned so badly, his wounds might never heal. They were quick, eager lads and they needed to be. This was not a profession for dullards.

Trestles, water tubs and such equipment as could be moved were rapidly cleared from the long workshop and stools, sacks and benches were brought in to make a place to eat and sleep out of the biting wind. One of the apprentices, shielding his arm with a thick leather gauntlet, stacked wood inside the red-hot gloryhole, the open furnace where glass was reheated between working. He was well practised at the art, leaping back as the sparks spat out, before covering the gloryhole to keep the heat in overnight. The heat from all the furnaces, though they were well insulated, made it the warmest place we had stayed for weeks and in testimony to this our clothes soon began to steam in the warmth, the smell of wet wool and sweat mingling with the wood smoke.

It is only when you get truly warm that you realize how cold you have been. As I eased my sodden boots towards the warmth of the furnace, I felt as if I would never be persuaded to move from that spot again.

Like those in the rest of the country they had long used up their flour, beans and peas, but they were more fortunate than those in towns for they could forage in the forest for fruits, herbs and fungi and the boys were all expert with the slingshot and catapult. They had set a large pot to bubble over a fire. Judging by the mutton bones in it which had been boiled so often they broke at a touch, the pot was never entirely emptied. At every meal they simply added to it, water and a few handfuls of whatever they could find – wild onions, wild garlic, sorrel, nettles, and anything they could bring down with their slings.

Pleasance and Adela were soon supervising some of the boys in making extra food to supplement their pottage. Even Zophiel seemed caught up in the excitement and brought out our last remaining cask of flour and some salt butter to add to the provisions. With the help of Osmond and Jofre and one of the boy's ferrets, several plump rabbits were soon being spit-roasted over the woodchip fires, while some pigeons were rolled in clay and left to bake on the edge of the fire in the embers, so that the meat would stay sweet and succulent inside.

Pleasance had shown a couple of the lads how to make rastons in one of the cooling ovens, loaves sweetened with wild honey and scooped out to be stuffed with a mixture of breadcrumbs, butter, and onions, then heated again until the butter melts. I swear there is nothing so warming to the stomach on a cold winter's night as sweet bread, hot from the oven, dripping with melted butter, truly a feast for St Barbara's Day.

After the meal the apprentice boys, stomachs stuffed to bursting, dozed off where they sat, until one or another was prodded awake by the journeyman Hugh, who sent them yawning and shuffling to stoke the fires under the iron pots in the clearings and stir the mixture of wood ash and water. The boys would take it in turns to tend the fires until the water had evaporated, leaving the potash behind to be used for melting the glass. Others took turns in stoking the furnaces and pumping the bellows, for the heat in the furnaces had to be kept up until they were required in the morning.

Sheltered from the wind and made as drowsy as the apprentices by the warmth of the furnaces, the rest of us settled down to a long evening of gossip and drinking. Talk inevitably turned to the subject we had all tried so hard to forget. It was Hugh who told us about the village, staring morosely into the bottom of his tankard.

'Started there ten days ago. Leastways, that's when they found the first corpse, but God knows how long the poor soul had been dead. Neighbours noticed this terrible stench coming from one of the cottages. They banged on the door, but no one answered. No one could recall seeing anyone go in or out of the place for a couple of days. So in the end the neighbours broke the door down and found the wife lying dead in her bed. Died in agony she had, judging by grimace on her face and the way her body was all twisted up. No sign of the rest of the family. Seems as soon as they realized what it was that ailed her, they took off in the middle of the night and fled the village in secret. Likely, the poor soul was still alive when they left. Still, who can blame her husband? There was nothing he could do to save his wife. Perhaps he thought he was doing right, getting the children to safety before they caught it. Maybe she even told him to go and leave her.'

'I imagine he was more concerned to save his own skin,' Zophiel said. 'He left without troubling to warn his neighbours, leaving them to find the body and risk the contagion.'

Hugh glanced up. 'Happen you're right, but I don't hold with judging a man till you've walked in his shoes. No man can put his hand on his heart and say for certain what he'd do if his life was threatened. The pestilence is a cruel death, so they say.'

'Have many fallen to it in the village?' Adela asked fearfully.

'Near a dozen a day, we heard. Not that we've been near the place these last few days. Some of the lads are from there, but the master won't allow them to go home. Says if they go, they'll have to stay in the village. They can't come back here for fear they bring the contagion with them.'

'Poor boys,' said Adela, gazing tenderly at the tousled heads, 'they must be so worried.'

'Aye, but it won't do them any good to go home. If their families have got it, there's nothing they can do. Time enough to find out who's dead and who isn't when it's over. Did you see any signs when you came past?'

Osmond was about to answer, but I nudged his foot. I could see several pairs of eyes watching us anxiously. It would not help them to know about the pit, nor that there looked to be many more than a dozen bodies being pulled off that haywain.

'The light was too poor to see much,' I told them. 'And we kept our distance when we smelt the sulphur smoke and heard those bells ringing.'

Hugh grimaced. 'They'll keep ringing till there's not a man left standing to pull on a bell rope. They say noise drives the contagion out, especially the pealing of church bells. At least we don't have to listen to it. Be enough to drive anyone mad, those bells ringing morning, noon and night. But I suppose anything's worth a try. I'll tell you this for nothing,' he said, stretching and nudging another sleepy apprentice to his feet, 'something's got to work, because all those prayers the priests and the monks are sending up might as well be wood smoke for all the good they're doing.'

The master glassblower shook his head. 'Enough already, Hugh. Our guests will think you have no respect.'

'Aye well, ever since the summer we've had the pardoners through here in their droves, frightening the wits out of folk saying if they don't buy their indulgences before it's too late, not only will they die of the pestilence but they'll be tormented in purgatory for years after. Not cheap either, those bits of paper they sell. And who knows what's written on them in their Latin? Could be lists of the King's whores for all we know.'

One of the apprentices sniggered.

'Think that's funny, do you, my lad?' Hugh dragged the boy outside by his ear, the grin on both their faces showing that they both knew Hugh was only in jest.

Michael chuckled too. 'You must please excuse him. He is a good man, like a father to the boys, but he has no time for those he thinks take advantage of the weak. A pardoner came through here just after the pestilence came to the village and started preaching to the boys, telling them that they could buy indulgences for their dead parents. The boys are young; naturally they were upset. Hugh threw the man out. He did not take kindly to that.'

Rodrigo leaned forward impatiently. 'Enough of the troubles now. Tell us of yourself. How does one of my countrymen come to be here?'

The glassblower beamed and clapped his hands together in satisfaction. 'It is a long time since anyone has asked me that.' A hundred white and purple scars covered his hands and dark hairy arms. He was a small man, squat and out of proportion, with short, bandy legs, but a huge barrel chest from all the years of blowing and big, muscular arms, so that his top half looked as if it belonged to someone much taller and had been placed on the wrong legs. His face was wrinkled and pitted, but his brown eyes were dancing with life.

His real name, he told us, lowering his voice to a confidential boom, was Michelotto, but he called himself Michael, for in his experience the English did not trust foreigners. His father, a widower and a glassblower like himself, had brought him out of Venice before the glassmakers there were confined to the island of Murano.

'These days,' he spread his hands and shrugged, 'they do not allow anyone to leave the island. The Doge, he worries that if they leave they will betray the secrets of glassmaking to other nations. So what if they are the finest glassmakers in the world and the best paid, what good is that when they are little better than slaves? My father, may he rest in peace, was wise to get out when he did. Me, I stay nowhere for long. As soon as the trees are used up around us we have to move to a new site. Glassmaking burns up so much wood, you see, every two or three years we must move on, but not like you, *ragazzo*, you move every day.'

He leaned forward and affectionately ruffled the hair of Jofre who sat on a low stool at his feet. He had insisted on keeping the boy at his side all through the meal, like a favoured grandchild, feeding him with the choicest portions of meat from the tip of his own knife. Jofre revelled in the attention and could hardly take his eyes off Michelotto, drinking up every word he had to say about his life in Venice. Jofre asked eagerly if the glassblower knew his mother, but the old man shook his head sadly, knowing how much it meant to the boy. He had left Venice so long ago, he said, he hardly remembered any names now. The squares and the canals he still dreamt about, but like the faces of the people in his dreams, he could no longer remember their names either. He saw the disappointment in the faces of both Rodrigo and Jofre.

For a moment he sat despondently, then an idea seemed to occur to him, and excusing himself, he rose and slipped off into the darkness. A few minutes later he returned, something shining in his hand. It was a small, tear-shaped flask, such as a lady might use for perfumed oils. Cupped in his hand, it was dark and opaque, but when he held it up to the light of one of the torches, the glass glowed with rich blue and purple ripples and tiny flecks of gold sparkled all over it.

'See, that is what I remember, the light of Venice is like glass itself. I remember the way the evening sun sent golden sparks dancing over the waters of the lagoon. I remember the pearl light of the winter's dawn and the hot, fierce red of the sun as it sets in summer, making the white marble blush pink under its heat. I remember at night when the waters of the canals turn dark as sable, how the moonlight glitters on the dark water like a silver fret on the black hair of a beautiful woman. That is what I try to make in my glass. I capture the light of Venice in my glass.'

He held out the little flask to Jofre, who took it carefully in both hands, holding it up to the light of the torches, twisting it to every angle, a look of sheer wonderment on his face as every turn brought a new subtle shift of colour and pattern. With a sigh, Jofre made to hand the flask back to Michelotto, but the glassblower folded Jofre's fingers around the flask. 'Take it. It is yours. You look at this and think of your mother, no? Maybe you think of me sometimes too.'

As the yawns multiplied around the group, we finally pushed aside the benches and stools and rolling ourselves up in our cloaks, lay down in the warmth of the furnaces to sleep. Michelotto and Rodrigo slipped off somewhere, I guessed back to Michelotto's own hut, where the two of them would doubtless continue to talk long into the night over a drink or two. Rodrigo was hungry for talk of home and it would not displease the old glassblower to remember the old times either. Jofre was already asleep, the beautiful little tear-shaped flask carefully wrapped and stowed safely in his pack, but not until after he had unwrapped it several times to hold it to the light once more.

In many ways Jofre's behaviour had improved since the whipping and for the past month he had not, so far as any of us knew, been gambling in the towns or villages, leastways he had not come back drunk and there were no angry locals demanding money that he owed them, but Rodrigo was still worried about him. Jofre had always withdrawn into himself on occasions, but since the whipping, the frequency of these silent moods had increased. He no longer displayed the outbursts of anger which used to make him storm off; instead he seemed frozen, as if trying to cut himself off from any feelings or emotions at all.

Jofre obediently practised when he was told to and with more concentration than he had shown for months. What he played was technically correct, but mechanical, as if he was deliberately divorcing himself from the music, trying to play without being affected by it. Rodrigo was angry and frustrated. He could hear better than any of us how passionless the music was and treated this as one of Jofre's sulks, his revenge for the beating. But I sensed that Jofre was not trying to frustrate Rodrigo; he was genuinely afraid to let himself feel any emotion after the flood which had engulfed him that night in the barn. That evening as he listened to Michelotto speak of Venice, I saw the first glimmer of life I had seen in Jofre's eyes for weeks. As I lay down to sleep that night, I hoped that the evening might be the turning point and the boy who played and sang like an angel might be back with us again.

The sound of thundering hooves and screams woke me. It was still dark, but the clearing seemed to be full of riders weaving their horses in and out of the burning fires, scattering the terrified apprentices. I grabbed Adela's arm and, with Osmond on her other side, we hauled her bodily into the shelter of the trees behind the workshop, well away from the exposing light of fires and torches. We pushed her down behind a thick trunk and told her to keep still. I threw my cloak over her head, so that should anyone glance that way the whiteness of her skin would not betray her. Then I dragged the reluctant Osmond away from her. If there was going to be trouble, Adela's best hope was to lie still, a dark hump unnoticed in the shadows, and it was vital that we didn't draw attention to her whereabouts.

Zophiel too was crouching on the ground behind one of the huts. He had grabbed one of the apprentices by both arms and was shaking the cowering boy.

'I know they're soldiers, idiot boy, but whose arms do they bear?'

'I don't know, sir,' the terrified boy wailed.

'Then tell me what they look like,' Zophiel hissed.

'Two . . . two gold lions, sir, passant . . . guardant . . . on a red ground.'

'Was there anything above them? Think, boy, think!'

'A mitre, sir.'

'A mitre, you're sure about that? And below the mitre, was there a Virgin and Child?'

The boy screwed his face up in concentration. 'There was something, I don't know, sir, I didn't get a proper look.'

Zophiel groaned. 'The Bishop of Lincoln's men.'

He released his grip on the boy who fled into the trees without a backward glance.

'What do they want here? We're nowhere near Lincoln,' Osmond whispered.

'The See of Lincoln stretches down as far as London, they have lands everywhere,' I told him. 'Zophiel, we should . . .'

But Zophiel had vanished.

I heard a bellow of rage that I recognized. It was Rodrigo. Osmond and I hurried into the clearing.

In the centre of the clearing was Michelotto in the grip of two soldiers. His arms were twisted behind his back and one soldier had locked an arm around the struggling man's throat. Though the soldiers towered above him he was still putting up a good fight. Two other soldiers held Rodrigo, who was also struggling in their grip, and the rest of the soldiers, still on horseback, had corralled Hugh, three or four of the apprentices, Jofre, Pleasance and Narigorm against one of the huts. Of Cygnus and Zophiel there was no sign.

I didn't notice the man who sat quietly on a palfrey in the shadows until he trotted forward and dismounted. It was plain from his broad-brimmed hat that he was a pardoner. He was a thin, spidery man, not much taller than Michelotto, and though his face was weather-beaten from his journeys, it still managed to retain an unhealthy pallor beneath the surface, as if he slept too little and brooded too much. It was probably as well he had chosen a life as a pardoner, for his physique suggested he would have fared badly at any profession that demanded physical labour. But he was clearly no ordinary pardoner, for he seemed to carry some authority over the Bishop's soldiers. At a nod from him, they dragged Michelotto forward.

He looked the glassmaker up and down before speaking. 'Yes, this is the Jew. Well, well, pestilence breaks out in a village though there is none else for miles around, and what do you know, we just happen to find a Jew living on their doorstep. Now, isn't that a coincidence?'

Michelotto jerked violently, almost wresting one hand free. 'I am no Jew, pardoner.'

The pardoner smiled as if he had made a joke. 'A glass-blower from Venice who is not a Jew, I find that hard to believe. The reason so many have died in Venice is thanks to the swarms of Jews they shelter.'

'My family, they were Jews, but we converted when I was a child. I have papers to prove it.'

'The worse for you then. They hang Jews, but they burn heretics . . . slowly.'

'I am no heretic.' Fear was beginning to show in Michelotto's face, as well it might.

'Any Jew or Muslim who converts to the one true faith, then goes back to his old ways, like a dog returning to its vomit, is a heretic. A Christ-killing Jew is bad enough, but worse is a Jew who has been shown the mercy of our Lord and has spat on it.'

'But I have not gone back. I am a good Christian. When I can, I attend mass. It is not easy in this job to go always when I should, but I go when I can. Ask the priest.'

'The priest is dead of the pestilence. One of the first to fall sick, don't you find that significant? But then a heretic Jew would murder a good Christian first.'

'But I did nothing to him. I have not seen him for weeks.'

'But I thought you said you attended mass regularly. Now it seems you are saying you do not. And you prevent your apprentices from attending also, do you not? Trying to corrupt their innocent souls and make them as wicked as your own.'

Michelotto struggled against the hands that held him. 'No, you are mistaken. I do not stop them. I would never –'

'But you forbade them to go to the village last Sabbath, did you not?' cut in the pardoner. 'Just as you ordered your journeyman to prevent them from buying indulgences.'

'Now look here.' Hugh pushed his way forward from behind the horses. 'It was me that ordered you off our works for frightening the lads with your talk of death. The master knew nothing about it, till I told him. You can't hold that against him.'

'Can't I?' the pardoner rejoined, smiling. 'A master is responsible for all the actions of those he employs. And I trust you will not be so foolish as to deny that he forbade them to go to mass on Sunday.'

'That's because there was pestilence in the village. He wanted to stop them catching it,' Hugh said indignantly.

'When they are in mortal peril it is all the more reason that they should go to mass to cleanse their souls. But you say your master would rather save their bodies and damn their souls to hell. That sounds like Jewish logic to me. Perhaps he has corrupted you also.'

Michelotto shook his head at his journeyman. 'Enough already, Hugh, no need to make trouble for yourself.' A look of defeat had crept into his face. He turned wearily back to the pardoner. 'What must I do to convince you that I am no Jew? You want me to swear on a cross, I will do it.'

Smiling, the pardoner shook his head. 'And have you blasphemed our Lord? If you do not believe in Christ, then the oath would have no meaning. No, I have another test for you.'

He sauntered back to his horse and removed a wrapped parcel from the saddle bag. Slowly and dramatically he began to fold back the wrappings. Michelotto tensed in the grip of the soldiers, waiting to see what instrument of torture would be revealed. I glanced apprehensively around at the furnaces; there were too many places to heat a branding iron or pincers. Michelotto was used to burns, but how long could any man stand the irons?

The pardoner nodded to one of the mounted soldiers, who dismounted and came to stand beside him. He gave the parcel to the soldier who carried it across to Michelotto and waved the contents of the package under Michelotto's nose. We all let out our breath; inside was nothing more threatening than a rancid mound of pieces of meat. The flesh had a greenish tinge and stank, but it was not a branding iron.

'Pork,' the pardoner said with an evil grin. 'All you have to do is eat a little pork. A Jew or a Muslim could not eat it, but to a Christian it is good wholesome fare. All you have to do is eat the pork, without vomiting, and I shall know you are a true Christian and let you go.'

'But the meat is gone bad,' said Hugh fiercely. 'You cannot expect anyone to eat that.'

The pardoner gestured to the soldier. 'Does this meat look good to you?'

The soldier grinned. 'So fresh, I swear I heard it squealing just now.'

The pardoner turned back to Hugh. 'Perhaps, my young fellow, you find it smells bad because you cannot stomach good Christian pork meat either. I wonder why that could be?'

'I will eat it,' Michelotto said, his voice flat and resigned.

'No,' Hugh pleaded.

'What choice do I have?'

The two soldiers held his arms tightly while the third grasped his hair, dragging his head back, and thrust piece after piece into his mouth, scarcely giving him a chance to swallow before the next piece was crammed in. Pleasance, clutching Narigorm, buried her face in the child's hair. The rest of us were forced to turn away in the end too. He tried to hold the foul meat down as long as he could, but they would not let him rest or draw breath. He vomited as they knew he would.

The pardoner, smiling, turned away. 'Bind him and tie him behind the horses.'

Michelotto sank to his knees, heaving over and over again. One of the apprentice boys, braver than the others, dashed forward and held a flask to his lips. A soldier aimed a kick at him, but the pardoner held up his hand.

'No, let him drink. Wash the meat out of his stomach. I don't want him vomiting all the way. It puts me off my breakfast. Besides, I want to bring him in alive. I don't want him dying on the road, depriving the populace of their sport.

Good for morale, a burning, let's them know the Church has got everything under control.'

The soldiers finally released Rodrigo and turned to mount their horses. Rodrigo ran across to the pardoner who was already in his saddle. He grabbed the pardoner's arm.

'This man has done nothing. You must give him a chance to defend himself. You are a man of God and you know in all conscience that was no fair test. Let him answer properly.'

'Have no fear, good fellow, he will be heard. They will hear him all over the Bishop's palace before we've finished with him. We do not burn men until they have confessed and by the time we have finished with him, he will be begging to confess.'

'You would torture a man in the name of a merciful God?' Rodrigo asked bitterly.

The pardoner's eyes glittered in the torchlight. 'Just a moment, do I detect the same accent as Master Michael's? Another Venetian? Could it be we have two Jews for the price of one? Well, well. It is my lucky night.'

Michelotto looked up. 'This man, a Venetian? He is a bastard Genoese. It is bad enough you call me a Jew, now you accuse me of being countryman to this whoremonger. Take me if you are going to; I'd rather burn than have to spend another minute in the company of a Genoese.'

Michelotto spat at Rodrigo, and a glob of purple wine-stained spittle landed on his cheek and rolled slowly down his face.

The soldiers laughed and turned their horses in the direction of the track.

The pardoner swept his gaze round the clearing. 'You may spread the word. We shall root out all Jews wherever we find them and believe me, we shall find them.'

Within minutes they had gone, dragging Michelotto behind them on a long rope. We all stood, listening to the hoofbeats fade into the distance. One of the apprentices silently and mechanically began to straighten the overturned benches. One by one the others joined him as if they didn't know what else to do.

It had begun to rain again. I walked over to Rodrigo, who still stood staring down the track, though there was nothing to be seen or heard except the wind in the branches and the pattering of the raindrops.

'He denied you to save your life, Rodrigo.'

Rodrigo did not answer. There were tears in his eyes.

Hugh stumbled across to us, his face wretched. 'It is all my fault. If I hadn't thrown the pardoner out, he'd not have come back here with the soldiers.' He pounded his fist into the nearest tree trunk. 'I am such a fool, a stupid, hot-headed fool.'

'He'd have come back anyway,' I assured him. 'However much they cream off the sale of indulgences, pardoners are always greedy for more. They're always on the lookout for something they can report to their masters for an extra purse and the Church makes good use of them as spies. As you said yourself, the prayers and masses haven't stopped the pestilence. Catching a few Jews reassures the people that something is being done to keep them safe. But God help Michelotto, it will be better for him if he does die on the road.'

We finished clearing up as best we could, then I lay down once again in the warmth of the workshop and closed my eyes. I was dimly aware of others stepping round me to find their own sleeping places, but I was too tired to open my eyes to see who they were.

*

For the second time that night I woke with a start. I thought I heard the distant howl of a wolf. Around me I could see Rodrigo, Jofre, Osmond and Adela all sitting up. The howl had woken them too. One of the apprentice boys whimpered in his sleep, but they slept on, huddled together in the corner of the workshop, too exhausted by the night's events to be woken by anything. I heard Osmond murmuring to comfort Adela. I lay still and listened for a few moments, but heard nothing more. One by one the others lay down again. But I couldn't settle.

I got up as quietly as I could and slipped outside to relieve myself. It was still dark. The wind roared in the branches overhead and it was cold after the warmth of the workshop. In the clearing, fires glowed ruby-red under the iron pots, but the flames had died down. I was just slipping back to the workshop when a movement caught my eye. Narigorm sat near one of the potash fires, her runes scattered in front of her.

'Too late for that now, Narigorm,' I said. 'We could have done with the warning before the soldiers came.'

'Nine for knowledge. Nine for nine nights on the tree. Nine for the mothers of Heimdal. And so Morrigan begins it.'

'Begins what?' I asked her.

She looked up and opened her eyes wide as if she had only just realized I was there. 'One has gone. Now we are eight.'

'What do you mean, one of us has gone?' I was tired and irritable. 'Zophiel? He'll be back, I can promise you that. He'd not go anywhere without his precious boxes and he can't carry those on foot.'

'Not Zophiel.'

Another thought struck me. Cygnus. I didn't remember seeing him at all after the soldiers came. The sight of them must have frightened him out of his wits. It was hardly surprising if he had run off and if he had, there was no reason for him to come back.

'You mean Cygnus?'

She shook her head. I knew she wanted me to guess again, but I was in no mood to play childish games. I was cold and weary. I wanted to lie down again. I turned to go.

'Pleasance.'

I turned back to her. 'Did you say Pleasance? Don't talk nonsense. She was standing with you all the time the soldiers were here, why should she have run off now?'

By way of an answer Narigorm pointed to a rune lying half-way across the line of one of the circles. The figure etched on to it was a straight line with two short lines coming down at an angle as if a child had drawn half a pine tree.

'*Ansuz*, the ash tree, Odin's sign. He hung on the tree for nine days to learn the meaning of the runes.'

'What does this have to do with Pleasance?' I asked, but Narigorm only looked down at the runes again.

I searched the runes, trying to see if I was missing something. There was no shell or feather among them, but then I saw there was something else lying on the bare earth. In the dim light cast by the fires I had almost missed it, a little sprig of some plant. I picked it up and peered at it closely. The long spike of tiny yellow flowers, though dried, was unmistakable. It was the herb agrimony and it had been bound with a coarse red thread, the same thread that midwives use to bind agrimony to the mother's thighs to help ease the passage of the baby.

I crouched down and looked into Narigorm's ice-blue eyes.

'Narigorm, stop playing games, tell me where Pleasance has gone.'

She looked at me for a long time, without blinking, before she finally spoke.

'Pleasance is dead.'

15. The First Death

We found Pleasance early the following morning. Hugh had ordered the apprentices to help us search and in the end it was one of them who came back, white and trembling, to say he had found her body. He delivered his message in faltering tones and promptly vomited, but after a mug of ale was finally persuaded to lead us back to where she was.

Hugh, Rodrigo, Osmond and I followed the boy through the trees, leaving Jofre at the glassworks to look after Adela and Narigorm. We walked for about a quarter of an hour, and I was beginning to think the boy had lost his way or imagined the whole thing when he suddenly stopped in his tracks and pointed. A body was dangling from the high branch of an ancient oak tree. Even though her back was towards us, I recognized her immediately. Her long skirts clung wetly to her legs. Her limp arms dangled uselessly by her sides, the hands purple where the blood had pooled. The thick veil she always wore to cover her hair was missing and her dark hair was loose. Long wet strands of it snaked down over her shoulders. Her head was lolling at a strange angle.

She was hanging by a length of rope to which a leather

noose had been tied. As the body rocked back and forth in the wind, the wet rope made a mewling sound, like a new-born infant, as it rubbed against the branch of the tree. As we stared aghast, there was a sudden gust of wind and the body twisted round as if to greet us. Her eyes were wide open and seemed to be staring straight at us. The apprentice boy behind me gave a high-pitched yelp and fled.

Osmond was the first to pull himself together. He climbed up the tree and, legs astride the branch, inched forward until he could reach far enough to saw at the rope with his knife. He worked carefully; there was no point in hurrying for we could see from the angle of the head that her neck was broken. Rodrigo and Hugh caught the body as it dropped and eased it down on to the fallen leaves. Her sightless eyes stared up at us. I passed my hand over them to try to close them, but the rigor of death was already beginning to set in and her face was stiff. She had been dead for some hours.

The leather thong had bitten deep into her neck. As Rodrigo cut it loose and pulled it away, her pierced amber wolfstone slid into view. It had been hidden by her hair. It was only then that I realized the noose had been fashioned from her own necklace.

'She was fortunate,' Rodrigo said. 'The wolfstone, it jerked against her neck and broke it. She died instantly. That is a blessing. I have seen men die by hanging and it is an agonizingly slow death.'

'But to break the neck in that manner means she was not hauled up by the rope. She must have been pushed off from something high,' I said.

Osmond crouched down beside the body. 'Like a horse? If the soldiers set her on a horse, then pulled it away?'

Rodrigo shook his head. 'That would not break her neck, not if she swung back at an angle. It has to be a sharp drop downwards.' He looked up at the high branch. 'If she jumped from that branch, that would have done it.'

'You think she killed herself then?' I asked.

Hugh, at my elbow, took a deep breath and crossed himself. 'God's blood, don't say that. Better she was murdered than that she took her own life.'

'They could have broken her neck and then hanged her,' Osmond said.

'I hardly think so.' I jumped as I heard Zophiel's unmistakable drawl behind me. 'Why go to the trouble of hanging her if she was already dead? It's plain the woman killed herself. She was the sort of hysterical female who would be given to such fits of melancholia.'

Rodrigo rose and glared at Zophiel. 'Where have you been hiding all night? Do you know anything of this?'

'I really don't see that I have to account to you for my whereabouts, Rodrigo. I'm not your pupil. But since you ask, I was not, as you put it, *hiding*, I was in the wagon guarding our provisions. Someone had to, with those louts rampaging through the camp.'

'It is a pity you did not stay and meet the pardoner, Zophiel. You would have got on well.'

Hugh looked from one to the other, evidently puzzled by the antagonism between them. 'Maybe whoever did it hanged her to make it look like suicide, instead of murder.'

'The journeyman makes a good point.' Zophiel raised his voice slightly. 'Has anyone thought to enquire where our young friend Cygnus spent the night?'

We looked at one another.

Osmond said hesitatingly, 'He's right. It could be . . .'

I shook my head. 'I don't dispute that a man who has used only one arm for his whole life has the strength and dexterity to break a woman's neck. There are many ways that might be accomplished. But to hang a dead body from a tree at that height, that requires two hands. The rope end was not tied off at ground level, which means someone would have had to climb that tree to haul her up, just as you had to climb it to cut her down. And how would he lift a dead body up? The rope did not reach from the branch to ground.'

'But if the body was lying on a horse under the tree,' Osmond said, 'that might lift it high enough. Xanthus will stand like a lamb for Cygnus.'

Hugh shook his head. 'From what I've seen of him that Cygnus is a soft lad. I doubt he's got it in him to wring a chicken's neck. If she was murdered it is more likely it was by a passing stranger. Could have been one of the charcoal burners in the forest. They're a strange lot, living by themselves for months at a time. No womenfolk with them, most of them. They say even the pigs are nervous of them and it's not for fear of being made into bacon.'

'Or,' Rodrigo said quietly, 'she may simply have taken her own life.'

Hugh looked down at the bedraggled figure at his feet. 'Aye, well, that too,' he said soberly. 'By rights we ought to raise the hue and cry and send for the coroner. It is up to him to decide how she died, but . . . look, we've had enough trouble here. If the pardoner is brought in to testify, it's us that'll get the blame whatever. He's got it in for us. And I've the lads to think about. With their master gone and their families more than likely dead, I'm all that stands between them and starvation. We're the only ones who know about the woman. I'm guessing she's no relatives to come looking for her, so . . .' He trailed off, a pleading expression on his face.

'You mean bury her quietly here and not report it,' I said.

'God's blood, not here!' he said quickly. 'Her ghost would never give us a moment's peace. She's died violently, by her own hand or by someone else's; either way, her spirit would revenge itself on any in the forest. She'll not rest till we're all in the grave with her. You'll have to take her with you. Bury her well away from here where she can do no harm and then you can travel on till you've left her ghost far behind.'

We left the glassworks before noon. Although Hugh waved us off and wished us well, it was with a profound look of relief on his face. The wagon now bore an extra bundle. We had wrapped the body up where it lay in the forest, in case we should meet anyone as we carried it back to the glassworks. Hugh had fetched us some old sheepskins to tie round the body to disguise her shape, so that to the casual observer it might look like a bundle of skins. At least it was winter, so there were no flies to be attracted to the corpse. It was the first time I was grateful for the cold wind and rain, though it was not cold enough to keep the body for long.

When we brought the body back, Hugh and Rodrigo carried it straight to the wagon while Osmond and I went to look for Adela and Narigorm. We found Cygnus sitting with his good arm around Adela, comforting her. Osmond ran forward and dragged him away from Adela, demanding to know where he had been last night.

Cygnus's explanation was as plausible as Zophiel's. He had fled as soon as the soldiers had charged into the clearing, without even waiting to see whose colours they bore, naturally assuming they had come for him. He ran as deep into the forest as he could, finally crawling into a dense thicket of bushes where he had lain all night. Having fled in the dark without paying any heed to direction or landmarks, it had taken him some time to find his way back to the workshop in daylight. In fact he said he would still be wandering around had he not heard one of the apprentices yelling Pleasance's name.

Although Cygnus knew by now that Pleasance had been found hanging, he told his story guilelessly without any sign that he thought he was under suspicion. Osmond continued to eye Cygnus with distrust, but even he had to admit Cygnus's story was no less credible than Zophiel's.

Adela was distraught. Though Pleasance spoke little, the two of them often spent time together preparing meals, with Adela chattering away enough for both of them, and Adela had come to regard her almost as a favourite aunt, the only woman she had for company.

The manner of her death shocked Adela deeply. 'But she was the kindest and gentlest of people. She'd never have harmed anyone. Who could have done such a wicked thing to someone like her?'

But none of us had the answer to that.

I was worried that once the news had sunk in, Adela's shock and sadness would give way to fear. Her baby was due in three weeks, and she had pinned all her hopes on Pleasance to deliver her child safely. Childbirth was a dangerous time for both mother and child, but Adela had convinced herself that as long as Pleasance was there neither she nor the child could come to any harm. Only if we were able to get shelter at an inn, or nunnery, was there any chance of finding another experienced woman to help her through her labours, and with the pestilence now on three sides of us the chances of finding a roof over our heads, never mind a midwife, seemed slim indeed.

We kept our promise to Hugh and walked for two, maybe

three hours before we buried Pleasance. In the end it was fear of having to spend the night camping near her grave that determined the place, for we needed enough daylight to dig and then move on some distance before night fell. It was not easy to find a spot. The forest floor seems soft, but dig a few inches and you soon run into a thick tangle of tree roots. Finally, we glimpsed a place off to the left of the tracks where several old trees had fallen in a past storm and lay uprooted and rotting, already half-covered by ferns, bone-white fungi and pillows of dark green moss.

We scraped away beside one of the fallen tree trunks with hands, sticks and the one spade which Zophiel had for digging the wagon out of ruts. The sweet, rich smell of leaf mould clung to our skin and mud streaked our faces before we'd dug anything deep enough to be called a grave. When we finally called a halt we had a long, shallow hole partly tucked under the curve of the trunk.

'That won't be deep enough to stop animals digging up the body,' Zophiel said. 'Cover her with rocks and cover them with earth and leaves, so the grave can't be seen.'

We slid her into the hole. There was a soft thud as Rodrigo heaved the first rock on to the body.

At the sound, Adela moaned, 'No, don't, please,' and sank to the ground, clutching at her belly. Osmond led her back to the wagon while we continued to cover the body with rocks and stones. I wondered if we were really doing it to keep the scavengers from mauling the corpse or if, like Hugh, we too feared her ghost and wanted to fasten it in its grave.

The ground looked dug over, darker than the surroundings, but it was on the far side of the trunk, hidden from the track. In a day or so the soil and leaves would weather to look no different from the rest. Come spring the grave would have settled and there would be nothing to distinguish it from the rest of the forest floor.

There was nothing more to be done, but it seemed indecent simply to walk away. I glanced over to where Narigorm stood impassively staring down. She had not shed one tear for her nurse and protector. Even though Zophiel was not what you'd call grief-stricken, he at least seemed perturbed by the events. Narigorm, betraying neither shock nor grief, had watched the burial with curiosity as if she was watching ants strip the flesh from the body of a squashed frog. As if she felt me watching her, she raised her eyes and stared into mine. Her words from last night echoed in my head as if she was speaking them aloud, but her lips were not moving. *And so Morrigan begins it.*

It was Jofre who broke the spell. He stepped forward and stuck a cross into the mound, which he had fashioned from two bound sticks. Zophiel immediately wrenched the cross out of the ground again and tossed it into the undergrowth.

'Idiot boy, what is the point of us trying to disguise her grave if you're going to draw attention to it?'

Jofre flushed. 'But there's no priest to bury her, we said no words, we can't just bury her like a dog.'

'Why not? If she killed herself, no priest would bury her. She's fortunate to have a grave. You've passed enough corpses lying where they fell to know that.' Zophiel picked up the spade. 'Now, unless you want to spend the night with the corpse, I suggest we move on. There is barely an hour or two of daylight left.'

He strode away. The rest of us muttered furtive little prayers over the grave, crossing ourselves rapidly before we too turned away. Jofre was the last to leave. When he thought he was unobserved, he quickly retrieved the handmade cross and laid it flat on top of the grave. I said nothing; like him, I too wanted to do something for Pleasance.

As we trudged on along the track, I dropped back behind the wagon with Rodrigo. I pulled on his arm, signalling him to slow down until the others were out of earshot.

'Tell me honestly, Rodrigo. Do you think it was murder? For if it was, I can't see a stranger's hand in this. Pleasance wouldn't have gone so far into the forest at night except with someone she knew and trusted, especially with soldiers about.'

Rodrigo stared ahead at the backs of Cygnus and Jofre despondently dragging their feet through the mud. 'Maybe she went to find Cygnus to tell him it was safe to come back.'

'It would have been a fool's errand in the dark if she'd no idea where to look. And I still cannot fathom how Cygnus could have hanged her. Anyway, what reason would he have to murder her, unless . . .' I thought of what Hugh had said about the charcoal burners. Was it possible that Cygnus had tried to rape her as perhaps he had already raped and murdered a little girl? I'd be more willing to believe that of Zophiel than Cygnus.

Rodrigo shook his head. 'He did not do it. I know in my heart it was her own hand that tied the noose and her own feet that jumped.'

'But why would she hang herself, Rodrigo? There are enough poor souls dying who would give all they owned to stay alive, even if it was for just another day. What cause did she have?'

He turned and studied me for a moment. 'You do not know, Camelot?'

I shook my head.

'You remember that night we spent with Walter and his

son? Zophiel talked about burning Jews because they were to blame for the pestilence. He said how in England there were Jews still hidden among the Christians. Then last night when the soldiers came for Michelotto, again the question of the Jews. And you saw what the pardoner did to him and what he threatened? Torture and burning?'

'You think Pleasance was distressed about what they would do to Michelotto?'

'For him, yes, of course. But she was also distressed, as you put it, about what they would do to her if anyone discovered her secret. Pleasance was a Jewess, Camelot. Did you not realize?'

I suddenly remembered the look on Pleasance's face that night in Walter's cottage, the way she trembled. And I had stupidly thought she was afraid of Jews.

'Are you sure? Did she tell you that?'

He pressed his lips in a grimace. 'In a way she did. That night in the old widow's inn when she told the story of how she had been midwife to a wolf, you remember?'

I nodded.

'She said that the cave to which she was taken was full of demons, except that she did not use the word demon, she called them "*sheidim*". It is a word I have never heard used in this land, but I heard it often where I grew up. In Venice there was a quarter where the Jews lived. There were some fine gold- and silversmiths among them. Glassblowers too, before, as Michelotto said, they were sent to Murano, though that was before I was born.' He wiped the rain out of his eyes.

'Jews were tolerated because they brought wealth to the city from the traders who came to buy from them and the taxes they paid, for they were taxed twice as much as the Christians. Besides, whenever the priests wanted a silver casket for their relics or a fine gold chalice for their church, who else could they call upon who had the skill to make anything as fine as the Jews? They mostly kept to their own quarter, for the Christians would have little to do with them, but I was drawn to them by their music from the day I could walk.'

Now that we were on the subject of music, his face lit up as it did whenever he picked up his lute.

'The Jews are fine musicians. You should hear them play for their weddings.' Rodrigo sighed as if he longed to hear it again. 'The music would begin so softly and slowly, played by just one man, each note so pure and clear like the drops of water dripping from a leaf, and gradually the other musicians would join in and the drops would turn to a trickle and the trickle to a waterfall which crashed about your ears and made your feet dance as if they were bewitched. Some said that is exactly what their music did, bewitch you, and that the Jews intended it so. They wanted to make you dance until you dropped dead from exhaustion for if you died while you danced, unshriven and unheeding, your ghost would be compelled to dance for eternity among the tombs and in the wastelands and you would never find rest. Priests said it was their way of stealing Christian souls.

'One priest in a nearby church was so convinced of it he would order the church bells rung to drown out the devilish music whenever it was played. He told Christians to hurry past their high walls with their fingers stuffed in their ears, but I did not. When I was a small boy I was forever wandering there in the hope of hearing that music. After a while they got used to me standing in the doorways, listening, and would beckon me in, even showing me how to play a few notes. That is where I first learned to play. My parents were frightened when they discovered where I went, for everyone knows the stories of how Jews are said to kill little boys and use their blood to make their Passover bread. The stories are nonsense, of course, for anyone who knows about the Jewish ways knows that they abhor blood and even soak their meat for hours to remove all drops of it lest they sin by consuming it. But my parents believed the tales and forbade me to go near them, but their music drew me back, whatever my parents threatened.' He smiled fondly at the distant memory. 'Perhaps the priest was right after all and I was bewitched.'

He paused as our way was blocked by a particularly wide puddle, mud and leaves still swirling in it from the wagon wheels that had rolled through it. We stepped off the track and threaded our way through the trees to avoid it. When we rejoined the track again, Rodrigo took up his tale.

'When I was older and trying to earn every penny I could to buy my own lute, the Jews paid me well to be a *Shabbes goy* for them.'

He smiled at my puzzled expression. 'You do not know this word either?'

I shook my head.

'Their religion forbids them to work from sunset on Friday to sunset on Saturday. They take work to mean any kind of household task, so that they cannot light fires, or even candles when it gets dark. They cannot even stir the food in the pots, so they employ Christians to do these things for them, and it was then that I used to listen to the stories the old women told to tell to pass the time, tales of *sheidim* and of angels, of brides possessed by *dybbuks* who slay their husbands on their wedding night and foolish old men brought to wisdom by their daughters.'

'That's where you heard the word Pleasance used?'

'I do not think she meant to say it,' Rodrigo said gravely.

'Maybe she did not know that it would mark her out. Words are woven into stories; they cannot easily be separated.'

'So when Adela drew attention to it by asking what it meant, you tried to cover for Pleasance, telling us it was a local village word.'

Rodrigo nodded. 'I hoped that no one else would understand. I prayed they would not. I feared Zophiel might, for though he would not know the word, he is clever enough to realize it was no English word, but his mind was distracted by the wolf and only half on the tale.'

He lowered his voice and glanced uneasily ahead, though the wagon was some way in front of us by now. 'Zophiel would not have hesitated to expose her if he suspected, and she knew this. Zophiel plays cat and mouse with Cygnus by threatening to hand him over; maybe she thinks he plays the same game with her. And after she saw what they did to Michelotto, she thought it better to take her own life than wait for them to come for her.' Anger flooded his face. 'It is that pardoner and Zophiel who together are to blame for her death. Zophiel's vicious words . . .'

I remembered what Pleasance had said the morning we were stuck in Northampton: 'sometimes you have to leave'. I wondered if she had any inkling then of how final that leaving might be. If only she had walked away from us that day.

Rodrigo turned to me, his face suddenly pale. 'But what if Zophiel did realize she was a Jewess? The pardoner said they hanged Jews. What if he hanged her for a Jew?' He gripped my arm fiercely. 'Camelot, is it possible? Do you think he killed her, not just with words, but with his hands?'

'But why? I can see that a man with his hatred of the Jews would want her dead if he knew what she was, but why kill her himself in secret rather than hand her over to the Church? I'd have thought a man like Zophiel would get far more satisfaction from seeing her humiliated and executed in public.'

'But he has not handed over Cygnus either, though twice now he has had the chance. I am beginning to think perhaps Zophiel has his own reasons for not wanting to draw attention to himself with the authorities.'

16. The Chantry

'What say you, Camelot?' Cygnus asked. 'Are they dead or fled?'

It was a good question, for the chantry chapel certainly appeared to be abandoned. The chapel stood hard against the central arch of the stone bridge as if it was propping it up on one side. The stone pillars which supported the base of the chantry rose out of the middle of the fast-flowing river below. Two steps led up from the bridge to the heavy wooden door of the chapel itself, but peering down over the bridge wall, I could see that there was a second chamber underneath the chapel, hanging just a foot or so above the churning water. I hoped it was a sacristy and not a burial chamber. It made me shudder to think of bodies being interred there, suspended for ever above that dark, rushing water.

The chantry was newly constructed. Many of the saints and grotesques which ran around the roof were still just rough shapes blocked out by an apprentice in readiness for a master stone-carver to chisel in the fine detail. The walls and slate roof were complete, though none of the stonework had yet been painted.

But although the building was not finished, it already

had an air of neglect about it. Drifts of brown leaves had accumulated in the corners of the steps and the door and more were blocking waterspouts on the roof. Several blocks of masonry were piled against one of the walls, some half-worked as if the workmen had just downed tools that afternoon, but the cut faces of the stones were covered with a green bloom, indicating they had not been moved for some time.

I walked back to join Cygnus and the others by the wagon. 'Whoever was working here looks to have departed in some haste, but whether it was into the next town or the next life, is hard to say.'

'Let's pray it was not into the next life, if Adela is going to have her child here,' Cygnus replied.

Adela, sitting on her usual perch on the wagon, looked aghast. 'I can't give birth to my baby in a chapel.'

Cygnus tested the door before replying. The iron handle was stiff but the heavy door was unlocked. He pushed it open but did not go in. An odour of musty dampness oozed out, but there was no hint of the putrid smell we had come to dread.

'Why not? It's solid, and once we have a fire going it will be warm and dry. Besides, it's unfinished, so it cannot yet be consecrated, in which case it is just an unused building, not a chapel.'

Zophiel's eyes blazed. 'It is nevertheless a sacred building and it would be a desecration to pollute it with childbirth.'

Cygnus wiped the rain from his face and pointed up to a sculpted panel immediately over the door, depicting the Virgin and Child, the only carvings on the outside of the chantry which had been completed. 'Surely Mary would not consider childbirth a desecration of her chapel?'

'Hers was a sinless birth, but this . . . this . . .' Zophiel was so outraged that for once he could not finish his sentence.

Rodrigo, who had been leaning over the bridge staring at the raging water below, straightened up and glared pointedly at Zophiel. 'Murderers and thieves claim sanctuary in churches. Why not an innocent mother and child? Do you think that the birth of a baby pollutes the house of God more than the blood on the hands of a murderer?'

Rodrigo still blamed Zophiel for Pleasance's death. Whether she had taken her own life or had it taken from her was one and the same to him, Zophiel was responsible, of that he was certain.

I tried to bring us back to the purpose before war broke out between them again.

'Cygnus is right; there is no reason why as travellers we should not take shelter in a chapel for a few days. Consecrated or not, the Church permits it. But we still don't know if it is safe to enter. We haven't resolved what happened to the workmen. This work was stopped abruptly. Granted the chapel does not smell of death, but there is a chamber below it. If we find someone dead down there, it will be too late, we will already be exposed to the contagion.'

Cygnus nodded. 'Then I'll go in alone and search the place. If someone lies dead in there, I'll call out to you from inside and you must go on without me.'

Rodrigo stepped between Cygnus and the chapel door, holding up his hands. 'No, no, Camelot is right, if you stumble across a body, it will be the end for you. You heard Hugh at the glassworks, the woman they found in the village had died in agony. We cannot let you put yourself in such danger. If we cannot be sure it is safe, we should all go on.'

'We are in danger at every turn at the road,' said Cygnus. 'We could walk into someone who is dead or dying round any corner. If we don't take this chance there's every possibility that Adela will have to give birth on the road. The baby could come at any time and we don't know if we shall find anything better.' He gestured to the road that led away from the bridge. There was not a house or barn within sight. Nothing but leafless trees and open scrubland lay in that direction as far as the eye could see and what lay beyond was concealed by the rise of a distant scarp. 'We can't risk going on for much longer.'

He pulled the neck of his hood up over his mouth and nose and twisted it firmly in position. Then he thrust Rodrigo aside. We stood in the rain and waited.

We all knew Cygnus was right. The business of where Adela would give birth was becoming more pressing by the day. Although many women, of necessity, deliver their babies on the roadside, many women die there too, and Adela, for all her Saxon blood, had not the strength of a woman bred to such hardships. It was almost Christmas and as Cygnus said, the baby could come at any time. Jolting along in the wagon over washed-out roads, stones and potholes in the chilling rain was surely enough to open any woman's womb. Adela had already begun to have the false pains which often precede labour and these had terrified her so much she had convinced herself that unless she found a midwife to help her when the time came, she would die in childbirth. Since Pleasance's death, Adela's spirits had sunk so low that not even Osmond could coax a smile from her, and despite his entreaties to eat, if not for her sake then for the baby's, it was all she could do to swallow two or three mouthfuls. I began to fear that her dark forebodings would prove justified and she would not survive the birth.

We had, several times, suggested taking her to a nunnery for the nuns have well-equipped infirmaries and great medical skill. Indeed, many wealthy women send for the nuns to assist them in their confinement. But at the mere suggestion of a nunnery, Adela became hysterical, shouting that she'd rather die on the road than go into such a place. I told her we weren't suggesting that she took the veil, merely that she was delivered of her baby there, but to my great surprise even Osmond seemed vehemently opposed to the idea.

So since neither could be persuaded to it, we had no other option but to look for an inn that was still open to travellers and prepared to take in a woman so obviously near her time. Most innkeepers are not, as we soon discovered. For as they told us, their other customers would soon be demanding their money back if they'd paid for a bed only to be kept awake all night by a woman screaming for hours. Then, they said, there's the mess which someone has to clear up, as if their serving maids didn't already have enough to do. And who's going to pay for a ruined pallet, they'd like to know. Not to mention, they added, lowering their voices to a stage whisper, the trouble it brings if the woman dies. With things being as they are, no innkeeper wants it spread abroad that he has a dead body on his hands. They were not heartless men, but business is business in these troubled times.

The last town we'd passed through, a mile or so back, had brought us no nearer to a solution. At first sight it had appeared promising. At least the town gates were wide open and the jovial gatekeeper refuted any suggestion of the pestilence having reached them. According to him, everyone was as fit as a flea inside. This hysteria about the pestilence was nothing but a pig's fart. He wasn't worried about being struck down, for only those with a guilty conscience need fear it and his own conscience was as clean as a newborn babe's for he went to mass as often as any man could. He eyed Adela shrewdly and directed us to the Red Dragon, an inn near the main square, which he said was run by a decent enough old biddy who could brew a good drop of ale when she'd a mind to. She'd not turn anyone away, whatever their condition, if she was offered a little extra for her trouble. Had some friendly girls working for her too, he added, giving Zophiel a broad man-of-the-world wink. Our hopes rising, Zophiel led Xanthus through the gates.

If every town has its own smell, this one was the stench of the midden. The main street was wide enough for a wagon to pass, but ankle-deep in slimy mud, and the open sewers were clogged with refuse, so that the foul water spilled out over the road. On either side of the main street, a maze of snickets and lanes ran between huddles of squalid wooden houses and workshops, their overhanging top storeys almost touching the house on the other side. These mean little alleys were so dark and cramped that daylight never reached into their depths, where pigs, dogs, chickens and children scavenged and fought among the piles of stinking rubbish. As soon as we entered the town, a mass of bow-legged urchins swarmed alongside the wagon begging for coins. Several of the bolder ones tried to clamber into the moving wagon to see what they could steal and it took several cuts of Zophiel's long whip to send them packing.

We found the Red Dragon Inn easily enough. It looked as filthy and neglected as the other buildings in the town and an unappetizing smell of sour ale and boiled cabbage hung about it. Despite the cold and rain, a girl lounged in the doorway. Her hair had tumbled from her cap and her kirtle was stiff with grease. There was a ring of sores around her mouth, though she was, as the gatekeeper had told us, friendly enough and her face lit up at the sight of us. She sauntered across the street, swinging her wide hips. Her gaze roved first to Zophiel, then to Rodrigo, Jofre and Osmond in turn as if deciding which to try her luck with. She seemed to conclude that Zophiel was the man in charge. With a saucy grin, she nudged him aside with her hip and caught hold of Xanthus's bridle to lead her into the yard.

'You come along with me, sir,' she said. 'Stable's round back. I'll show you.'

But Zophiel seized her wrist and thrust her firmly aside, pulling Xanthus forward and leaving the disappointed girl shouting in our wake that the beds were clean and she'd warm them herself for us.

'Zophiel, that was the Red Dragon we just passed,' Osmond said, catching up with him. 'Aren't we stopping?'

'Would you really have your wife give birth in there?' Zophiel snapped. 'If she did manage to survive the birth, she'd be dead within the week from the dirt and stench.'

'It might have been better inside,' Osmond said weakly.

'If that slut had the cleaning of it, I very much doubt it.'

Osmond looked up at the white-faced Adela, who was swaying from side to side with the movement of the wagon. Her eyes were closed and her forehead furrowed as if she was in pain.

'There might be another inn or lodgings somewhere in the town, if we ask.' Osmond sounded desperate.

'Look around you, boy. The gatekeeper said they don't have the pestilence, but that ignorant fool will still be denying it exists when they are slinging him into the burial pit. There could be a dozen dying already in the backrooms of those filthy houses and we'd not know it until it was too late. You and Adela can stay here if you want, but you'll be on your own. Shall I stop and get her down? Because believe me, I'd be only too happy to leave both of you here.'

Osmond dropped his gaze and shook his head.

*

Cygnus was inside the chantry for a long time. His examination of the chapel had not taken long, but then he called out that he was going down to the lower floor. We heard nothing more. Xanthus shifted restlessly in the shafts, her head down against the pouring rain. Strange how you seem to get wetter in the rain when you are standing than when you are walking, more conscious of the coldness seeping down your neck. Zophiel was impatient to move on, muttering that it would be God's punishment if the boy did meet death in there after what he'd had the audacity to propose. Finally he turned and pulled on Xanthus's bridle.

'Come,' he said coldly. 'We are leaving.'

Narigorm, curled up as usual in the well at the front of the wagon, lifted her head. 'Not yet,' she said. 'It's not time to leave yet.'

Zophiel, furious now, ignored her and tried to pull the horse forward but Xanthus braced herself and refused to budge. She seemed to know that Cygnus was missing and was not going to take a step without him. Zophiel was reaching from the whip when there was a loud flapping above our heads and several pigeons flew out of the small bell tower. Minutes later, Cygnus's head appeared at one of the small openings in the tower.

'It's safe,' he called. 'There's no one here. I've searched everywhere.'

Zophiel turned and stared hard at Narigorm, but she scrambled from the wagon and in a moment had disappeared though the chapel door.

We followed her cautiously. It was cold and damp inside, colder even than standing outside on the bridge, but it was surprisingly light. On each of the three sides of the chapel were three square-headed windows, with smaller, higher windows on the east side. Niches were hollowed out round the walls which were intended one day to contain the figures of saints, perhaps of the Virgin Mary herself, but these had not yet been filled. At the east end of the chapel was a raised dais on which stood a stone altar elaborately carved with the five glorious mysteries of the Rosary. Unlike the carving on the outside of the building, these had been painted, the robes of the figures picked out in rich blues, greens, yellows and reds, and touches of gold. Directly behind the altar, wooden scaffolding had been erected against the wall on which the painting of a scene appeared almost complete, but the other walls of the chapel were as yet bare.

To one side of the sanctuary was a door opening on to a narrow spiral staircase leading to the crypt below. It was smaller than the chapel and lit only by two loop windows high up on the wall. In one corner was a small angled recess containing a privy hole which emptied straight out over the river. A heavy door on the north wall led to the outside. When the river was lower there was probably a small island in the middle of the river to which the door gave access, a way into the chantry for people and supplies arriving by boat. But now the steps outside leading up to the door were all but covered by the turbulent water. If the river rose another foot, water would pour in under the door straight into the crypt.

A few planks and trestles were scattered about the chamber, together with some empty flagons, barrels and a brazier with blackened pieces of wood and a few charred bird bones in the bottom. A heap of fine grey wood ash still lay in the pan beneath. Some old fowling nets and tangles of line heaped in the corner suggested that the workmen had supplemented their rations with whatever they could catch in the river. But other than this jetsam, the crypt was empty of furnishing.

Although it was damper and colder than the chapel, we decided to both cook and sleep in the crypt. The brazier had evidently been brought in by boat through the crypt doorway and would not easily be carried up that narrow staircase. Cygnus also pointed out that the windows in the chapel had been designed to allow any light from candles inside to shine out over the approaches to the bridge, and while there was no good reason for travellers not to take shelter in a chantry, we did not want to draw attention to our presence at night, for who knew what vagabonds and cut-throats might be abroad?

Zophiel stated his intention to sleep without a light up in the chapel, for that was where we had stored all his boxes from the wagon. No one was of a mind to lug them all downstairs, and as Rodrigo told Zophiel when he protested, if the river level rose and we had to leave quickly we would not want to have to abandon his precious boxes, now would we? Xanthus and the wagon were concealed among the trees on the far side of the bridge on the opposite side to the town. And so we settled in and prepared to stay until Adela's baby was born.

Osmond knelt in the sanctuary beside the altar grinding a small quantity of *terre verte* in a mortar. I recognized it as the colour the painters use to paint flesh tones. As I watched he carefully added a few drops of oil and continued to grind vigorously with his pestle. He beamed up at me as I moved closer. His eyes were shining in a way I had never seen before.

'I hope this will work,' he gabbled excitedly. 'I've always used eggs to bind the colour before, but at this time of year, even if we could find a hen or a goose that has not been eaten, they will not be in lay. I found some old pigeon's eggs in the bell tower, but they were so raddled, they were useless. Rodrigo says some painters in Venice use oil to bind the pigment. I've never heard of it myself, but he's usually right about these things. He's given me a little of the oil he uses to keep his lute and pipes from drying out and cracking. I didn't want to take it in case he can't get more, for his instruments are his life, but he insisted.'

I could not help smiling at his earnestness. 'Rodrigo is a generous man, especially to a fellow artist. So what do you intend to paint?'

By way of an answer he nodded at the eastern wall of the chapel which was covered in scaffolding. 'I shall finish that. Whoever began this was a good painter. I hope I may do it justice.'

I moved nearer to examine the painting. It was of the Virgin Mary. She wore a stiff blue and gold mantle which she held open, and beneath the mantle, as if they were sheltering in a cave, a crowd of diminutive figures knelt serenely in prayer, like dwarfs beneath the giant queen. Two figures in the foreground were painted larger than the rest, a bejewelled merchant and his wife. The other figures appeared to depict the merchant's family, his children, parents and siblings. Also protected under Mary's cloak were several tiny houses, two ships and a cluster of warehouses, all the property belonging to the merchant.

Outside of the shelter of Mary's mantle there were other figures, but they were not praying. They were fleeing in panic, for above Mary sat Christ on his throne, surrounded by angels and demons who were firing arrows and spears down on to the world below. The missiles bounced harmlessly off Mary's cloak, but those outside of her protection cringed in terror as the spears and arrows rained down upon them, piercing them through torsos, limbs and eyes.

Most of the painting had been completed except for Mary's face and hands, which were sketched in red on the white wall.

Osmond came across and stood beside me.

'Mary Misericordia,' he explained 'Our Lady of Mercy who protects those who pray to her. And these,' he gestured to the merchant and his wife, who knelt in the foreground, 'must be the benefactors who commissioned this chantry, so that the priests could pray for their souls. They must have great wealth to build such a chapel. I can't understand why it has been abandoned when they were so near to finishing it, and at a time when you'd think they would need the masses of the priests more than ever.'

'Maybe the merchant and his family have already fallen to the pestilence or he has lost his fortune and can no longer pay the workmen. Whatever the reason, if the craftsmen didn't receive their money when it was due, they wouldn't stay and work for nothing. I suspect this will not be the last building to be abandoned before it is completed.'

'I thought nothing could touch the wealth of the merchants. These last few years as the harvests failed, they seem to have grown even richer. They grew fatter as the poor grew thinner. I know my father did.'

'Your father was a merchant?'

He nodded, frowning, and turned his face away. I waited, but he did not say more. I didn't press him. A man's history is his own business.

'Then I pity him. This pestilence will bring a change in many fortunes, for better or worse.' I glanced at the paint and brushes in his hand. 'So, I fear you can't hope to be commissioned to finish this painting, not while the pestilence rages, anyway.'

He smiled, his dark mood vanishing in a trice. 'But I don't

want to be paid. I'll finish this painting as an offering, so that the Virgin will smile down on us and Adela will be safely delivered of a healthy child.'

He swung himself up on to the wooden scaffolding and eyed the space where the Virgin's face should have been, first from one angle and then from another.

I stood and watched him for a while, but Osmond was already absorbed in the first tentative brush strokes and seemed to have forgotten I was there. I walked to the door and looked back at him. His brow was furrowed in concentration, yet the expression of his face was one of utter contentment as the rapid strokes of the brush grew more confident in his hands.

'You realize that if the craftsmen ever return here after we are gone, they will think the face of the Virgin has miraculously appeared on the wall. The chantry will grow rich from all the pilgrims coming here to see the miracle.'

He laughed without taking his eyes from the wall. 'Then I must paint the most perfect face in England to be worthy of such a miracle.'

Few people passed over the bridge in the next few days. It was winter, and a wet winter at that, not a time for travelling unless you had to. Those families displaced by the flooding or fleeing the pestilence had not made it this far, preferring to take shelter in the towns which were still open. There was more hope of finding work and cheap lodging in a town, or if they could not find work, there would be a greater chance of receiving alms in the crowded streets than on a lonely road. Those travellers who did cross over the bridge were on urgent business and most scarcely gave the unfinished chantry a second glance, except occasionally to cross themselves and mutter a prayer for a safe journey from horseback as they passed. It was obvious that the chapel was unfinished and unconsecrated, so no one bothered to stop to light a candle in it. And we were careful to show no lights at night in case we attracted those whose business was not so honest.

Then it was Christmas morning. We heard the church bells ringing in the town for the Angels' Mass at midnight and again for the Shepherds' Mass at dawn, but we didn't answer the call. As for so many throughout the land, for us this Christmas would not be as any Christmas before. In many churches, the bells would not ring and the candles would not be lit, for there would be no one left to light them.

They say that at midnight on Christmas Eve the bees in the hives sing a psalm, all the cows in the byres kneel down and all the sheep turn to the east. They say too that every wild beast falls silent at that hour. If they are right, then what we heard after the chimes of the midnight bell died away was, as Osmond said, nothing more than the baying of a town dog provoked by the bells. But though he said it soothingly as Adela clung to him, I don't think even he believed that. We'd heard that same cry too often before to mistake it now. It was the howl of a lone wolf.

Osmond held Adela tightly in his arms. 'Even if it was a wolf, we have thick stone walls and a new stout door to protect us. Not even a mouse could get in here.'

'But it must be ravenous to come so close to a town.'

'Even if there's a whole pack of them, we are safe in here. Now, go to sleep, Adela.'

But even if Adela could sleep, I could not. I could not get that howl out of my head. There were wolves in the forests, but with a bounty on every wolf's head, they had been driven into the remote places far from highways, farms and towns. It was true that in recent years hunger had brought some packs close to crofts and isolated villages in the dead of winter, but we had kept to the main highways, we were forced to with the wagon. So why had we heard a wolf so many times on our journey, and why only ever one, unless there was only one – the same one – following us? It wasn't possible, it didn't make sense, and yet still I shuddered.

The crypt remained cold and damp; the heat from the brazier barely penetrated the room. The sound of rushing water, which was not so noticeable during the day, grew louder in the silence of the night and several times I woke from a fitful doze, sure that the river was in flood and pouring into the chamber.

Cygnus, who had been muttering in his sleep for several nights, also suddenly woke with an anguished cry and sat up trembling in the dim light cast by the brazier.

Narigorm was watching him. She was sitting upright, hunched against the wall, wrapped in a blanket. Something small fell from her hand with a faint clack on to the stone flags. She swiftly retrieved it. Pulling the blanket more tightly about her, she rested her chin on her knees, then turned her head to stare into the firelight. I wondered if she had slept at all. This biting cold was hard on all of us, even the young.

Cygnus rose and tiptoed up the stairs. He did not return.

'Osmond, are you awake?' Adela whispered. 'I think Cygnus might be ill. Did you hear him cry out? Should we go after him?'

'He's not ill,' Osmond muttered sleepily. 'When a man screams like that in his sleep it means he has a guilty conscience. I don't want you to be alone with him. He's dangerous. Who knows what goes on in the head of a creature like that?'

'But you can't still think he murdered –'

'Will you both shut up and go to sleep,' Jofre snapped irritably from the corner.

We must have finally slept, for when we all woke again daylight had penetrated the gloom of the crypt. The damp seeping up from the cold stone floor had turned my bones to ice and it took several minutes of standing in front of the glowing brazier before my stiff and aching back was ready to move. But Osmond, despite the disturbances in the night, had woken in a remarkably cheerful mood. He was determined that something should be done to celebrate Christmas Day and had soon persuaded Jofre and Rodrigo to help him net some ducks on the river, while Zophiel rather more grudgingly agreed to turn his hand to trying to catch some fish.

Rodrigo and I were still struggling into our damp boots long after Osmond and Jofre had bounded upstairs. The others had followed, all except for Narigorm who was still sitting hunched beside the smouldering brazier, her doll in her lap.

'You'd best stir yourself too, girl,' I told her. 'If the lads catch anything we'll need a good fire to cook it. You and I will search for kindling and wood. You take the town side of the river and I'll take the other.'

'I don't want to collect wood. I want to hunt for birds.'

Rodrigo chuckled. 'Leave that to Jofre and Osmond, *bambina*. The river is too fast. It is not safe for one as small as you.' He patted her hair affectionately. 'Come now, as you search you can think about a plump duck roasting on the wood you collect. Imagine how good that will taste, *si*?' He took her gently by the hand, pulling her to her feet. Her wooden doll clattered to the floor.

Rodrigo bent down to pick it up. 'I will put her safely . . .'

He was staring aghast at the doll in his hand. The rags were still wound around the doll's body, but they had been pulled back from its face. And now that they were removed, we could see that the doll no longer had a face. The brown wool hair had been ripped off; the carved nose and ears had been chipped away; the pretty eyes had been scratched out, the mouth obliterated. Rodrigo stared from the mutilated doll to Narigorm and back again as if he could not believe a child capable of such a thing.

'Why have you done this? Osmond spent many hours carving and painting this for you. It will hurt him that you have destroyed it, Adela too.'

Any other child would have looked ashamed or tried to make excuses, but Narigorm neither blushed nor answered defiantly. She regarded Rodrigo calmly.

'It's mine and I didn't like its face. Now it can be anyone I choose.'

As we emerged from the chantry, I noticed that for the first time in months the sky was lighter. The wind had turned, the clouds had rolled back and there was a patch of blue in the sky, just enough to make the Virgin a new cloak. I realized I had not looked up for months. You don't look up in the rain. I stood for a few moments gazing up at the bare branches of the trees waving in the breeze and the rooks flying overhead, their ragged wings tossed in the gusts of wind. A flock of starlings, the pale sun glinting iridescent from their purple feathers, wheeled towards the distant scarp and a single pigeon winged its way towards the town. I supposed birds must have taken to the wing through all those months of rain, but it was as if only that morning they had remembered how to fly.

I found Cygnus on the far bank, tethering Xanthus in a new patch of grass, her coat gleaming red-gold as the light caught it. Even she seemed to sense the weather was on the turn, lifting her head and flaring her nostrils as if to taste the wind. But I could see at once that Cygnus was not caught up in the mood of excitement. His face was drawn and there were dark circles around his eyes, making them appear blacker than ever. His movements were listless and everything seemed an effort for him. I hadn't noticed before how tired he looked. Xanthus nuzzled him gently and he rested his cheek against her flank and closed his eyes.

'Are you unwell, Cygnus?'

He started at my voice and straightened up. He gave me a weak smile. 'Have no fear, Camelot, it's not the pestilence.'

'There are other kinds of sickness.'

'I'm not sick, Camelot, just tired.' He reached down, tore up a hank of grass and fed it to Xanthus.

He turned to stare at the water surging beneath the bridge and finally, after a long pause, he turned back to me. 'I dream of the swans, Camelot. That's what disturbs my sleep every night. They're waiting for me. I see them swimming up the river, first a pair, then three, then four. I want to swim out to them, but I can't. I see them coming, more and more from every direction until the river is full of white bodies. Their wings arch, their necks bend and their dark eyes turn towards me, glittering in the darkness. They wait silently and I know they are waiting for me. Then suddenly they all begin to flap their wings. Their wings are beating me about the head. I have to crouch down to protect myself, the air is full of their feathers and I can't breathe. I'm gasping for air and all at once they are in the sky flying away from me. I call out to them to wait, but they can't hear me.'

Cygnus covered his face with his hand as if he was still protecting himself from the beating wings.

I moved closer and put my hand on his shoulder. 'It's the crypt, Cygnus. It's too close to the river. The noise of the water crashing against the pillars is so loud it penetrates my dreams too.' I tried to laugh. 'You'll think me an old fool, but I have nightmares that the water is pouring in and I am drowning.'

Cygnus didn't smile.

'Why don't you try sleeping up in the chapel for a night or two until you are rested, Cygnus? The dreams will stop then, I'm sure.'

He didn't reply. He hesitated for a minute, then turned to face me, stripping off his shirt until his folded wing was exposed. He unfurled his wing and as he did so, more feathers fell from it and were caught up by the wind. There were large gaps now in the wing, and in the bright winter sunshine, those feathers that remained were no longer smooth and white, but matted and grey. Cygnus held out his good arm and caught a falling feather in his hand before it was whisked away by the wind. He held it out to me, like a child offering a flower.

'Why is this happening, Camelot? I thought all I had to do was believe in my wing, but I'm losing my faith and the swans sense it, they know I am betraying them. They come to make me believe again, but the new feathers do not grow. I can't believe in them any more. I can't believe enough to make them grow again.'

Osmond and Jofre tumbled through the door of the chantry, their arms linked and waving limp ducks in the air like favours at a tournament. Osmond was dripping wet and Jofre was caked in mud, but Jofre's eyes were sparkling and his cheeks flushed with cold and exertion. Rodrigo and Zophiel followed behind them at a more sedate pace, carrying fish and nets. Between them they had caught three ducks and even a few small trout, despite Zophiel complaining that the river was too churned-up and fast-flowing for good fishing. But even so, among eight hungry people, the ducks and fish would not go far, especially as we had little else to add to them. Still, we had reason to be thankful for it was a better meal than many would have that day.

Osmond threw his birds on to the floor of the chapel and told, amid much laughter, how he had accidentally slipped down the bank into the water and had only been saved from a full ducking by Jofre grabbing him, before his head went under. Adela, once reassured that he had neither broken any bones, nor cracked his head, fretted that he would catch his death of cold. So she insisted he strip off his wet clothes while she fetched dry ones from their pack in the chamber below. Osmond meekly did as he was bid and stood naked waiting for her to return, shivering and hugging his arms around him. He had lost weight these past few weeks and gained muscles which sculpted his body. Beads of water glistened on the fine golden hairs of his chest and he slapped at his body to warm it, for Adela, encumbered by the great bulge of her baby, was taking a long time to find him some clothes.

His teeth chattering, Osmond picked up his wet shirt and chucked it at Jofre's head. 'Don't just stand there staring, idiot. Fine friend you are, saving a man from the river only to let him freeze to death. For pity's sake, get me a blanket or something.'

Jofre seemed to come out of a trance and reaching for his own cloak held it out, but Osmond, numb with cold, fumbled and dropped it.

Zophiel looked up from sorting the nets and lines. 'What's the matter with you, boy? Anyone would think he was a naked woman you were too scared to touch. Wrap the cloak round him and give him a good rub with it. Get his blood flowing to warm him. The last thing we need is him falling sick of ague.'

Jofre flushed scarlet and picked up the cloak from where it had fallen, but Rodrigo stepped quickly forward and took it out of his hands.

'I will do it. You are as cold as he is. Go down to the brazier, get warm.'

Jofre stumbled towards the stairs without a word. Rodrigo wrapped the cloak around Osmond's shoulders and pummelled him vigorously, until Osmond laughingly protested that he'd rather die of cold than be beaten to death. At that moment Adela returned with dry clothes.

We ate in the chapel. None of us could bear to go down into the dark, damp crypt to eat our Christmas feast. The winter sun shining through the windows, though not warming, filled the chapel with a light that we had craved for so long, and we drank it in like hungry prisoners who have been kept for months in a dungeon. Dappled lights from the river below were reflected up on to the white wall of the chapel, sending an endless pattern rippling across its surface, like shoals of tiny rainbow fish.

In defiance of Osmond's warning, Adela went out of her way to include Cygnus in the light-hearted chatter and ensure that he received a good share of the meats. Cygnus had returned in a melancholic humour, but even he could not fail to be seduced by the irresistible aroma of roasted duck and trout and, recognizing Adela's efforts to include him, tried his best to conceal his melancholy thoughts.

We ate our food slowly to make it last, not easy when

you are hungry, washing each mouthful down with ale that was beginning to turn sour. We cracked open the ducks' skulls and scooped out the roasted brains, no more than a mouthful, but every mouthful counts, and sucked at the feet which had been set to boil with the last handful of beans. When every piece of flesh had been stripped from bird and fish, we tried to pretend to one another that we were full, though our stomachs told us we were lying, and sat chewing the ends of the duck bones to extract every last flavoursome mouthful.

Rodrigo wistfully began to describe the Christmas banquets he had enjoyed in his lord's employ: the dancing and singing, the gaming and cock fights and the lewd games played by the young men and women, in which all normal decorum was cast aside for the Christmas season. He told us, much to Adela's giggling embarrassment, how the men had fastened huge false cocks on themselves and chased the women. How men and women changed clothes and played at being the opposite sex, the men mincing and simpering in their kirtles, while women strode about belching and shouting orders. Then the women would climb on to the men's backs and ride them like horses in races around the hall and end in a great tangled tumble among the rushes, giggling and laughing.

Then, Rodrigo said, came the feast itself with its endless procession of pages and servants bearing in stews and breads, puddings and pies. There were swans, geese, partridges, larks and great haunches of venison. And to crown the feast, a succulent roasted boar would be carried by four servants staggering under the weight of it. It would be glazed so that its skin shone in the torchlight and garlanded with holly, ivy and mistletoe and set about with roasted crab apples and dried fruits.

Rodrigo's descriptions of the food were making us as hungry as if we had not eaten at all, and in the end, to stop him talking about food, Zophiel told him to do his duty as a musician and play something. Rodrigo smiled broadly as if he had just been waiting to be asked. He took up the pipes for once instead of his beloved lute and began to play the familiar strains of an old carol-dance. Cygnus, his dark mood pushed aside for the moment, got to his feet and gravely bowed to Adela.

'Will you honour me with a dance, m'lady?'

Osmond started to his feet as if to protest, but Adela had already laughingly refused with a shake of her head and her hand on her swollen belly. 'You do me great honour, m'lord, but I fear I could not waddle, never mind dance.'

Cygnus then turned to Narigorm and took her by the hand, pulling her to her feet. 'Then, little mistress, I must beg a dance from you. Will you join us, m'lord Osmond, for we must have four at least?'

Osmond, already standing, looked as if he would refuse, but at Adela's urging he finally conceded, made a stiff bow, then looked round for a partner. A dark look from Zophiel was enough to warn all of us that while it might be Christmas, there were still some liberties that should not be taken, not if you valued your life. So, since he obviously considered that my dancing days were long over, Osmond marched across and grabbed Jofre by the hand.

'Come, pretty maid, you shall dance with me. Now don't be shy,' he added as Jofre tried to pull away.

'Come on, Jofre,' Adela called out. 'You must or you'll spoil the fun.' Jofre reluctantly allowed himself to be dragged into the ring. Rodrigo started up the carol again and the four of them pranced around, weaving round one another in a parody of a dance. Soon they were all laughing helplessly as they repeatedly turned the wrong way and collided. They tried to shout out steps to one another which left them in worse confusion, until Adela, tears of merriment streaming down her face, begged them to stop for she had a stitch in her side from laughing too much. While little Narigorm, giggling louder than any of us, begged to do it all again.

Breathless and still laughing, they collapsed on to the floor of the chapel. Osmond, scarlet in the face, waggled a finger at Zophiel.

'Come, we let you off the dance, so now it is your turn to entertain us.'

Zophiel smiled, not ungraciously. 'I see, my friend, that you have appointed yourself King of the Feast, but it is the custom, is it not, that the one finding the bean in his pudding is the rightful lord. You must present your bean, if we are to obey you.'

Osmond laughed. 'I fear we have eaten every bean in the place.'

'Surely not, my lord.' Zophiel leaned forward and, placing one cupped hand under Osmond's chin, tapped him smartly on the back. As Osmond opened his mouth in a gasp at the slap, a dry bean shot into Zophiel's cupped hand. The surprised look on Osmond's face made us all burst out laughing. It was an old trick, but neatly done.

'Now that you have presented your bean, my lord, your wish is my command. What would you have me do?'

'Amuse me, my man,' Osmond said, leaning back against Adela's legs and waving his hand regally.

Zophiel bowed his head and after rummaging around in his boxes, returned with several objects concealed under a cloth. He first withdrew from the cloth a wooden goblet and placed a white marble ball in it. He covered the goblet and when he showed us the contents again, the ball had turned black. Next a dead toad in a glass bottle was brought back to life and hopped around, trying in vain to leap out. Then Zophiel placed an egg on a cloth and when he passed over it with a stick, the egg rose by itself several inches into the air, before dropping again on to the cloth.

At each new trick, Adela clapped her hands with delight like a small child and the others smiled, gasped and laughed in turn. Only Jofre had fallen silent. He did not join in the applause and laughter, remembering, no doubt, the time he had first encountered Zophiel and had been goaded by him into betting heavily on the outcome of such tricks. He had good reason to be wary; we both knew that at any moment Zophiel might choose to remind him of it and humiliate him in front of the company. But Zophiel, it seemed, had entered into the Christmas spirit of goodwill and for once was refraining from tormenting anyone. He smiled with satisfaction at our gasps of admiration and bowed gravely after each round of applause.

'And now we must have a story,' Osmond commanded, turning expectantly to Cygnus. 'No Christmas feast is complete without one.'

Narigorm wriggled around to look at him. 'Not Cygnus, Adela should tell it. She must, she's Queen of the Feast, so she must do something.'

Adela shook her head. 'Cygnus is the storyteller. I don't know any stories.'

'Tell us about how you and Osmond fell in love then,' Narigorm persisted.

Cygnus smiled encouragingly. 'Come on, Adela. I'm sure that is a romantic story, a better one than ever I could tell.'

'No, leave her, let her rest,' Osmond protested.

Zophiel snorted. 'She can speak while she rests, can't she, or is she too feeble even to do that? I, for one, would be intrigued to know your story. You have never told us what brought you on the road. I imagine your parents did not approve of the match, which is why you find yourself homeless.'

Adela glanced at Osmond. His face was flushed, but it was hard to know if it was from anger or embarrassment. She bit her lip, then began.

'When I was fourteen years old my parents betrothed me to a man named Taranis. He was twenty years older than I was, wealthy and powerful, and I was afraid of him for although he was courteous, he had cold eyes and I saw from the way he treated his servants that he was cruel. He was impatient to marry straight away, but I pleaded so desperately against it that my parents persuaded him to wait a year until I should prove more willing. But they were adamant that sooner or later I must marry him. As the month of my wedding crept closer, my despair grew deeper. Each day when I went to the well to draw water, I would look down and see my own reflection mirrored in the dark cold depths, and each day I saw myself growing paler and thinner.

'Then, on the night of my fifteenth birthday, I had a dream. A man, a stranger to me, climbed in through my window and came quietly to my bed. He was young and strong. His eyes were soft and full of gentleness. He told me that I was the beat of his heart, the breath of his life, his soul's desire. He touched me and I melted to his touch. He kissed me and love leaped up in my breast. All night we lay in each other's arms. Then, as the cock crowed, he slipped away. I begged him to come again and he promised he would on condition that I told no one of my dream for if I did he would be lost to me for ever.

'The next few weeks were the happiest of my life. My

nights were spent in his arms and my days were spent dreaming of the nights. Now when I went to gaze down into the well, I saw the flush of love bloom on my cheeks and the laughter dancing in my eyes. But my cousin grew suspicious. She could see I was in love, and she coaxed me and teased me about it for days. "What harm can it do to tell me? I'm your cousin; you can trust me."

'I was bursting to share my great joy with someone, so in the end I told her. But my cousin was filled with jealousy and went straight to Taranis and he told her what to do. That night when I fell asleep, unknown to me, she bolted the window and the door.

'At midnight I heard Osmond's voice at the window. "Why have you shut the window against me? What have you done? I cannot come to you again."

'I ran to the window and flung it wide, but it was too late – he was gone. The next day when I went to the well and looked down into the dark, icy water, I saw not the reflection of my own face, but the face of Osmond. His eyes were open, but he could not see me.

'I went to the ancient woman who keeps the bees, for she has many wise ways, and I asked her how I could reach Osmond.

'"He lies at the bottom of the well. He is not yet dead, but he is dying. Taranis has conjured a Sending from the bone of a dead man and sent it against him. As the Sending draws nearer, he will grow weaker and in three days he will die."

'"How can I stop it?" I begged her.

'"With the bone of his bone. You must go to the grave at midnight and take the thighbone of the corpse Taranis used to conjure the Sending. You must drill a hole in it and descend with it to the bottom of the well."

'I did as she said, though I was very frightened. At midnight I went to the graveyard. Shadows ran under the moon and voices whispered through the yew trees. There were many graves and I did not know which one Taranis had used. But then I heard the voice of a man crying, "Give me back my bone." I crept forward and saw the skeleton of a man risen half out of the grave, trapped up to his kneecaps in grave mould. I was terrified, but I thought of Osmond's face and so I ran forward and snatched away his thigh bone. But though I had faced fear, I knew I could never jump down into that deep black water.

'The next day I returned to the well and, looking down, saw the face of Osmond again. His eyes were closed as if he was sleeping. But I was too afraid to jump in for I knew I would drown.

'On the third day, I looked down into the well and Osmond's face was as pale as death. I wept bitterly. Osmond was dead and I could not bear to live. My fear of life without him was greater than my fear of death. I closed my eyes and jumped.

'The icy water closed over me and I sank down and down into the blind, black depths, but when I opened my eyes, I discovered I was in a round chamber. The walls shone with many pale colours like the rainbows in a waterfall. The floor was as soft as moss and in the middle of the chamber stood a great round bed, hung about with curtains glistening like green water weed. Osmond was lying on the bed. His skin was as cold as stone, his lips blue and his breath was very faint. I tried to shake him, but I could not rouse him, I kissed him, but his lips did not respond to mine. Then, as I sat in despair watching over him, I saw a fly crawling across his face. I tried to brush it away, but it kept buzzing around his head. I raised the thighbone to try to kill it, and the words of the old woman came into my head, "With the bone of his bone".

'As I said the words the fly alighted on the bone and crawled into the little hole. I stopped the hole with my finger and at once Osmond's eyes opened and he sat up.

'I told him what had happened, and he quickly sealed the hole in the bone with a rag torn from his shirt, for he knew the fly was the Sending sent by Taranis to kill him. Now that the Sending was trapped in the bone, Osmond commanded it to take us from the well and far away across the hills, for we knew that once Taranis had discovered the Sending had failed, he would conjure another, more powerful one. As soon as we were safe, we wrapped the bone in a baby's caul and tossed it into the middle of a bog where the Sending could do no harm.

'For six days we were happy, radiant with joy. Osmond's eyes shone with my smiles and my mouth sang with his kisses. All through the day we walked hand in hand, delighting in each other's company, and all night we lay side by side, joyous in the heat of our passion.

'But on the seventh day my cousin looked into the black waters of the well and saw me lying naked on the silken sheets beside Osmond. Full of rage and jealousy, she went to Taranis. He conjured another Sending, a more terrible Sending, in the form of a flayed bull that dragged its bloody skin behind it. As it drew close, Osmond grew sleepy and I could not rouse him. It carried me off from Osmond's bed while he slept. It set me down in a great granite castle. The floors were made of white marble and the beds were made of iron. Taranis placed a heavy chaplet upon my head that bruised my skin. He weighed down my neck with chains of emeralds and about my wrists he twisted bracelets of rubies that cut me whenever I moved. I wandered from room to room, weeping, for everything was cold and hard; there was no warmth or softness anywhere in the castle. He tried to force himself upon me, but I fought him. He tried to woo me with gifts, but the gifts that he brought me were dead things.

'So I fled the castle and wandered though the land seeking Osmond until my clothes were torn to rags and my shoes were worn away. And naked I came at last to the sea and to the shore of the singing rocks.

'I went to the first rock and asked, "Where can I find my love?"

'The rock said, "Give me payment for my song."

'So I cut off my hair and gave it to the rock, but the rock's song was without words. And without my hair I was ashamed.

'I came to a second rock and asked, "Where can I find my love?" And I cut off my breasts and gave them to the rock, but the rock's words had no letters. And without my breasts I could not suckle a child.

'To the third rock I gave my feet, but the rock's letters were without meaning. And without my feet I could not dance.

'To the fourth rock I gave my hands, but the rock's notes had no pattern. And without my hands I could neither weave nor spin.

'To the fifth rock I gave my eyes, but the rock's song was without a tune. And without my eyes I could neither write nor read.

'To the sixth rock I gave my ears and if the sixth rock answered me with a song, I could not hear it.

'Then I came to the seventh and last rock, and asked, "Where can I find my home and my love?"

'And I let the rock cut out my tongue. And without my

tongue I had no voice. All that was left of me was my tears and my tears fell into the hollow of the rock and become a pool on the shore of the sea.

'But all this while, Osmond had been searching for me. He had found the castle of Taranis, and there they had fought until Osmond had overpowered him and killed him. Hearing the commotion, my cousin came rushing in, but all she found left of Taranis were three tiny drops of blood on the white marble floor.

'Osmond seized her and threatened to kill her likewise unless she told him where I was. She looked into the well and there, in the black water, she saw the singing rocks and the pool of tears. But she warned him that at the next spring tide, the sea would break over the pool of tears and he would never find me for I would become just a drop of water in the vast seas.

'Osmond searched for me for many weeks and finally, on the evening of the first of the spring tides, he came to the singing rocks, and at the first rock he found my hair and smelt it. He found my breasts and caressed them. He bathed my feet. He kissed my hands. He cried into my eyes. He whispered love into my ears and poured honey on my tongue until finally he came to the pool of my tears. But it was growing late and the waves were already crashing on to the rocks, each higher than the last. He had all that was me, yet he did not have *me* and he did not know how to make me whole again. He called my name forwards and backwards, he tried to scoop up the tears and carry them away, but they slid through his fingers, and all the while the sun was sinking and the waves were crashing higher and higher until they almost touched the lip of the pool.

'Then, as the next wave rushed towards the rocks, he remembered the words of the old woman. "With the bone of his bone." He quickly drew out his knife and cut off the third bone of his little finger and dropped it into the pool of tears. At once I lay whole again in the pool, but I did not breathe. I was like one drowned, for the wave had splashed into the pool and my spirit had already begun to float adrift out into the wide vast sea. But as Osmond reached out to touch my face, three drops of the blood from his bleeding finger dropped into my mouth and my eyes opened. And our tears then were tears of joy.'

Adela reached over and drew Osmond's paint-stained hand towards her, kissing it, before holding it up to show the missing top of his finger. Osmond blushed and hastily pulled his hand away.

Cygnus clapped his hand enthusiastically against the stones of the floor. 'Well done, Adela. That is a beautiful love story. It is you that should be the storyteller, not me.'

Rodrigo slapped him lightly on the back. 'Come, Cygnus. You must better it.'

Cygnus protested he could not, but instead told us the comic tale of the fools who try to rescue the moon from the river. As he told the tale he gibbered and capered around the chapel, making such a mime of trying to rake out the moon from an imaginary river that we were all soon helpless with mirth again. Only Jofre did not join in the laughter, but sat lost in his own thoughts.

It may not have been as grand as the Christmas festivities that Rodrigo had described, but for a few hours at least we had contrived to forget our own fears and the misery of what lay outside the chapel. But now the afternoon was drawing to a close and shadows were lengthening in the chapel. The merriment had died away and we sat reluctantly preparing ourselves for another cold night down in the crypt. I thought of Pleasance lying alone in the dark forest and felt guilty at laughing again so soon.

Osmond sprawled on the floor, his head resting on Adela's outstretched legs. He was lost in his own thoughts, gazing up at the painting at the far end of the chapel, as if he was itching to get back to it.

'How goes the painting, Osmond, are you making progress?' I asked.

'Her face is finished and I have made a start on her hands. It's usual to leave the face until last, but I don't know how long we will be here and I wanted to complete that at least.'

'Can I see?' Narigorm asked suddenly.

Osmond smiled indulgently. 'Of course, you shall see it when it's finished.'

'But you said her face was finished. Why can't I see her face now?'

Osmond, laughing, shook his head. 'Don't be so impatient.'

Adela joined in. 'Please, Osmond. It would be such a comfort to me to know she can at last look down upon us. And as you say, if we have to leave before she is finished, we may never see it.'

Osmond was visibly torn between his desire to show off his painting and his wish to keep it covered until it was complete. But Adela's pleading won out and he rose and climbed up the scaffolding, pulling aside the cloth which hung down from the scaffolding plank. He leaped down from the scaffolding and stood aside.

He hauled Adela to her feet and led her across to the sanctuary. We moved behind them and stood looking up. Adela gasped, her eyes bright with tears, and buried her head in Osmond's shoulder. It was plain to see why she was moved. The face of the Madonna was beautiful and it was unmistakably that of Adela, even down to the wisp of flaxen hair which peeped out from underneath the white veil.

Most artists take the face of the woman they love – their wife, daughter or mistress – as the model for the Madonna. There have been popes and bishops who have insisted the face of their whores should be used as the face of the Virgin, so we should not have been surprised that Osmond should take his own young wife as the model.

Rodrigo broke the silence. '*Bellissima*, Osmond. She is lovely. The face, the eyes, such gentleness and compassion.'

Osmond, beaming with pride, said modestly, 'It is thanks to you, Rodrigo. It is the trick you taught me with the oil. The paint dries much more slowly than using egg tempera, so it is possible to work more slowly and carefully to blend the tones and shadows.'

He was right. The face had a lifelike quality that I had never seen in a painting before, the skin so warm and the eyes so alive that it looked as if at any moment the smiling lips would part and speak.

Rodrigo bowed. 'Not my oil, but your talent. You have a great gift and you have a model beautiful enough to inspire any artist.'

He kissed his fingertips to Adela. Smiling delightedly, she raised her face and kissed Osmond on the cheek.

We all looked round as the heavy door to the chapel suddenly slammed behind us.

Zophiel called out sharply, 'Who's there?' He strode across to the door.

'No one,' Narigorm said. 'Jofre went out. He slammed the door.' Then, seeing our puzzled expressions, she gave her knowing little smile. 'Jofre doesn't like it that Osmond painted Adela.'

Adela looked puzzled. 'Why? Does it offend him that a pregnant woman is painted as the Virgin?'

With a cold lump in the pit of my stomach, I suddenly realized what Narigorm was hinting at and tried to stop her saying it. How could the little brat have known, unless she had overheard Jofre and me talking in the barn that night after his whipping? But even if she had, nothing had actually been put into words. Was she really that astute?

I broke in quickly, 'Jofre quickly gets bored once he has nothing to entertain him and goes off on his own. He's always done that. It's nothing to do with the painting.'

Narigorm fixed me with a wide, innocent stare. 'But it has. Jofre is jealous. He wants Osmond to paint him, not her.'

I glanced at Rodrigo who looked distraught.

Zophiel too had seen the expression on Rodrigo's face. A look of triumph spread slowly across Zophiel's sharp features as if he had just discovered a great secret.

'So that's the way our young friend bends, is it? I've always wondered about men who choose to spend their life playing pretty tunes instead of earning their living in manly toil. Now it seems I was correct.'

'I'd hardly call magical tricks and exhibiting mermaids manly toil, Zophiel,' I said coldly.

But before Zophiel could reply, Osmond broke in. 'What are you trying to suggest, Zophiel?'

'Isn't it obvious? Haven't you noticed how he's always watching you and Adela? It has been so ever since you joined us. I thought it was your wife he fancied, but now it seems you spoke truer than you know when you called him a pretty maid this afternoon. Haven't you noticed how eager he is always to go out alone with you to hunt for the pot?'

Osmond blushed furiously.

'Of course he's eager to go out hunting with Osmond. What could be more natural for a lad?' I said firmly. 'The two of them are closest in age. A young boy like Jofre doesn't want to spend time in the company of old dotards like us; he wants to be around other young people.'

Zophiel looked highly amused. 'But most young men would prefer to spend their time flirting with a beautiful woman, than hunting with her husband. If I were you, Osmond, I'd keep my backside against the wall whenever he's around.'

Osmond was looking more angry and uncomfortable by the minute. 'But I swear I've done nothing to encourage him. I'm not like that. How could he think I was one of those . . .'

I glared at Zophiel who was smirking, thoroughly enjoying the look of panic and embarrassment on Osmond's face.

'He doesn't think anything of the sort, Osmond,' I said. 'If Jofre seeks out your company it's because he has come to regard you as an older brother. You can paint, hunt, swim, do all those things which any young lad would admire. Furthermore, you have a beautiful wife. What young lad wouldn't hero-worship you? He wants to be like you and naturally he wants to win your approval, nothing more. Did you never feel the same at his age for someone you admired?'

'No, I did not,' he said firmly.

Adela came and took him by the arm. 'You did. Don't you remember how you used to trail after Edward D'Fraenger when you were young? You'd try all kinds of tricks to get him to notice you and . . .' She broke off abruptly and shot a scared glance at Zophiel. 'I mean . . . that's what you told me once.'

Rodrigo, looking suddenly old and drawn, walked towards the door. 'I must look for Jofre; it will be dark soon.'

'Wait,' Cygnus called after him. 'I'll come too. I need to check on Xanthus.'

Zophiel watched the door close behind them. 'Perhaps music is not the only thing Rodrigo has taught Jofre. It's easy for a master to corrupt an innocent young pupil to his own perverted taste. It would explain why he is so indulgent with him. He has an unusual fondness for the boy, wouldn't you say?'

'You see evil in everyone and everything, Zophiel.'

'Because there is evil to see, Camelot.'

17. The Stew

Rodrigo and Cygnus searched for Jofre until well after dark, but it was futile to keep looking when he evidently did not want to be found. He could have run a mile or more in any direction or he could be sulking just a few yards away in the dark, ignoring their shouts. All we could do was wait for him to return whenever he was ready.

Jofre did return, but not until the small hours of the morning. Zophiel had, of course, insisted on barring the chapel door as soon as it got dark, but Cygnus, Rodrigo and I had elected to sleep upstairs in the chapel, so were all awoken by his urgent hammering on the door.

'Wake ... up, wake the master of the house, I'm come a-wassailing,' he sang out in a childish falsetto.

Zophiel shouted to him that he wouldn't be allowed into the chapel until he had sobered up and that a night in the cold would serve him right. But drunks seldom go away on being told to and Jofre continued to bang and sing until Rodrigo finally pushed Zophiel aside and unbarred the door. When he opened it, Jofre, who had evidently been leaning against it for support, tumbled straight into Rodrigo's arms and thence to the floor where he lay giggling. A small barrel rolled out of his arms, making a loud rumble on the stone floor. Zophiel stopped it with his foot, took out the stopper and sniffed the contents.

'Wine.' He tipped a few drops of the red liquid into his cupped hand and tasted it. 'Strong too. Where did he get this?'

Rodrigo grabbed Jofre by the front of his shirt and dragged him to his feet. Jofre swayed unsteadily. 'You heard him, *ragazzo*, where did you get this?'

Jofre hiccuped. 'My friend gave it . . . to me.'

'What friend?' Rodrigo shook him.

Jofre flung his arms wide. 'I have lots of friends . . . lots and lots. A dragon and knights and big, big Saracens with curved swords. There were lots of swords . . . and a dragon. Did I tell you about the dragon?' He sank to his knees and closed his eyes, swaying.

'Mummers,' I said. 'He must have run into a crowd of mummers and gone drinking with them. If there's a drop of strong drink to be found anywhere in a town, you can be sure the mummers will sniff it out. Likely some of the taverns have been holding back a few barrels for the Christmas celebrations.'

Rodrigo released his grasp on Jofre's shirt and the lad crumpled on to the floor, curled up like a baby and instantly fell asleep.

Rodrigo turned away in disgust and strode over to the window, looking out down into the dark, swirling river.

He slapped the wall and turned back to face us, a mixture of anger and bewilderment on his face. 'Why does he do this? He was behaving better these last few weeks. I thought he had learned his lesson.'

'You can't blame any young lad for getting drunk at Christmas,' I told him. 'I dare say anyone who can afford it is drunk tonight in the town.'

'Which means,' Zophiel said tartly, 'that Jofre went into the town and has been drinking in some rat-hole where he could have picked up any contagion and brought it back here. And those drinking dens are teeming with thieves and cutpurses, anyone of whom could have got our young friend here to tell them where he was staying. Are you still going to excuse him, when they follow him out here to cut our throats and take whatever we have?'

'And just what have we got that is worth stealing, Zophiel? What are you so anxious to protect?' I snapped.

But if I hoped to goad him into revealing anything about the contents of his precious boxes, I was wasting my time. Even when woken in the middle of the night, Zophiel's wits were still scythe-sharp. He eyed me coolly.

'The wagon, a horse, your *genuine* relics, Rodrigo's instruments, why, even an old rag is worth the stealing to a man who is naked. We may not be rich, but still we have much that some might covet, don't you agree, Camelot?'

We had all longed for the rain to stop, but now that it had, the weather grew colder and the wind icier. The weak sun which shone through the clearing skies may have raised our spirits, but it did nothing to warm our chilled bones. Food was our biggest concern. Our stores were gone and we were reliant on what we could gather or catch and that was no easy task.

But hunger was not the only thing which kept each of us locked in our own silent thoughts. Cygnus looked even more exhausted and wretched than before. Despite sleeping in the chapel, nightmares repeatedly disturbed his sleep, much to the irritation of Zophiel, who told him that if he couldn't control his own mouth, he should sleep outside in the empty wagon where only Xanthus would be disturbed.

Adela, now that Christmas had come and gone with no sign of the birth, was becoming more fretful and demanding by the hour. Torn between wanting the baby out of her body, and fear of the labour beginning, she was afraid to let Osmond out of her sight to go hunting in case the pains started and he wasn't there. Osmond not only had Adela to fret over, now he could hardly bear to look Jofre in the face. He went out of his way to avoid being alone with him and made a point of asking Zophiel or Rodrigo to help him with the netting of birds or hunting, tasks neither of them was skilled at, but Narigorm eagerly offered to go in their stead. And Osmond, though reluctant to take her, had to admit that even experienced hunters would be hard put to match her persistence and patience when stalking prey. Any offers of help from Jofre were refused with some feeble excuse which both baffled and hurt him. Zophiel took every opportunity to goad him, but even so Jofre did not at first appear to see the connection between Zophiel's taunts and Osmond's coldness.

It was on the feast of St John the Apostle, two days after Christmas, that matters came to a head. Jofre, Zophiel and I were alone in the chapel. We had woken to find our breath hanging like white mist in the air and a hard frost outside. Every blade of grass sparkled white in the watery sunshine and the ruts of mud were frozen into rock-hard ridges. The river was too fast-flowing to freeze over, but the puddles in the road had turned to glass. Xanthus stood under the trees, stamping her feet and snorting puffs of steam through her pink nostrils. Cygnus had already gone out to lead her to the river to drink, for her own bucket of water, put out the night before, was frozen solid.

Osmond and Adela were jubilant when they saw the glittering branches of the trees. It was what we had been waiting for, what all England had been praying for. Surely the pestilence would now die away, as all summer fevers did, banished by the ice of winter. I fervently prayed it would be so, but as Zophiel had said, this summer we'd had no heat to breed the fever and still it had burned. But then, if the winter frosts did not kill it, what in heaven or earth could?

I was about to set out to see what I could forage when Osmond came up from the crypt below, his fowling nets over his arm and Narigorm at his side. On catching sight of Jofre, he hesitated, but then recovered himself and strode purposefully towards the chapel door without glancing at him.

'Wait, Osmond,' Jofre called. 'If you're going fowling, I'll come with you.'

Osmond grabbed Narigorm by the shoulder and held her in front of him as if she was a human shield.

'No, I can manage the nets with Narigorm. Why don't you take the sling into the woods? If we don't find many ducks, we shall need some pigeons or partridge, and maybe you'll catch some rabbits, that'll be good eating.'

Jofre did not appear to notice Osmond's embarrassment. He picked up his cloak. 'I can go sling-hunting later. The banks will be icy and the river's in flood. Narigorm won't be able to hold you if you slip. You could both be swept away. Better the two of us go, then we can look out for each other.'

'I said no,' Osmond snapped.

Jofre recoiled at the vehemence of his tone.

'We'll get many more birds between us, Jofre, if we work separately from now on,' Osmond muttered, and rushed Narigorm out of the door before another word could be said, leaving Jofre standing in the chapel looking like a puppy that's been kicked and doesn't know why.

'It appears you have been jilted, my pretty maid,' Zophiel drawled. Jofre gave no sign that he realized he was being addressed. He dropped his cloak and crossed to the window, where he stood looking out, lost in thought.

'Leave him alone, Zophiel,' I warned quietly. 'We don't need any more trouble.'

Zophiel ignored me. 'What a picture, a broken-hearted maiden standing at the window, watching her lover depart. You should write a song about it, Jofre.'

Jofre turned at the mention of his name.

'Did you say something, Zophiel?'

'I was merely remarking on what a tragic picture you make; the jilted virgin waiting in vain for her lover. But then, you are not exactly a virgin, are you, Jofre? I imagine you have had numerous lovers already.'

Jofre was too preoccupied to follow the subtleties of this conversation, but he reddened slightly at the mention of lovers.

'Not as many as you've had, Zophiel,' he replied insolently.

'No? Pity.' Zophiel studiously brushed some dirt from his sleeve. 'Too bad this one's married then.'

'If you're talking about Adela, I have no interest in her except as a friend.'

I winced for I knew he had walked right into Zophiel's trap.

'No, I thought as much. Your tastes don't run to skirts, do they, Jofre? I've heard it said that some men find the meat of the cock more to their taste than the breast of the hen. Personally, I find it loathsome and revolting. Still, as

I say, how unfortunate for you this particular cock is married. Who knows, you and your *master* might have managed –'

Jofre, suddenly comprehending, flushed with anger. He flew at Zophiel, his fists raised.

Zophiel, laughing, neatly sidestepped him.

I stepped between them. 'Leave it, Jofre, can't you see he's trying to bait you? Go and take your anger out on the birds with your sling, where it will do some good.'

I bundled up his cloak, thrust it into his arms and pushed him towards the door.

As I opened it, Zophiel called out, 'I'm afraid your friend Osmond will be keeping his clothes on in your company from now on, boy, but if your tastes run to cock birds, you might try a bit of swan. I'm sure he'd be grateful; after all, a freak like him can't be getting much either.'

It took all my strength to stop Jofre smashing his fist into Zophiel's face, something I was itching to do myself.

I returned to the chapel late in the afternoon with half a sack of beechnuts, hazelnuts and acorns. It had taken several hours to gather what little I had for, judging by the churned-up soil, either wild boar or the local pigs had been foraging heavily in the area for mast. The beechnuts would take an age to shell, but we had little else to do in the dark evenings and they could be dried for flour, if we could restrain ourselves from nibbling them for long enough. The door was unbarred and I was surprised to find the chapel empty, but I could hear Cygnus's voice drifting up from the crypt below. It sounded as if he was telling Adela a tale to keep her occupied. I barred the door to the chapel before joining them and found the two of them huddled round the brazier in the crypt. They smiled as I came into the room.

'No sign yet, Adela?' I asked her.

She shook her head.

'It'll come in its own time. Be thankful you can rest now for when the baby does come, you won't have a minute's peace for years to come.'

Cygnus rose and pulled his purple cloak around his shoulders. 'If you can keep Adela company, Camelot, I'll go and see to Xanthus.'

'I'd best come up with you and bar the door behind you. Zophiel will be furious if he comes back to find it open and all his boxes left unguarded.'

Cygnus clapped his hand to his mouth. 'I left the door unbarred, didn't I? That's how you got in. I was thinking of other things and then Adela called up and . . .'

I chuckled at his horrified expression. 'No harm done, but I suggest you don't mention it to Zophiel, otherwise you may find yourself tied to the wagon again.'

I barred the door behind Cygnus and turned again to look around the chapel, just to reassure myself that, as I said to Cygnus, there was no harm done. I checked the pile of Zophiel's boxes in the corner. The stench of the mermaid permeated the room – seaweed and that bitter perfume of myrrh and aloes. I had grown so used to the smell by now that most days I no longer noticed it, then at other times, without warning, I would smell it afresh and the memories would come flooding back – the day they brought my brother's head home.

It was months after the news came that Acre had fallen. And in all those months we didn't know if he was dead or alive. He might, we told one another, even now be on his way home to us. He could be wounded. He was being nursed somewhere until his strength returned and then he'd come limping home. One day, when we least expected it, he'd walk back through the door. We went on hoping that until the day we were summoned to the solar and saw the casket on the table in front of my father and smelt that odour.

I wouldn't have recognized his head. The face was wrinkled and dark like leather, the eyelashes and beard startling white. The lips were drawn back from the teeth in an awful grin, the eyes squeezed shut as if horror-struck by something he had seen and couldn't bear to look at. They said it was his head, but I wouldn't believe it until I saw the little piece missing from his left ear where a hound had bitten him as a boy. Strange how, in the end, it is only our scars which distinguish us. My father held the head between his two hands as if my brother was again a little boy standing at his knee to receive his blessing. He did not weep. 'I can bury my son now,' was all he said.

People blamed them, you know, blamed the knights for not holding on. Even though Jerusalem had fallen many years ago, still as long as we held Acre, people believed that one day we would take the Holy Land again, but once Acre fell, a dream fell with it. They had destroyed the one last thread of hope and people could not forgive them for that. My father was one of them, saying the knights that had fled were traitors, betraying Christ and their King. My father said he'd rather his son came home on his shield than as a coward. We begged him not to say it, but he had spoken and it was too late.

Do you think words have the power to kill? Who knows where they go once they are spoken aloud; they drift off like seeds in the wind. 'Speak no evil,' my nursemaid used to say, 'for tiny demons lurk everywhere just waiting to catch your words and use them to tip their arrows with poison.' My father had spoken and now my brother was dead.

I heard Adela calling anxiously from below.

'Coming,' I said.

I glanced again at the boxes; none of them seemed to be missing. At least Zophiel wouldn't find out that Cygnus had left the door unbarred. I turned to go back down to Adela. The late-afternoon sun shone in through the window, sending long shafts of light across the stone floor. Layers of dust had accumulated since the builders abandoned the chapel. We hadn't troubled to sweep it. What was the point when we continually trailed mud in? But now, as I turned to go, I noticed something I had not seen before. Several of the boxes had been moved, swivelled out and then pushed back into their original positions, leaving fresh fan-shaped trails in the dust. Most likely Zophiel himself had moved them before going out to fish. He constantly checked them, so doubtless he had done so again that morning. For a moment I was tempted to try to open one until I heard the sounds of voices outside, Osmond and Narigorm returning. I went to unfasten the door.

Jofre didn't come back for supper. No one had seen him all day. Zophiel was adamant that no food should be left for him, since he had not contributed so much as a plucked sparrow to the pot. I have to confess that no one, not even Rodrigo or the tender-hearted Adela, put up more than a token protest, for we were so cold and hungry that even if we had wanted to save some food, I doubted we could have resisted eating his share.

As darkness fell, so the air grew colder. Down in the crypt we stacked the brazier with wood and huddled round it in our cloaks. The wood was still too damp to burn well and gave off more smoke than heat. The river rushing below seemed louder than ever. Sometimes we heard the grinding of a branch or some other object forced against the pillar of the crypt by the surging water. The stone amplified the noise so that it sounded as if some huge beast was gnawing away at the foundations of the chapel.

We were just preparing to settle down for another cold night when we heard the wolf again. A wolf's howl, however often you hear it, still sends shivers down your spine. Adela cried out in alarm, and both Zophiel and Rodrigo started to their feet.

'Is the door still barred?' Zophiel asked sharply. 'No one has been out since I barred it tonight?' He looked round at us as if he thought we might have sneaked up and opened it while he wasn't looking.

'But Jofre is still out,' Rodrigo said. 'He may be walking home. The howl came from the side of the river nearest the town. Jofre will be in danger and if he is . . . not able to defend himself . . .'

'Drunk, you mean,' said Zophiel. 'Yes, I'm afraid you may be right. When our young friend is in his cups, he's incapable of defending himself against a marauding rabbit, never mind a wolf.' The thought seemed to give him considerable satisfaction.

'Then you will go with me to find him?'

I was astounded that Rodrigo should think for one moment that Zophiel would go and I was not surprised by Zophiel's sneering refusal. 'You really think I am going to give up my sleep to go looking for that drunken little sod? Serve the boy right if he does get eaten.'

But Zophiel's hands were trembling and I knew his refusal had less to do with his contempt for Jofre than his fear of being out there in the darkness with a wolf prowling round.

We heard another howl and stiffened, listening. Adela, cringing at the sound, gazed fearfully up at the ceiling as if she thought the beast might leap through the chapel window above our heads. Osmond pulled her tightly to him. This time not even he could pretend it was a dog.

'Wolves guard the paths of the dead,' Narigorm said suddenly. My stomach lurched. Narigorm was crouching just outside the circle of flickering yellow light cast by the brazier. Her face and body were concealed in the dark shadows of the crypt, but her hands were in the pool of light, hovering over the runes. There were only three in front of her, not the whole set. I could see nothing else on the floor with them – no shells, no herbs, no feathers. I had watched Narigorm work the runes often enough to know that using only three meant she was asking a question of them. A simple question, but the answer would not be simple, that I did know. And was the wolf the question or the answer?

Zophiel strode across the room and seized the child's wrist, pulling her hand away from the runes.

'What do you mean?' he asked in a dangerously quiet tone.

Narigorm lifted her head. Twin flames reflected in the pupils of her eyes, like fire burning in ice. 'Wolves bring the spirits of the dead home, however far they have travelled.'

Cygnus shifted uneasily. 'I've heard that tale before. My mother used to tell me that the spirits of the newly dead travel the ancient straight tracks to get back to their ancestral homes. Wolves guard the tracks to make sure that the spirits of the dead are not taken from the path by demons or witches. Is that what you meant, Narigorm?'

Narigorm didn't reply but sat motionless, gazing up at Zophiel. Man and child stared at each other, both expressionless. It was Zophiel who looked away first. He dropped her arm as though he had been stung and turned abruptly on his heel.

As if a spell had been broken, Rodrigo reached for his stave and cloak. 'I am going to find Jofre.'

I leaned on my stave and prised myself stiffly to my feet, wrapping my cloak more tightly around me.

'I'll go with you, Rodrigo. I may be too old to make much of a fighter, but there is safety in numbers. A wolf won't attack a man in a crowd. Who else will come?' I looked at Osmond, but he studiously avoided my gaze and stared at the floor.

The night was clear and frosty, each star bright and sparkling in its sable bed. The moon was rounded but not quite full; tomorrow it would be. Now, though, it was bright enough to flood the bridge with opal light. Below us the water, black now, roared and surged beneath the arches. The silver moonlight glinted on its surface like scales on the back of a giant fish.

Once off the bridge, the road curved away in the darkness, running between scrubland littered with tree stumps. Rodrigo had brought a lantern as the law demands for those brave or foolish enough to be abroad at night, proof that our business was honest. An honest man, the law says, will go abroad openly and not wish to conceal his presence or identity. But what does the law say of those dishonest men who can then see the light from miles around, proclaiming a traveller ripe for the plucking? Who will protect the law-abiding from the law? Still, that night I feared the wolf more than man and the light would at least help keep that at bay. Cygnus had bravely joined us and he glanced uneasily around at the bushes on either side of the road where shadows ran and branches growled.

Suddenly Rodrigo stopped dead and pointed. 'Over there,' he hissed. A pair of eyes, low to the ground, glowed in the flame. For a moment neither we nor it moved, then it turned its head and began to slip away. We caught sight of the red bushy tail and breathed a sigh of relief; a fox, only a fox. We continued on our way. Our eyes and ears began to hurt with the strain of looking and listening for any sign of the wolf, but there was none.

There was no sign of Jofre either on the road, even though the curfew bell in the town had rung an hour since. We reached the town gate. A steep embankment, topped with a wattle fence, marked the town boundary. It was in poor repair, not much defence against anyone except old dotards like me who can no longer scramble over fences. A town like this could not afford a wall. As we expected, the cart gate in the wooden gatehouse which straddled the road was firmly shut.

I rapped on the wicket gate with my staff. A small grilled shutter in the gate opened, revealing the head of the night watchman.

'What's your business?' he growled.

'We come looking for a lad.'

'No accounting for taste.'

I ignored the remark. 'This man is the boy's master. He's come to fetch him home. The boy should have been back hours ago. You know what these young lads are, always chasing some pretty girl. Can we come in and find him?'

'Gates are locked for the night.'

'All the more reason to find him and to fetch him home. This lad's a bit of a handful once he's had a drink or two, he gets rowdy, disturbing good folks in their houses, chasing their daughters, smashing things. You don't want to be dealing with endless complaints on your watch, now do you? Let us in and we'll haul him out of here before he causes any trouble.'

The watchman hesitated.

I pushed a coin through the grill at him. 'For your trouble.'

That seemed to persuade him and the small wicket gate in the main door swung open.

Once inside we described Jofre to him, but he only shrugged, impatient to return to warming his backside at his fire. He told us no lads had passed through this gate, but then he had only been on watch since the curfew bell and Jofre had probably been in the town long before that.

We walked three abreast down the main street, hoping that we might see Jofre making his way towards the gate. The town looked even more squalid under the yellow-orange glow of the night torches. Most of the houses were dark and shuttered and only the glimmer of candlelight here and there showed through the cracks. But despite the curfew bell there were still people abroad. The taverns were open and every now and then a group of revellers would spill out. Occasionally a man would be thrown out, landing on his backside in the street if he was lucky, or face down in the sewer if he was not. The alleys and snickets were darker than before, but the odd squeal or yell which emanated from their depths suggested they were not deserted.

We drew level with the Red Dragon Inn. It was brightly lit and sounds of raucous laughter rang out from inside. However hard up they were, there were plenty of people determined to make the most of this Christmastide, whatever the rumours of pestilence or perhaps because of them.

The door of the inn opened and a girl threw a pail of slops out into the street. We all jumped back.

'Careful, girl,' I yelled. 'Mind where you're throwing that.'

She looked up. It was the same serving wench we had seen lounging outside the inn on the day we came past.

'Beg your pardon, sirs, I . . .' She suddenly smiled in recognition. 'Aren't you the gentlemen came by with a wagon a few days back?' She put the pail down and tugged at the front of her dress, revealing even more of her ample breasts. 'Managed to shake off that old tight-arse who was leading the mare, did you? Does he ever crack a smile, that one? If you're looking for a good time, you've come to the right place. You come along in with me, sirs. We'll soon see you right.'

I took a step forward. 'Maybe another time, but just now we're looking for the young lad who was with us. I don't know if you remember him. Slim, dark hair and brown eyes.'

'I remember him all right. Came here a couple of nights back with the mummers. Good-looking lad, nice manners, gentle too. He could share my bed anytime and there's not many I'd say that about. But he wasn't interested in getting between my sheets, if you get my drift. Always the way with the good-looking ones, either they're monks or mollys.'

'Have you seen him tonight?'

'Maybe.'

I fumbled in my purse; Rodrigo saw what was required and proffered a coin. The girl took it with a small bob and tucked it into her bodice.

'He's in the stew.' She caught Rodrigo's arm and pulled him a little way up the street until we came to the entrance to a dark alleyway. 'Up there second right. You'll see the sign.'

'You are sure he is there?'

'I'm sure. Someone in the Red Dragon saw him go in. More to the point, they saw who he went in with.' Her smile vanished and she gripped Rodrigo's arm urgently. 'You want to get him out of there, quick as you can. Like I say, he's a nice lad and I wouldn't want to see that pretty face of his messed up.'

Rodrigo looked alarmed. 'You think someone is going to hurt him? Why?'

'Look, if anyone asks, I haven't said anything, right?'

We nodded.

'The other night when he came in with the mummers, he started getting friendly with one of our local lads, more than friendly, if you get my drift. If your lad had gone for anyone else, no one would care what he did or who he did it with, so long as he could pay for it, but Ralph is trouble. His old man is Master of the Butchers' Guild. He owns a deal of property in the town, fingers in a lot of pies, and he'd stick them in a lot more if he could. I reckon he knows the way his son leans, must do, but he won't have it. He's arranged a marriage between Ralph and the daughter of a baron who owns a dozen farms round these parts. You can see how it would be a good match; the baron produces the beasts, the butcher slaughters them. Keeps all the profits in the family, especially as the girl is the baron's only surviving child.

'Trouble is, the baron wants grandchildren, lots of them, and he wants a son-in-law who'll put his back into the getting of them. If the girl's father gets a whiff of anything amiss before the wedding, it'll be off quicker than milk in a thunderstorm and Ralph's old man wouldn't take too kindly to that. Take it from me, you want to get your lad away from Ralph before his old man gets wind of it, that's if he hasn't already.' She looked round anxiously. 'There's many round here in debt to him and might think to pay it off with a little tattle.'

We thanked her and turned into the narrow little alley she had indicated. The overhang of the darkened houses blocked out the sky so that only a slim ribbon of stars could be seen between them. The alley stank of piss and worse, but fortunately whatever filth we were walking on had frozen over and we did not have to wade through it.

As the serving girl had told us, the stew was easy enough to find by the sign of the bath over the door. The woman who admitted us was friendly until she discovered we had not come to bathe and told us to clear off. But when we described Jofre, her attitude changed and she seemed grudgingly grateful for our arrival.

'Aye, well, you'd best get him out of here. I don't want trouble.' She jerked her head in the direction of one of the rooms. 'He's in there.'

We entered. The warm room was hot and steamy, smelling of wet wood overlaid by the clean sweet smell of thyme, bay and mint. Three big wooden bathtubs stood in a circle in the centre of the floor with triangular wooden canopies over the top to shield the bathers from draughts and keep the steam in. The bath-house owner clearly took great care of the customers for the tubs were lined with linen to prevent splinters. Between the tubs were several small tables. Ewers of ale and wine, and plates of roasted meats, cheese, pickled vegetables and fruits preserved in honey lay within easy reach of the bathers. I felt my stomach growl with hunger.

We didn't recognize the two young men and the girl in the tub facing the door. They wallowed up to their necks in the hot herbed water, naked save for cloths wrapped around their hair. I longed to join them. The thought of soaking my cold aching limbs in a hot tub for an hour or two seemed like heaven. It's years since I have been able to do that. Stewing in a hot tub is one of the many pleasures I have had to forego.

The occupants of the other two tubs were screened by the canopies. We moved forward. One of the young men, catching sight of us, raised his hands.

'We're full here. Try the other rooms.' Then, grinning at Rodrigo, 'We can always squeeze you in though.'

Rodrigo said gruffly, 'I have not come to bathe. I have come for my pupil.'

There was a sudden violent splash from the third tub as if someone had been startled.

I walked round. There were only two in this tub, a young man older than Jofre by a couple of years, stockier too. Even with his hair concealed by an unflattering linen cap, he was good-looking with his hazel eyes, square jaw and full lips, in many ways not unlike Osmond. The other occupant of the bath, pressed as far back under the canopy as he could get, was Jofre, his eyes wide with alarm.

In the light of the tavern girl's warning, I knew we needed to do this as quickly and quietly as possible. It was important that Rodrigo didn't lose his temper, not here. I turned to him. 'Go find one of the serving wenches to bring him his clothes.'

Rodrigo hesitated, but Cygnus grasped the situation at once and led him away.

I turned back to Jofre. 'Come on, lad, get yourself dried. It's after curfew; we need to get back to the gate before the watch changes.'

But Jofre, mutinous now after his initial scare, was not in a mood to come quietly. 'Why should I?'

His face was flushed and I realized at once that the cause had as much to do with the half-empty ewer of wine on the table as the heat of the bath.

The other lad, whom I took to be Ralph, draped his arm casually around Jofre's wet shoulders.

'He doesn't have to go. He can stay the night in the town.'

'He's apprentice to a master and his master bids him go.

He's bound by law to obey him. As you, Ralph, are bound to obey your father's wishes.'

He looked startled that I knew his name.

'And what, sir, is my father to do with you?'

'Nothing at all, and I'd like to keep it that way to preserve all our skins. If you care anything at all for Jofre, you'll encourage him to leave now for his sake, if not for yours.'

By the time Rodrigo and Osmond came back into the room with his clothes, Jofre had been persuaded to clamber unsteadily out of the bath and was attempting to dry himself. He allowed the serving maid to dress him. When the girl had finished, Jofre tossed a handful of coins on the table, with the carelessness of a young lord. He glowered at Rodrigo, then leaned over the bath and kissed Ralph passionately and defiantly on the mouth, before finally allowing himself to be conducted outside. It crossed my mind to wonder where he had got the money, but this was not the time to ask him, for as we emerged into the alley, I thought I saw a man leaning against the wall of a house a few yards away watching us. I took a firm grasp of my stave, but when we reached the place there was no one to be seen. I was annoyed with myself for jumping at shadows; still, the quicker we got out of the town, the more relieved I'd be.

Jofre walked between us, shivering in the frosty night air after the heat of the bath. He was silent and I prayed that Rodrigo would have the wisdom to hold his tongue as well, at least until we were safely back in the chantry. There were too many dark alleys and lurking shadows in this place to want to draw attention to ourselves. I glanced back over my shoulder several times, but could see no one following, though that did not make me feel any easier. There could have been a whole army hidden in the shadows. Rodrigo and Cygnus glanced nervously around too at every group of men who passed us, but no one challenged us and we finally saw the town gate ahead of us.

The watchman held out his hand for another coin to open the gate. 'So you found the young rascal, did you? Taking him home for a thrashing, are you?' He chuckled with satisfaction. 'You'll smart for this one, boy.'

I felt Jofre stiffen beside me and whispered, 'Hold your tongue, lad,' as I pushed him through the gate. I gulped in the clean cold air of the night with relief. All we had to worry about now was the wolf.

18. Birth and Death

The following day was Childermas, named for the day they massacred the Holy Innocents and the day Judas Iscariot was born, the unluckiest day of the year, they say. Some people refuse to get out of their beds on Childermas. They think the day so unlucky that they won't venture on any journey or sell goods at the market, or buy any beast, for they say, what is begun on Childermas Day will never be finished. And that particular Childermas seemed determined to live up to its ill-fated reputation.

The day began no worse than any other. We'd managed to bring Jofre back to the chantry without incident or argument and, thankfully, without encountering the wolf. Zophiel had doubtless been ready with a few well-chosen words, but he didn't get the chance to deliver them for Rodrigo hustled Jofre straight down to the crypt without giving Zophiel time to say more than, 'So the wolf did not devour him. What a disappointment.'

Rodrigo himself had not said a word to Jofre all the way home. The cold air and the long walk rapidly sobered the lad up and several times he glanced apprehensively at Rodrigo as if trying to read his mood, painfully aware that his master's silences were more dangerous than his rages. When we reached the crypt, he turned to face Rodrigo, clearly expecting a confrontation, defiance written all over his face, but Rodrigo had simply said, 'It is late, Jofre, get some sleep.' Then he turned away to his own sleeping place and lay down without another word. Jofre stood dumbfounded for a moment, absently rubbing his backside, then he too lay down in his corner and buried his face in his cloak.

But whatever retribution Jofre feared, I sensed that this time Rodrigo was not angry. Jofre's drinking and gambling, refusing to practise, wasting his talent, these things made Rodrigo angry, but not this, he did not blame Jofre for this. He'd known for a long time it was inevitable and he was afraid for him.

Breakfast was a subdued affair. Everyone was tired from the disturbances of the previous night and to break our fast we only had a thin broth boiled from the previous night's carcasses. It was quickly drunk and wearily we began to prepare ourselves for another long day out in the cold in our search for something to put on the table.

Jofre had studiously avoided meeting anyone's eye all through breakfast and now, before anyone else was ready, he hastily gathered his bag and sling.

'Going hunting,' he muttered to the floor. 'Be back before dark,' he added with a nervous glance at Rodrigo. He made for the stairs leading up to the chapel, but he only got as far as the second step.

Zophiel, descending the stairs from the chapel above, pushed Jofre back down into the crypt so savagely that the boy stumbled and fell. He scrambled to his feet and tried to make for the stairs again, but Zophiel blocked his way.

'Not so fast, my young friend. I want some answers first. Where did you go last night?'

Rodrigo stepped forward. 'He is my pupil, Zophiel. It is no business of yours where he went.'

'I think it's very much my business, Rodrigo, when it was my money he was spending.'

'You gave him money?'

'I did not *give* anything to him, Rodrigo. Jofre stole it.'

Taken aback, Rodrigo turned to look at Jofre who was staring wide-eyed at Zophiel. A dull red flush spread over the lad's face, though whether this signified anger or guilt was impossible to say.

'I thought we knew all your pupil's vices – indolence, drunkenness, gambling, *sodomy*.' He spat this last word out. 'But now it seems we must add stealing to this ever-lengthening list. Well, boy, I'll ask you again, where did you go last night?'

'I didn't steal anything,' Jofre said, his jaw clenched in fury.

Zophiel moved a step closer. 'So now we can add lying to the list as well, can we?'

'Jofre does not steal,' Rodrigo said firmly.

Zophiel kept his cold stare firmly fixed on Jofre's face. 'I notice, Rodrigo, you wisely avoiding saying – he doesn't lie. Perhaps you don't know your pupil as well as you think. Did he ever tell you, for instance, that the first time we met, Jofre lost a purse full of money to me on a wager he insisted on making to show how clever he was? He was most anxious that you did not find out about that. Perhaps he thought he'd steal from me to even the score.'

Jofre raised his chin and glared at Zophiel. 'You're the liar, Zophiel. I've never stolen any money from you.'

Zophiel smiled humourlessly. 'No, but you stole something else, didn't you, something you could sell for money in that rat-hole of a town.'

He produced a small box from under his cloak. It was about the size of a lady's jewel casket, except that this was made of plain wood, banded with iron. The lock had been prised open. He tipped it forward. A heap of straw fell with a whisper on to the flags.

'Empty, as you see. But yesterday morning it was not.'

He threw the box violently into the corner where it landed with a crash, making Adela cry out in alarm.

Zophiel ignored her and grasped Jofre by the front of his shirt, pushing his face into Jofre's. 'Who did you sell it to, boy? Answer me.'

Rodrigo pushed Zophiel aside and grasped Jofre's upper arms, swinging him round to face him. 'In the stew, you had money. Where did you get it from? You have earned nothing for weeks. Answer me, Jofre.'

Jofre, wincing, tried in vain to wriggle out of Rodrigo's iron grasp. 'I'm not a thief. I swear I didn't take anything from Zophiel. I won the money gambling on dog-fighting. I didn't tell you because I knew you'd be angry. But I didn't steal it, I swear.'

Rodrigo searched the boy's face for a few moments, then released his grip, shaking his head as though he no longer knew what to believe. Jofre backed away, rubbing the bruises on his arms.

'So you won it gambling, did you, Jofre?' said Zophiel, his tone icy now. 'I congratulate you. Your luck must have changed; you've never won at gambling before. You're as useless at that as you are at lying. So, tell me, boy, where did you get the stake money? Were your new friends so generous they let you play for free, or was the wager the contents of that box? Is that what you put up as your stake, boy, my property?'

'I never touched your fucking boxes.'

'Is that so? You know,' said Zophiel thoughtfully, 'it is Childermas today, is it not?'

Jofre looked bewildered.

'When I was a child,' Zophiel continued, 'our teacher whipped every boy in the school on Childermas to remind them of the suffering of the Holy Innocents. It's a pity to let these old customs die out.' Without warning he twisted Jofre's arm behind his back and began pushing him towards the stairs. 'I have the horse-whip upstairs. Perhaps that will loosen your tongue.'

Jofre, unable to break free, turned frantically towards Rodrigo. 'Rodrigo, please, stop him. I didn't do it, I swear!'

Rodrigo stood with his head bowed and his arms folded, unable even to look at him.

Cygnus started forward. 'Wait, Zophiel. It was me, my fault.'

Zophiel swung round, but did not relax his grip on Jofre. 'You stole from me?'

Cygnus shook his head. 'No, no, on my oath I did not, but I did leave the door to the chapel unbarred yesterday in the afternoon. I was distracted. I forgot to bar the door behind Rodrigo when he went out, then I went downstairs to talk to Adela, leaving the chapel empty. I was telling her a story to amuse her and it wasn't until Camelot came back that I realized how long we had been talking.'

'You were alone with Cygnus?' Osmond said sharply, rounding on Adela.

'Why shouldn't I be? Osmond, you know this is foolish nonsense. Cygnus wouldn't . . .' She broke off gasping, clutching at one of the trestles for support.

'Adela, are you ill?' I asked.

But Adela shook her head. 'It's nothing. A little touch of gripe, that's all.'

Zophiel cut in. 'Camelot, is this true?'

I turned back to him and nodded. 'The door was unbarred when I returned and Cygnus and Adela were down here. I'm afraid anyone could have come in and taken whatever it is that has been stolen. What is it that has been taken, Zophiel?'

He ignored the question. 'You didn't think to mention this?'

I shrugged. 'So few people pass this way and I couldn't see anything that was obviously missing when I looked about. From the dust in the floor it appeared that a few of the boxes had been moved, but you frequently check the contents yourself, Zophiel, as you did this morning, so I assumed you'd moved them yourself before you went out.'

Jofre wriggled in Zophiel's grasp. 'You see? Anyone could have taken one of your precious boxes and I wasn't even near the chantry yesterday afternoon. I was in the town. So let me go!'

He gave another violent squirm and succeeded this time in twisting himself free. He turned and glowered at Zophiel.

'Apologize, Zophiel, apologize for calling me a thief.'

'Not so fast, my young friend. Camelot is right, so few people pass this way, and if it had been a chance thief, why take the contents of a box that was under several others? Why not take the first thing he could grab, or take it all, and why bother to put everything back exactly as before? That takes time and he'd want to be out and away as fast as he could before he was discovered. No, my young friend, I think you slunk back here and finding the door unbarred and the room deserted, you took your chance, knowing that if one of us returned unexpectedly no one would question your presence. You put everything back just as it was, in the hope that I wouldn't notice the theft straight away, so I wouldn't link it to you. And I would not have done, if Narigorm had not come to tell me she'd read in the runes that something had been taken from me.'

I turned to look at Narigorm who was crouching as still as a spider in the corner. She glanced up wide-eyed from under her white lashes, but her face was without expression.

'No, my young friend,' Zophiel continued, 'what Cygnus tells me does not exonerate you; it merely explains how you did it.'

He grabbed Jofre again and pushed him up against the wall, pinning him to the wall by his throat.

'I could take you to the town bailiff and hand you over to be hanged, but I'm a merciful man. I'm not going to hand you over. I'm going to take you upstairs and I'm going to flog you, boy, until you admit the truth, even if I have to flay your back to the bone. Let's see if your cocksucking boyfriends still find you as pretty then, shall we?'

Jofre brought his knee up sharply and caught Zophiel hard in the balls. The man staggered backwards and doubled over, groaning. Jofre darted towards the stairs, as Zophiel hissed through gritted teeth, 'You'll pay for that, you lying little pervert.'

Jofre turned, tears of rage standing out in his eyes.

'Don't you touch me, Zophiel. Don't you ever touch me again. I know all about you. I know what's in those precious boxes of yours. And I bet there are others who'd love to know what you've got hidden. I don't need to steal anything from you, Zophiel; I can just sell what I know, that should be worth quite a bit, don't you think?'

Zophiel froze, the colour suddenly drained from his face. Jofre ran lightly up the stairs. We heard his feet on the floor above and then we heard the outer door slam shut. The sound seemed to startle Zophiel out of his trance and he staggered to the stairs and heaved himself up, gripping hard on the stone handrail. Again the door above us crashed shut.

Before any of us could follow there was a sharp cry behind us. Adela was leaning against the wall, clutching her belly. There was a splashing sound and a puddle of water trickled out from under her skirts. I hurried towards her.

'Here, help her to sit down,' I yelled at the dumbfounded faces around me.

Adela pushed our hands away. 'No, no.'

'Come now, Adela,' I said soothingly. 'You should be pleased the baby is at last on its way.'

'Not today. It can't be born on Childermas. The child will be cursed.'

'Your waters have broken, Adela, it's coming whether you like it or not. The best you can hope for is a long labour, so that it is not born until after midnight, but that, my girl, I would not wish on anybody.'

I turned to the others who stood around staring, immobilized. 'Osmond, you had best stay with your wife. Narigorm, we'll need water when the baby comes. You'd better fetch it now; I'll have other errands for you later. Cygnus, Rodrigo, there is nothing you can do here. You'll be more usefully employed in finding us some food. However long this takes we'll need to eat, and I don't think we can expect much help from Jofre or Zophiel today.'

I went to my pack and took out a small package wrapped in a scrap of soft leather. I led Rodrigo and Cygnus upstairs where I unwrapped the small bundle in front of them. Inside lay a shrivelled, blackened finger. The stump where the finger had been severed was covered in a cap of engraved silver, set with tiny fragments of turquoise and garnet. I wrapped it again and thrust it into Rodrigo's hand.

'Take this to the town and try to sell it.'

'But this must be valuable. I cannot do it justice.'

'You've watched me sell a saint's bones often enough to know how it's done. Besides, Cygnus will be able to spin a good tale about it even if you can't. That serving girl at the Red Dragon will know who might be interested. The money will buy the services of a midwife, there must be some woman in the town who has the skill. Then use what's left to buy anything that will fill our bellies. There's still food to be had in that town somewhere, judging by the spread in that stew, and we'll want more than a few starlings today. If there's money enough, then bring some good sweet wine too, for Adela will be needing it before the day is out.'

'I must also look for Jofre,' Rodrigo said. 'If Zophiel finds him first, he will kill him.'

Cygnus grinned broadly. 'No chance of that. Jofre is half Zophiel's age and he had a head start. Besides, that was some wallop Jofre gave him. That ought to slow him down for a bit.' His expression changed to one of concern. 'Do you think Jofre really knows what Zophiel keeps in those boxes, or was he just saying the first thing that came into his head as a way of getting back at Zophiel?'

I looked at Rodrigo and we both shook our heads.

'Either way, it hit the mark,' I said. 'But, Cygnus, don't you know what's in them? Back at the ford you started to tell us you'd seen something.'

'Not exactly seen. When I was hiding in the wagon during that day on the road, I dared not move in case any of you heard me, and that night, when I was alone and you were all inside the cottage, it was much too dark to see anything. I confess I did try to open some of the boxes, but only because I was looking for something to eat. I was starving. Mostly the ones I tried were locked. There was one that wasn't, but that just had what felt like a small plate inside, and Pleasance came out then, so I didn't have a chance to try the other boxes. It was only afterwards, when I saw how anxious Zophiel was about them, that it struck me as odd. The mermaid I can understand, but who bothers about a little plate? I doubt even a beggar would trouble to steal that.'

Rodrigo frowned. 'But you said the plate was in an unlocked box. It is what a man keeps in a locked box that –'

From the crypt there was a sharp cry from Adela and Osmond came bounding up the stairs. 'Come quickly, Camelot, I don't know what to do.'

'There is nothing to do yet. Just hold her hand when the pains come.'

Rodrigo and Cygnus scuttled to the door as if afraid they too would be called back down. Grown men who ride boldly into battle flee like startled rabbits when faced with the horrors of a birthing chamber.

Cygnus closed the door behind him, then opened it again and stuck his head round.

'One thing I forgot, Camelot, which saint does this finger belong to?'

'Whichever saint they're prepared to pay the most for. But don't get carried away, make it a minor saint, eh, Cygnus, not St Peter. That would be pushing our luck.'

It was a long day. The pains came slowly at first and Adela wouldn't rest. She ranged around the crypt, muttering prayers and even trying to conceal her pain when a wave overtook her as if, by denying it, she could prevent the child from coming until a more auspicious day. When by mid-afternoon the pains began to come faster and stronger, we made Adela as comfortable as we could, sitting her on the upturned half of a barrel, propped up by packs under her arms. When the pains came she screamed and when they subsided she cried. Osmond was alternately pacing the floor and clutching Adela's hands as if he could wring the child out of her. He looked paler and more distraught than she was and his panic was doing nothing to calm Adela.

He reluctantly helped me to undress her down to her shift, but recoiled at the suggestion he should lift the shift and massage the base of her back and her buttocks to help ease her pains.

'But she's your wife,' I told him. 'You've seen her naked before.'

'You do it,' he said, backing away.

'But she doesn't want an old man, she needs her husband.'

He shook his head vehemently. A fleeting expression of guilt and abhorrence crossed his face and in that instant I understood what I think, deep down, I had known for many weeks. Only a woman's father or brother would recoil so violently from touching her naked body at a time like this. When Osmond climbed through that window to Adela's bed, he had not been a stranger to her. I knew now why he feared the baby would be cursed.

I had no choice. I did what I could and for a while it seemed to work. But after a while not even the massaging helped. The pains redoubled and Adela was straining to push. I felt between her legs and I could feel the crowning of the baby's head. Adela's skin was tight around it. At least the baby was coming out the right way round. But it would arrive soon and there was no sign of Cygnus and Rodrigo with the midwife. I knew that if this proved anything but a straightforward birth I would not have the skill to help her.

I tried to think. It was many years since I had assisted at

the birth of a child and I tried desperately to remember what the midwives had done then. Fragments floated back to me – a reed to suck mucus out of the baby's mouth and nose and something to tie the cord. That much I remembered. Some threads from a new clean cloth would do, but where were we to get new cloth? Something to swaddle the child in, we'd need that too. But first we needed the reed. I told Narigorm to run down to the river to find some hollow reeds, but she shook her head.

'Pleasance already has reeds.'

'Pleasance is not here, Narigorm.' I snapped in exasperation. 'All would be well if she was, but she's not. Now, please go to the river as I asked.'

Adela screamed as her belly was convulsed by another wave of pain.

Narigorm stared at her indifferently for a moment, then said, 'The reeds are in Pleasance's pack. She got everything ready for Adela's baby weeks ago. 'Case it came early, she said.'

I didn't know whether to kiss her or slap her for not revealing this before.

Pleasance's pack didn't contain much: several packs of dried herbs, a few jars of ointments, the poppy juice sleeping draught, undergarments, and a linen-wrapped package. I opened the package and laid out the contents: a roll of swaddling bands, red thread to tie the cord – red for a firstborn child – some reeds, as Narigorm had said, and some agrimony to make the mother sneeze. There was also a knife with letters on it in a script I did not recognize and a small silver amulet in the shape of a hand with the same letters repeated on the open palm.

The afternoon was drawing to a close by the time we heard hammering on the door above. It was Cygnus and he was alone. He heaved a sack of beans off his back, untied a wine flagon from around his waist and stretched his shoulders with relief.

'I'm sorry, Camelot, we tried all the midwives the serving girl knew. They all said the same, any midwife who assisted at a Childermas birth would bring misfortune to all births she attended for the year to come. None would come with us, however much we offered them.'

He lowered his voice to a whisper. 'They also said a child born on Childermas will either die or take the life of the mother. They couldn't both live.'

'Because they won't attend the births, that's why,' I muttered angrily.

There was another shriek from downstairs and Cygnus winced. 'How goes it?'

I shook my head. 'I can feel the top of the child's head, but the opening has not widened any more for some time now. I fear she is too small for the baby. The pains are strong, but the birth is not progressing and Adela is exhausted.'

Osmond came running upstairs. 'Is the midwife here?'

'There are none able to come,' I told him as calmly as I could.

He seized a handful of Cygnus's shirt and shook him. 'You were supposed to fetch a midwife hours ago. What have you been doing? Do you want Adela to die? Do you enjoy seeing women dead? Is that what excites you?'

'Stop it, stop it,' I shouted, pushing Osmond away. 'Rodrigo and Cygnus have tried as hard as anyone could. None of the midwives will attend a Childermas birth.'

Osmond backed away and crouched against the wall, his head in his hands. 'How can I tell her that? She's already convinced she is dying.'

I glanced helplessly around the chapel, then my gaze came to rest on the painting of the Mary Misericordia.

'Do you remember what Adela said on Christmas Day about taking comfort from the thought of Mary looking down on her? Perhaps if she sees the mantle of Mary above her she'll take strength from it. Bring her up here. The sanctuary dais is just the right height for a birthing stool; it could have been made for the purpose.'

Adela did indeed seem calmer when we eventually managed to haul her up the narrow circular staircase, but she was in pain and her strength was ebbing fast. We sat her on the edge of the dais. Her face was white and her shift was soaked with sweat. I tried everything I could remember: warm cloths on her belly; making her sneeze to expel the infant. None of it helped. I laid Pleasance's silver hand amulet on her belly and then gave it to her to hold when the pains came. She squeezed so hard it cut her hand, but still she did not open wide enough to get the child through. The skin between her legs was stretched as tight as a drum.

As dusk fell, Rodrigo returned, looking despondent. He'd searched high and low but had been unable to find Jofre, but if he couldn't find him, then neither could Zophiel. Jofre was wisely lying low somewhere until Zophiel's temper had cooled. He'd come back eventually, he always did.

Rodrigo was devastated when he saw how ill and weak Adela was. He drew me aside. 'We must get the baby out. She cannot go on longer.'

'I've tried everything I know. The opening's too small for the child to pass through.'

'Then she must be cut between her legs to make the passage wider.'

'You've done this, Rodrigo?'

He shook his head. 'They did it to my lady when she was

in labour. I heard her serving women talk about it. Of course, I did not see it.'

'I've seen it done once, Rodrigo, but it takes a skilled hand. Then if she lives, she must be stitched or she'll bleed to death.'

'That I can do. I did it once before for a wound on my brother's leg, a long time ago. It is not the same, I know, but what else can we do?'

Adela gave another shuddering moan, arching her back. Sweat ran down her face. She was not screaming any more. She didn't have the strength. Osmond staggered away from her, running his fingers through his hair.

'What am I to do, Camelot? This is all my fault. I should have left her with the nuns. I shouldn't have tried to help her. At least she would have been safe there. They would have taken the baby, but she would have lived.'

I shook him. 'Enough!' Then I added more gently, 'There's nothing to be gained by blaming yourself for what's done, we have to think what to do for her now.'

Rodrigo said urgently, 'You must cut her, Camelot, or they will both be lost. At least you have seen it done. Where and how long to make the cut, these things I do not know.'

'Cut her!' Osmond cried, gripping my arm, but I brushed him aside.

'Rodrigo will explain. I'll fetch Pleasance's knife. It's clean and sharp.'

My hands were shaking as I descended the stairs to the crypt.

Narigorm sat by the brazier, her runes scattered before her in three circles drawn in wood ash on the floor. I guessed what she was asking them and I told myself I did not want to know the answer. I gathered the bundle of things Pleasance had made ready and walked back across the crypt to the foot of the stairs. Above me I could hear Adela moaning and the others talking to her in soothing voices.

I stopped, one foot on the stairs, and without looking round at Narigorm, I spoke softly into the darkness behind me.

'Will we soon be nine again?'

There was a silence so long that I thought Narigorm hadn't heard me, but when I turned to look at her she was staring at me. Her pale eyes glittered in the flames from the brazier.

'If one is added, one must be taken away,' she said, as if the matter had been settled long ago.

Then Adela will not survive this, I thought, and as I dragged my tired, aching body back up the stairs, I was aware that my hands were no longer shaking. Perhaps it was the certainty that Adela's life was no longer in my hands that made me suddenly detached and calm.

I made Osmond sit behind Adela on the sanctuary dais so that she could lean back against him. Adela held his hand and grasped Pleasance's little silver amulet in the other. We gave her a little wine which she sucked thirstily, but I wouldn't allow her more. She mustn't be so dulled that she could not push. We spread the pile of straw that Zophiel had shaken from his empty box on the floor of the chapel between her legs.

Then I lifted her shift. Pleasance's knife was sharp and unblemished. I sliced the tight skin swiftly and surely, front, back. Adela screamed then. Blood flowed on to my hands and splashed down on to the chapel floor.

'Rodrigo, spread your hands on her belly. When she pushes, you must bear down gently but firmly. Adela, push now, push.'

The head came free, purple and covered in Adela's bright

red blood. Red for the firstborn. I managed to wriggle one finger under the child's slippery armpit.

'Again, Adela.'

She was leaning back, her eyes closed. She moaned through clenched teeth and shook her head.

'You can, Adela. You will. Think of Mary, think of her birth, you can do it.'

She leaned forward, her eyes screwed up in pain and concentration. She shrieked as I pulled and the baby came slithering out in a gush of hot fluid over my knees. It flopped across my legs and lay still, the skin blue, the eyes closed. It was a little boy. He was perfect, but he wasn't moving. I put the reed into each nostril in turn and sucked out the mucus and then did the same with the mouth. But the baby did not take a breath. I took another reed and blew into each nostril – nothing. Into the mouth – nothing. Adela tried to struggle upwards, calling for the child, but Osmond held her against him, his head bowed over her, covering her face. The others watched silently as I tied the purple cord with the red thread and cut it.

'Massage her belly to help the afterbirth come,' I said as I picked up the baby by the ankles and gave him a sharp slap on his buttocks. Still he didn't cry. Cradling the flopping infant in my arms, I walked swiftly away over to the far window.

Narigorm stood in the doorway, watching. I didn't want to see the expression on her face. Without warning my emotions returned; anger swept over me in a wave. I could not accept this, first Pleasance, now this child. I would not allow the runes to win. I would not allow Narigorm to win. I didn't want to see that triumphant smile on her face. The baby's head hung limply over my arm. I began rubbing at the chest and limbs, as if I could rub through to the life that

345

lay beneath the skin and release it. Behind me I could hear Adela sobbing, asking over and over again why the baby was not crying. I rubbed still harder and suddenly felt a jolt beneath my fingers like a little hiccup; then there was a thin, piercing cry. I looked down. The baby's chest was moving, heaving in and out, his tiny fists flailing as if ready to fight the world.

At once the room behind me erupted with shouts and laughter. Rodrigo was shaking Osmond's hand. Adela stretched out her arms and I placed the infant on her chest. He was covered with blood and white mucus, but underneath his colour was beginning to turn pink. His tiny fists opened and closed as if he was reaching for something we could not see. Adela lay back, a wan smile on her lips, but her face was deathly pale and covered in sweat and I realized she was shivering violently. Blood was running from between her legs on to the sanctuary dais and dripping on to the chapel floor.

I looked back at Narigorm still standing in the doorway. Was she right after all, that if one was added another would be taken away? Was Adela about to give her life in payment for her son's? I pushed Rodrigo aside and began to knead her belly hard.

'Cygnus, fetch coverings. Rodrigo, you must be ready to sew her as soon as the afterbirth has been delivered.'

I ripped down the front of Adela's shift and put the baby to her swollen nipple. They say if the baby suckles it helps to expel the afterbirth, but the child was too weak to suck. After what seemed like an age, the afterbirth finally came away, but the last convulsion of her belly took all her remaining strength and Adela closed her eyes and fell back into Osmond's arms. The silver amulet fell with a tinkle from her limp hand on to the sanctuary floor.

While Rodrigo's deft musician's fingers stitched, I took the baby, washed him clean and swaddled him in the bands Pleasance had made ready. I blessed her for that and though it was doubtless blasphemy, I prayed that if the dead could do anything for the living, she would watch over Adela now. It was many years since I had swaddled a child. I held the sleeping infant up to my face, drinking in the sweet smell of his damp, dark hair, feeling the warm little fingers curl like rose petals round my rough finger, watching the tiny mouth purse in its sleep as if he was thinking great thoughts. It was as if I was holding my own baby sons again. I felt the weight of them, the shiver of joy when they were laid in my arms. Each so different, yet each burrowing into the warmth of my skin as if they knew I could keep them safe. I thought of my little sons and I wept for the first time in many years.

Rodrigo touched me on the shoulder. 'I have finished. It is the best I can do.'

I thrust the infant into his arms and went to Adela. She lay white and still in Osmond's arms. Her skin was cold and clammy to the touch. Blood still ran from between her thighs. I pressed a cloth between her legs, but it was quickly soaked through. I couldn't think how to staunch the flow. Her life was running out between my fingers.

Cygnus, touched me lightly on the shoulder. 'Wait, there is something. My mother once . . .'

And before I could ask him what he meant he had raced for the door to the bridge. It seemed like hours before he returned, but in reality it was probably only minutes, long minutes as I pressed the cloth hard against Adela until my fingers ached. Then he was back, a mound of bright green sphagnum moss dripping between his fingers. He wrung it out and thrust it towards me.

347

'Pack this inside her. It will staunch the blood.'

We packed. The clear water from the moss mingled with the blood on the flags. As fresh blood splashed into the puddle, oracular shapes formed and dissolved until at last the drops of blood ceased to fall. We pulled her legs together and tied Cygnus's belt tightly around her thighs to keep them still. And swung her round until she lay flat on the sanctuary dais, pale and still as a marble effigy.

Osmond was kneeling beside Adela. He had finally unpinned her veil and her flaxen hair clung to her forehead, damp with sweat. I saw now why she had refused to remove the veil before, not even to sleep. For beneath it, her hair had been savagely cropped.

Osmond tenderly stroked the poor shorn locks. 'She will be all right now, won't she?' he pleaded, his face as drawn as Adela's.

'Cygnus has gone to make her some hot mulled wine. I've told him to put some amaranthus in it to stop the bleeding. Pleasance had some of the powdered flowers in her pack. We'll try to rouse her to drink a little of that and then let her sleep awhile. We'd best make her a bed here on the sanctuary platform; if we move her too soon the bleeding might start again. Let me sit with her. You go and admire your son, you've not yet held him. What will you call him?'

But Osmond rose and staggered away from the dais without making any answer.

All through that night, Rodrigo, Osmond and I took it in turns to sit with Adela, sponging her forehead and spooning broth and herbed wine into her a sip at a time. We warmed hot stones for her feet in the ash pan of the brazier and rubbed her hands to restore the warmth as the night grew colder. I squeezed and rubbed her full breasts, collecting the thick yellow milk in a bowl and feeding it to the infant drop by drop from the tip of my finger.

I must have fallen asleep towards morning, for when I jerked awake I found myself sitting on the chapel floor beside Adela, my head in my arms resting on the dais. A pearly-pink light was ghosting through the window. Downstairs a mewling wail broke the silence, but as I tried to make my stiff legs stand, Adela woke and turned towards the sound. She was pale, but even in the dim dawn light I could see at once that the life had come back into her eyes. She struggled to get up to go to the child, but I pushed her gently down.

'Wait, I'll bring him to you.'

When I bent to lay the child in her arms Adela smiled, touching his downy cheek with the tip of her finger. I crouched behind her, supporting her shoulders. I turned the infant in her arms and helped him to find her breast. He didn't seem to understand at first, but I nudged her nipple against his soft pink lips until finally his mouth closed round it and he began to suck. She relaxed against me and for a few moments I too felt that unutterable joy as I looked down into the face of a suckling child again.

I shifted slightly to ease the pain in my stiff back and heard the scrape of something metallic against the sanctuary stones. I reached down and picked up the small silver hand with its strange lettering, Pleasance's amulet. I looked up at the Madonna with her outstretched mantle and wondered which of them had kept Adela and her child safe, the Christian Virgin or the ancient Jewish amulet. Did it matter which Adela had put her faith in? Perhaps Mary too had held a Jewish amulet when her son was born. All I knew for certain was that we had beaten the runes. The runes, the omens and the midwives had all lied. We were nine again and one had not been taken. Childermas was over and they were both alive.

19. One Is Taken

A tentative knock sounded on the door of the chantry.

Rodrigo was on his feet in an instant, relief written all over his face. 'There is Jofre at last.'

Jofre hadn't returned to the chantry the previous night. None of us, except Rodrigo, were concerned about his absence during the day. We knew that if he had any sense, he'd stay well away until Zophiel's bruised balls were a little less tender. Zophiel himself had not returned until long after the curfew bell and when he did he was still in a foul temper.

'Did you catch up with Jofre?' I asked innocently.

He glowered. 'Like the vermin he is, he's gone to ground. But he'll have to show up here sooner or later. And when he does, I'll make him wish he'd never been born.'

But our concern over Adela that night had driven all other thoughts from our heads, so it was not until breakfast the next morning that we realized Jofre hadn't returned at all. As soon as the bell for prime sounded from the town, Rodrigo set off to look for him. I knew what was on his mind. Had Jofre spent the night with Ralph, despite the warnings about Ralph's father? The young take warnings as challenges and after Zophiel's humiliation of him, Jofre might seek out Ralph as a matter of defiance. Rodrigo searched all the likely haunts, but there was no sign of Jofre. Even the serving girl at the Red Dragon hadn't seen him. Finally he admitted defeat and came back to the chantry hoping to find Jofre waiting for him, but he was not.

The knocking came again, but before Rodrigo could reach the door, Zophiel stretched out his hand to block his way.

'Be warned, Rodrigo, this matter of the theft is not over. You're the boy's master, so I will give you time to get the truth out of him in any way you see fit, but my patience is limited. If you do not discover the truth, I will, and,' he added still more coldly, 'there's still the matter of his assault on me. I expect you to punish him well for that, or, as his master, it's you from whom I shall demand recompense.'

The knocking sounded again, more urgently this time, and Rodrigo, pushing Zophiel's arm aside, went to unbar the door. But it wasn't Jofre who stood in the doorway, it was the serving girl from the Red Dragon. Her chest was heaving as if she had been running and despite the coldness of the day, her face was flushed and sweating.

She plucked at Rodrigo's sleeve. 'Please . . . sir,' she panted, 'you must come. Your boy . . .' she pointed with a shaking finger in the direction of the town. 'They found him . . . little lads found him . . . on their way to the river.'

'Is he hurt? Is he in trouble?'

The girl looked away.

Rodrigo caught her wrist and pulled her round. 'Tell me!'

'Please, sir, I . . . I'm sorry, sir, but he's dead.'

Rodrigo stared at her without comprehension. 'No, he is drunk. He knows I will be angry, so he is staying away until he is sober. But he will be back soon.'

Pity creased the girl's face. 'Sir, he isn't coming back. They found a body.'

Rodrigo snatched his hand away. 'You are mistaken. He

drank too much and now he is sleeping. How could he be dead? I spoke to him yesterday. He was going hunting. He said he would be back before dark. And I said . . . the last thing I said . . .'

Rodrigo collapsed against the wall, and slid down until he was crouching on the floor, his head in his hands.

Osmond pulled the now tearful girl inside and closed the door behind her. He put his arm around her. 'Tell us what happened.'

'I don't rightly know, sir. My two little nephews, just little lads they are, set off for the river, across the common land. Then they came running back into town saying they'd found a body in the bushes. Covered in blood it was. They said it had been . . .' She closed her eyes and shook her head as if trying to shake the words loose. For a moment she stood, her mouth working convulsively, but no sounds coming out. Then she swallowed hard. 'Some men went to look. The bailiff's sent for the coroner.'

'Have you seen the body?' I asked.

She shook her head.

'Then how do you know it's Jofre?' I asked gently.

She glanced over at Rodrigo who raised his head, a look of hope in his eyes.

'One of the men recognized him. Said it was the new lad who'd been hanging round with Ralph. They all know Ralph, sir.'

'But they do not know Jofre,' Rodrigo said. 'It is some other boy.'

'Where is the body?' I asked.

'Still where they found it. They can't move it until the coroner gets here.'

'Then I'll go and see it,' I said. 'If it is him, the coroner will require someone who knew him to swear to his identity.'

'But it is not Jofre.' Rodrigo still crouched on the floor, like a cornered animal, trapped somewhere between hope and despair.

'I'll go with you, Camelot,' Cygnus said.

Rodrigo wiped his hand fiercely over his eyes and took a deep breath. 'I will go. He is my pupil, my responsibility. I will go.'

It was easy to see where the body lay – a dozen or so men stood around it. A little way off two small ragged boys stood with a woman who might have been their mother. The town gate was closed, but that did not stop a gaggle of urchins taking it in turns to scramble up to peer out over the town fence in the hope of glimpsing something of what was happening below. There were more faces peering out of the upper windows of the houses nearest the fence.

One of the men broke away from the knot as we approached, holding his arms out as if we were geese to be shooed away. The serving girl ran ahead a few paces and murmured to the man. He looked over at us, pursed his lips, then nodded reluctantly and beckoned us forward.

'Bad business, bad business. Ella here reckons him to be one of your lads. He's not a pretty sight, but you'd best come and look, the coroner will want a sworn identification for his records.'

'You wait here, Rodrigo, I'll go,' I said.

'No, I have to see. If it is him, I will only believe it if I see it with my own eyes.'

At a nod from the bailiff the men parted and let us through. The body was lying some distance from the main track, concealed from view of both track and town by scrub and bracken. Someone had covered the body with an old cloth and the bailiff leaned down and twitched it back from the face. Jofre's dark, glossy hair flopped back from his forehead, stirring in the breeze as if moved by a human breath. Under the olive skin, the face was blanched and the lips blue. I thought at first the face was covered in mud, but then I realized it was smears of dried blood which had run from several long deep scratches. There was a large purple bruise on the left cheek and temple. The eyes were open and staring, a look of abject terror on his face, and no wonder for there, on his neck, was a huge gaping wound, like an open mouth screaming. His throat had been torn out.

Rodrigo gave an anguished cry and fell to his knees, his hands reaching out to Jofre's hair as if he was trying to soothe him. The bailiff grabbed him.

'Can't let you touch the body,' he said, pulling the cloth back over Jofre's face. 'Have to wait for the coroner.'

It took three men to pull Rodrigo away, but suddenly the fight seemed to go out of him. He stumbled away into the scrub, fell to his knees and vomited. Then he sat, his arms wrapped over his head, rocking and sobbing in a tongue none of us could understand.

The men turned away, embarrassed.

The bailiff watched him for a few moments before saying unnecessarily, 'It's his lad then? Poor beggar. 'Course, it's up to the coroner to decide, but I reckon it must have been a wolf. Watchman says he's heard one howling these past few nights. I thought he was daft and said as much. There's not been a wolf in these parts for years. But it looks like he might have been right after all.'

He glanced up as the serving girl approached.

'My sister wants to take her little lads home now. They're cold and hungry. They've been hanging about for hours.'

The bailiff shook his head. 'You can go on home if you

want to, Ella, but I've told your sister and now I'm telling you. They found the corpse, so the law says they have to stay here till the coroner's questioned them.'

So we waited. Some of the men also wanted to go, arguing that they were not witnesses, just the town's representatives, but the bailiff was having none of it. So, grumbling, they lit a fire and sat round talking in low voices and drinking the generous quantities of ale brought out by Ella, courtesy of the town's coffers. The little boys who were leaning silently against their mother cheered up when they were given a hunk of cheese and an onion apiece. Rodrigo sat by himself away from us all, staring at the ground. Cygnus went across and sat down near him. He didn't try to engage him in conversation, but merely sat so that he would know he was not alone.

The afternoon wore on. It was bitterly cold. A raw wind sprang up and the cloth over Jofre's body billowed as if the body beneath was rising. A couple of the men went across and anchored it with stones. Above, in the sky, a pair of kites wheeled round in lazy circles looking for prey, their wings glinting rust red in the bright glacial sun. Finally, as the shadows began to lengthen, the town gates opened and a small man on an overlarge dun-coloured mare rode out, followed by a young lad who rode saddleless on a mule. From his pained expression the ride had been long and hard. The night watchman followed behind them on foot.

The bailiff stumbled to his feet, his legs so stiff from the cold that he almost fell and hobbled across to the rider. Removing his leather cap, he bowed low, as though he was greeting royalty.

'Body's over here, coroner, sir.'

The coroner tossed him his reins as if he was a stable lad. 'Let's get on with it then. I want to be finished before dark.

No sense hanging about. Are you ready, Master Thomas?'
he bellowed at his clerk.

The clerk, who was rubbing his aching backside, hastily
donned a small writing board which hung suspended from
a strap around his neck and scrabbled in the mule's pack
for parchment, quill and a flask of ink, getting more flustered
by the minute.

The coroner impatiently tapped the side of his boot with
his riding whip. 'Now, who found the corpse?'

The bailiff thrust the reins of the coroner's horse at one
of the other men and pointed to the two lads who, now that
strangers had arrived, were once again clinging to their
mother's skirts.

'These two lads came across the body when they were
taking a short cut to the river this morning, bit after ten or
thereabouts.'

'Did they raise the hue and cry?'

'In a manner of speaking,' the bailiff said cautiously. 'They
told their mother.'

'Anyone identify the corpse?'

I glanced at Rodrigo, still sitting away in the scrub. He
hadn't even looked up when the coroner arrived.

I stepped forward. 'The body is that of Jofre, apprentice
musician.'

'You're the boy's master?'

'No, sir, I am a camelot. Jofre and his master are among
a group of us who travel together for safety. His master's
over there, but he's very distressed.'

The coroner glanced over at Rodrigo. 'I imagine so, all
that time wasted training the boy, now he'll have to start
again with another, I suppose. Apprentices are more trouble
than they're worth, bone idle and ungrateful, the lot of them.
So when did the boy go missing?'

'Jofre left our lodgings yesterday morning. We are lodging outside the town. We believe he may have come into the town, but he didn't return last night. One of our company gave birth last night. It was a long and difficult labour. It kept us all busy, so we didn't start looking for him until first light.'

He nodded. 'Quite. So the boy was in the town all night.'

'Begging your pardon, sir, but it wasn't all night.' The night watchman hovered nervously at the coroner's elbow, twisting his hood in his hands. I had the impression that he'd been pushed forward, for he kept glancing behind him as he spoke. 'The lad left the gates alone at curfew, sir. Locked the gate behind him myself. Likely he was attacked on the road on the way home. But it wasn't in the town, sir, that it wasn't.'

'Good, that narrows the time down then. Let's take a look at this apprentice of yours, shall we?' He turned to the townsmen. 'Gather round, everyone. As jurors the law requires that you view the corpse.'

The men made a wide circle round the body, and Cygnus and I joined them. The bailiff dragged the corner of the cloth and this time uncovered the whole corpse. There was a gasp and several of the men including Cygnus turned away. The young clerk's hand shook so violently that a great blot of ink fell across the parchment, obliterating several lines. Even the coroner hesitated for a moment, swaying on his heels, then he stepped forward and looked down.

Jofre was lying sprawled naked on his back. His body was covered in blood, not only from the wound in his throat, but from what appeared to be dozens of jagged bites. But the worst thing, the thing that made even the night watchman gag, was that his genitals had been ripped away, leaving a raw and gaping wound.

The coroner swallowed hard. 'Now, men, observe the teeth marks and scratches on his body and limbs. The throat has been ripped out, and the ... and the private parts. Typical of a dog attack to go for the throat. I'm sure you've seen something similar yourself when a dog starts savaging sheep. Turn the corpse over, if you please.'

The bailiff moved forward and beckoned one of the men, but he backed away. Finally another came forward and together they rolled Jofre over.

'Ah yes, as you see, men, more teeth marks and scratches. I would suggest this boy has been attacked by a dog, more likely a pack of them. Have you had any trouble from dogs worrying sheep hereabouts?'

The bailiff spoke up. 'No dogs, coroner, but these past nights there's been reports of a wolf howling. Watchman heard it, sir. Others heard it too.'

The coroner raised his eyebrows in a manner that reminded me of Zophiel. 'A wolf? In these parts?'

Several men nodded emphatically.

'Seems unlikely. But if you say so, a wolf it is then.'

He prodded Jofre's leg with the toe of his boot as if trying to rouse him.

'Stiff, but in this cold weather that won't tell us much by itself, hard frost last night, but it fits with what the night watch says, that he was attacked on the road going back to his lodging sometime after the curfew bell. Well, men, I must ask you to talk it over amongst yourselves and give me your verdict, but I don't think there's much doubt what happened. No need to debate this overlong. I'm sure you're as anxious as I am to close this business and get to the tavern.' He rubbed his hands. 'I'm sorely in need of hot mulled ale and a hearty meal, as I dare say are you.'

'Wait!' Rodrigo burst through the ring of men. I don't

know how long he had been standing looking at Jofre's body, but his face was drained of colour.

The coroner turned. 'Ah, yes, the boy's master.' He held out his hand. 'My condolences, sir. Once the verdict has been returned you may remove the body for burial.'

I saw the men around us stiffen and glance at one another, but the coroner didn't appear to notice.

Rodrigo ignored the proffered hand. 'You say a wolf or a dog did this, but that is impossible.'

The coroner shrugged. 'Up to the jury, of course, but you can see the bite marks.'

'I can also see that the body is naked. He must have had clothes when he left the town. You think a wolf or a dog strips a body before it attacks it?'

The coroner looked slightly taken aback. 'Watchman, what have you to say? Was the boy dressed when he left the town?'

The man shuffled forward, looking anywhere but at the body. 'I think so, sir.'

The coroner began tapping his whip impatiently against his boot again. 'Come now, man, you think so? You surely remember whether or not someone walked through your gates naked.'

The watchman glanced nervously behind him again.

'It was dark, sir . . . he had a cloak . . . he could have been naked under the cloak.'

'Why, in God's name, would a man walk around naked in midwinter? You men, did anyone here remove his clothes?'

Several men shook their heads, but no one met the coroner's eyes.

Rodrigo was on his knees bending forward. 'These marks on his buttocks and legs, the skin is scraped off. Earth and stones stuck in the wounds.' He looked up. 'The body was dragged across the ground.'

A big, burly man walked up. His nose was squashed sideways as if it had once been broken in a fight. He scowled at Rodrigo. 'Wolves drag their prey off to eat it, any fool knows that.'

'A sheep or a child, yes, but to drag the weight of a man? And what happened to his clothes?'

The man's face darkened. 'I dare say he took his clothes off himself. Look, we all know what your lad was into. Maybe he'd arranged to meet someone outside the town gates. So busy giving him one, he didn't notice the wolf till he sprang. A bare backside, all white in the moonlight, heaving up and down, the wolf must have thought it was a pig. And he wasn't far wrong, was he? Anyhow, we've got our verdict, coroner. Killed by a wolf, we're all agreed.'

The coroner nodded, rubbing his hands against the cold. 'Excellent, excellent. Have you taken that down, boy? You must also record that since the wolf caused the death, the wolf in question is declared deodand. Bailiff, it's your duty to see the beast is hunted down, and since the town has been negligent in allowing a dangerous animal to attack travellers within its boundaries, the price for its head must go to the Crown, not the hunter. The town will hand over the bounty for the wolf's head at the next assizes. Make sure you record that, Master Thomas.'

The bailiff and the men looked mutinous. This was nothing but a thinly disguised fine, and they knew it. Coroners always found a way to fine you for something, however careful you were. The coroner began walking back to his horse, but Rodrigo ran after him and grabbed his arm.

'Is that all you are going to do? Will you not question

other people in the town? If he was out here with someone, then they must be found to testify.'

The coroner shook him off impatiently. 'What is the point? We know what happened.'

I stepped forward. 'Forgive me, sir, but we don't know. A lone wolf would only kill for hunger. Having made a kill, it would settle down to eat, not run off. There are no signs that the flesh was gnawed or the entrails eaten. And a single wolf could not make all these bite marks both behind and in front of the person he had leapt upon. As you said yourself, sir, it looks as if the boy was attacked by a pack of dogs and the dogs could have been deliberately set upon him.'

'Come now, who would do that?' The coroner took the reins in his hand and mounted his horse. He leaned down wearily. 'Watchman, did anyone follow the boy out here with dogs?'

The watchman said hastily, 'No, sir, no one left after curfew. More than my job's worth to let anyone in or out after curfew. That's a thing I'd never do, sir. Value my skin too much for that.' He flashed a scared glance in my direction.

For a moment I was tempted to reveal our visit a few nights before, but the watchman looked so terrified, I couldn't do it to him. I had a feeling he was being threatened into lying by someone he feared much more than the law.

I looked up at the coroner. His mount was skipping sideways restlessly, impatient to be off. 'Sir, threats were made against the boy in town because of his friendship with a young man called Ralph. At least send for this Ralph and ask him if he saw Jofre last night.'

'I can save you the trouble of that, coroner.' I turned to

see the man with the broken nose standing directly behind me. 'Ralph left the town early yesterday morning. Gone to stay with his future bride's family. He'll not be back till after they're wed.'

'Then he'll be no help to us in this matter. Besides, the verdict by the jury has been recorded, can't go changing it now.' The coroner looked at Rodrigo. 'Best thing you can do now is take the body up to the church for burial, then start looking around for a new apprentice. I dare say you'll find plenty of likely lads who –'

The town gate burst open and a man came running out, shouting his message before he had even reached the group. 'Bailiff, you're wanted . . . come quick . . . Yeldon has fallen . . . to the pestilence.'

The coroner's eyes opened wide in alarm. 'God's teeth, that's only three miles west from here.'

The bailiff and most of the men were already hurrying back towards the gate. The coroner stared after them, then wheeled his horse around in the direction of the river.

'Come, Master Thomas, don't lag, we've some hard riding ahead.'

'But I thought we were going to have supper,' the clerk wailed.

'In there? Don't be a bloody fool, man. If someone brought them news of the pestilence, the chances are they brought the pestilence as well.' He glanced over at Rodrigo. 'As for you, Master Musician, if you've any sense you'll bury your apprentice and get back on the road as fast as you can, otherwise he won't be the only one you'll be burying.' He dug his heels into his horse's flank and urged her towards the bridge and away from the town.

Most of the townspeople had disappeared inside the gate, but Broken-nose and another equally big man hung back.

As Rodrigo and I turned to walk back towards Jofre's body, they moved in front of us, blocking our way.

'Don't even think of burying your boy in the churchyard,' Broken-nose growled. 'Cos you won't get the body as far as the church gate.'

I stared at him. 'Are you denying him a Christian burial, after all that's happened?'

The man shrugged. 'Just a friendly warning, save you wasting your time. Everyone in town knows he was killed by a wolf –'

'You know as well as I do that it wasn't a wolf that killed him.'

The man grinned. 'Coroner's recorded a wolf and if it's written down in his records it must be true. Thing is, there's not been a wolf in these parts for years, so there's rumours going round the town that this weren't no ordinary wolf. It was a werewolf, that's what they're saying. Thing is, if your young friend's been killed by a werewolf, then he'll not rest easy in his grave. Those killed by werewolves become vampires, that's what priest says. Pestilence may have reached Yeldon, but it hasn't come here and it's not going to cos we've got no vampires here. And we'll do whatever we have to do to keep it that way. Understand?'

We trudged back to the chantry in silence. Rodrigo would not allow either of us to help him carry Jofre. He bore the stiff body like a man carrying a heavy burden in penance, staggering under its weight, but shaking us off if we tried to steady him. Behind us, the sun began to set, a blood-red disc hanging over the dark buildings of the town.

Osmond, lantern in hand, came out to meet us. He began to ask what had happened, but Rodrigo walked past him without reply and gently laid the wrapped body on the sanctuary dais where only a few hours before Adela had given birth to her son. One look at our faces was enough to caution Osmond not to ask any more. Even Zophiel was silent.

We could do nothing until the rigor had worn off. At Osmond's urging we went down to the crypt and picked at some food, but for once, none of us was hungry, except for Narigorm who ravenously consumed her own portion and more. Rodrigo said nothing and ate nothing. He only drank. Drank too much wine for an ordinary man on an empty stomach, but we didn't try to stop him.

Adela sat near the brazier, her hair once more concealed beneath the tightly pinned veil. She was rocking the baby, who whimpered fretfully, screwing up his tiny face in a series of grimaces. Adela was able to sit up now, but her face looked more drawn than ever, as if you could see the face of an old woman lying just beneath her skin. I knew the slightest movement must be causing her great pain from where I had cut her, but she tried hard to conceal it. She watched Rodrigo anxiously as if she was desperately trying to find words to speak, but no words came.

We said nothing to the others of the news from Yeldon. The coroner was right, we had to move on quickly. If Zophiel found out, he would insist on leaving that very night, but with Jofre lying upstairs I knew Rodrigo would refuse and that would only lead to trouble. We had to risk staying another few hours for his sake as well as Adela's. She was not strong enough to travel yet. And she would have to be told that the frosts had not, after all, stopped the pestilence, but not now, I could not bring myself to tell her now.

Eventually, when we could put it off no longer, we all went upstairs, leaving Adela alone in the crypt with Narigorm and the baby. Cygnus fetched water and I lit some rushes. There was little point in concealing our presence any more. Then tenderly, as if he could still be hurt, Rodrigo peeled back the cover from Jofre's body. Osmond gave a strangled cry and rushed towards the barred door. He only just succeeded in opening it before retching violently, losing what little supper he had eaten. Even though I already knew what lay beneath the covers, I found myself swallowing hard to keep the bitter gall from rising into my mouth.

I glanced at Zophiel. He stood a little way off, staring down at the body, his face a blank mask. But his right hand had moved to the hilt of the knife in his belt and he was gripping it so hard the knuckles were bloodless.

Cygnus, Rodrigo and I washed Jofre. We turned him over carefully and tended to his back first. It was easier than staring into those huge open gaping wounds. The dried blood was hard to remove and when we did the teeth marks showed up blue and ragged against the cold waxy skin. Now that the dirt and blood had been washed away the wounds on his back were more numerous than even I had first thought. He had been repeatedly bitten as if animals had leapt up at him over and over again while he ran or struggled.

Finally we had to turn him over again and face what we did not want to look at. Rodrigo gently wiped his face, washing the blood out of his curls, until his hair glistened wet under the flickering rushlights. The large purple bruise on Jofre's face looked more livid than before under the smoking yellow light.

Cygnus suddenly broke the silence. 'This is a clean cut! No wolf did this. Look!' He pointed at the place where Jofre's genitals had been ripped away. 'See the edges of the wound – this wasn't bitten or torn. It's been sliced.'

Rodrigo pushed him aside and stared. Then he called to Osmond, 'The rushlight, bring it here.'

Osmond did so, holding the light lower, but letting it wobble as he looked away. Rodrigo impatiently snatched it from his hand. He moved it up towards the wound in Jofre's throat. Here the bite marks were unmistakable, the flesh around the wound jagged and torn, but Cygnus was right, the wound in his groin was too clean at the edges. There were bite marks around it as if something had been snapping at the place, drawn by the smell of blood perhaps, but teeth had not inflicted this horrendous injury.

Rodrigo held the rushlight close to the body, examining every inch, then stopped.

'See, bruises on both his arms. Someone has held him tightly.'

Zophiel shifted slightly in the shadows. 'You gripped his arms yourself down in the crypt yesterday when you were questioning him about him being a thief, remember?'

'He is no thief!' Rodrigo sprang at him, knocking the bucket of bloody water flying. He had Zophiel by the throat, but Zophiel's reflexes were as quick as his own and in a flash his knife was pricking Rodrigo's ribs. Osmond ran forward and pulled Rodrigo away, but it was not without a struggle.

'You are to blame for this,' Rodrigo choked out. 'If you had not falsely accused him, he would not have run off.'

'You no more believed the boy than I did, Rodrigo, and he knew that. Your opinion mattered far more to him than mine. If either of us caused the boy to run off . . .' He let the rest of the sentence hang in the air.

Rodrigo's shoulders slumped; for a moment I thought he was going to fall, but he stood swaying, his arms now limp at his sides.

Zophiel, still breathing heavily, lowered his knife. 'I was merely trying to point out that you yourself gripped the boy hard enough yesterday to cause bruises. No one blames you for that. I also held him when I questioned him – who knows, I might have caused a mark or two myself. Simply because he has bruises on his arms does not mean he was restrained last night.'

'He's right, Rodrigo,' Osmond said soothingly. 'The bruises mean nothing.'

'And having his member sliced off, that means nothing too?' Rodrigo shouted. 'Jofre was murdered. Whoever did this mutilated him and set dogs on him or left him for the wolf. Either way it was murder. And I am going to kill whoever did this. I swear it.'

I gripped his arm. 'Rodrigo, we know as well as you do that Jofre was murdered, but you have no hope of finding his killer. The townspeople will defend their own. No one will talk to us, we are travellers, outlanders.'

Osmond nodded. 'Camelot's right. You go stirring up trouble and they'll turn on all of us. Even in this place, we could not defend ourselves against a mob. Think of Adela and the baby, Rodrigo. You'd not do anything to hurt them.'

'You do not understand,' Rodrigo said softly. He walked across to Jofre's body and knelt down in the pool of blood and water. He laid a hand on the boy's chest and bowed his head. His fist clenched around the hilt of his knife.

'*Giuro dinanzi a le tue ferite ti vendicerò!*'

I did not understand the words, but there was no mistaking the tone. I shivered.

We covered the body again and lit candles at Jofre's head and feet. All night Rodrigo kept vigil over him. Osmond slept downstairs with Adela, the baby and Narigorm, but the rest of us slept in the chapel, staves and knives in hand, just in case the townspeople should decide to ensure the body could not rise up and walk.

I lay in the darkness, aching with tiredness from having slept so little the night before, but I couldn't sleep. In the dim light of the candles, I could just make out the outline of Rodrigo. He was kneeling before the painting of Mary, his arms held wide as if on a cross. He stayed there swaying a little, but holding his arms up as if he had imposed a penance on himself or was preparing to undertake a sacred oath. Cygnus sat cross-legged at the foot of Jofre's body, his head bowed. Under his shirt, his wing moved restlessly, fluttering as if trying to escape the bindings. Then from outside came the sound we had all been dreading, the howl of the wolf.

'Put those candles out!' Zophiel was on his feet, his knife in his hands, and this time there was no disguising his fear.

He ran from window to window peering out. The yellow candle flames flickered over the still form of Jofre's body, so that it looked as if he stirred beneath the sheet. Cygnus lifted his head and looked round, but Rodrigo didn't move from his position beneath the painting. Another cry. The howl seemed to have a new note in it that night, stronger, more triumphant, like the sound of a beast that has made a kill and is calling others to join it.

'Put the candles out!' Zophiel shrieked.

I rose, half fearful he was going to strike Cygnus in his panic. 'Whether we show a light or not makes no difference now, Zophiel. Whatever is out there knows we are here and I am beginning to believe it has always known where we are.'

20. Alchemy

The following morning none of us could bring ourselves to broach the question which hung unspoken between us. Where was Jofre to be buried? It was not a decision we could delay. We dared not risk another night in the chantry. If the pestilence had reached the town and people started to flee, they would come this way, people who might already be carrying the sickness. But Rodrigo was adamant that Jofre should not be buried in unconsecrated ground. At first he wanted to carry him with us to the next church, but we persuaded him that questions were bound to be asked if we turned up with a mutilated corpse. One glance at the body and the next parish would hardly be more willing to let him lie with them than the townspeople had been.

'Bury him here,' Cygnus suggested. 'Though the chapel isn't yet consecrated, it's bound to be one day and in the meantime, there is the painting of the Vir . . .' He trailed off awkwardly.

'And where exactly do you plan to bury the body?' Zophiel snapped. 'If the chapel was built on solid ground you might dig up the floor, but dig here and you'll fall straight through to the river. Do you propose simply to leave a body lying about in the chapel?'

Osmond, who had been pacing the floor, stopped and pointed upwards. 'Under the altar. It must be hollow, a solid block that size would be too great a weight for the vaulting below. It's a ready-made tomb. If we can prise a panel loose, or even the top, we can put him in there. We can replace the panel and I'll paint over it.'

Rodrigo pressed his hand in gratitude. 'You are a good man, Osmond.'

Osmond flushed with embarrassment. 'Rodrigo, I never meant to drive Jofre away. It was just the shock when Zophiel said . . . I never realized, you see. If I hadn't stopped him coming fowling, then he would never have gone into town. He might still be alive . . . What they did, it was . . . he didn't deserve that.'

Rodrigo squeezed Osmond's shoulder. 'You must not blame yourself. You did not do this to him.'

Osmond, uncharacteristically, flung his arms round Rodrigo and hugged him. 'I'm so sorry, Rodrigo, I know he was like a son to you.'

Rodrigo returned the embrace, then thrust him away, tears shining in his eyes. 'Come, show me the altar, perhaps together we can move the top.'

Zophiel, for once, had the grace to wait until we could hear them moving about upstairs before he spoke.

'They're wasting their time. Osmond seems to have forgotten we've no lead coffin to seal the body in. He can paint the altar as much as he likes, but it won't stop the stench that will linger for months, years even. When they come to finish the chantry and smell it, they'll open the altar up. It won't take long for people round here to work out who it is. Then the corpse will be tossed in the river, or dismembered and scattered. Rodrigo would do better to bury the body in an unmarked grave in the woods. If they can't find it, they can't dig it up again.'

'But they won't dare throw the bones away if they think it's a monk who's interred there,' said Cygnus, looking at me.

'And why, pray, should they think that?' Zophiel asked coldly. He had obviously still not forgiven Cygnus for failing to put out the candles.

'Camelot has some monks' robes in his pack. Remember, Camelot, the ones you bartered for at the monastery? Cloth stays whole long after the body begins to decay. All they'll see will be the monk's habit.'

'You are determined to make a mockery of God in everything, Cygnus, but be warned, God is not mocked.' Zophiel, a look of disgust on his face, swept up the stairs and disappeared.

The baby, woken by Zophiel's raised voice, began to cry.

Cygnus came over and knelt beside me as I rummaged in my pack for the habits. He glanced over at Adela who was occupied with the child, then whispered, 'Has it occurred to you, Camelot, that Zophiel was also missing around the time Jofre was killed? He didn't return until well after the curfew. He must have walked back along the same track. Surely he would have seen or heard something, unless he was the one who –'

'Don't say it. I know what you're thinking. Just pray that thought does not cross Rodrigo's mind. If Rodrigo accuses Zophiel, then I fear for the lives of both of them.'

We interred Jofre's body in the altar. Osmond carved a large wooden cross, such as monks wear, to place in his hands. Jofre seemed to belong in monk's robes. Perhaps that is where he would have come eventually or should have gone, among the pure clear voices that sing of a higher love than the love of women. We closed his eyes, and now that the rigor had worn off, the look of terror had melted from his face. The cowl over his head and the high-necked robes concealed his wounds so that he looked at the last like a sleeping child.

Rodrigo knelt and gently kissed the cold blue lips, smoothing the downy cheek with his hand as if he tucked his own son into his crib. He did not cry. He had gone beyond that into a grief too deep for tears. And I thought of Jofre's mother. Jofre had died without ever knowing if she had survived. Did she live without knowing her son was dead? It is hard to bury your own children. It breaks your heart in a way no other death can ever do, for you are burying part of yourself in that grave. Rodrigo had wanted to take Jofre home to her. It was too late now. Why do we always leave it too late?

The top of the altar grated, a mournful, hollow sound, as we slid it back into position. I looked up to see Narigorm standing in the doorway to the stairs. She was holding something that gleamed in her hand. As I turned to her, she held it up in the stream of watery sunshine that glinted through the chantry window. I saw again the blue and purple rippled with golden flecks, the glass tear that held the light of Venice.

Rodrigo saw it at the same time I did. He took it from her, cradling it in his palm.

Finally Cygnus said gently, 'Shall we open the lid again and put it in his hand?'

Rodrigo hesitated, then he shook his head. 'It was made for the living so that they could remember what was lost. The dead cannot remember. One day I will give it to Adela's son, for he was born in the same hour that Jofre was murdered.' He turned back to stare at the altar. 'But not yet, there is something I must do before I can part with this.'

The words rang in my head like the pestilence bell. *Born in the same hour that Jofre was murdered.* The words had been in my head all along, but I had refused to let them take form. I turned to look at Narigorm still standing in the doorway, her eyes fixed on the sanctuary dais where the child had been born and Jofre lay dead. In the gloom of the doorway I couldn't see her expression, but I could sense her satisfaction. The blackness of the deep stairwell behind her swelled up around her as if its very darkness was her shadow. *If one is added, one must be taken away.* The runes had not lied after all.

Even when there is no desperate cacophony of bells echoing from the village, even when there is no thick yellow pall of sulphurous smoke, you learn to recognize the warning signs. The mills, standing like watchtowers, are silent, their sails still and locked, no rumble of the grinding stones or procession of chattering women passing to and fro with their family's flour. The watermills are also silent, no splashing of paddles, no rasping of stone upon stone, no shouts of men. And when you hear the silence, you come to hope that it is only because there is no more grain left to grind.

More chilling are the mills which are not silent, where sails spin out of control and you can feel the vibration of the grinding stones under your feet. The ghost mills, where the stones grind and grind, but no flour trickles out. Where sails and paddles batter themselves to splinters, because there is no one left to stop them. You see sheep lying dead in the field and dogs rotting in the ditches. And then you turn, turn away quickly and take the next road, any road that will take you away from the village, for you know they have something worse than hunger in their midst.

More and more of the towns and villages were falling to the pestilence. It came without warning. At dawn people would be about their business with no hint of sickness among them; by sunset a dozen would be lying dead and then it would run through the streets like fire. There was no telling who it would strike; fit young men would fall as quickly as ailing old women, without pattern or reason. So we began to fear even to enter a healthy village, in case it struck while we were there. And there was no point risking death for food, because no one had any left to sell. Most of the villagers were hungry themselves and any fortunate enough still to have food kept it hidden for themselves, and who could blame them?

And so we kept travelling east. We turned and twisted like eels funnelled towards the trap, but still we found ourselves facing the rising sun. Each time I tried to turn us towards the north, our way was barred by bridges washed away, roads made impassable by fallen trees, tracks blocked by villagers for fear of the pestilence. These obstacles were to be expected, natural, and yet a nagging disquiet was beginning to take root inside me, as if there was something, some force I could not name, compelling us towards the east. Why had Narigorm whispered those words, 'We're going east, you'll see.' Was she simply saying what the runes predicted or was she more than just the messenger?

The others hardly seemed to notice the direction we were travelling in, for if our days were haunted by the fear of stumbling into the pestilence, our nights were haunted by something that was beginning to hold a greater terror. The wolf was still with us.

Those first two nights after we left the chantry we heard

nothing and I began to believe that the bailiff had done his job and had the beast hunted down. Then on the third night we heard it again, just as before, and this time none of us could pretend it was not the same animal. As we travelled on, so it followed, the howl never nearer, but never further away. It didn't call every night, and in a way that was worse, for we lay awake rigid in the darkness, listening for the sound. Sometimes when we did not hear it for several days, we told ourselves it had gone and then without warning the howl would split the night again.

We never saw so much as a glimpse of it, not a shape on a hilltop in the moonlight, not a pair of yellow eyes shining in the forest, not a paw mark in the mud and not even the remains of a kill. But each time I heard that howl in the darkness, I thought of the savage bites on Jofre's body, the gaping hole in his throat and the look of terror on his face and I shuddered.

It had taken us some time to reach the healer's cottage. The road which ran up into the low, long hills was only used by farm carts. It was wide enough for the wagon, but full of potholes and sharp rocks, and we had to travel even more slowly than usual so as not to risk breaking a wheel shaft or laming Xanthus.

The cottage lay on a rise at the far end of a narrow, steep-sided gully, close to a waterfall that tumbled over rocks before crashing down into a deep, fern-fringed pool. A boulder-filled river ran the length of the gully and curved around the base of the hillock to run parallel with the road. There was no track leading from the road up to the cottage, only a narrow path worn between huge rocks by those who had trodden the way over the years. There was no sign of its owner either, except for a trickle of smoke meandering out of the hole in the roof into the frosty morning air. But a hearth fire was a good sign; at least the householder was well enough to make one.

Osmond helped Adela down from the wagon. Her face was pale and tired. The infant lay in a woven basket in her arms, staring listlessly up at her. He screwed up his face as if he wanted to cry, but no sound emerged. Adela shivered. Ever since we brought home Jofre's body, a chill had settled into her. No matter how close to the fire she sat, or how many blankets were heaped upon her, she couldn't get warm, as if the cold had pierced her bones like a wolf's bite. It had been over a month since the birth, but her strength was not returning and she was making herself worse by worrying about her son. The baby, though he had fed well at first, was now getting weaker by the day, his eyes sinking into hollows and his flesh melting away.

Adela's growing anxiety for her son had turned to fear when, one evening as we made camp, Narigorm suddenly cried out, 'Look, it's the omen of death,' and pointed to a white dove circling above the wagon where the baby lay sleeping. Adela had snatched the infant from the wagon and Osmond had driven the dove away, but the damage was done. Adela was convinced that the sign was meant for her child, and I became increasingly haunted by the fear that if she continued to torment herself, we would be burying two more of our company before the month was out.

We needed a skilled healer. We didn't dare go into the towns in search of an apothecary or a doctor, even if any remained alive, and though I knew enough about herbs to treat common ailments, I did not know how to cure this. Pleasance would have known and we felt her loss more keenly than ever. She had stood in the shadows, quiet and unassuming, tending a blister there or a belly ache here. We had taken her for granted until she was no longer there, like an ancient tree you don't truly see until it is felled, and then only from the empty space in the sky do you suddenly grasp its stature.

We enquired of those we passed on the road for someone skilled in herbs, but most, like us, were far from home. They shook their heads and trudged on. Finally, a goose-girl we passed on the road told us of this cottage.

'Everyone in these parts goes to her,' she said. Then, as she shooed her hissing flock onwards, she turned and called after us, 'She's a sharp tongue, that one. Mind you don't get on the wrong side of her or she'll send you away with a flea in your ear.'

Her words rang in my ears as we stood looking up at the cottage. There was no sense in taking Adela up there if the woman wouldn't help her.

'You all wait here,' I said. 'I'll go up alone. An old man by himself won't be any threat to her.'

The cottage was small, round and windowless, built into the side of the gully and made of boulders and rocks, with a thatch of reeds. A leather curtain served as a door. A few hens scratched among the herbs in the sloping garden which was bordered by a blackthorn hedge. An old rowan tree grew close by the cottage door. Its bright red berries had long gone, but fruit of some kind hung from its branches, pale brown, like parchment, some no bigger than a thumb, others as large as a man's fist, but I couldn't make out what they were.

When I reached the wicker gate I stopped, intending to call out so as not to startle the woman, but before I could do so a voice rang out from inside the cottage.

'Come in. I don't bite.' The leather curtain at the door was pulled aside and a woman stepped out. She was tall and willowy with long iron-grey hair which she wore braided in two plaits like a young girl. 'Heard your wagon coming along the track. Sound carries up here. Not many use that track, even fewer since this pestilence came upon us.'

'We don't have the pestilence,' I said hastily.

'I know. If you had, I'd smell it. So are you coming in?'

I opened the gate and took a few steps up the path. A couple of hens bustled away, indignant at having their scratting disturbed. The woman's face turned in the direction of the sound and I saw that her green eyes were covered in a milky-white film.

'You've come for my help,' she said. It was a statement, not a question.

I gestured in the direction of the wagon, then stopped, feeling foolish. Though I have one blind eye, I still rely on my one good eye instead of my other senses. The voices of the rest of the company drifted up the gully as they made camp.

'We've a young woman travelling with us. She gave birth to a boy a few weeks ago, but her milk is drying up and the baby is weakening.'

'There are many reasons why a woman's milk stops before it should. But before I can tell which herbs will help her, I'll need to feel the breasts, see if they are empty or swollen, cold or hot. Bring her here. I don't go down to the track. In the meantime, I'll give you something to help the child. Come.'

Without waiting for me she disappeared inside the cottage. I followed her, but my footsteps faltered as I drew near the rowan tree and saw what was hanging from the branches. Dozens of dried foetuses dangled in the breeze – lambs', calves' and human babies'. Some were so tiny it was impossible to tell if they were human or animal; others were perfectly formed infants, but no bigger than a man's hand. The dried bodies rattled softly as they struck one another in the breeze.

As if she could see what I was staring at, the woman spoke from inside the darkness of the hut. 'These past years, more and more women have miscarried. Cattle and sheep are losing their offspring too. Evil spirits enter the womb and the woman becomes pregnant, but these offspring are born before their time. If their bodies are buried, the spirits are set free to enter the womb over and over again, preventing the woman from carrying a human child.'

She emerged holding a wooden bowl full of thick white liquid and continued to speak without pause. 'The rowan tree traps the evil spirits and binds them so they cannot re-enter the womb. Rowan wood is powerful against curses and evil spirits, even stronger when it is living.' She thrust the bowl towards me. 'Feed the baby as much of this as you can, a little at a time but often.'

I sniffed it.

She heard me and laughed. 'It's only eggs, shells and all, dissolved in spirit of angelica and beaten with a little honey. It will nourish the baby. The stronger he grows, the harder he will suck and it will help the milk come. Now, mistress, go and send the mother to me and I'll see what can be done for her.'

'*Master*,' I corrected her. 'But thank you, I will send her.'

She frowned. 'Master? But I would have sworn . . .'

She reached out a hand to touch my face, but I jerked away and hurried off before she could say more, leaving her standing by her rowan tree among the dead babies.

Later, Osmond helped Adela up the boulder-strewn path and stood outside the cottage while the woman examined her. They returned to the camp with bunches of herbs which the healer assured her would stimulate the flow of milk. Adela, though still exhausted, looked happier than she had done for days. But Osmond was not reassured. The healer had warned him that herbs alone would not help Adela for long. Unless she took more nourishment to build up her strength after the birth, the milk would dry up completely. She needed more than a diet of scrawny wild birds and herbs. She needed red meat and red wine for her blood, if she was to produce good milk for the child. But the healer knew of no one who had any meat or wine left for sale.

'I hear they have food and wine in plenty at Voluptas,' she told him. 'But it would take a cunning tongue to persuade them to sell it. Some have tried, they tell me, but no one has succeeded.'

It was as if she had thrown down a challenge and one that Zophiel, when he heard of it, could not resist.

The friar came closer to the grill in the gate and peered first at Zophiel, then at me.

'You can turn lead into gold?' he asked incredulously.

'You do not believe it is possible?' Zophiel raised his eyebrows in that too familiar gesture of his, a sure sign that he was laying a trap for some innocent to blunder into, but for once I hoped this trap would catch its prey.

The manor they called 'Voluptas' or 'Delight' was as remote as the healer's cottage. The ideal place for those who wanted to hide away from the problems of the world, and those at Voluptas did. According to the healer they were mostly from London, twenty or so men and women, wealthy, handsome and young for the most part, having fled when the pestilence first struck the city. But it was said the man who proclaimed himself their leader was not rich, handsome or young, he was a poor friar, but one with a great gift, for he knew how to stop the pestilence.

From what we could see of him through the grill, he wore the robe of the White Friars, but this was not made of the coarse cloth with which friars usually like to humble the flesh; this was made of soft wool, thick and warm against the biting cold. His flesh was soft too and well rounded, his stubby fingers plump and dimpled at the knuckles. He held a posy of sweet herbs against his nose as he spoke to us, but they were hardly needed, for the heavy perfume which wafted from his own body was surely enough to dispel any unwelcome odours we might bring.

The friar moved the posy far enough away from his mouth to speak. 'Many believe it is possible to turn lead into gold,' he said cautiously,

Zophiel smiled. I had no idea where this was leading, but I already knew from what the healer had told Osmond that my relics would buy nothing here. The people at the manor did not put their trust in saints, but in this friar, and he put his faith in neither God nor the devil.

'From where does the pestilence come?' Zophiel asked.

The friar looked puzzled at this change of subject. 'From a surfeit of melancholy, an imbalance in the humours,' he said abruptly. He was plainly anxious to get back to the subject of gold.

But Zophiel hadn't finished. 'And how is this imbalance to be corrected and the pestilence prevented?'

The friar sighed impatiently. 'As we do here, by immersing ourselves day and night in the noble arts, by eating good food, dancing, playing sweet music, smelling pleasant odours, giving free reign to the pleasures of the flesh in all its forms, denying the body nothing it craves. People fall ill when they allow themselves to dwell on unpleasant thoughts and fears, when they deny the body that which it wants and make the flesh miserable. That is why so many have fallen to the Great Mortality, they dwell upon it, and so their body falls prey to it. I don't allow it to be mentioned within these walls. We think only of beauty and pleasure here. But never mind that,' he waggled his beringed fingers impatiently, 'you spoke of changing lead into gold. What does sickness have to do with the gold?'

Zophiel smiled. 'You know, my friend, that all things are composed of the four elements, earth, water, fire and air, and the three principles, salt, sulphur and quicksilver. Lead differs from gold only in the proportions of these things of which it is composed.'

'Yes, yes, this is well known.'

But Zophiel would not be rushed. 'Sickness, as you have so wisely said, comes from an imbalance in the humours of the body. If you keep the mind and body in their equilibriums, the body cannot fall sick, and if the body is sick it may be transformed into a healthy body by correcting the balance of humours. And so, my friend, it is with all things in the universe. Sequitur, one only has to find the right balance of elements and principles to turn base metal into gold. Just as you, my friend, through your wisdom have discovered that beauty and pleasure combined is the alchemic substance that transforms base sickness into the purity of health, so others have found the substance that transforms metals from corruptible lead to the purity of gold.'

'You have discovered the alchemist's stone?' The man's eyes lit up hungrily. 'But this is what alchemists have been seeking for years.'

'Not a stone, my friend. As you have discovered, it is not taking blood *from* the body that restores the balance of the humours, as doctors have so long misguidedly believed, but adding beauty and pleasure *to* the body. So the alchemists did not understand what they were searching for; it is not a stone that will transform, but a liquid, an elixir.'

The friar's eyes shone. 'And you have discovered how to make this liquid? You must be a wealthy man indeed.'

Zophiel sorrowfully shook his head. 'Alas no, I have not discovered it, though I live in hope, my friend, but in my travels I have found one who has. He gave me a few drops of this precious elixir in return for some modest service I performed for him.'

Here Zophiel pressed his hand to his chest and bowed humbly, implying that the service in question had been far from modest.

'Alas, I have already used most of what he gave me to keep body and soul together in these hard times. But when I heard of the transformation you had performed on the body, I couldn't resist coming here to show you what could be achieved. I knew that only a man like you would truly understand what you were witnessing. With the last remaining drops I would be prepared to demonstrate the wonder of it for your edification.'

The friar hesitated, torn between wanting to keep us out and witnessing the great dream. He spoke to someone standing near him and we heard sounds of someone moving away from the gate. Finally we heard the rattle of chains and locks.

'You may come in, but only as far as the gatehouse. I do not wish the women to see . . .' He hesitated, staring at my scar.

I smiled wryly; doubtless he was thinking that my purple scar and eyeless socket were neither a thing of beauty nor of pleasure.

Once inside the gate, it was I who stood and stared. After all the ravaged villages and towns, the gardens stripped bare, the crops rotting in the fields, Voluptas seemed like an hallucination brought on by hunger. Here were well-tended orchards and herb gardens, clipped and neat, ready for the first spring buds. Turf seats nestled among banks of thyme and camomile, ready for lovers when the days were warm again. Irrigation channels ran with clear water and were doubtless teeming with fish, whilst the white doves pecking around the herbs suggested that somewhere there was a well-stocked dovecote too. There was not a single thing to distract the eye from the pleasure. It was a world that existed out of time.

But we weren't permitted to linger over these sights, for the friar hustled us into a small stone room to one side of the gate. A few minutes later several men came hurrying up. They were not wearing friars' robes. The fine cloth, rich colours and warm furs they sported were proof that only the rich came here to think their beautiful thoughts. The friar knew what he was about; preach comfort to the rich and you will grow fat; preach hell to the poor and you will starve with them.

Zophiel asked for a small brass brazier to be brought and some charcoal and he made a great show of heating the charcoal and testing its heat on fragments of wood and the blade of his knife until he was happy that the temperature was correct. He produced a small crucible, held it over the brazier, and with a flourish dropped three drops of a clear, viscose liquid into the heated crucible. It vaporized into a cloud of thick white smoke. He held up a small nugget of lead, grey and dull.

'Watch closely,' he commanded.

Everyone bent a little nearer. They saw the lead fall into

the crucible. They saw the smoke turn from white to purple to black. Everyone held their breath and then the smoke cleared.

'Observe.'

There was a gasp as they saw the glint in the pale afternoon sunshine. Zophiel asked the friar to hold out his hand and as he tipped the crucible over the soft, fat palm, a small nugget of gold rolled into it, exactly the same shape and size as the nugget of lead.

I waited until we were outside again and I was sitting beside Zophiel in the wagon. Not even a nugget of gold could wrest a barrel of flour from the friar, but we were trundling back to the camp with a large cask of wine and a live sheep trussed up in the back of the wagon, which was more than I had dreamed possible.

I glanced sideways at Zophiel. His thin pale face wore an expression of smug satisfaction and his eyes had lost that hunted look that had haunted them ever since the day of Jofre's murder. It had been months since Zophiel had the chance to work a crowd and his success had restored the old arrogance. He had done well and he knew it.

'Gold covered by grey wax, I assume, Zophiel. Heat it and the wax burns off under the cover of the smoke. Behold, the gold beneath is revealed. Clever.'

He inclined his head graciously in acknowledgement, flicking his whip across Xanthus's back to make her quicken her pace. She ignored him.

'But if you already had the gold, why not simply offer to exchange that for the provisions we needed? Why that mummery, which they might easily have seen through?'

A smile twitched over his thin lips. 'You're losing your touch, Camelot. They are wealthy men. They didn't want gold. What use is gold to them? There is nothing to buy with it. They wanted proof that they were right.'

'Are you finally admitting that you can sell a man hope? Have I at last succeeded in teaching you that?'

He laughed and flicked his whip again, harder. He was in a better mood than I had seen for weeks.

'No, Camelot, not hope. Hope is for the weak; have I not succeeded in teaching you that? To hope is to put your faith in others and in things outside yourself; that way lies betrayal and disappointment. They didn't want hope, Camelot, they wanted certainty. What a man needs is the certainty that he is right, no self-doubt, no fleeting thought that he might be wrong or misled. Absolute certainty that he is right, that's what gives a man the confidence and power to do whatever he wants and to take whatever he wants from this world and the next.'

We camped that night at the base of the healer's gully. We built fires and Zophiel slaughtered the sheep. His hands were skilled at that too. A flash of his knife across its throat and the beast dropped like a stone without a struggle or a cry. Zophiel caught the blood in a bowl and set it aside, then he and Osmond skinned and gutted it. Narigorm helped them, squatting on her haunches, as she dragged the steaming purple entrails into the bucket.

The healer had told us that Adela should eat the liver and heart, so these I stuffed into the paunch with the kidneys and pluck, boiling it in the blood, along with the sheep's head and trotters. We set two legs to roast on spits. The remainder of the carcass we wrapped and hung from the top of wagon, out of reach of scavenging dogs or foxes. In this cold weather it would keep for several days.

We sent up some roasted meat, a trotter and a little of the wine to the healer by way of payment for the herbs. I declined to take them to her, but Zophiel offered to go. I had no wish to speak to the healer again.

Darkness came quickly and the air grew colder still. The clear indigo sky was frosted with stars. Using the river as a defence on one side, we lit a semicircle of fires so that we could sleep between the river and the fires for protection. Then we sat under the stars warming our stomachs with the sweet roasted meat and picking the flesh off the trotters steeped in the rich blood gravy. Never had meat tasted so solid and satisfying. We stuffed ourselves until our bellies were swollen, and still had appetite to crack the bones and greedily scoop out the melting yellow marrow fat.

Adela, though still tired, looked brighter. I hoped the healer was right and the milk would soon flow richly. The baby lay sleeping in her arms. He had taken several spoonfuls of the egg and already his eyes seemed less hollow and his skin smoother.

The baby had been named Carwyn, which means *blessed love*. Despite his precarious grasp on life, he had not been named until he was several days old. For even had we been thinking of anything else but Jofre's mutilated body, we could never have named an innocent child on the day we buried Jofre, tying him for ever to the name of death.

It was Adela who named him. Osmond smiled wanly at her choice, but he never used the name. He never held Carwyn or tended him, even when he cried. There was something about the baby which he couldn't bring himself to approach. He no longer sat with his arms about Adela as he used to do of an evening, but sat apart now, like Joseph in the paintings of the Nativity. Guarding, protecting, yes, but standing aside, no longer part of the mother and child.

I had not told Adela and Osmond what I had guessed and I would not betray them to the rest of the company. I did not want to see the disgust in the eyes of Rodrigo and Cygnus or the pain in Adela's and Osmond's. And what right did we have to condemn them for being in love? 'Bone of my bone,' isn't that what Adam said of Eve?

Besides, little Carwyn was the only thing that could bring a trace of a smile to Rodrigo's face. He doted on the baby and often cradled him in his arms while Adela rested. His own eyes gentled as he looked into Carwyn's dark blue ones and for a few minutes he looked again like the Rodrigo I had first seen in the inn all those months ago.

Since Jofre's death, he had withdrawn into himself. His face was haggard and not just from the meagre diet. Before, I had seldom known him to go a day without practising his music. He said it was vital to keep his fingers supple. But since that day he carried Jofre's body home, he hadn't played a single note. I think he was punishing himself by denying himself his greatest joy, because he blamed himself for Jofre's death. My heart ached for him, but I couldn't find the words to comfort him.

The only one of us unaffected by Jofre's death was Narigorm. She did not change; things changed around her. Unlike most girls her age, she showed not the slightest interest in the new baby, almost as though she thought he was already dead. I tried to shake the thought off, but her way of looking straight through Carwyn, as though he was not there, frightened me. Osmond still took her hunting with him. He spent more time with her than with Carwyn. Yet even he would come back from these expeditions troubled by how much pleasure she took from the act of killing small creatures. But as Zophiel said, children enjoy the triumph of catching a bird or fish. It's a game to them.

Zophiel had been in a buoyant mood ever since we had returned with the wine and sheep. He recounted the tale of Voluptas with self-deprecating modesty, which from him always sounded more arrogant than a man who openly boasted. But as the moon began to rise, filling the gully with pale light and long shadows, his unease returned and he began to dart anxious glances about him, his hand straying to the knife in his belt. We all of us had drawn our knives and staves close to hand as the sky darkened. We had good reason to. Night was the domain of the wolf.

I stared up at the top of the ridge above the gully. The moonlight brushed the brow of the hill with a silver sheen, but nothing up there was stirring. I could hear nothing except the crackle of the fires and the water in the river rushing over the stones and boulders. As I sat in the stillness of that valley, listening to the babbling of that river, I suddenly felt as if I was back in the hills of home. I could almost see the sleek otters hunting in the streams, the water so cold and clear it numbed your fingers. I could almost taste the sweet purple bilberries crammed into my mouth, staining my lips and fingers blue. And the wind, the clean, pure wind that in winter snatched your breath away and in summer tasted like white wine. I knew it was impossible, but that night I'd have given anything just to stand there and drink in the solitary peace of it, just one last time.

I started as something huge and pale glided silently down the gully just beyond the light of the fires. Glimpsing it only out of the corner of my eye, I couldn't make out what it was. Then I heard the deep sonorous 'oohu-oohu-oohu': an eagle owl out hunting for his supper.

Cygnus shivered at the eerie sound and pulled his cloak tighter around himself. 'What if the wolf smells the sheep carcass on the wagon?'

'It'll be drawn to the spot where we slaughtered and skinned the sheep,' Osmond said. 'The smell of blood there will be stronger.'

They had deliberately butchered the animal a good way off from the camp, so as not to attract any scavengers, but now that it was night, it seemed uncomfortably close. The next valley would have been too near. Cygnus glanced in the direction of the spot, but it lay in the shadow of the hill, too dark to see anything moving there.

'But what if it follows the scent back to the camp?'

'It will not,' Zophiel said. 'It'll find all it needs there.'

'But there is nothing except some blood-soaked grass. That'll only whet its appetite.' Cygnus's voice shook slightly.

'There's meat there. I returned to the place and left some.'

I drew my stave closer. 'That will divert it tonight, for which I am profoundly grateful, Zophiel,' I added hastily. 'But aren't we in danger of encouraging it to continue to follow us for food?'

'I assure you, Camelot, that if it takes the meat tonight it will be its last meal. The meat is laced with wolfsbane. Come now, you didn't think I would simply leave it as a gift? Whatever or whoever takes that meat will not live to see dawn and then we shall be rid of it for good.'

'Whoever?'

'Was it not you, Camelot, who first told us the tale of the werewolf? Surely you don't dismiss the idea? After all, you have the scar to prove it.'

Rodrigo broke in as if he had only just realized what Zophiel said. 'Wolfsbane? You carry this poison with you?'

Zophiel laughed softly. 'You take me for an assassin? No, I suspected the healer would have some. It grows well near water and it is, I'm told, effective when applied to the bites of venomous creatures, even the bite of a werewolf.'

'The healer gave it to you?' I couldn't imagine her handing over a quantity of deadly poison to anyone, especially a man like Zophiel.

'Let us say, she was persuaded to do so.'

Osmond was on his feet in instant. 'What did you do to her, Zophiel?'

Zophiel flinched backwards, but quickly recovered himself. 'Nothing, my friend, a little bargaining, that is all.'

'What could you have that she would want?' Osmond asked suspiciously.

'It is more a question of what she has. It's well known that witches use blackthorn rods to procure abortions. If they are caught with such a rod, I believe the punishment is to burn them on blackthorn pyres. She has a blackthorn hedge big enough to set a whole coven alight.'

'You threatened her, after all she's done for us?' Osmond shouted.

Rodrigo too was on his feet. Faced with the fury of both Osmond and Rodrigo, Zophiel tried to scramble up, but all three froze as the unmistakable sound of the wolf's howl echoed along the gully, reverberating through the darkness. We stared around frantically, but none of us could tell where the sound came from. Again and again the wolf howled and each time the sound seemed to surround us. First we heard it on one side, then on the other. Osmond and Cygnus ran to the fires, poking them and piling more wood on to them until the flames roared up and golden sparks exploded into the darkness. Rodrigo, his stave firmly grasped in both hands, peered this way and that, trying to see where the attack might come from. Adela crouched on the ground, bending over the baby in her arms, trying to shield him with her own body. Zophiel wheeled around wildly, his knife raised and his lips moving soundlessly as if he was praying.

The only one who did not seem to comprehend the danger was Narigorm. She stood motionless, silhouetted by the fire, one hand extended as if she was reaching out to touch the sound. Then it was gone and silence rolled back from the hills, a silence that blotted out the crackling fire and dark rushing water, a silence more unnerving than the howl. We held our breath and listened.

I don't know if the others got any sleep that night. We took it in turns to keep watch and stoke the fires, but even when I knew others were on watch, I couldn't sleep. Finally I saw, with relief, the thin edge of light come creeping over the distant hill. I must have slept then for when I woke, the sun was up and Adela was stirring a pot over the embers of one of the fires. A thin plume of smoke rose vertically into the pale pink sky. My cloak was so stiff with frost it crackled as I tried to rise.

I glanced up at the healer's cottage. No smoke rose from her hearth. Perhaps she had not yet risen. I didn't blame her. If I'd spent the night in a warm bed I wouldn't hasten to get out of it. Zophiel and Rodrigo still lay asleep recovering from their last watch, but Osmond and Cygnus had already gone to search for wood and Narigorm was drawing water from the river.

I was finishing a second bowl of broth when I saw Cygnus and Osmond striding back to the camp, their breath hanging white in the air as they hurried along. Both had bundles slung over their backs. It appeared their forage for firewood had been successful. But as Cygnus strode past me I could see that something was wrong. Zophiel had just risen and was crouching by the river, splashing water on his face. Cygnus strode up to him and pulled at the knot in the thong round his neck, letting his bundle drop with a dull thump on to the frozen ground. It wasn't firewood he carried, but the lifeless body of an owl, a large one. The black beak was wide open as if it had been gasping for air.

'This is what you killed with your wolfsbane last night, Zophiel. No wolf, just this poor creature.'

Zophiel straightened up and turned, shaking sparkling droplets of water from the tips of his long fingers. He barely glanced at the owl lying on the ground at his feet.

'Any signs the meat had been gnawed?'

'A few strips torn from it, but they were probably taken by the owl.'

Zophiel prodded the feathers with the toe of his boot. 'Eagle owl. Valuable hunting bird. It might be wild, but most likely some careless falconer lost it. I wouldn't want to be in his shoes; they'll take the price of it from his hide. Still, it's worthless now, you may as well throw it away.'

Cygnus was trying to keep his temper in check, but he was losing the battle.

'Never mind the value of the bird, Zophiel,' he shouted. 'What about the meat you left out? A few scraps of raw meat laced with poison would have been enough to kill a hungry wolf. But you put out a whole leg and part of the side too. Adela and the baby need that meat. It would have fed all of us for at least a day. You took it without even consulting us. Now, because you've poisoned it, we can't even use the bone for broth. I know you're terrified of the wolf, Zophiel, but this was a stupid and needless waste.'

Zophiel's expression had grown increasingly venomous as Cygnus spoke. At the mention of his terror of the wolf, his eyes flashed dangerously, but unlike Cygnus, his voice was controlled and quiet.

'May I remind you that it was my skill and my gold that

bought that sheep and the wine, therefore the sheep and wine were mine. The fact that I chose to share them with you, as I have also shared my wagon and my provisions, is something you should be thanking me for on your knees. Had I not chosen to be generous, you, like Adela, would have gone hungry yesterday. What I chose to do with the remains of the carcass was entirely up to me.'

'We all share what we have, Zophiel,' Osmond protested. 'There's many a night you've dined on what I hunted or what Camelot bartered for one of his relics.'

Zophiel ignored the interruption and continued to stare malevolently at Cygnus.

'I sacrificed the meat, meat which I also could have eaten, in an attempt to keep all of us from the fate of our headstrong young friend. I trust you will allow that it is worth the sacrifice of a day's food. I hope you've not forgotten what Jofre's body looked like when it was recovered. It's hard to eat a slice of mutton without a throat. I suggest you keep that in mind before you venture to criticize me again. And as for wasting the meat, we'll lay it out again tomorrow night and the night after if we have to. Who knows, if we're lucky, we may succeed in ridding the world of another of your feathered cousins.'

He kicked the body of the owl out of his way and began to walk away from the riverbank. As he brushed past Cygnus, he knocked hard against him with his shoulder. Cygnus slipped on the frosty grass and staggered backwards, teetering on the edge of the river bank. Unable to regain his balance, he fell backwards into the water. The river was not deep, but it was icy. The shock made him gasp, just as the wave caused by his splash broke over his face. He choked as the water filled his mouth and lungs. Unable to get a foothold on the slippery boulders and weighed down by his heavy, waterlogged cloak, he panicked, his eyes bulging, thrashing wildly with his one arm.

Rodrigo ran across the grass and splashed into the river. He grabbed Cygnus, just as his head was going under again. He pulled him upright, dragged him to the bank and hauled him out.

Cygnus sank to his knees on the grass, coughing and spluttering. Rodrigo thumped him on the back as he fought for air. He remained where he was on the ground, breathing in painful shallow pants and shivering uncontrollably.

Rodrigo put a hand on his shoulder. 'Take off your wet clothes and come to the fire. Narigorm, fetch a blanket.'

But Cygnus was unable to move. Rodrigo crouched down and began to peel the sodden cloak from his back. As he helped the shivering boy out of his wet clothes, Rodrigo looked up at Zophiel who was watching the proceedings with amusement.

'You deliberately pushed him in, Zophiel. I saw you.'

'His temper needed cooling.'

'You know he cannot swim.'

'Then it's time he learned. Isn't that what swans do, swim? Surely that is the point of being a swan, that and making a fine roast for the table. After all, they're no use for anything else.'

He paused, stared and suddenly threw his head back, roaring with laughter.

'But what have we here? It seems I was mistaken. Our little prince is not a swan after all.'

We turned and followed Zophiel's mocking gaze. Cygnus still knelt on the grass. But he was stripped to the waist now and we saw at once what Zophiel meant. There was no wing, no feathers, just a soft pink fleshy stump, about the length of his foot, with six tiny protuberances ranged along the bottom, buds of flesh, no bigger than a woman's nipples.

Zophiel was grinning broadly. 'Naturally, if I had known he was just a poor cripple, I would never –'

Cygnus flinched at the word *cripple*, but Zophiel did not get the chance to finish his sentence. In one swift movement, Rodrigo had crossed over to him and struck him hard across the mouth with the back of his hand. Zophiel fell backwards on to the grass, but he recovered swiftly. Holding his left hand to his mouth, he struggled to his feet. I glimpsed a flash of sunlight reflecting off something in Zophiel's right hand. I tried to shout a warning, but Osmond reached Zophiel first. He grabbed Zophiel's wrist and twisted. The knife fell to the frozen ground.

Osmond kicked it away. 'Oh no you don't, Zophiel, you asked for that.'

For a moment Zophiel stood glaring at Rodrigo, then he wiped away the blood trickling down his chin from a rapidly swelling lip.

'Have a care, Rodrigo,' he said quietly. 'This is the second time you've raised your hand against me. I will not tolerate a third.'

21. The Standing Stones

There was still no smoke rising from the healer's hearth by mid-morning when we were packing up to leave the camp. I was becoming increasingly concerned, but the others were too preoccupied by the argument between Rodrigo and Zophiel to notice.

As they went about their tasks, the tension between Zophiel and Rodrigo was palpable. Osmond was keeping an anxious eye on both of them in case tempers flared again and he had to leap in to separate them. It was like watching a pair of growling dogs, knowing it is just a matter of time before they savage each other. Cygnus, on the other hand, was so sunk in misery and humiliation that he hardly seemed aware of his surroundings. He shook off Rodrigo's hand when he tried to help him to his feet, snatched the blanket and took himself off to dress alone. Dry, but with his teeth chattering uncontrollably, he returned to the camp. He wouldn't look at any of us. When Adela tried to get him to drink some hot broth to warm himself, he pushed it away without a word and went to prepare Xanthus for the wagon. But not even Xanthus's nuzzling drew a response from him.

As we packed, I kept glancing up at the healer's cottage. I had vowed never to go back there, but I knew I couldn't leave without finding out if something was wrong. Once again I felt responsible. If I had taken the roasted meat and wine to her the day before and not Zophiel, he wouldn't have had the chance to threaten her. What if he had gone beyond threats? What if he had pushed her, as he had Cygnus, and she was lying injured or worse?

It's madness in these times to approach a dwelling where no hearth fire burns. I knew that, yet still I climbed the path to the healer's cottage. I called out as I reached the gate, but there was no reply. The garden was as I'd seen it the day before, the hens still clucking and scolding among the herbs. I walked cautiously up the path. The strange fruit on the rowan tree hung heavy with frost. The tiny bodies sparkled as they slowly revolved in the light breeze.

When I reached the cottage and still got no reply to my calls, I pushed aside the heavy leather curtain and held it up so that the weak winter sunshine would illuminate the dark interior. Rocks which were part of the hillside jutted into the room, forming natural ledges and shelves on which were stacked pots and clay jars. Bunches of dried herbs hung from the roof timbers. The black iron pot suspended over the fire in the centre of the room was empty and the fire below was banked down so that hardly a whisper of smoke escaped. Only a few blood-red lines in the grey ash, like tiny veins, showed that beneath, the fire still glowed. The furnishings in the room were simple: a wooden clothes chest, two low stools and a narrow bed raised only a few inches above the beaten earth floor. The bed was occupied by a lanky grey cat which was curled up in the centre, regarding me impassively with big green eyes.

'Where's your mistress then?'

The cat blinked and licked a paw.

I backed out and looked around the garden, peering

behind bushes to see if the healer was lying unconscious somewhere, but there was no trace of her. Perhaps she had been so frightened by Zophiel that she had fled. I scanned the gully and the hill above, but there was no sign of anyone. The waterfall roared down over the rocks into the dark pool below. If she had fallen in there and been dragged down by the force of the water I had no hope of seeing her beneath the churning foam.

I turned to go, pausing only to leave a small flagon of Zophiel's wine by the door. Zophiel didn't know he had made her the gift, but I thought it was the least he could do.

I'd closed the gate and was on the path down, when the voice called out behind me, 'If that is wine you left at my door, I thank you.'

I turned. The gate was open and the healer was standing with one hand on it, but whether she had opened it from the inside or the outside, I couldn't tell.

I walked a few paces back up the path, near enough to speak without shouting, but not so close that she could touch me.

'I came to apologize for Zophiel, the man who came to you last night . . . and to assure you that whatever he said, we will not let him carry out his threats.'

'Your friend is a terrified man and with good cause judging by the howls I heard last night. I pity him. That's why I gave him what he wanted, not because he threatened me.'

'You heard the wolf then.'

'I heard it. Your friend did not succeed in killing it.'

This was a statement not a question. I wondered just how sharp her hearing was. 'It didn't take the bait. But we're leaving. I think it will follow us, so you don't need to fear it.'

'I fear priests and others who believe the Christ of compassion is best worshipped with bone-fires and racks, but not that wolf. I know I am not its quarry.'

I looked down at the camp. I could see Cygnus backing Xanthus between the wagon shafts. 'I must go, but many thanks for your help. The woman and child are already improving.'

'I'm glad.'

I turned away and took a couple of paces down the path before turning back; the healer was still standing there, one hand on the gate, as if she expected me to say something else.

'Forgive me, but I'm curious. Where were you, just now? I couldn't see you anywhere. Did you hear me calling out to you?'

She smiled. 'I heard you. I was there.'

An image of grey fur and green eyes flashed into my head and before I could stop myself I blurted out, 'The cat?'

She laughed. 'You also think I am a witch? No, not the cat, the waterfall. Water is transparent, yet it can conceal better than a solid door. There's a cave behind it. I discovered it long ago and my mother knew it before that. If people looked they would see it, but they don't. If you want to conceal yourself, the best place is often in plain view. But then I think you have already discovered that.'

The journey that day was more fraught than usual. The ground was frozen hard, which made Xanthus's job easier and the going quicker, but despite the winter sunshine, a storm cloud had settled over the company. Adela tried to keep up a bright stream of chatter, but it had no effect. Zophiel's swollen and evidently painful lip was a constant reminder of the humiliation he'd suffered and he was never one to bear such humiliations in silence. Only Narigorm was spared Zophiel's taunts. He had been wary of her ever since that night in the chantry crypt when she had spoken of wolves guarding the paths of the dead, but his unwillingness to challenge her did not extend to the rest of us. He vented his spleen first on Rodrigo, then Cygnus and finally on Adela, goading them at every opportunity until Osmond came close to giving him a black eye to match his lip. Rodrigo, ignoring Zophiel, tried desperately to engage Cygnus in conversation, but Cygnus, answering only in monosyllables, made it plain he wanted to be left alone.

To make matters worse, the track now began to skirt the edge of an ancient forest. Though the sun sparkled from the frost on the bare black branches of the trees, the forest made everyone uneasy. There were no leaves on the trees or bushes, but the thick trunks and tangle of last year's brambles made it hard to see far into the woods. After the fears of the night before, we were all on edge. Anything might be keeping pace with us in the shadows, slinking behind the trees. And it was not just beasts we had to worry about, there are human predators too. A band of cut-throats might easily be concealed around the next bend and every bird call, every rustle might be their signal.

As the afternoon wore on and there seemed no end to the forest, we quickened our pace, not even stopping to eat, until we came to a fork in the road. The main track ran on through the trees, but a smaller, rougher one appeared to lead away from them into open country once more. None of us wanted to spend the night sleeping near that forest, so by common consent we turned Xanthus on to the rougher track.

The sun was low and the cold chill of night was already rolling in. Apart from the dark line of forest at our backs, the only thing to be seen in any direction was a distant ring of standing stones. The dark stones stood out starkly against the vast expanse of pinking sky. It was a bleak and barren place. I shuddered to think of the nature of the gods they might once have worshipped here.

It soon became apparent that the track led to the stones and nowhere else. After all that effort we had been following a dead end, but it was too late to turn back before nightfall so we continued pushing the wagon towards the ring of stones.

The stones in the circle were about the height of a man and twelve in number. A taller rock, like an ancient warrior queen, stood a little way outside the ring and, between this and the circle, several smaller stones lay fallen in two rows as if prostrating themselves before her. Even close up it was an eerie place, but there was comfort in it too for the stones had withstood centuries of storms, invasions and disasters and had survived unchanged and unchanging.

At the base of the queen rock we found a deep, curved stone basin, like an oyster shell, but large enough for a man to sit in. It was placed so that any rain which fell on the rock would trickle down its surface and drip into the basin beneath. The stone surface of the basin was green with slime, but once we had broken through the thin layer of ice, the water beneath was clean and clear. At least we had water enough for Xanthus to drink and for us to cook with.

The sun was sinking rapidly and almost before it was gone, the first stars appeared, bringing with them an ice-sharp edge to the wind. We finished preparing the supper. Zophiel had laid out the poisoned bait again, some distance from our camp, but I don't think any of the rest of us believed it would work. Perhaps he didn't either. It was an amulet, a talisman, something to ward off disaster when you are powerless to prevent it. Despite what he said, Zophiel needed hope as much as the rest of us. As the skies darkened, he began pacing restlessly, peering out from between the stones in all directions, but he did not step outside their protective circle.

'Don't you want to eat, Narigorm?' Adela called over her shoulder, as she ladled mutton into my bowl.

Narigorm crouched in the shadow of one of the stones. She was hunched over, peering at something on the ground in front of her which lay within the light cast by the fire. My chest tightened into a dull ache as I watched her hands hovering in that familiar way over the ground.

'Narigorm, did you hear what Adela said? Come and eat now!'

Adela looked round in surprise at the sharpness in my voice, but Narigorm didn't move.

'I didn't realize,' Adela said in an anxious voice. 'It's best not to disturb her, Camelot, not when she's reading runes. It might . . . bring bad luck. I'll save her supper for her.'

The ancient stones loomed taller in the darkness. Strange shapes danced across them in the light cast by the flames, as if a host of people circled us just beyond our sight and we glimpsed only their shadows.

I took a bowl of mutton and walked across to Narigorm, deliberately standing between her and the fire to block the light. I held out the bowl, hoping the rich, hot steam rising from it would make her realize she was hungry.

'Please, Narigorm,' I said weakly, 'why don't you leave that and come and eat? No runes tonight, there's a good girl, not in this place.'

'What harm can it do?' Osmond said. 'Maybe she'll be able to tell us how to get rid of this wolf. If we even knew why it's following us, I'd feel better.'

404

What harm can it do? I'd never told him or any of the company what Narigorm had read in the runes the night Carwyn was born and Jofre died. I had tried to convince myself that her words had meant nothing. We'd all been worried for Adela and the baby that night. Narigorm had only said aloud what we all privately feared. The death of Jofre had been a coincidence, nothing more. You can read anything into a fortune-teller's predictions; they deliberately make them vague enough so they always seem to come true. Perhaps she'd not really learnt of Pleasance's death in the runes either. She could have followed her and seen her hanging. Nothing mystical about that, at least that's what I tried to tell myself.

Narigorm picked up a rune and held it up in the firelight. The symbol on it resembled a pot on its side.

'*Peorth* reversed.'

Osmond glanced at the symbol, then quickly averted his eyes. 'Is that to do with the wolf?'

'*Peorth* means a secret someone has not told.'

He laughed uneasily. 'We all have those. Let me think. When I was a boy I was madly in love with my mother's serving maid, but I was too shy ever to tell her. There, is that the secret?'

Narigorm shook her head. 'When *peorth* is reversed it means a dark secret, a dark secret that will soon be exposed.'

I heard a sharp intake of breath from somewhere behind me, then Osmond said quietly, 'Camelot is right. You should eat now.'

But Narigorm held up a second rune inscribed with two V shapes carved into it, interlocking and opposite.

'*Jara*. The time of harvest. The time to reap.' In the firelight her white hair writhed with red and orange flames. She gazed up at Osmond. 'When *jara* lies with *peorth*, it

405

means someone will reap the punishment for their dark secret soon.'

A look of utter panic crossed Osmond's face and he glanced at Adela who was staring equally wide-eyed, her ladle arrested in mid-air, spilling its contents on to the grass.

'That's enough now, Narigorm,' I said sharply.

I intended to say more, but Zophiel spoke from the shadows.

His voice sounded curiously strained, almost pleading. 'The runes only show what might be. We have the power to change the outcome. The runes are only a warning about what will happen if we do nothing to prevent it.'

Narigorm lifted her head and stared at him. The light from the flames twisted across her pale face, as if vipers writhed across her skin. Then, without answering, she picked up a third rune and held it up. This one was like an angled cross.

'*Nyd*,' she said. 'It's the fate rune. It means there's nothing that can be done to change the other two. The fate written in them cannot be changed. The dark secret will be revealed and it will be punished.'

In the silence that followed, no one moved. The only sounds were the crackling of the fire and the high-pitched keening of the wind as it funnelled between the stones.

Finally it was Rodrigo who broke the silence. 'Who are these warnings for, Narigorm? Do you know that?'

She reached down and picked something else from the ground in front of her and held it up in the firelight. It was not a rune this time, but a tiny ball of black marble.

'Whoever dropped this,' she said.

We looked from one to the other, perplexed, then Adela blurted out, 'Zophiel, isn't that the ball you used in the cup trick on Christ . . . ?'

She broke off. Zophiel was standing pressed flat against one of the stones, his eyes wide and horrified. Even in the dim light of the fire we could see he was trembling violently. He drew his hands up over his face and slowly, like a man who has been stabbed, he slid down the stone until he was crouching on the ground.

'You have to help me . . . you have to stop him . . . you can't let him kill me . . .'

No one moved. We were all too stunned. We had seen Zophiel scared before, but then he had been angry, bellowing orders. To see him reduced to a quivering wreck was far more horrifying. I crossed over to him and laid my hand on his arm. He flinched, but didn't shake it off.

'Zophiel,' I said as gently as I could, 'who are you talking about? Who's going to kill you?'

'The wolf,' he whispered.

'Come on now, Zophiel, this howling night after night is tormenting all of us. I know it is not natural for a wolf to be following us like this, but these are strange times; men and beasts alike are hungry. But if you're thinking of what happened to Jofre, he was alone, and anyway it's far more likely he was killed by a pack of dogs deliberately set on him. As long as we stay close together a lone wolf will not attack us.'

Zophiel moaned, his face still buried in his hands.

'Have you been attacked by a wolf before, is that why you've always . . . ?'

He shook his head, but still did not raise it to look at me.

Then a sudden thought struck me. 'Zophiel, when we were in the cave, the night we first heard a wolf howl, you said that if the wolf was a beast, the fire would frighten it off, but if it was a human wolf then the fire would attract it.

Is that what you think is out there, some kind of human wolf?'

He flinched.

'Zophiel,' I said urgently, 'if you know what this creature is you have to tell us. We have to be aware of what we're up against.'

There was a hiss as Osmond thrust a glowing stick into a beaker. He walked across to where Zophiel crouched.

'Hot wine,' he said awkwardly, thrusting the beaker at Zophiel. His face wore an expression of both embarrassment and pity.

Zophiel took the beaker, though his hands were shaking so much I finally had to help him hold it. He winced as the warm wine made contact with his cut lip, but he gulped the contents of the beaker down greedily.

I handed the empty beaker back to Osmond. He stood looking down at the trembling figure hunched against the stone.

'Camelot's right. You must tell us. We need to be prepared.'

Zophiel pressed his hand over his swollen lip and stared at the ground, then finally he nodded.

'A wolf story,' he said with a shaky laugh. 'We've heard Camelot's and Pleasance's, now you want mine. Why not? If the runes are to be believed, you'll find out soon enough. At least if I tell you, it will be the truth, not the lies others will tell of me.'

For a long time Zophiel remained silent, then he began, his voice still trembling, but gradually regaining its usual control.

'There once was a boy from a poor family, isn't that how you begin a story, Cygnus? He was one of five brothers, but this boy was different from his brothers, quick to learn and

clevei
that.
more
boy i
could
was s
beat
were
and p
from
and n
his he
'H
ally t
wealt
were
poor
they

procurement. He ceaselessly rooted out sin
found it, ministering to the stinking poor o
and remonstrating with drunks and who
to his own health. He still had faith
faith that if he was zealous in his d
would reward him with a pa
talents could be better appr
Zophiel started as if h
out into the darkness, dra
of the stone, dra
blanket as if he
one of his o
a man fir
out th
fea

services for months at a time, leaving the young priest to the care of the souls.

'Finally the young man did at last succeed in gaining a living in the city of Lincoln, but though that great city is wealthy, his parish was not. It lay in the poorest part of the town. No wealthy guilds endowed the church with chantries or silver chalices or even enough to mend the leaking roof. The church didn't lie on the pilgrims' route to the shrines of St Hugh or Little Hugh in the great Cathedral. It lay at the bottom of the hill by the stinking quayside. Only the poorest people, dock rats, drunks, whores and common sailors, came there. The rich merchants and ships' captains worshipped in the more prestigious churches.

'Still, the priest worked hard and went daily to the Cathedral to get himself noticed, hoping for a better

wherever he
n their deathbeds
res, without thought
then, our young priest,
uties, God and the Bishop
rish where his learning and
eciated.'

e had heard something. He stared
pressing his back into the hard granite
wing the shadow of it over him like a
could disappear into it, vanish, like a ball in
wn conjuring tricks. But however dark a place
ds to hide, the smallest glimmer of light will pick
whites of his eyes, and we saw them now, wide with
, gleaming like bleached bones in the moonlight.

Osmond fetched him another beaker of wine and he took a large gulp before resuming his tale.

'Then one day a miracle happened. It was the middle of winter, there had been a heavy fall of snow, and the boats had to break a channel through the ice as they came to the quayside. The priest was saying the third office of the day. There was a handful of people in church, mostly the old or beggars come in to keep out of the cold, not that the church was much warmer than the street. Suddenly the door burst open and a woman came staggering in, carrying a little boy who lay limp and still in her arms. He'd been playing on the ice and slipped through. They'd fished him out, but it was too late, the boy was dead. The mother begged the priest to pray for him. There was nothing that could be done, but the woman was so distressed that the priest took the boy from her and carried him through into the sacristy, but in his haste he stumbled and fell on top of the child. The jolt of the fall or the weight of the priest must have pushed the water out of the boy's lungs, for when the priest stooped to pick him up, the child coughed and began to draw breath. He carried the child back out into the church and his mother was overjoyed to discover the boy was alive. No one had seen the priest drop him, and before he had a chance to explain, everyone was talking about how the priest had prayed over a dead child and brought him back to life.

'News of the miracle spread and people began to flock to the priest for help, the poor at first, but then the wealthy who left money and fine gifts at the church. They sent for him to come to their homes to lay hands on their sick and they were generous in their gratitude.'

'The priest cured others?' Adela interrupted.

Zophiel laughed bitterly. 'Miracles are like murders; after the first one, each becomes easier than the last for, with each success, the miracle-worker's certainty in himself becomes stronger. But curing the sick and raising the dead is not enough. People want drama. They want the grand gesture, just as at the mass the ignorant populace must have the pageant and the spectacle to appreciate the power and the glory of God. Offer them a quiet prayer and a simple laying-on of hands and they think nothing important has happened. So they must be given sweat and blood. Pass your hands over a man's head, wrestle and groan and pull out a stone and tell him this is what has been causing his headache. Cry aloud in an agony of words, let them see the effort it costs, then hold up a bloody lump of gristle saying, "This I wrested from your belly."'

Rodrigo shook his head disgustedly. 'You called Camelot a liar for selling people relics and now you tell us this.'

'I was not selling them the fake bones of saints and telling them to put their faith in lies. Don't you understand? I was actually curing them. I only showed them the stones to make

411

them appreciate what I was doing for them, but it was my hands that were healing them. I had the power to heal. God was working through me. He showed me that when I brought that child back from the dead. He chose me because my soul was pure, because I had worked to make it so.' Zophiel was breathing hard, trying to regain control of himself.

'So what went wrong, Zophiel?' I asked quietly.

'A girl. A stupid little whore and her mother. She was the youngest daughter of wealthy parents, a girl of about fourteen. She was overindulged and spoilt. She wouldn't eat and when she was coaxed to, she would make herself vomit what she had eaten. She would lie for days sometimes, not speaking, just staring up at the ceiling. There were fits too, convulsions, not frequent, but enough to make her parents worry for her marriage prospects. The physicians couldn't help her so they summoned me, as so many did in those days. I laid hands on her and pronounced her cured, but that very night she had another convulsion, worse this time than before.

'Since she refused to accept that she was cured I knew that she was persisting in some grievous sin. I examined her alone and finally she admitted that she was touching herself in her private places, arousing herself. I ordered her to stop, but though she swore that she had, I knew she had not, for her sickness continued. After that I saw her alone daily to hear her confession. I gave her penances, but still she persisted in her sickness. I stripped her and whipped her with a birch to help her cast out her lust. But she was so steeped in depravity that her wanton lust reached out to me. I began to dream of her naked body. When I tried to say mass she invaded my prayers. I knew she was trying to bewitch me. I whipped her harder and I whipped myself harder still. I whipped myself until I was bloody. I punished my own flesh in every way imaginable, by fasting, by denying myself sleep, by wearing iron spikes on a belt which dug into my flesh, but nothing prevailed against her.

'As her sickness persisted, rumours began to creep round the town that I had lost my healing powers. Other clergy who were jealous of my miracles said that I had lost my power to heal because of some grievous sin. And then the girl's mother came to my church. She flew at me, accusing me of having lain with her daughter, said her daughter had told her as much. Said she was going to tell her husband.'

Zophiel's hand, the knuckles gleaming white in the moonlight, emerged from the darkness of his cloak and in the moonlight I saw the glint of silver from the knife he gripped.

'I swear by God's holy blood I did not have carnal knowledge of the girl. However much she had tempted me, I was true to my vows. I had kept myself pure. But that day as her mother stood screaming at me in my own church, I knew God had abandoned me and I could not defend myself against her lies. I knew what would happen. There would be the humiliation of an arrest, and even though I could claim trial in an ecclesiastical court, a charge of raping the young daughter of a wealthy and powerful man would not be treated lightly. It was my word against the girl's and the punishment would be severe. I cursed myself for ever being alone with her.

'Even if I were found innocent, even if that wretched girl could be made to confess her lies, I knew no one would believe in my miracles again, no one would come to me for healing. I would lose everything I had worked for, the money, the respect. All my efforts would have been for nothing, I would be back in the sewer that I had struggled so hard to escape from. After all I had done for God, I did not deserve that.

'I could not sit there and wait for them to come for me. So I cast off my priest's robes, packed what I could and by nightfall I was on the road.'

There was a long silence when Zophiel finished his tale. He sat with his head once more in his hands as if trying to blot out the memory of that day. Sadness welled up inside me, not for the man crouching by the stone, but for the youth, long gone, who once had tried so hard, had so much faith.

Finally the silence was broken by Adela. She stared at him incredulously. 'You were a priest?' she said, as if she had only just taken in what he had told her. 'But how could you be? You're a magician, a conjuror.'

Zophiel raised his head and laughed bitterly. 'You think they are different? When a conjuror performs, people see what they want to see. The conjuror holds up his cup, says his abracadabra, and behold, a white ball turns black; a toad becomes a dove; lead transforms into gold. When a priest holds up his cup and incants his Latin chant, the people say, behold, wine has become blood, bread is become flesh.'

'That is blasphemy!' Osmond sounded more shocked than I'd ever heard him. 'Rodrigo is right, you are a hypocrite. You accused Cygnus of sacrilege when he suggested Adela could give birth in the chapel. And for you, a priest, to say –'

'Do you know what blasphemy really is, Osmond? Blasphemy is a woman. That is the thing which is an abomination before God. They are the succubi that leech upon the soul of man. They tear down all he has built and bring him to nothing. They lead him from God into the snares of the devil, no man is safe from them, for even if he resists their seductions, they will find a way to bring him down. And one day you will discover that for yourself, Osmond. One day she will do to you what women always do to men; she will damn your soul.'

Adela, covering her face with her hands, scrambled up and fled towards the wagon. Casting furious looks at Zophiel, Osmond ran after her.

Cygnus rose to his feet, his face contorted in fury. 'How dare you speak of women like that, especially Adela? She's shown you nothing but kindness. Are you forgetting it was a woman who gave birth to you?'

But Narigorm interrupted. 'There's no wolf in this story. You said this was a wolf story.'

'Narigorm's right,' I said. 'What has this tale to do with the wolf?'

Zophiel drained the last dregs from the beaker of wine.

'It has everything to do with the wolf. The wolf that has been following us is a human wolf, as you surmised, Camelot. I knew he had found me the night we heard him when we were in the cave. He's been tracking me ever since.'

'Because of the girl?' I asked.

'No, not the girl, she does not matter to anyone. If it had been the girl they would have sent the sheriff's men after me. Out there somewhere watching us are not the sheriff's men; it is the Bishop's wolf. The wolves are the men the Church pay to recover what's been taken from them. They pay them well, but only if they recover what is lost. They work alone, tracking their quarry for months, years sometimes, to recover some stolen relic or jewel. They work outside the law. There are too many precious items in churches and abbeys whose provenance would not stand up to close scrutiny in court. Which bishop or abbot can swear his relics and jewels were not once the property of someone else, someone who might in turn demand them back? The Church's wolves do not arrest people and bring them to trial. The Church cannot risk that. The wolves have their own brand of justice and they are the judge, jury and executioner of it.'

'But I don't understand, you made no mention of theft. What did you steal?'

'I stole nothing. I took only what was mine. I earned them. They were given to me in gratitude by those I had healed. It was the power in my hands that healed them, not the Church. They were mine to take.'

I shook my head in disbelief. 'You took the gifts that had been given to your church as thanks offerings?'

'That small metal plate I felt in the unlocked box, the night I hid in the wagon. I've just realized what it was,' Cygnus said suddenly. 'It was a paten for holy bread, wasn't it? No one would make a plate that small for anything else.'

'That piece is of little value, but it is mine.'

A look of comprehension was spreading across Cygnus's face. 'But if Jofre got curious and searched your boxes and he saw it, he would have realized that there was something odd about a magician travelling with an object that only those in holy orders should ever touch. That's what he meant in the chantry when he threatened to sell the information of what was in your boxes. He wouldn't have known who you were, but he knew no layman would have come by such an object honestly.'

'So,' said Rodrigo furiously, 'I was right. You threatened to hand Cygnus over to the sheriff's men, but you had no intention of doing this. You were a fugitive yourself. You could not risk standing up in court as witness against him. You tormented him with your threats because it amused you. And you accused Jofre of being a thief when you –'

'They were mine to take,' Zophiel repeated stubbornly, ignoring Rodrigo whose eyes were blazing with anger.

'What I don't understand,' I said, 'is if they knew you had taken them, why didn't this wolf seize the items as soon as he found you?'

'He didn't know for certain I had taken them. You don't think I simply walked out with them? I'm not that stupid. I was careful to make it appear that the church had been broken into. The church was surrounded by thieves and foreigners. They'd break in and steal anything just to get the price of a drink or a whore. It was easy to cast suspicion on others. The wolf had no proof, so he had to wait for a chance to look inside the wagon, or maybe he hoped I'd be foolish enough to try to sell one of the pieces.'

'And we unwittingly protected you, because there was always one of us around,' I said.

'Until that day in the chantry, when this useless cripple left the door unbarred, the day a silver chalice was taken from my boxes.'

'And that's what you accused Jofre of stealing,' I said.

'The wolf took the chalice. It was a warning.'

Rodrigo's fists clenched in fury. 'Then you knew Jofre had not stolen it.'

I grabbed his arm, mindful of the knife in Zophiel's hand.

'I did not know that morning, I swear. I believed it was Jofre. I thought he had taken it and sold it in the town. I went there that morning to try to recover it, but I could discover no trace of it. Then I realized the wolf had taken it as a warning to me.'

Rodrigo's breathing was heavy and laboured. I could feel the tension in his body. I prayed he would be able to keep control of his temper, for neither Cygnus nor I would be able to stop him if he lost it.

'And what happened to Jofre . . . was that also a warning?' he asked, his voice cracking with choked-back tears.

Zophiel didn't answer.

I shivered. The wind was picking up and flames from the fire twisted in the gusts. Rodrigo sat with his fists pressed against his mouth, as if he could not trust himself to speak.

A thought struck me. 'But if you know the wolf is human, why lay out the poisoned meat? A man wouldn't fall for such a trick.'

'He must be using dogs to track us under the cover of darkness. He can't risk following us too closely in open country; we'd see him. If we can get rid of the dogs, we might lose him. Besides, if he thinks the meat has been dropped by mistake or stolen by the dogs, he might be tempted to share it with them. All those weeks out there, he can't have found it any easier to find food than we have.'

'You left meat poisoned with wolfsbane for a man!' Cygnus cried. 'Don't you know how cruel and agonizing a death that is?'

Zophiel's face was contorted into a mask of fear and hatred. 'Yes, of course I know. Agonizing but rapid, which is more mercy than the wolf has shown me.'

In spite of all he'd done, I felt a sudden wave of pity for him. Even though I had no love for the man, I would not have wanted my worst enemy to torture himself like this.

'Zophiel,' I said as gently as I could, 'it's been over a month since the chalice was taken. Surely if he was hunting you, he would have made his move by now? What would be the sense in delaying? He would have had you arrested weeks ago if he had proof.'

'Why are you all so stupid?' Zophiel screamed. 'Haven't you listened to a word I've said? Don't you understand? There will be no arrest. There will be no trial. They relish their work, these men. To them, murder is an art. They want you to know they are there watching and that they can take you any time they please. They enjoy tormenting the victims first. How can you fight a man when you can't even see him? I look at faces in a crowd and I know any one of them could be him. I could brush past him on a crowded street and I wouldn't even know it. He is out there, biding his time, waiting until there are no witnesses. Then he is going to kill me ... he's going to kill me and there is nothing I can do to stop him.'

As if it had been listening to these words, a wolf's howl suddenly rang out above the wind. Zophiel started so violently that the knife jerked from his trembling fingers and fell noiselessly on to the grass. He was still on his hands and knees, desperately groping around in the dark for it, when the second howl reverberated around the stones. He collapsed on to the ground, pressing his hands to his ears, and began to sob.

22. Stains in the Snow

We heard the singing long before we saw the procession. It was still dark and the stars shone brightly, but a faint pearly shimmer on the eastern horizon whispered that dawn was not far off. We were already awake. None of us had got much sleep with the thought of the Bishop's wolf out there somewhere watching us. Although Zophiel had regained much of his customary composure once the howls of the wolf had died away, his revelations had left us all tossing and turning, unable to settle. Zophiel himself had paced the stone circle half the night, before weariness and wine finally caught up with him. Towards morning it had grown so cold that any pretence at sleep had become impossible. One by one, we had risen and crept close to the fire to sit in silence, warming our hands on beakers of a weak bone broth that had been simmering all night in the embers of the fire pit.

The sound of the chanting reached us in snatches above the wind. At first I thought it was the wind itself, singing through the stones, but as it grew louder, more constant, I realized it was human voices. Zophiel and Rodrigo hurried across to Osmond who was still on watch and was peering across the dark heath in the direction of the forest.

Then we saw distant dots of light bobbing and weaving

in the darkness. We all stood grasping our knives and staves as the lights came slowly towards us and finally we made out a line of people carrying flaming torches that trailed streams of fire and smoke behind them like pennants in the wind. Osmond hurried Adela and the baby to the wagon and pushed them underneath it. Shoving a blanket towards her, he urged her to cover herself and keep still. He made Narigorm do the same.

About twenty men and women were walking towards us in a long line. Despite the torches, they did not look or sound like a lynch mob. We stood nervously among the stones and waited, gripping our staves. Our fire was well banked down in the fire pit, and the stones were still in darkness, so they didn't appear to notice us at first, but they must have caught sight of the wagon for the leader suddenly raised his arm and they all stopped.

They stood watching us, as we stood watching them. We still had darkness on our side, for though they were well illuminated by the torches, we were concealed among the stones and they could have little idea of how many we numbered. Eventually they came to some sort of a decision and started forward again. The line was a little more ragged, but the singing grew louder and finally we could make out the words.

'*Ave Maria, gratia plena, Dominus tecum.* Hail Mary, full of grace, the Lord is with thee.'

As they drew level with the circle of stones, we saw their faces turn towards us, searching the darkness anxiously, but they didn't enter the circle of stones. Instead they walked round them until they came to the line of fallen stones leading to the tall queen stone at the end. Still chanting, they processed up through the line of prostrate stones and there they paused to stick their torches in the ground. Then, as we stood in silence and watched, they began to strip off their clothes until each of them was naked.

'*Benedicta tu in mulieribus, et benedictus fructus ventris tui, Jesus.* Blessed art thou among women and blessed is the fruit of thy womb, Jesus.'

They stood facing the east, their arms hugged around themselves, shivering in the bitter wind. Their leader positioned himself directly in front of the queen stone. He was a small, frog-like man with no neck and a rotund, sagging body, but in contrast, his legs and arms were long and spindly. He jiggled up and down on the balls of his feet in an effort to keep himself warm, his pale flaccid buttocks wobbling in the torchlight. His followers were still singing, but the sound was muffled now by clenched jaws and chattering teeth.

'*Salve, regina, mater misericordiae, vita, dulcedo et spes nostra, salve!* Hail holy queen, mother of mercy, hail our life, our sweetness and our hope.'

As the pale disc of sun edged up just over the horizon, the leader struck his fists down on to the ice in the bowl at the foot of the queen stone and stepped in. He ducked down quickly and scooped the freezing water over his head and shoulders three times, before hastily scrambling out. No sooner had he stepped out than the next stepped in, men and women, one after another, the first rays of the sun sparkling from the drops of water as they dashed them over their shivering bodies. Once the ordeal was over, each dressed as rapidly as numb fingers and wet bodies would allow. They didn't dry themselves, but pulled their shirts and shifts over their goose-pimpled flesh and stuffed wet feet back into woollen hose. Through all the bathing and dressing, the round of *Ave*s continued shakily, but unabated.

It was only when the women laid little bunches of snowdrops around the base of the stone that I finally remembered it was Candlemas Day, the purification of the Virgin, but which virgin, I wondered, for despite their *Aves* this was hardly a Christian site. It was not like me not to keep track of the days, but this business of the wolf was depriving me of what few wits I had left.

The leader came across to us and nodded gravely.

'You will forgive us, brothers, for intruding on your camp, but we always bathe here at dawn on the quarter days. We didn't expect to find anyone here. No one comes here as a rule but us.' He sounded somewhat put out.

'A penance to purify the soul?' said Zophiel. 'This is a heathen place to make such an act of contrition.'

The man drew himself up to his full height, which had little effect since he was still over a head shorter than Zophiel.

'Heathen?' he said indignantly. 'Did you not hear us singing to the Blessed Virgin? People have been coming up here for generations. The water which runs down that stone has healing powers. Why, cripples who could not walk a step have been carried here and put in that basin and they have walked back down that path on their own two feet.'

Zophiel snorted. 'We have a cripple among our company. Born without an arm. Do you think your water will grow him a new one?'

'It's easy to mock, my fine fellow, but you'll be laughing on the other side of your face when you fall sick with the pestilence and we do not.'

I stepped in quickly. 'Forgive my friend, good sir, he didn't sleep well last night. He is in a choleric humour.'

'Then perhaps he should try the water,' the man said acidly.

'I'll see that he does. I take it you know these parts well?

423

Tell me, the main track over there, does it continue through the forest for many miles?'

The man considered this for a long time, before finally saying, 'It does.'

'Is there a crossroads or a road that forks off it?'

He considered the matter again. 'There is.'

I tried not to get impatient, but trying to extract any information from this fellow was like trying to milk a flea. 'How far along the forest road before you reach a fork?'

'About a mile.'

'Does this fork go anywhere?'

'Same direction as this. Crosses the heath, but lower down.'

'Forgive me, sir, but I meant, is it a dead end like this one or does it lead somewhere, to a village or town perhaps?' I could see Osmond grinning behind the man's back and I tried not to meet his eye.

'Leads to the sea. Take you a couple of weeks or more to get there, mind.' Then, taking a reckless plunge, he added, 'But if you take that road you'll not get to anywhere before nightfall and you'll want to be somewhere before then.' He glanced up at the sky. Heavy clouds were rolling in from the north. 'Wind's shifted. We'll see some snow before long.'

He turned to go, then stopped as a new thought struck him. 'There's a drovers' hut near a pinfold along that heath track. You might make that, if the snow holds off long enough. It'll be a bit of a roof over you. There's a spring there to water the horse. But,' he added, glowering once more at Zophiel, 'it's not a healing spring, so if you want to get rid of your friend's choler, I'd give him a good bath here first if I were you.'

With that he turned on his heel and stalked off, leading his band of shivering supplicants back down the track towards the forest road.

'Well done, Zophiel,' Osmond said, 'You've certainly ensured we can't look for lodgings with them. They'll be waiting for us with pitchforks and burning brands once the news spreads.' He turned to Rodrigo and me. 'Do we make for the drovers' hut? If it's going to snow, we'll need more shelter than these stones.'

We all nodded.

'Break camp quickly then,' Zophiel said. 'Our helpful little friend omitted to tell us just how far the drovers' hut was, and if the track is anything like this one, I don't want to be travelling it in the snow. Cygnus, see that Xanthus is well watered before we move out, unless, of course, you want to try the water yourself first. Who knows, if our diminutive friend is right, pray nicely and you might grow another wing.'

Men say many things under the cover of darkness which, come the cold light of dawn, they bitterly regret revealing and Zophiel was no exception. He was clearly furious that he'd been forced to confide in us the night before. And as usual with men like Zophiel, they don't blame themselves, but those who witness their moment of weakness. He was not going to forgive any of us for having seen his wretched state the night before and it was evident he had no intention of giving way to his fear again. But then it is always easy to dismiss the terrors of the night when it is day, not so easy when darkness falls.

The baited carcass had caught nothing except a half dozen ravens which lay dead around the leg. None of us really expected to find a wolf lying there, nevertheless we hoped, for the alternative was to accept that whatever was following us was no animal. Rodrigo burned the carcass before we left. At least there would be no more dead birds.

It was around noon when we found the drovers' hut. Our little friend was right; it was 'a bit of a roof'. The hut was long and narrow, made from wattle and daub. Good for sheltering from summer storms, but not from winter's cold. The roof was an equally flimsy affair of overlapping wooden tiles cut from the ends of logs, but it looked sound and was steeply raked, which would be a blessing if the snow did fall. The most substantial thing about the hut was a rough stone chimney at one end.

The wooden pinfold nearest to the hut was large enough to contain a flock of sheep. There was a stone water trough inside, so it would hold Xanthus well enough. Several older pinfolds lay some distance away, made of rough stone walling which had collapsed in places. The hut itself was bare inside except for a stack of wool sacks, which served as beds for the drovers, shepherds and stockmen who used the hut. A small sack of withered turnips lay in one corner. I wasn't sure if Xanthus had ever been offered such fare before, but if we couldn't find fodder she might be grateful for them, as would we.

We set the last of the mutton to boil over the fire. It was going to be a meagre supper, but the water would collect the fat and flavour and make a thin broth for the morning. I made Narigorm sort through the sack of turnips and toss in a few of the better ones. They were woody and shrivelled, but they might be edible if we stewed them long enough.

As I stirred the pot, Adela sat nursing baby Carwyn. Her milk was flowing a little better now and the baby was stronger, but it wouldn't last if we couldn't find more food soon.

As if she had read my thoughts, Narigorm looked up. 'There's no more meat left after this, is there? If Adela doesn't eat meat, the baby will die, won't it?'

I saw the stricken look on Adela's face and said hastily, 'Don't say such foolish things, Narigorm. We still have the herbs the healer gave us. Carwyn is in no danger.'

'There'd be another day's worth at least, if it hadn't been wasted on useless baits,' Osmond said, glowering through the open door at Zophiel who was collecting boxes from the wagon.

'Recriminations won't restore the meat,' I said. 'Let's make sure we lay a piece of this aside for Adela to eat in the morning. The rest of us can do without tomorrow.'

Zophiel came in with the last of his boxes which he stacked as neatly as ever in the corner.

'Do we have to have those in here?' Osmond grumbled. 'There's hardly enough room for the seven of us as it is.'

'There'd only be six, if your wife had learned to keep her legs crossed. I have to put up with being kept awake half the night by your mewling brat.'

'And we have to put up with being kept awake all night by your howling wolf,' Osmond snapped. His fists clenched, but Rodrigo laid a hand on his shoulder to restrain him.

'Zophiel,' I said, 'why don't you simply leave the treasures from the church for the wolf to find? I know, I know,' I added hastily, seeing the look of outrage on his face, 'they're yours, you earned them, but surely your life is worth more than a few bits of silver? They're no good to you if you're dead.'

'Do you really think that would make him leave me alone? The Bishop may want his treasures, but the wolves feed on fear and blood. It's about exacting revenge and punishing their victim, not simply recovering what has been taken.'

'But you said yourself the Bishop would pay him well if he recovers the items. So if he retrieves them he'll be anxious to hurry back to Lincoln to claim his reward. He won't want to waste time waiting for a chance to find you alone.'

'If Lincoln has been hit by the pestilence, that city is so crowded it'll run through it faster than flood waters. The Bishop won't risk his corpulent posterior by exposing it to the city's foul humours. He'll have left long ago and our wolf will be in no hurry to seek him out. If the Bishop lives, the wolf may return to Lincoln once this pestilence is over or he may simply disappear and keep the treasures for himself; after all, what he's paid will be a fraction of what they're worth. Who's to know he did not perish in the pestilence? Another good reason for killing me; after all, I might take it into my head to throw myself on the mercy of the Church and confess all, including that he now has the items. No, Camelot, I am not simply going to hand my property over to a hired killer. I can wait too. He may be stalking me, but there is something stalking all of us, including the wolf. For all his assassin's skill, he can't fight pestilence or hunger. Whichever kills him, I trust it will be painful and lingering.

'Besides,' he added with a cold smile, 'our diminutive friend at the standing stones said this road leads to the sea and so I will finally get my passage to Ireland. The Bishop of Lincoln's reach is long, but it does not stretch that far. In Ireland I will be safe, safe from the pestilence, safe from the wolf.'

It was useless to argue with him, but I wondered if Zophiel would still be speaking as easily of waiting when night fell and the wolf howls began again. If the man at the standing stones was correct, we had at least two weeks' journey ahead of us before we reached the sea, and once the wolf realized where Zophiel was headed, he'd surely try to stop him before he boarded a ship.

Zophiel peered out of the door at the swollen clouds. 'At least if it snows today, he won't bother us tonight. He won't want to leave tracks, his or his dogs, which could be followed back to him. So all we'll have to keep us awake tonight is that brat. Did you know the ancients used to leave sickly infants outside in the snow? It either killed or cured them. Perhaps we should revive the custom.'

Adela clasped Carwyn to her, as if she feared Zophiel would snatch him from her arms.

Cygnus, glancing at the furious Osmond, said quickly, 'You'll sleep sounder under a roof, Zophiel, you won't even hear little Carwyn.'

Zophiel's eyes narrowed. 'Meaning what exactly, Cygnus?'

Cygnus hesitated. 'If I was being hunted, I'd be nervous about sleeping in the open. The howling would terrify anyone. I feel sorry . . .' He trailed off miserably, as he saw the look of fury in Zophiel's face.

'I trust I shall never sink so low as to need the pity of a cripple,' Zophiel snarled. 'What use are you to anyone, Cygnus? You can't hunt. You have to get Rodrigo to fight your battles for you. Tell me, Cygnus, what exactly is the point of you?'

Only Rodrigo's iron grip on his shoulder kept Osmond from launching himself at Zophiel.

Zophiel swung his cloak over his shoulders. 'I'm going to find fodder for Xanthus; we'll need as much as we can get if it does snow. I can't afford to have a dead horse on my hands.'

'But if the wolf is following, you shouldn't go out there alone,' I said.

'Let him go, Camelot,' Osmond said. 'Serves him right if the wolf does get him.'

Zophiel made a mocking bow. 'Your concern is touching, my friend, but he will not risk striking in the open in daylight.' He strode out without a backward glance.

Osmond's face was flushed with fury. 'I know being pleasant would be asking too much of him, but considering that little weasel begged for our help last night, you'd think he'd try to curb his tongue, seeing that we are all that stand between him and the Bishop's wolf.'

Cygnus muttered something about needing to see to Xanthus and rushed out into the cold.

'If Zophiel doesn't leave Adela and Cygnus alone, I swear I'm going to kill him,' Osmond muttered, his jaw clenched. He pulled on his cloak. 'I'll see if I can find anything for the pot. If I take it out on a few birds or rabbits, it might stop me pounding Zophiel to a pulp.'

Adela waited until he was out of earshot. Then she turned anxiously to Rodrigo. 'Go after him, Rodrigo, please. Stop him doing anything stupid. I'm afraid Osmond might really lose his temper and hit him. He'll use his fist, but Zophiel always goes for his knife and Osmond is not as good at defending himself as he likes to think.'

Rodrigo reached over and took her hand. 'I swear I will not let any harm come to him, Adela.'

She smiled up at him. 'You're a good man, Rodrigo.'

Rodrigo squeezed her hand, but he did not return her smile. He followed Osmond outside.

Our friend at the standing stones was right about the snow. By mid-afternoon the first flakes began to fall and soon they were swirling fast in the driving wind. Rodrigo and Osmond both came hurrying in within minutes of each other, banging the door behind them and sending smoke billowing back into the hut. Osmond dropped a pair of snipe on to the floor.

'Best I could do. Missed more than I hit and there wasn't much to hit. Everything's gone to ground. Seemed to know the snow was on its way.' He crouched down at Adela's feet and looked anxiously up at her. 'I'm sorry. I'll try again tomorrow. If this snow stops I may be able to track a hare or two to their form.'

She brushed the snow from his shoulders and smiled affectionately. 'You've done well to catch anything. Is it bad out there?'

'The snow's whipping so hard into your face you can't see a thing.'

The door crashed open for a third time. Cygnus stood in the doorway. Adela glanced up at the sudden blast of cold air and screamed. We all stared aghast. Cygnus's hand was covered with bright red blood.

Osmond, recovering from his shock, started forward. 'What happened, Cygnus? Are you hurt?'

Cygnus looked bemused, as if he didn't know why Osmond was asking.

'The blood on your hand!'

He stared down at his hand as if seeing it for the first time. 'Blood . . . yes, there was a lot of blood . . . I had to hurry.'

He swung a sack down from his shoulder and as he pulled off his cloak we saw the front of his gipon was also soaked with blood. He peeled back the neck of the sack and exposed the freshly skinned leg of a sheep.

'Adela needs meat. If the snow lasts we may not get more food. The sheep was old. It'll be tough, but if we boil it –'

'You slaughtered a sheep?' Relief spread across Osmond's face. 'But who on earth did you buy it from? I walked for ages and I couldn't see a cottage.'

Cygnus stared down at the blood on his hand again. 'I didn't buy it.'

Adela gasped. 'You stole it? That's a hanging offence. Tell me you haven't risked that to get meat for me.'

There was a shocked silence in the room; for a moment all you could hear was the crackling of wood on the fire.

Cygnus shrugged, avoiding looking at her horrified face. 'I buried the marked skin under some stones. No one will come here in the snow and if they do, who's to know this isn't the same sheep Zophiel and Camelot bought?'

I swallowed hard. 'If they find you covered in blood, eating fresh mutton in a drovers' hut, believe me, they won't stop to ask questions.' I was just as shocked as Adela. The penalties for sheep-stealing were merciless. I couldn't believe that Cygnus, of all people, would take such a risk.

'Camelot's right, you must wash that blood off quickly,' Adela said. 'Give me your gipon and your shirt. If I wash them in cold water before the blood has a chance to dry, we'll get the stain out.'

'No!' Cygnus snapped, then, seeing Adela's hurt expression, he added more gently, 'No, thank you. I can wash it. I don't want you to get blood on your clothes.'

We couldn't bring the sheep back to life, so there was nothing for it but to eat the evidence. We put the head, trotters and offal to boil straight away and hung the rest of the carcass up in the sack outside where the snow would keep it fresh. The wind had temporarily abated and snow was falling thickly now. It was lying and already the ground of the pinfold was white. By the time Cygnus returned from the spring clad only in his cloak and breeches, he was shivering violently and covered in snow. We hung his wet clothes near the fire to dry, where they steamed. But Cygnus insisted on braving the snow again to lead Xanthus to the side of the hut. He tethered her close to the back of the chimney in the lee of the hut where she could feel the warmth from the chimney stones.

Snow was driving in through the open window which overlooked the pinfold. There was no shutter. The shepherds and drovers who used the hut needed to keep an eye on their charges. I volunteered to go out to the wagon to find something to fasten one of the wool-filled sacks across the window to keep out the snow and the cold.

Xanthus was leaning gratefully against the warm chimney back, her head lowered. Her mane was already white with snow. Cygnus had tied some old sheepskins across her broad back to keep out the cold, and snow was forming a thick crust on top of them. It occurred to me that I should also fetch a spade from the wagon. If it carried on like this all night, we might have to dig our way out of the hut door.

At least we would have food to fill our bellies for the next few days. Whilst I was grateful for that, I cursed Cygnus with every name I could think of for taking such a stupid risk. I thought of the day we had first seen Cygnus telling his stories in the market place, and of the purple, swollen faces of the men slowly choking to death on the end of a rope in that same square. Cygnus knew only too well what they did to men who stole sheep. Osmond had asked me that day what would drive a man to risk such a punishment. Had Zophiel's taunts driven Cygnus to do something so dangerous, or was it what he once said to me, that no one who lets a child come to harm could ever be forgiven? Had he risked the rope for Adela and baby Carwyn?

But maybe he was right; no one would come looking. If

the sheep had been left to wander out on the heath in this, then they were strays or no longer had a shepherd to tend them. Why should we starve and watch a baby die when there was food for the taking? It was hard to adjust to, but the old laws and the old order were crumbling about our ears. There was a new king and his name was pestilence. And he had created a new law – thou shalt do anything to survive.

I returned to the hut, shaking the snow from my cloak. As Osmond nailed the wool sack across the window, a sudden thought struck me.

'Where's Zophiel? He can't still be looking for fodder in this? Did anyone see him when you were out?'

Osmond shook his head. 'Just as well I didn't. I'd probably have thrashed him.'

'Cygnus? Rodrigo?'

Rodrigo sat hunched over the fire. He didn't look round. 'I saw him earlier this afternoon.'

'It'll be dark soon. Perhaps we should go and look for him. He may be lost.'

'There's another hour of light left,' said Osmond. 'Maybe he walked a long way and it's taking him time to get back. Anyway, I'm in no hurry for him to return.'

We waited, but Zophiel did not return. The light was fading fast. Eventually even Osmond had to agree we needed to go out to look. If Zophiel had slipped and broken a leg, he might be lying out there helpless, though I dreaded to think what sort of patient he would make if he was hurt. Pain and frustration would do nothing to sweeten his temper.

Adela clutched at Osmond's cloak. 'What if the wolf's out there?'

'If you mean the Bishop's wolf,' I said, 'Zophiel's right. He'll not risk coming close in the snow and leaving tracks.

Besides, there's no reason why he should harm us,' I assured her, trying to push the image of Jofre's mutilated body out of my head.

'All the same,' said Osmond, 'since those wretched boxes of his are in the hut, I think Rodrigo should stay here with Adela, Narigorm and the baby. Rodrigo's the most able of us with the stave if it should come to a fight.'

Rodrigo, when pressed, said he'd last seen Zophiel walking in the direction of the far pinfolds. Pulling our cloaks tightly around us against the stinging wind, Cygnus, Osmond and I set off towards the pinfolds, fanning out so as to cover more ground between us. The snow was ankle-deep, deeper where the wind had blown it into drifts against walls and bushes. We carried torches lit from the fire, waving and calling in the hope that if Zophiel was lost he would at least see the lights or hear the shouts.

It was hard work, tramping through the snow; several times I came close to slipping and breaking a leg myself. Though the wind had eased a little, the snow was still falling hard and my guttering torch did little more than illuminate the millions of soft white feathers drifting down around us. In the distance I could just make out the bobbing torches of Cygnus and Osmond. I stopped to catch my breath. The sounds of Osmond's and Cygnus's shouts drifted back, but otherwise there was a suffocating silence.

We searched until it was completely dark and my hands and feet were so cold they hurt. Then I saw the two torches moving back towards me. Osmond and Cygnus had evidently decided it was futile to continue. I also turned back. He could be anywhere out on that heath. We didn't have a hope of finding him in this.

As I neared the furthest pinfold from the hut, I saw something move on the other side of it. I stopped, holding my breath, unable to make out what it was. I could feel my heart thudding against my chest, but then it moved again, and I realized with a rush of anger and relief that it was Narigorm. She had evidently been standing there for some time for her clothes were encrusted with snow. She was staring up into the sky, letting the white flakes fall silently on to her white hair and lashes.

'What on earth are you doing out here, Narigorm?' I shouted. 'Have you no sense?'

She turned, as if she had just been patiently waiting for me to come. Then she pointed at the ground inside the pinfold. The snow there was smooth and white, glittering in the torchlight. But then, near one of the walls, I spotted three dark smudges. I leaned over the wall as far as I could. Dark stones, maybe, sticking out of the drift. I moved the torch and realized it wasn't something jutting out of the snow; it was the snow itself that was stained.

I walked round the pinfold wall until I came to the opening. Now that I was inside, I could see there was a shape under the snow. From a distance it looked like a drift, but close up it was unmistakably the blurred form of a body. My heart pounding, I knelt down and scraped away until I found the fabric of a hood. I pulled it back. Zophiel was lying face down on the ground. There was no question that he was dead. I looked down at the three dark red patches staining the snow, melting it slightly. I brushed away the snow with numb fingers.

A pool of blood had oozed out of a wound between his shoulder blades, the kind of wound a dagger would make if it was thrust in hard and then wrenched out again. Chances were, Zophiel would not even have seen his assassin until he felt the knife plunge in. I brushed the snow from the side where a second, larger patch of dark blood stained the whiteness. My fingers encountered something both spongy and sharp. I had to fight to keep from retching. I swallowed hard and, gritting my teeth, grabbed at the cloth at Zophiel's shoulder, pulling the body up on one side.

The killer had not been content to leave it as a simple murder. Zophiel's arm had been severed between the shoulder and the elbow. From the end of the raw, bloody mess, the bone protruded white and jagged. I guessed by the staining on the other side of the body that the killer had done the same to his other arm. As I turned the body, something fell from it into the snow. Narigorm bent swiftly and picked it up. It was Zophiel's knife. It was covered with blood. Unless Zophiel had managed to wound his attacker, which seemed unlikely, then whoever had cut off his arms had probably used Zophiel's own knife to do it. It was sharp enough to slice through flesh, but not bone, that would have had to be snapped.

So the Bishop's wolf had caught up with him after all. Zophiel had said that he wouldn't strike once the snow had lain and risk leaving tracks. But he had forgotten that falling snow quickly covers tracks, even bodies. The wolf had timed it well. He must have struck just as it was beginning to snow and the falling snow had concealed him, his tracks and his deed.

23. A Corpse Lies Bleeding

Osmond and Cygnus stood in the pinfold staring down at Zophiel's body as the snow continued to cover it.

'We should raise the hue and cry,' Osmond said, his voice trembling.

'And send for the coroner?' I said. 'What if he happens to be the same one who attended Jofre's death? Two violent deaths from among our company in a month – we'd be hard put to explain that. I don't think that coroner would believe stories of the Bishop's wolf; we can't even describe him. And don't forget we have a stolen sheep in our hut too, in case you were thinking of asking him to stay for supper. No, unless we all want to be hanged, I think we should bury him before anyone else chances on the body.'

'But the ground's frozen solid,' Osmond protested. 'We'd never manage to dig even a shallow grave.'

'The earth floor in the drovers' hut won't be frozen,' I said.

The torch shook in Osmond's hand. 'Are you seriously suggesting we bury him in the hut and then sit on top of his grave and eat our supper?'

'Since the bad harvests, many people have taken to burying their relatives under their thresholds or floors, if they can't pay the soul-scot.'

'But not when they've been murdered and mutilated,' Cygnus said, glancing down at the body and quickly looking away. 'It's not like dying in your own bed. His spirit won't rest. It'll seek vengeance.'

The snow was still falling hard. I could see the faces of the others were stiff with cold and I could hardly feel my own. 'For now, let's cover him with the fallen stones from the wall. That and the snow will conceal him if anyone chances along here. And it will give us time to decide what to do.'

Even that was not as easy as it sounds. We had to drag the body over to the fallen part of the wall, where a heap of stones would not look out of place. Then we had to lift the stones on to the body with numb and painful fingers. It takes more stones than you might think to cover a man.

When we returned to the hut we found that Narigorm had already told Adela and Rodrigo about the body, in gory detail no doubt. They sprang up as we returned, searching our faces anxiously to see if it was true. Osmond hugged Adela to him, though I think that was as much to seek comfort for himself as to comfort her, for of the two of them, he was the more shaken. It was hardly surprising, for the sight of that mutilated corpse was enough to make even the strongest stomach heave.

Rodrigo clutched his head with both hands as if he was trying to keep it from bursting. Finally he said, 'You left the body where it was?'

'We covered it with stones for the moment,' I told him. 'But it can't stay there. If any shepherd or drover moves the stones to repair the wall, they'll find it at once. Even if the body has begun to decay by then, with the arms missing, no one finding it is going to think the stones fell by accident and killed him.'

'But with the snow, maybe no one will come.'

'The snow won't last for ever; they could be driving cattle or sheep this way within weeks, days even. If anyone finds the body and spreads the word, that man at the standing stones is bound to remember he directed us here. He's hardly likely to forget Zophiel. We have two choices: either we report it ourselves and trust that the coroner will believe the story about the Bishop's wolf, or we hide the body so it's not found. I think hiding the body is our only option.'

He nodded and turned away, crouching down by the fire and staring into the flames.

'What about Zophiel's boxes?' Adela asked fearfully. 'The Bishop's wolf might come in here to get them tonight.'

I shook my head. 'He's just murdered a man. He won't take the risk of being seen by all of us. But we should put them back in the wagon. Make it easy for him to take them and at least then we'll be rid of him. Although it's too late to help poor Zophiel.'

'Well, I for one am not going to pretend that I'm sorry Zophiel is dead,' Osmond suddenly burst out, glaring round at us. 'Look how he treated Cygnus and Adela. You're not sorry he's gone, are you, Cygnus? Or you, Rodrigo, not after the way he tormented Jofre?'

Neither of them looked at him.

'Osmond, don't,' Adela pleaded.

'What's the point of pretending? Why can't we be honest? He was a spiteful, vindictive, malicious man.'

'Osmond, don't talk about him,' Adela wailed, crossing herself. 'He's been murdered. He died without being shriven. His ghost will still be here. It'll hear you.'

We ate. We hadn't eaten since dawn, but I don't think

anyone tasted the food, except Narigorm who devoured hers with more than her usual relish. We chewed and swallowed to fill our bellies, but took no pleasure in it. We might as well have been chewing the old turnips as fresh mutton. We moved around one another in an awkward and uncomfortable silence, but I suspect no one's thoughts wandered far from the mutilated body lying out there in the dark. We covered ourselves with cloaks and blankets and slept, or pretended to, for it was an excuse not to talk.

None of us was surprised to hear the wolf howl that night. We propped ourselves up on our elbows and listened. The sound came from the direction of the far pinfolds, as if whoever or whatever was calling was standing on the pile of stones and howling his triumph into the night. He had made his kill. Justice was done. Honour was satisfied.

As the howls died away I became aware of another sound: someone in the hut was crying. I saw Rodrigo get up and go across to Cygnus. He wrapped his own cloak around the boy's shoulders and held him in his arms, rocking to and fro as if he was comforting a frightened child.

'It is the last time we shall hear it,' he said. 'It will leave us alone now. We are safe now that Zophiel is dead. We are all safe.'

'I heard the swans again,' Cygnus sobbed.

'No, no, *ragazzo*, it was the wolf you heard, but it is the last time.'

'Didn't you hear the swans? Didn't you hear their wings as they flew over? The feathers big and white, falling down, smothering everything. I couldn't breathe. It was so cold and their wings beating down . . . the sound of their wings. You must have heard them.'

'There are no swans. There is no water here. It was the snow that made you think of white feathers.'

He sat with Cygnus, stroking his hair, waiting until his breathing became steady again. Then, his arm still across the boy, he lay down, but I don't think he slept.

The following morning I went out early. It had stopped snowing, though the sky was heavy and it was bitterly cold. The boxes were still in the wagon where we had left them. I walked towards the pinfold where Zophiel's body lay. The ground was covered in a fresh layer of snow which had smoothed over our trampling footsteps, covering too the bloodstained grass where Zophiel's body had lain. There was no sign of any tracks, either human or animal. If the wolf had stood on that pile of stones howling the news of his kill into the night, the snow had covered all traces of it.

I glanced uneasily around me. Was he out there watching us still? Zophiel had been right; the Bishop's wolf was a man who took pleasure in murder and revenge. Death alone had not been enough to satisfy him. The severing of the hands was a common punishment for a thief, but why not simply cut off the hands at the wrists? It would have been easier than slicing through an upper arm. Had the wolf taken the arms as proof that he had brought his fugitive to justice or so that Zophiel's punishment would pursue him into the afterlife, for if Zophiel could not find his limbs on Judgment Day he'd face an eternity without them? I thought of the mutilation of Jofre's body. Had the wolf been responsible for that too? I knew with a sickening jolt that none of us would be safe from a man like that until he had taken what he sought.

The freeze continued throughout the next day and night. We mostly kept to the hut, eating the stolen mutton and waiting for the weather to change. Then, on the third day, we woke to clear skies and a bright sun and by mid-morning the snow was beginning to drip from the roof and melt in our footsteps. If this thaw kept up, we could travel in the morning, but so could others.

We could no longer avoid the question that none of us had been ready to face. What was to be done with Zophiel's body? Did we take it with us and hope to find a burial place, as we had with Pleasance, or leave it behind? There was no real choice. It had been hard digging in the forest even with the ground softened by months of rain. But after such a spell of cold weather, even once the snow melted, the ground was likely to remain frozen for several days. And the open heath was no place to spend hours digging a grave in frozen ground, not if you wanted to do it unobserved.

Rodrigo, Osmond and I took it in turns to dig in the darkest corner of the hut where we hoped the disturbed earth would be least noticeable. Fortunately, because it was only intended as an overnight shelter, the builders had not troubled to mix the earth with straw and clay to make it hard, though it had been compressed by the many feet of those who had used the hut. We worked in silence. Adela kept her face averted and cradled Carwyn tightly in her arms as if she feared the grave might swallow him.

It took as long to remove the stones from Zophiel's body as it had that first night to lay them. The corpse was frozen and stiff. We rolled him in a blanket and carried him back to the hut where we laid him, still covered, in the centre of the floor.

'We should pray,' said Adela awkwardly. 'He was a priest.'

'If he was a priest he could have said the prayers over Jofre. He could have given him a Christian burial,' Rodrigo said bitterly.

I put my hand on his arm. 'Jofre was given a good burial,

443

better than Zophiel will have. Jofre lies under an altar and the image of the Virgin watches over him.'

'Zophiel could have anointed his corpse.'

'Friends who loved him washed him and laid him to rest; that is all the anointing he needed.'

In the end we stood around the covered body and muttered what we could remember of the *Placebo* and the *Dirige*, the vespers and matins for the dead. With no priest to lead us we got no further than the first few verses of the psalms, but it was a service of a kind and perhaps it would shorten his days in purgatory.

Osmond and Rodrigo bent to pick up the roll of blanket containing the body, but I stopped them.

'We should strip the body and put it in the grave without a covering. The earth will absorb the fluids and he will decay faster. There will be less of a stench coming up through the ground. And if he is dug up, there's less chance he can be identified. Someone who saw him up by the standing stones might recognize his clothes. We'll bury the mutton bones with him too,' I added, carefully avoiding meeting Cygnus's eyes. 'If he's found, they may think stockmen caught him stealing sheep and took matters into their own hands. No one will blame them for that in these times and it may stop them looking further.'

No one moved. I knew none of them wanted to touch the body. I felt bile rising in my throat at the thought of it, but since I had suggested it, I had no choice.

Osmond put his arms round Adela and turned her away.

I peeled back the blanket. Zophiel's face stared up at me. The skin was blanched and waxy, but the nose was almost black. His eyes were open and the lips drawn back so that he looked as if he was in the act of making some sneering comment.

I worked as quickly as I could, trying not to look down at the arms. Though the skin was beginning to thaw and soften in the warmth of the hut, he was still too frozen for me to be able to move the limbs. So I cut away the clothes with my knife, piece by piece. They would have to be burned in any case. When he was finally naked, I had no choice but to ask the others to help me lift him.

Cygnus and I each grasped an ankle. Rodrigo stood behind the head and slid his fingers under Zophiel's shoulders, while Osmond, gritting his teeth, eased his hands under the cold naked buttocks, but we had not raised the body more than a few inches when there was a sudden cry from Narigorm that made us drop the body with a thump on to the hard earth.

'Look,' she said, pointing. 'The wounds are bleeding again.'

A watery red liquid was dripping from the ends of his severed arms. Osmond stepped sharply backwards, crashing into the wall behind him.

Narigorm took a pace nearer. 'When a murderer touches their victim's corpse the wounds open and bleed again to show everyone who the murderer is. That means,' she added triumphantly, 'that one of you must have murdered him, doesn't it?'

We stared at one another. Horror was written on every face except Narigorm's. No one moved or spoke and at our feet, the severed stumps continued to drip their accusing blood.

24. The Swan Knight

We left the drovers' hut as dawn was inching over the horizon. Patches of green were appearing all over the heath and the bushes dripped in the early-morning sunshine. Drifts of snow still lay against the walls of the pinfolds and the hut, but the track was rapidly turning to a thick, muddy slush, which the wheels and Xanthus's hooves sprayed over us as we trudged along beside the wagon. Every traveller knows it is madness to journey in a thaw. The mud makes the pace slow and the snow conceals rocks and potholes which could easily break a limb or a wheel shaft, but none of us wanted to spend another hour in that hut.

The night before, Osmond had taken Adela and Carwyn to sleep in the wagon, for she had become terrified that Zophiel's vengeful spirit would enter the hut where his body now lay buried beneath the floor. They say that infants should never sleep in the same room as a corpse, for spirits who are torn violently from their own bodies can enter the open mouths of babies while they sleep and possess them.

Rodrigo, Cygnus, Narigorm and I stayed in the hut. We had sprinkled the grave with salt, placed four candles around it and sat up to keep watch all night. We had taken the excavated earth that would not fit back in the grave and spread it across the rest of the floor, trampling it down hard so that the colour in the corner would look no different from the rest of the floor. Now, if we were lucky, no one would ever know they were lying down to sleep on top of a corpse. Perhaps we sleep on corpses every night and do not know it.

All through that long night we did not talk and we dared not sleep. We stole glances at one another in the candlelight. Could he have murdered Zophiel? Or him? But it was impossible to believe that anyone other than the Bishop's wolf could have done it.

Osmond had threatened to kill Zophiel and was hot-headed enough to have punched him, maybe even stabbed him in a fight, but Osmond would have fought face to face. He would never have stabbed Zophiel in the back or mutilated the body in such a terrible manner.

As for Rodrigo, it was unthinkable. Of all of them I knew and trusted him the most. True, he had twice attacked Zophiel, and I had seen the day he whipped Jofre that once he made up his mind to do something he saw it through with an iron resolve, but why do it now? If he really believed Zophiel had murdered Jofre as Cygnus had suggested, he would have taken revenge long before this; he'd had countless opportunities.

No, if any among us had cause to kill Zophiel now it was Cygnus. Vengeance smoulders a long time in a man who is repeatedly humiliated and builds a great heat in him, so that if he does turn on a bully, the attack will be savage. Had all the blood on his hand and clothes come from the sheep? And there was still the shadow of the deaths of Pleasance and the little girl hanging over him. Juries had convicted men on much less. But whatever the evidence, I could not believe that gentle Cygnus had murdered them or Zophiel.

It was the wolf who had killed Zophiel, I was certain of that and, as if to confirm it, the sound we most dreaded shattered the night again – the long-drawn-out howl of the wolf. Cygnus started and stared wildly at the grave. He scrambled to his feet with such haste that he fell back against the wall behind him. The four candles had burnt low. They were guttering and smoking in pools of wax, but it was not those flames which held Cygnus's horrified gaze. A small blue ball of flame hovered above the centre of the grave.

'A . . . corpse-light,' Cygnus, stammered. 'Zophiel . . . his spirit.'

He ran to the door and as he opened it, the light vanished and the four candles were extinguished as a blast of cold air rushed into the room.

Something made me turn to look at Narigorm. I could just make out her white skin by the light of the moon shining in through the open door. She was crouching, staring at the spot where the light had been. She held her hand out towards the grave, palm out, fingers spread wide as if she was trying to grasp the light. It was the same gesture I had seen her make that night near the healer's cottage when we heard the howl of the wolf.

The journey across the heath track was not an easy one. We were used to tramping through mud, but slush is worse, colder for a start and more treacherous. Cygnus was leading Xanthus, and although the mare was used to Cygnus feeding, grooming and harnessing her, she knew at once that something was wrong. Zophiel had always led her when she pulled the wagon. She laid back her ears, rolled her eyes, and dug her heels in. Cygnus tried to coax her but to no avail. After the sleepless night he'd had, Cygnus's nerves were already stretched to breaking point, and Xanthus's refusal to move reduced him to tears. He was not angry with the horse. On the contrary, he seemed distraught that Xanthus was missing Zophiel. He had taken far more care of her than Zophiel had ever done and yet it was Zophiel the horse wanted.

You can pull a lady's palfrey forward by the bridle, but when a horse as big as Xanthus refuses to budge, no amount of pulling has the slightest effect. In the end Osmond was forced to do what Cygnus would not and use the whip on her. Xanthus finally walked on, but she kept tossing her head furiously, trying to yank the bridle out of Cygnus's hand. He had to keep a tight hold to stop her biting him and anyone else who came within range of her teeth.

Zophiel's boxes were still in the wagon. The wolf had not yet claimed his prize. Perhaps, as Zophiel had said, he wouldn't risk leaving tracks in the snow. The others wanted to leave the boxes behind in the hut. Believe me, I too wanted to leave them, but I knew we couldn't. There was no cover near the hut where the wolf could hide, so he must have moved some distance away before daybreak. If a drover or a traveller found boxes full of church artefacts in the hut before the wolf got to them, they would know at once they were stolen. It was not like finding a few coins you could slip into your pocket and say nothing. Word would soon get out and our friend at the standing stones would surely remember whom he'd seen with a wagon capable of carrying a stack of boxes. There was nothing for it but to take them with us, knowing the wolf would follow, and leave them where only he would find them.

At intervals the track branched off in the direction of distant hamlets, but we didn't take these paths. We hurried by as fast as Xanthus would permit, for few of the cottages had smoke rising from them. The farm strips around the hamlets were untended. Once in the distance we saw a child crouching by a door, knees drawn up and his face buried in his arms, but if he heard the wagon he did not raise his head – perhaps he would never raise his head again.

You can tell who's died of hunger and who of the pestilence before you even approach the body, which is a good trick to learn if you want to stay alive. The secret is to watch the birds. You'll see them gathering over a corpse that has starved to death, long before you reach it. The ravens come in first, bouncing to the ground and ambling over like monks, eyeing the corpse sideways, then coming in for the first stab. Above them the kites wheel and wait, their feathers gleaming like ox-blood in the sun. Once the ravens have opened up the corpse, they fly in, closing their wings at the last minute to turn sideways, snatching a piece of flesh in their claws before soaring back up to devour it on the wing.

But neither ravens nor kites will go near a pestilence corpse. No animal will approach it, however hungry they are. The corpse lies unmauled and rots without the help of any scavenger. Its bones lie unscattered where it died and will continue to lie there until sun, rain and winter storms give it the dignity of a burial. That's why you have to be on your guard. Keep your eyes on the ground, probe the drifts of snow, search the mud carefully, for otherwise you can stumble straight into them.

Perhaps it's the stench which warns birds and animals to stay away, as if the body had rotted away inside before the victim had even stopped walking. But that had ceased to be a warning to us, for the stench hung in the air everywhere we went. It carried for miles, filling our nostrils until even the food we ate tasted of its foulness. The stench was no warning any more. All England was rotting.

That night we camped out in the open, near a tumble-down round tower, a spot chosen for Xanthus more than us. She'd had little to eat since the snow first fell and we needed her to remain strong. The snow had melted around the tower and the grass and herbs grew lush among the fallen stones and hollows. Adela, Osmond and Carwyn slept in the wagon again and the rest of us slept beneath it. It was to be the last time we used our little ark for shelter. For it was there, the following morning, that we left the wagon for the wolf to find, concealed from the track behind the tower. We knew he'd find it. He had found us. We had heard his howl again in the night, letting us know that he was still with us. Even in open land he still had the power to follow us unseen. And he was not giving up.

Osmond was all for unloading the boxes and taking the wagon on with us, but I wanted to be sure that the wolf knew we had left all behind. There was a chance that if he saw the wagon tracks rolling on, he might think we still carried the boxes and follow us, instead of looking for the hidden boxes. Besides, without the wagon we could take to the smaller tracks, the little paths that did not pass through towns or villages but led to the remoter places where the pestilence might not yet have reached. Without the wagon we could finally turn to the north, for we would not need a road if we were on foot.

But we didn't leave Xanthus. How the wolf was to move his bounty was his affair. He might be on horseback for all we knew, probably was, but we would not surrender Xanthus to him.

There was something else I would not leave – the mermaid. Zophiel could not have stolen her from the church. If we left her for the wolf, she would be thrown away or else sold to be exhibited to another gawping crowd, if there ever was another crowd or another fair again. The rest of the company thought I was mad to insist on taking such a useless and cumbersome object, and I could not explain to them why I could not leave her. But each time I smelt the myrrh and aloes I thought of my brother's head in my father's hands. I thought of his body lying somewhere in Acre, hacked to pieces, his head severed by a Saracen's sword and stuck on a pike for the crowds to stare at. I thought of his servant risking his life to take it down in the night and bring it home across mountains and seas: the only piece of my brother he could bring back to us, the only piece we could lay to rest. In the end it was Rodrigo who gently took the box from me and strapped it to Xanthus's back. He alone did not ask why.

We strapped our packs to Xanthus and set off again, praying that this time the wolf would not follow. It was easier for us to travel without the wagon, except for Adela who now had to walk. But now that she was no longer pregnant, she seemed to relish the freedom. She tied Carwyn on her back and tried her best to keep a steady pace, though she was still weak. We had to make frequent stops to allow her to rest, for she tired easily, but we were all grateful for those, especially Xanthus who ate everything she could reach each time we halted, as if she thought she might never see another blade of grass again.

Narigorm was obliged to walk too. She had walked alongside the wagon before, but mostly when she had chosen to do so. Although she could easily keep pace with Osmond when they went hunting, now, deprived of her little rat's nest in the well of the wagon, she trailed a few paces behind us, watching, listening, but rarely saying a word, her face revealing nothing of her thoughts.

Without the wagon, the gap where Zophiel used to be

had disappeared. It was possible to walk for an hour or two without seeing him lying in the bloodstained snow and without thinking of the wolf. And the mood of Rodrigo, Cygnus, Osmond and Adela seemed to grow lighter the further we walked from that tower. Without the heavy wagon to push and pull through the slippery mud, they realized they could go anywhere, whether there was a track or not. It was as though like the trickster, Sisyphus, they had been rolling a great boulder up a mountain and now they were unchained. The wolf had got all he wanted and they were free of him too.

As if to emphasize our liberation, that afternoon we came to a broad, fast-flowing river. The bridge had been washed away, so we turned aside from the track and followed the river downstream, letting its meandering guide us, until dusk began to close in. We camped a few yards from the river, in the shelter of a small thicket of birch and willow scrub. Osmond and Narigorm had caught some ducks which bubbled in the pot over the fire and we gathered hungrily around the fire as dusk began to settle, tucking into the stew of birds as fast as Adela ladled out the bowls.

The edge of hunger blunted, I paused and looked round at the others. Everyone, except Narigorm, seemed unnaturally buoyant, like boys released early from the schoolroom. They were convinced that our troubles now lay behind us. But perversely, the further we had walked from the wagon, the more panic-struck I had become. I was the one who had argued we should leave the wagon behind, but without realizing it, I had come to treat it as home, the place to return to each night, the one solid and constant thing in this world that was collapsing around us. Now, strangely, after all those years travelling alone on the road, with the wagon gone I suddenly felt cast adrift, naked and exposed as if

I was about to be swept away and there was nothing to cling to.

Ever since the flood waters had turned us east we had not been in control of our direction and that frightened me. Like an animal that senses a trap it cannot see, I sensed we were being driven by something that I could only glimpse as a shadow. Three of us had died violently since we had turned east. There was no connection that I could make sense of and yet a shadow, though it has no substance of its own, is always cast by something that has.

I glanced over at Narigorm. She was sitting a little way off, absorbed in her meal, tearing strips of flesh from a duck's leg. Not this time, she would not get her own way this time. I would not let the runes drive us any more. We had to take control of our destiny again. This time we would make for the north and I would not let her runes stop us. It was the only direction that might yet take us away from the pestilence. It was a slender hope, I knew, but better than the certainty of walking into death. I edged closer to the others and kept my voice low enough for Narigorm not to hear.

'Now that the wolf is off our backs, we need to make some decisions. We're going to need to find food, fuel and shelter. It's not so cold tonight, but it's only the beginning of February so we can't hope it'll last; there may be more snow to come. None of us knows how long this pestilence will continue. We should turn north again, try to find an isolated place untouched by it, a place where we can settle and fend for ourselves, well away from villages or highways, until the worst is over.'

Osmond looked up, his spoon half-way to his mouth. 'But why not continue to the sea? At the coast we'd be able to catch fish as well as birds. They say some people live off

454

what the sea provides and the sea can't be affected by the pestilence.'

'But the ports and the fishing villages will be, they more than most, and there are too many villages along the coast. If we go north and inland we can outstrip –'

'No, no, you cannot use that,' Rodrigo's voice cut in sharply.

Narigorm had wandered back to the pot on the fire and had speared a piece of duck flesh with a knife. She turned and looked at him.

'That is Zophiel's knife,' he said. 'What are you doing with it?'

'I found it. He doesn't need it any more and it's sharper than mine.'

'Throw it away.'

'Why should I? It's a good knife.' She dipped it once more into the pot.

'No, throw it away!' Rodrigo shouted. 'It has Zophiel's blood on it.'

Narigorm, with an exaggerated gesture, plunged the knife back into the pottage. 'I cleaned it. There's no blood on it now.'

Cygnus rose and in one deft movement took the knife from Narigorm's hand. 'Rodrigo's right,' he said quietly. 'You shouldn't be using it.'

He threw the knife in a wide arc over the scrub towards the river and we heard a splash. For a long moment Cygnus stared at Rodrigo, then he turned away, gazing out into the darkness towards the river.

Adela came bustling across and took the pot off the fire. There was little left in it, but she tipped the remains out into the bushes, wiping her hands on her skirt.

'You know it's bad luck to use a dead man's knife,' she

scolded. 'Don't you think we've had enough misfortune already, without bringing down any more?'

She pushed Narigorm back towards her place with an impatient little slap on her bottom as if she was a naughty toddler. Narigorm sat down, but she didn't look sulky or resentful, as I expected; she looked almost pleased with herself and for reasons I couldn't explain that bothered me.

As the evening wore on we all drew closer to the fire. The trees and reeds along the river rustled in the breeze and dark water slapped against the banks. Occasionally the squeak or cry of some bird or animal, killing or being killed, reached our ears, but otherwise it was quiet. A covering of clouds obscured the stars. It was dark, much darker than any night since Christmas. Only the light of the fire crackling in the fire pit illuminated our faces. Even though we told ourselves the wolf wouldn't trouble us again, with the coming of darkness the old tension returned and we sat listening for something out there in the night, something that did not belong here.

'Rodrigo, can't you play or sing for us?' Osmond finally burst out. 'It is going to be a long night. At least let's have something to while away the evening.'

'I will tell a story, if you like,' Cygnus said.

We looked at him in surprise; he had not told a tale since Christmas. It was a good sign. Perhaps now that Zophiel had gone and he no longer had to face the constant taunts about his arm, his misery would lift.

'Just so long as it isn't about wolves,' Osmond said, with an attempt at a laugh.

'No wolves, just swans.'

'Not swans,' I said quickly. 'You shouldn't dwell –'

He smiled. 'These are not my swans, Camelot. This is the tale of the Swan Knight, grandfather to the great Godfrey de Bouillon, knight of the Crusades. It comes from a song the minstrels sing, a courtly tale. Perhaps Rodrigo will know it.'

Rodrigo frowned, but didn't answer. Cygnus drew his cloak more tightly around him and began.

'King Oriant of Lillefort was a handsome young man, skilled in all the noble arts, but his chief delight was the bow and arrow and often when he was restless, he would go out at night to hunt by moonlight. One winter's night when he was hunting alone down by the lake, he heard the singing of feathers in the frosted air. Looking up, he saw a swan, stretched out across the darkening sky. She glided through the cobalt night on wings as strong as freedom and came to rest upon the silvered waters of the lake. She was a magnificent creature and King Oriant wanted to take her more than he had wanted any other beast or bird he had hunted. He drew back on his bowstring and aimed, but just as he was about to loose the arrow, she cried out in a human voice, and when he looked again, he saw walking out of the water towards him not a swan, but a beautiful woman with eyes as dark as the midnight sky and hair the colour of moonlight. And tangled in her hair was a single white swan's feather. The King fell instantly in love with her. He caught her in his arms and kissed her and as he did so, he pulled the feather from her hair. Feeling her feather gone, she begged him to return it for without it she would have to remain in human form, but the King refused, saying he would only return the feather if she became his wife.

'King Oriant carried his swan bride back to the castle. He hid the feather in a chest, in a tower, in a forest, on an island where she would never find it. And when on their wedding night she begged him for the feather, he refused her, saying he would return it to her only when she bore him a son. So the sylph was forced to remain with him and she bore him five sons. Each time a son was born she begged the King to return the feather and each time he refused, saying, "when you have given me another son, then I will return it to you."

'But the children of a king and a sylph are not mortal children and unknown to their father, each son, like his mother, could change himself into the form of a swan. Their mother placed around their necks golden chains, from which hung silver moons. As long as they wore the chains they remained in human form, but at night they laid aside their chains, transformed themselves into swans and flew out into the starry sky. Their mother warned them never to lose the golden chains, for if they lost them, they would remain as swans for ever. Then she begged her sons to transform into swans and search for her feather and after much searching they found the island, and on the island they found the forest, and in the forest they found the tower, and in the tower they found the chest, and in the chest they found their mother's feather. They brought it to their mother who slipped it into her hair, kissed her sons and flew away for ever.

'King Oriant was heartbroken that his wife had left him, but it was not long before his advisers persuaded him to remarry and he took a new bride. But though his young wife was lovely, she was mortal, and how can human beauty compare to the beauty of a sylph? Each time the King looked at his sons, with their eyes the colour of the midnight sky and their hair the colour of moonlight, he sighed. His new wife grew jealous and looked for a way to destroy his sons, for she knew that as long as he looked on them, he would never forget his swan bride. So she began to spy on them and soon discovered the secret of the chains. One night when the young men had transformed themselves into swans she stole the necklaces from their room, all save one, that belonging to the eldest son, Helyas, for he had hidden his chain in a mousehole and a spider had woven a web across it, so that she could not find it. Before dawn the swans returned and flew into the room. Helyas at once resumed his human form, but the others could not find their chains and as dawn broke they were forced to fly away.

'For seven years Helyas searched the castle looking for the chains and for seven years the swans returned each night and flew away each dawn. Then on the seventh day of the seventh month of the seventh year, Helyas at last found the chains. He hurried out to greet his brothers and as each swan landed on the water, he threw the chain around his neck and each brother resumed his human form. But in his joy Helyas did not notice that the chain of the youngest swan was broken, and when Helyas threw it, the chain fell from the swan's neck to the bottom of the deep lake and the youngest brother remained a swan for ever, bound to serve his brothers in that form.

'Many miles away the Emperor Otto was holding court at Nimwegen. The Duchess of Bouillon pleaded with him for justice against the Saxon Duke Renier who accused her of having committed adultery when her late husband was alive. As brother to her husband, he declared that her lands should therefore be forfeit to him. Adultery in a woman so highborn was a grave charge and the Emperor ordered her to prove her innocence in trial by combat. If her champion lost the fight she would be put to death and her lands given to Renier. But so fierce a warrior was Renier, so skilled with the sword and so merciless to those who opposed him, that no champion would come forward to stand for her.

'After three days of searching, still no champion could be

found and the Emperor ordered his soldiers to seize the Duchess and put her to death. But just as they laid hands upon the weeping woman, a cry rang out from the river and people turned to see an unknown knight gliding down the river towards them in a boat pulled by a swan. Helyas, eldest of the swan brothers, stepped ashore and offered himself as champion against Renier. The battle was long and bloody, both men were skilled and courageous, but right was on the side of the innocent Duchess, so Helyas was able to slay Renier.

'As a reward for his services the Duchess offered the hand of her beautiful daughter, Beatrix, in marriage, bestowing all her lands and wealth on the couple. Helyas agreed on one condition, that neither Beatrix nor her mother should ever ask him his name or his lineage. They both readily agreed and so the wedding took place.

'Seven joyful and prosperous years Helyas and Beatrix spent together and their union was blessed with a beautiful daughter, Ida, who had her father's dark eyes. Each day at dawn and at sunset, Helyas went down to the river to talk to his brother the swan, and each time she saw him feeding the bird with his own hand, Beatrix wondered about her mysterious knight, but she kept her vow and did not ask him who he was.

'But many other nobles in the land were jealous of the wealth and happiness of Helyas and Beatrix. "Who is this knight?" they asked. "Why would a man of noble birth wish to hide his lineage, unless he had disgraced his family's name?" The rumours reached Beatrix's ears. Even her own serving maids whispered among themselves that perhaps this swan knight she had married was no knight at all, that he was of common birth, ignoble birth even. Finally Beatrix could bear the whispering no longer and one night when

Helyas returned from the lake she asked him that question which she had sworn she would never ask.

'Helyas was a knight and the law of chivalry demanded that he answer her truthfully. But as soon as he had spoken the truth, he saw his brother swan appear in the river, drawing the little boat. Helyas stepped into the boat and sailed away.

'Their dark-eyed daughter, Ida, grew up to marry Eustace, Count of Boulogne, and Ida's son, Godfrey de Bouillon, became the great knight commander of the First Crusade, Defender of the Holy Sepulchre, who some now title the first King of Jerusalem.

'But as for Beatrix, she never laid eyes on her beloved husband again. The Swan Knight had vanished. She searched for him for the rest of her life, but she never found him, and when at last she knew she never would, she died of guilt and grief, for she had betrayed the most gallant knight in Christendom. She had learned the truth, but the truth had destroyed them both.'

There was silence as Cygnus finished his story. Then Adela gave a great sigh of satisfaction and touched Cygnus's arm. 'That was beautiful, Cygnus.'

But he was not looking at her. Instead he was looking intently at Rodrigo. For a long time they stared at each other, comprehension dawning in Rodrigo's face. He looked horrified, then he turned away and buried his face in his hands. Finally he raised his head again and opened his mouth as if he was about speak, but Cygnus shook his head.

'No, Rodrigo, don't say it. The guilt is mine. I am a coward. Zophiel was right; I am neither man nor bird. I have neither an immortal soul in the next life nor purpose in this one. I had nothing to lose. It should have been me who did it. Forgive me, Rodrigo, forgive me.'

He adjusted the heavy purple cloak around his shoulders and strode rapidly away into the darkness. Overhead we heard a singing in the air, three swans flying towards the river. Spreading their strong white wings, they glided down and disappeared from sight.

25. The Mermaid and the Mirror

We searched for Cygnus most of the night and found him just after dawn, about half a mile downstream. His body was floating face down in the river. His shirt sleeve had caught on the sharp broken ends of a clump of reeds and had held him against the bank, otherwise he would have been swept away. The purple cloak had floated out to cover his head. We knew from the way the body drifted lifelessly in the current that there was no hope, but Rodrigo plunged in recklessly as if he thought he could still save him, if only he could get to him quickly enough. Osmond and I helped Rodrigo to haul the body out. As soon as he had clambered out himself, Rodrigo fell on Cygnus's body, pushing and pressing him as if, by shaking him, he could get him to breathe. Finally, Osmond had to restrain him.

'It's no use, Rodrigo. He's gone. He's been dead for hours. He must have fallen in last night and the cloak pulled him under.'

Rodrigo pulled Cygnus towards him and sat cradling him in his arms, as if he was a sleeping child.

'What I can't understand is why we didn't hear a splash or a cry,' Osmond continued. 'Unless he had already walked too far from the camp.'

Rodrigo looked up at us, his face haggard. 'He did not want us to hear.'

Osmond's eyes opened wide. 'You're not saying he deliberately went into the river to . . . to drown himself? But he was sitting here last night with all of us, calmly telling us a story. Why would a man do that and then go out and kill himself? Why would he do that to us? We were his friends. None of us ever said anything cruel to him. The only one who tormented him was Zophiel and he's dead.'

I thought of what Osmond had said to Cygnus when he failed to return with a midwife for Adela. How quickly we forget our own cruelty.

'He did it because Zophiel is dead.' Tears were now rolling down Rodrigo's cheeks.

'What do you mean *because* Zophiel is dead?'

'I think Rodrigo means he . . . he drowned himself out of guilt,' I said.

Osmond sank on to the grass, shaking his head in disbelief. 'So are you telling me that Narigorm was right all along, that it wasn't the wolf that killed Zophiel, it was Cygnus . . . ? Not that I blame him. But why kill himself? Did he think we would turn him in?'

'No!' Rodrigo shouted. 'No, he did not murder Zophiel. *Il sangue di Dio!* Did you not hear what he said last night, the last thing he said? He said it should have been him. He thought he had forced me to become a murderer, because he was too cowardly to do it himself. Zophiel accused him of not even being able to defend himself and he thought I believed that too.'

Osmond's expression was growing more bewildered by the minute.

I crouched down and put an arm round Rodrigo's wet shoulders. 'But Cygnus was mistaken, wasn't he? You didn't kill Zophiel. It was the wolf.' I wanted desperately to believe that.

Rodrigo looked down at Cygnus's body. The eyes were closed, the face peaceful and smooth, all the anxiety of the last few weeks washed away. 'I killed him.'

It was impossible to tell if he was talking about Cygnus or Zophiel.

'No, Rodrigo, listen to me. You didn't kill anyone. You're not to blame for either of their deaths.'

Rodrigo spoke in a low monotone, his gaze fixed on Cygnus's face. 'When Zophiel left the drovers' hut, I went after him. I begged him to leave Cygnus alone before he drove him to his death as he had driven Pleasance and Jofre to theirs. He said they had brought their own deaths upon themselves. It was nothing to do with him, he said. Sodomites like Jofre, he said, are condemned in this life and the next. His death was God's judgment for his perversion. Then he turned his back and walked away. I threw the knife as he walked away from me.'

Suddenly, I remembered the two lepers on the road in the gorge who had beaten the traveller to death, how they had turned on Osmond. A picture flashed into my mind of Rodrigo throwing his knife, of the leper's screaming, then falling dead. With a sickening jolt, I knew he was telling the truth. Rodrigo had murdered Zophiel.

'And the arms?' Osmond asked shakily. 'You . . . cut off the arms?'

'With his own knife. I wanted to make it look as if the wolf had punished him for stealing, that is what I told myself, but maybe in my heart I wanted to make him like those people he despised so much.'

I stared at the rushing water, glinting like armour in the early-morning sun. Somewhere in there lay Zophiel's knife.

I spoke without looking at Rodrigo. 'When Narigorm used Zophiel's knife last night, you told Narigorm the knife had Zophiel's blood on it. But you weren't there when we found the body. So you wouldn't have known Zophiel's own knife had been used on him, unless you'd done it. That's what Cygnus realized last night. That's when he knew you'd killed him and he thought you'd done it for him. Like Beatrix, he learned the truth, and the truth . . .'

Rodrigo closed his eyes tightly as if he was in terrible pain.

We wrapped Cygnus's body in his cloak and tied him across Xanthus's back. We'd no idea what we were going to do with it. We broke camp and walked on, veering away from the river as soon as we could, for none of us wanted to see or hear it. We didn't discuss where we might be going; it hardly seemed to matter any more. I followed behind with Rodrigo, who walked in a daze without seeming to know where he was or who was around him. Even Xanthus seemed to sense what she was carrying and walked solemnly as Osmond led her. We had let Adela believe it was an accident, but I could see from the expression on Narigorm's face she didn't believe that. She knew Cygnus had killed himself, just as she knew Rodrigo had killed Zophiel, and we had not told her that either.

We saw the man and boy cutting peat on the moor a long way before we reached them. It was a lonely, isolated spot and the man must have been desperate for fuel to cut it half-frozen and wet. Several piles of peat turfs stood around the long trough he had dug out and more had been stacked on a small sledge ready to be dragged off. There was no sign of a dwelling nearby so they must have walked a long way

466

to the site, but without fuel, a family can die of cold and hunger if they can't cook what little they catch.

The barefooted boy spotted us before his father and gave a warning. Both stood, spades in hand, warily watching us approach. All around them lay great pools of water where men had cut peat for years and the trench where they worked was filling up as fast as they dug. Even if it did not rain again between now and midsummer it would take months for all the water to seep out from the land.

As we drew close, the man's gaze was fixed upon the unmistakable shape of a body lying across Xanthus's back. He crossed himself three times and took several hasty steps backwards, dragging the boy with him. I needed no runes to know what he was thinking. I tried to reassure him.

'Have no fear, master, he didn't die of contagion. An accident. He drowned.'

The peat-cutter crossed himself again, looking embarrassed. 'God rest his soul.' He advanced a couple of steps towards us. 'The corpse road lies yonder.' He pointed. 'You can just see the crosses marking it.'

In the distance were several shapes which I had taken to be bushes, but now I could see they were dark stone crosses. He plainly thought that was where we were making for, not surprisingly since we were carrying a corpse.

'Then a parish church lies at the end of the road?'

'St Nicholas at Gasthorpe. But it won't do any good to go there. There's no priest any more that can give you burial.'

'The pestilence?'

He crossed himself again as if the mere mention of the word might call it down upon himself. 'Priest left afore that. They'd been having a hard time of it these last years what with the bad harvests and then the sheep sickening. A lot of families starved. Couldn't grow enough on their bits of land to feed themselves and what they did grow mostly failed these last years. Couldn't pay church-scots or tithes, which didn't please the priest. But if a well's run dry you can threaten it with hell and damnation till Michaelmas and you'll still not get a drop of water from it. That's why the priest took off. No one's seen hide nor hair of him since. Then when the ... when it came, that finished the rest of the village off, leastways, those that stayed on their tofts anyway.' He crossed himself again. Even avoiding uttering the word aloud was not enough to ward off its evil.

He glanced again at Cygnus's body. 'You'll be lucky to find a priest anywhere in these parts.' He edged a little closer and lowered his voice, as if afraid, in this vast expanse of nothing, we might be overheard. 'Someone told me that the Bishop of Norwich said anyone now may shrive a dying man, if there's not a religious to be found to do it, and anyone may bury him too. I buried two of my little 'uns in the churchyard myself. No one to say the words, but at least they were safe in holy ground. There's nothing to stop you doing the same.' He gave us a confidential wink. 'After all, who's to know save the others that are already six feet under, and they've no cause to complain, have they?'

He shook his head wonderingly. 'Who'd have thought it? This time last year you couldn't piss without the blessing of a priest; now any Tom, Dick or Harry, even a woman, can baptize you, marry you, shrive you and bury you. And there's the Bishop saying, go ahead, do it yourselves, you don't need a priest. Makes you wonder why we've been paying all those scots and tithes to the priests all these years, doesn't it?'

The corpse road was hardly a track at all, just a series of small granite crosses set up at intervals to mark the way for those who had to carry their dead the many miles from the hamlets and villages that had no parish church licensed for burial. We followed them until we saw the outskirts of the village. The peat-cutter was right, it was deserted. The nearest cottages looked as if they had been abandoned for months and the field strips were overgrown with weeds.

Osmond tethered Xanthus to a tree, before turning to us.

'Adela and Narigorm should stay here with the baby. There may be corpses. We'll go in on foot.'

'But what about you, Osmond?' Adela wailed. 'You can't risk your life.'

Rodrigo began to unfasten Cygnus's body. 'She is right, Osmond, you stay. I can carry him. I can dig the grave. No one else needs to come.'

'I need to come,' Osmond said, flushing slightly. 'Said things I didn't mean. Never got round to apologizing. That story he told us, the night we found him stowed away in the wagon, about the cordwainer being the one who killed that child, I didn't believe it then, but I do now, have done for a long time, yet I never got round to telling him. I owe him this much, especially after what you both did for Adela and the baby.'

Rodrigo nodded and briefly grasped Osmond's shoulder. I realized bitterly that none of us had ever got round to telling Cygnus we believed him about the child. Osmond found the spade and Rodrigo heaved Cygnus's body across his shoulder.

'Wait.' A thought struck me and I started to untie the mermaid's box from Xanthus. 'We'll bury her in the church-yard too. It's as good a place as any to lay her to rest.'

Osmond stared. 'You can't, she wasn't human. You can't bury something like that on consecrated ground She was just a . . .'

'A freak, a beast? Isn't that what Zophiel used to say of Cygnus?'

He blushed and turned away.

So after weeks of trying to avoid the pestilence villages we finally entered one, not to find food for the living, but burial for the dead. Weeds were beginning to grow along the main street. Some of the cottage doors and shutters lay wide open – doubtless they had been looted for wood or anything usable after the owners abandoned them. More sinister were the ones nailed shut from the outside with large black crosses painted on their doors and windows. I wondered how many dead lay inside them. So near to a parish church, yet there would be no consecrated ground for them to rest in.

I had the feeling we were being watched, and turned. I thought I saw something dart into the shadows of a byre, but when I looked hard at the place I could see nothing. Rodrigo and Osmond kept turning their heads as if they too could sense something. The unnatural silence in the village was unnerving. It was almost a relief when a scrawny dog leaped out from behind one of the cottages and began to snarl and bark, still defending its toft for its owners long since dead. Osmond threw stones at it until it retreated, but it continued to bark its defiance.

As we passed one of the boarded-up cottages I noticed that the corner of the door had been chipped away from the inside as though someone had been still alive when the door was nailed shut and had tried desperately to escape. Whoever it was had not succeeded, for the planks on the outside of the door remained firmly nailed in place. I shuddered to think of the horror of their final hours. Had they succumbed to the sickness of the dead entombed with them, or had they cruelly starved to death?

The church was locked. Doubtless the priest had taken that precaution before he left. If the villagers could not pay their tithes they should have no access to God, or perhaps he thought they'd strip the place bare in his absence.

The churchyard had not been scythed and long, wet grass grew up over the little wooden markers. There were several stone tombs where the wealthier and more worthy had been buried, but a fox had dug its den beneath one of them and yellow bones and pieces of skull lay scattered about it. I reminded myself to collect them before we left – better for their owner that his bones be miraculously translated into relics than scattered by scavengers. We found a spot close to the wall where if there were any markers they had long since rotted away, and Osmond and Rodrigo took turns to dig. They soon unearthed old bones, but laid them carefully aside to be replaced in the hole when they filled it.

I dug a grave for the baby mermaid a few yards away between two rotting wooden crosses. My grave did not need to be wide or long; there was only a tiny body to fit into it. Then I carefully unwrapped the cage and the familiar smell of myrrh and aloes mingled with dried seaweed overwhelmed me. In burying her, it was almost like burying my brother a second time. I remembered standing at the tomb in the church when they opened it to lay his head inside, the cold, damp smell of decay rushing out, not masked by the incense and the candles which burned around us. I remember my mother's sobs and my father's set jaw, but I did not cry. I had cried that day my father had uttered those words, 'I'd rather my son came home on a shield than as a coward.' I had known that day he would not come home alive and I had cried then until I had no more tears left to shed. The day we finally buried his severed head my eyes were so dry that my eyelids rasped against them. It was all I could feel.

I tried to break the lock off the mermaid's cage with a sharp piece of stone. It took several attempts, but at last I opened the door and reached in. The little body was stiff, like a leather doll. I wondered how long she had been dead – months, years? I had forgotten to bring anything to wrap her in, so I laid her straight into the cold earth. Beside her I placed her little mermaid doll.

Then I picked up the little silver hand-mirror, intending to put that in the grave with the mermaid child. I rubbed the tarnished silver surface. It's many years since I looked into a mirror and I almost dropped it in the shock of seeing the face that peered out at me. They say mirrors cannot lie, but they speak a cruel and spiteful truth. It was as if I was looking back at a demon trapped in the mirror. Though I passed my fingers across my lumpy scar and empty eye socket many times a day, I had forgotten the horror of the sight of it. Now it came back to me as sharply as the day I had ordered that they bring me a mirror. They had begged me not to look, but I had insisted, and then I knew why the servants avoided looking at me when they spoke, why my sons stared and quickly looked away. Who could blame them?

Yet, even after all these years, inside my head I am still unscarred, unmarked. I am still as I was when I was young. Now I had to face the fact that not only was I scarred, I was old. My face had withered like the faces of the crab-apple dolls they make for children. My hair was silver, the blue of my good eye had faded to the grey of a winter's sky. My lips that had once kissed with such passion were thin and pale, and my wrinkled skin that had once been pale and smooth was now tanned almost as dark as the mermaid's by the wind and sun. They say when you look into a mirror you see your soul and my soul was monstrous and ancient.

I shuddered and quickly turned the mirror over. It was much thicker and heavier than I anticipated. Something had been inserted into the round frame on the back of the mirror, a polished piece of crystal, surrounded by a broad ring of silver, inscribed with symbols and studded with pearls. Beneath the crystal, and magnified by it, was a tiny fragment of bone. It was a relic, and a valuable one too, judging by the mount. I must have cried out in surprise for Osmond came across to find out the cause.

'A reliquary,' I said, holding it out so that he could see. 'It was there all along in the mermaid's cage.'

Osmond peered at it. 'I thought it was just a mirror.'

'It always lay mirror side up, the back was hidden.'

What had the blind healer said? – the best place to hide something is often in plain view.

'Whose relic is it?' Osmond asked.

I turned the reliquary around, examining the symbols carved around the frame.

'A broken chalice and a serpent. If this bird is meant to be a raven then this may be a relic of St Benedict. They say a jealous priest once poisoned the holy wine and bread and gave it to St Benedict. The serpent in the chalice represents the poison and when Benedict blessed the poisoned chalice, the chalice shattered. Then he called up a raven to carry off the poisoned host. The crosier is the symbol of authority as abbot, and can you see that, a book? That might represent the rule he wrote for monks and nuns.'

'And that? What is that, a plant of some kind?'

'A thorn bush. He used to hurl himself into thorns and

nettles to mortify his flesh and keep him from the sin of lust. And this symbol, I think, is the rod of discipline he wielded to wipe out corruption and licentiousness.'

'No wonder Zophiel had such a relic then. I'm surprised he didn't have the actual rod.'

'Pearls for chastity and purity, yes, I'm sure this is a relic of St Benedict. Whichever church had this taken from them has suffered a great loss. He's the saint to whom many pray for a happy and peaceful death, so this relic must have attracted many pilgrims.'

'Then this is something else Zophiel stole from Lincoln.'

'There's no doubt it's stolen. No one would conceal a holy relic in a mermaid's cage if they weren't trying to smuggle it away from its rightful owners. But whether Zophiel stole it is a different matter. It depends on whether he preserved the mermaid and put her in the cage himself, or if he bought the whole thing complete from someone else. Three abbeys in France argue over which of them has the bones of St Benedict and whichever has them, they stole them from the abbey at Monte Cassino. If Zophiel bought this locked cage with the mermaid already in it from a merchant or a knight returning from France, he might not have realized what was behind the mirror any more than we did. We didn't find keys to any of the boxes on Zophiel's body. We don't know that he had a key to this, unless it was concealed somewhere on the wagon.'

Osmond frowned. 'They call the Virgin Mary, "the mirror without stain". I suppose Benedict might have approved of his bone being in a mirror.'

'And the mirror absorbs and preserves the holiness of the relic and reflects evil back on to demons who look into it.' I winced as I said this, thinking of my own reflection.

'But Zophiel would never put a holy relic in a mermaid's

hand; that would have been the ultimate blasphemy to him,' Osmond protested.

'He may not have seen it that way. There was a mermaid who became a saint: St Murgen, a mortal woman given the body of a salmon to save her from drowning. St Comgall at Bangor baptized her because he wanted to be buried in the same coffin with her. They say there were so many miracles attributed to her after her death that she is counted as one of the Holy Virgins. Zophiel might have considered it the perfect hiding place for the relic of a man who was so insistent on chastity. It could have been Zophiel's ultimate conjuring trick, the object in plain sight, but no one seeing it, because their attention was distracted by the mermaid.'

Osmond looked down at the body. 'So if Zophiel did steal the relic from Lincoln he would have hidden it in the mermaid's cage, thinking that if the wolf took the other items back from him, he wouldn't bother with the mermaid and Zophiel would get away with this relic even if he lost the rest.'

'On the other hand,' I said, 'this may have been the one sleight of hand that fooled even poor Zophiel. He may have been carrying his most valuable treasure with him all this time and didn't even realize he had it.'

'*Poor* Zophiel,' said Osmond indignantly. 'You actually pity that wretch?'

'I pity any man who doesn't realize that what he desperately seeks he already possesses. This would have brought Zophiel everything he wanted – fame, money and respect. With this he could have bought a position of power and authority in any monastery or church he wanted.'

'Maybe that's exactly what he planned to do in Ireland, after he'd shaken off the wolf.' Osmond's frown deepened and he glanced over at Rodrigo who was methodically filling in Cygnus's grave. 'And if it is one of the pieces stolen from Lincoln and the wolf discovers it isn't amongst the treasures he's recovered, he'll come after us again, won't he? The Bishop will have told him exactly what's been taken.'

I hesitated, looking down at the crystal beneath which lay the tiny sliver of bone. Bone of the man whose rule had spread across all Christendom and now governed the lives of thousands of monks and nuns in the magnificent abbeys and monasteries built in his name. If this was a true relic, it was the only genuine one I'd ever had in my possession. But could it be genuine? Could it, after all these years, be the real thing?

People say they feel a power coming out of true relics. Some say it's like a wave of warm water washing over you, or a hot glow that rises up through your fingers until your whole body tingles. Others say it is a light of many colours that dances in front of your eyes or like the prickling of the skin you get after you've brushed against stinging nettles. But then people have claimed as much for the relics I have sold them, because they wanted to believe in them. Did I want to believe in this? Could I have the faith that would let me feel what I had created for others? My finger hovered over the spot where the bone lay, but I drew it back. I did not want to feel – nothing.

'Osmond . . . I don't think the Bishop's wolf was ever following us.'

He looked startled. 'We know he didn't kill Zophiel.' He glanced apprehensively in Rodrigo's direction again. 'But Zophiel was sure he was out there.'

'But as Zophiel himself said, look how hard it would be for a man alone to find food in these times, even with dogs. Why go through all that needless hardship, risking the pestilence, to track Zophiel for so long? Surely he'd have struck much sooner. He could have done it the night Jofre was killed; Zophiel was out alone then too.'

'But you heard the howls, Camelot, we all did. Something has been stalking us and if it wasn't the Bishop's wolf, then what? A real wolf?'

I shook my head. 'Why would a wolf do that? Even if it was a crossbreed, half-wolf, half-dog, that had attached itself to us, we would surely have seen it slinking round the camp.'

'But if it isn't a man or an animal, Camelot, what on earth is it?'

There was a screech behind us and we whipped round. A woman crouched a few yards away by one of the tombs, knees spread apart, her hands clawed in front of her as if she was ready to spring at us. She wasn't old, maybe in her twenties, but she was naked, her hair matted, her skin so encrusted with dirt it was hard to see what colour it was underneath. Flat pendulous breasts hung over ribs so painfully thin you could count every one, but in contrast to her stick-thin limbs, her belly was swollen and hard. God's blood, I thought, let that be with worms and not with child.

She pointed at me. 'I know you. You're death come to torment me.' She slapped the sides of her head viciously as if trying to beat something out of it.

I hastily stuffed the mirror inside my shirt and hissed to Osmond, 'Fill in the mermaid's grave before she sees what's in there. I'll deal with her.'

I took a step towards the woman who scuttled backwards on all fours again.

'I know you. Don't take me. Don't take me!' she shrieked.

'I haven't come for you,' I said as gently as I could. 'Won't you tell me your name?'

A sly look came over her. 'Never give them your name. They have power over you, if they have your name. If death doesn't know your name, he can't call you. Always asking me my name, but I don't tell him. Don't tell him.' She pressed her grimy hands over her mouth as if she feared the name might slip out by accident.

'You've spoken to death before?'

The woman raised her head, distracted by a flock of rooks wheeling and cawing overhead. 'He tries to trick me. He uses different voices, sometimes like birds and sometimes like rain.'

'How big is death?'

The woman began slapping her head again. Then she suddenly stopped and held up her hands in front of her face, palms out, the thumb and forefinger of each hand touching to make a womb-shaped space through which she peered. 'Tiny, tiny he is, like a man's prick.'

I reached down and picked up the cage that had contained the mermaid. 'Next time he comes, you can catch him in there.'

The woman put her head on one side, then shuffled closer, still crouching. She wrinkled up her nose, sniffing the unfamiliar odour.

'How?'

'Do you smell that? Death cannot resist that smell, he will creep inside and when he does, you can slam the door shut and keep him from taking you.'

I put the cage full of shells down in front of me and backed off a few paces to allow the woman to scuttle forward and snatch it. She retreated to a safe distance and sat there crooning over it as if it was a great treasure. I felt a hand on my shoulder and jumped.

Rodrigo was standing behind me. 'You should not take the name of death in vain, Camelot, he walks too close to us.'

'The cage will make her feel safer. Surely it's good to ease the poor woman's crazed mind.'

Once he would have smiled at that. I wondered if he would ever smile again.

We left the woman with her cage in the graveyard and retraced the way we had come. Not talking, but walking as quickly as we could, anxious to be out of this village of death as rapidly as possible.

As I stared at those blinded windows, at the desolation of that street, where once children had blithely played and laughed, I was seized with a desperate hunger to know if my own children still lived. They would be grown men by now and have children of their own. I could pass them on the road and not even recognize them. Had they survived this? I had given everything I could to keep them from harm. Had that all been futile? I looked at the abandoned cottages and I saw my own house with boards nailed across its windows, a black cross slashed on its door. Was there somewhere a grave with my sons in it, or worse, no grave at all?

We had reached the last few cottages when the naked woman leaped out again from behind one of the buildings and squatted in front of us in the middle of the street. In her hand she carried something bloody, half a rabbit, the fur still on it. She held it out towards us. 'Food,' she offered. She laid it in the dirt in front of us as I had done the cage and backed away a few feet. 'Food,' she repeated 'for death.'

Osmond grabbed my arm as if he really thought I was going to pick it up.

I shook my head. 'Thank you, but we have enough. You eat it.'

The woman looked at me slyly through her mane of

tangled hair, then she darted forward, picked up the rabbit and ripping back the fur, began to gnaw ravenously on the raw, bloody carcass.

26. The Place of the Hollows

Looking back, I know it was Narigorm who led us to the place of the hollows. I had finally turned us north and she had let me do it. I thought I had won, but I should have known better. She knew exactly what we were walking into, I'm sure of that.

The hollows lay between the trees, broad and shallow, like pools, but without any water. No trees or grass grew in them, nothing except strange spiky plants with red fleshy leaves, so that from a distance they looked like pools of blood. But as you walked across them you became aware of something else; the hollows were littered with the skeletons of small animals, the bleached bones and tiny skulls of rabbits, voles, mice, foxes, even birds. They were so numerous you couldn't avoid crunching them underfoot. Some were newly dead, the shreds of dried flesh and fur still adhering to them; others were picked clean and whitened by the sun of several summers. In one, the skeletons of a sheep and lamb lay side by side. Among them were hundreds of snail shells, empty, transparent, scattered like petals by the wind. The hollows held a particular fascination for Narigorm. She spent hours sitting on the edge of the copse studying them, doubtless hoping to see something killed there.

It had been nearly two weeks since we had buried Cygnus and with each passing day, Rodrigo was retreating further into himself. He no longer cared where he was going or what he was doing and it took the combined efforts of Adela, Osmond and me to rouse him to the simplest of tasks. He wouldn't even look at baby Carwyn now, as if he was afraid to love anyone or anything again in case, by doing so, he destroyed them.

Something changed inside Osmond too the day we buried Cygnus. He had already made up his mind that our best hope of finding food lay along the coast, but now he was convinced that Zophiel had been right, there would be ships at the coast, a boat that could take us all to the safety of Ireland. We could sell Xanthus, he said, to pay for the voyage and if that was not enough we could work our passage. I tried to tell him that there would be little chance of Ireland escaping pestilence, it had probably already fallen to it, but he wouldn't listen, for the wolf was on our trail once more and, like Zophiel, Osmond had come to fear the beast even more than the pestilence. He clung to the belief that only the sea could protect us from him.

Every sense was telling me that I should break away from the company and travel by myself. But I could not bring myself to leave Rodrigo, not in the state he was in, and in truth I was afraid to be alone. But at least I persuaded Osmond to turn north and make for the coast higher up. And I foolishly comforted myself with that.

But we never reached the sea. Between land and sea, beneath wide grey skies, lay a great expanse of marshland, the fens that guard the Wash. Pools and waterways meandered among the mudflats and reeds, glinting in the winter sun.

There was no crossing the marsh unless you had a boat and even then you would have to be born here to fathom your way through it, for it was a maze of watery branches, most leading nowhere except to certain death in the oozing mud. Here and there in the distance we could see small islands raised a few feet above the surrounding marshes, some big enough to support a small village of cottages and byres, others just a few sheep. The sharp smell of salt weed, mud and rich vegetation pervaded the air, pungent and cleansing after the stench of rotting corpses.

We skirted the edge of the marsh, keeping to the higher ground, until we emerged from the trees to see a spur of hard ground jutting out into the marshland. The spur was almost an island, save for a narrow strip linking it to the mainland. Stunted trees covered much of it and at the far end lay a deserted hermit's dwelling built of stone and shaped like a beehive. Beyond that, at the tip of the spur, was a roughly hewn stone cross jutting up between the dwelling and the marsh as if to ward off whatever creatures swarmed and bred in the dark depths of the sucking, belching slime. We decided we would camp on this almost-island for a night or two, then we would continue our journey around the marsh, for it must surely come to an end and we'd find a way to the sea.

The spur was defendable. That was why we chose it and that was what we needed, a stronghold where we could defend ourselves from the wolf. We'd heard him the night we buried Cygnus and every night of our journey since. Adela had grown more terrified as, night after night, she clutched Carwyn to her while the howls reverberated through the darkness. She was not alone; we were all so exhausted and on edge that we fumbled tasks we had been skilled at since our infancy and stumbled over our own feet as we walked.

Despite what I had said in the churchyard, Osmond was still adamant it was the Bishop's wolf who was stalking us to retrieve the relic of St Benedict. He needed desperately to believe that. A man, however powerful, is mortal. He has weaknesses. You can fight a man. And as Osmond stubbornly demanded again and again, if it was not a man and not an animal, then what, in God's name, was it?

But even Osmond agreed that there was no point in simply abandoning the relic. If the Bishop's wolf didn't realize we had done so, he would continue to follow us and we'd be in a worse state if we had nothing with which to appease him. The best course, he said, was to take the reliquary to a church in a village not affected by the pestilence and make a public show of giving it to the priest so that it would come to the attention of the wolf. Then let him steal it back, if he would, from them. But we had not found a village without the pestilence. Those few we came across lay deserted or dying, and the peat-cutter had been right, there was not a priest left among them.

In any case, I had no intention of surrendering the relic. It had become my talisman, our protection against whatever it was that was out there. You may laugh that after all those years I had finally come to put my faith in a fragment of bone. It's easy to mock such things when the sun is shining, but when the sun begins to sink and shadows ooze towards you from the trees and you sit shivering in the darkness, waiting, then believe me, you will cling to anything to defend you against the thing you most dread.

That first night on the spur, as the moon rose, the mist crept low over the marshes, streaming out in white ribbons over the pools and waterways, until it seemed we were an island floating on a sea of cloud in the dark sky. The sounds were magnified in the still night, the sucking and gurgling of the water, the croaking of the frogs, the cries of night birds and the shrill screams of prey fighting for its life. Osmond built fires and set torches across the narrowest part of the spur. He knew that would not keep the wolf out, but he reasoned the wolf couldn't cross without being seen in the light of the flames.

Rodrigo was on watch when the howling began. The rest of us, exhausted, were already asleep, but the howl woke us, that and the cry of fear from Rodrigo. Osmond was on his feet faster than I was, but I told him to stay with Adela and hurried forward. Rodrigo was kneeling, staring at something up in the woods on the mainland. I put my hand on his shoulder and he jumped violently.

'The wolf, have you seen him?'

He pointed. I peered into the dark mass of trees. A flickering light appeared and disappeared among the trunks. It shimmered ghost-white in the darkness, too white for any torch or lantern.

'Corpse-light,' he whispered. He stood up and started forward as if he was about to follow it, but I grabbed his arm.

'Don't be a fool, Rodrigo. Whatever or whoever that is, you can't tackle it in the dark.'

He stared down at me like a man who is drunk and can't recall where he is. 'He wants me to follow. He is beckoning to me.'

'The light's flickering, that's all. How long has it been there?'

He ran his hand distractedly through his hair, but before he could answer, another howl from the wolf rang out over the marsh. It seemed to come from the trees, but it was hard to tell. The howl swirled around us like the mist. I could feel Rodrigo trembling.

Osmond came hurrying up, his stave grasped firmly in both hands.

'See anything?'

'Only that light.' I pointed, but when I looked, there was nothing there.

Osmond drove the end of his stave into the ground in exasperation. 'God's blood, I can't take much more of this. He wants the reliquary. We have to find a way to give it to him. Why did you have to open that cage, Camelot? Why couldn't you have left the infernal thing alone?'

Rodrigo was in no state to continue the watch, so I sent him back with Osmond and stayed myself. In any case, all desire for sleep had long passed.

The marsh is a place unlike any other. It calls to you night and day. By day its voice is the cry of birds screeching and sobbing on the wind, by night the whispering reeds call forth a great slithering and hissing as though huge serpents were crawling through the mud towards you. When the moon breaks through the clouds you see them heaving and writhing, the starlight glinting off their scales. Pale lights glide across the marshes in the darkness as if unseen people were walking across the mud where you know by day it is impossible for any human to walk, elf-fire leading men to their deaths. The marsh is always hungry and it has a thousand ways to lure you into its maw. It's not a place where your thoughts are led to God, but to the monstrous creatures that inhabit this twilight world which is neither sea nor land, water nor earth.

The cold, damp mist began to creep in around me, until I was cut off from the sight and sound of any living creature. I could no longer hear the reeds whispering. A smothering silence had rolled in, heavy and palpable, like the silence that had followed the wolf howls that night in the gully.

Shapes gathered out of the mist, but dissolved before I could reach them. I had never felt so alone. I was in the deadlands, the limbo where souls wander nameless and formless, unable to speak or to touch. And in that blind silence I knew it was not the nature of death that frightened me, it was what lay beyond; not heaven, not hell, but spirit without a form, without a place to be. I would be nowhere. I would be nothing.

The day that I left my home, I had prayed that my children would forget me. I wanted to spare them the pain of remembering. But that night, as I crouched in the white mist, waiting, I knew more than anything that I wanted them to remember. I wanted to go on living in someone's memory. If we are not remembered, we are more than dead, for it is as if we had never lived.

I had told Rodrigo once that we are all exiles from the past. I thought I had no need of a past. I thought if you cut away your past you could create yourself anew. But to sever yourself from the past is to cut away the only rope that anchors you to this world and to your being. When you cut away your past, you cut away yourself. What had I become?

Dawn came at last and as the sun burned away the mist, the morning sounds crackled back into life – Carwyn wailing, Osmond swearing as he stubbed his toe, and Adela stoking the fire to a blaze and calling to Narigorm and Rodrigo to come and eat. They were just the ordinary sounds of people beginning their day, raucous, discordant, but they were the most beautiful sounds on earth, the sounds of living people.

Later that morning, as I tended the cooking fire near the stone cross, I heard the sound of splashing and saw a coracle being paddled towards the spur. Osmond had taken Rodrigo fowling. I'd sent Narigorm back to a stream in the trees on the mainland to fetch water and Adela sat nursing the baby in the shelter of the hermit's dwelling. So I alone hailed the man who sat a little way off watching me.

'Any sick?' he called out. It was by now the common greeting.

When I reassured him, he paddled closer.

He held up three long fat wriggling eels. 'Want them?'

I nodded gratefully. We bartered back and forth until he finally agreed to take a belt and a cloak pin belonging to Cygnus. He tied the eels in a bit of sacking and held them out to me on the end of the paddle and I returned the belt and pin the same way.

'Two men netting. Fair and dark. They with you?'

I nodded.

'They want to stick to the heights, treacherous bastard this marsh. Many a man's put his foot on something that looks solid and found himself up to his waist before he can yell. Once he's in there's no man can get him out.' He spat a great glob of yellow phlegm into the water. 'Outlanders see fen folk out there, think there's no harm, but fen folk know where to walk and even they get taken when the mists come up.'

'Do you come from one of the fens?' I glanced towards the island villages behind him.

He spat again by way of denial. 'Height man. Village beyond the trees.' He jerked with his chin in a direction north of the spur.

'Has your village escaped the pestilence?'

He shook his head. 'Came a week or two before All Hallows. Lost near enough half the village, but there's been no more gone sick since St Thomas Eve now. Reckon it's moved on to find some other poor bastards. You seen –'

He suddenly froze, staring over my shoulder, a look of

panic on his face. I whirled round, alarmed at what might be behind me, but saw only Narigorm coming towards us, pails of water in her hand.

The man fumbled for something in his shirt and pulled out a hazel twig which he thrust out in front of him as if he was warding her off.

'That's only Narigorm, a child who travels with us,' I reassured him.

He looked relieved and sheepishly lowered his twig, but he didn't take his eyes off her. 'Thought she was a nixie or ghost, she's so pale. It's not natural.'

He continued to stare and Narigorm, aware she was being watched, returned his gaze unblinking. He quickly averted his eyes and picking up his paddle, deftly swung the coracle into the channel again.

Without looking back he called out, 'Make sure she doesn't comb her hair while she's in these parts. She'll comb up the white hair on the back of the waves and whip up a storm. We've seen enough death round here.'

As I watched him paddle away I hoped for Narigorm's sake there would be no storm. If there was, I had a feeling he'd be back and he would not be alone.

Fortunately for all of us, the next few days were calm though cold. We were glad of the hermit's hut to shelter Adela and her baby. The floor of the hut had been dug deep below ground level, so that inside it was high enough for a man to stand upright, but not wide enough for anyone to stretch full length when they lay down. The rest of us mostly slept outside around the fire pit. At least on the marshes there was fuel and food too if you could catch it. For those who dared risk their lives, there were birds to be netted, fish to be caught and eels to be speared. We caught few birds ourselves from the heights. Osmond was so punch-drunk with exhaustion from the sleepless nights that he could no longer hit a bird with his sling and netting was best done on the water, but as the eel-man had said, it was too dangerous to venture into the marsh, so we traded what goods we could for fish and fowl from the men in coracles who paddled across to us. They came as much out of curiosity as a desire to trade, but they kept us fed, though we cast envious eyes on the distant islands where sheep grazed. Salt mutton is said to be the best in the land, but no farmer slaughters his sheep before lambing and if anyone, like us, was tempted to steal one, they were far out of our reach, safe on their islands.

We should have moved on after a day or two. We knew we would have to go soon, for we were running out of things to trade and we needed to be somewhere we could feed ourselves. But the truth was we were afraid to leave the safety of the spur. Osmond was convinced that if the wolf came, he would come by way of the heights, not the marsh, and at least we could watch the entrance to the spur. And though I was certain the wolf was not human, like the others, I had no desire to sleep out there in the woods with nothing to protect my back. Whatever it was, at least on the spur we would see it coming. The marsh might be lethal but, like the sheep on their islands, its very danger was our protection.

But the marsh could not protect us from the howling. Every night we lit the fires and torches across the entrance and waited with mounting tension until we heard the wolf's howl and then we strained into the darkness frantically searching for any glimmer, any sign of movement. Even though we took it in turns to watch, those who were not on watch did little more than nap, constantly alert for any new sound. Of all of us, it was Rodrigo whom it affected the most. He hardly slept at all at night and we couldn't let him take the watch for he was so tense we feared he'd rush out into the marsh, if he thought that was where the howling was coming from. Without us realizing, the spur had become our prison. We fooled ourselves that we were keeping the wolf out, but in truth he was keeping us in.

Finally, late one afternoon as we sat round the fire, matters came to a head. Carwyn was fretful and Adela, exhausted by sleeplessness and tension, burst into tears and began screaming that she could not take another night of howling.

'I'd rather take Carwyn and walk into the marsh with him, at least it would be over,' she sobbed.

Osmond rounded on me. 'This is all your fault, Camelot. If you had left that accursed mermaid with the other boxes in the wagon, the Bishop's wolf would have left us alone weeks ago. We have to leave the reliquary out for him tonight. He knows we're here. He knows we have the reliquary. He's never going to leave us in peace until he has it.'

'But we don't know that it was among the things Zophiel stole. And I've told you, I don't believe that the Bishop's wolf is following us or ever was.'

'Are you deaf as well as blind? Haven't you heard the howls? God in heaven, Camelot, see sense, you know something is following us. What else can it be?'

'Please, Camelot,' Adela begged, 'we have to give it up to him.'

'We agreed we would find a church –'

Osmond's fists were clenched. 'No, Camelot, we will do it now. You heard Adela, she can't take another night of this. None of us can.' He took a deep breath, trying to regain control of himself. 'We will leave the reliquary where the spit joins the mainland, mark it with something that will show up in the dark, white cloth or stones, the Bishop's wolf will find it. Then it will be finished.'

Adela looked at me beseechingly. 'Please, Camelot. If the wolf gets tired of waiting and comes into our camp one night, he could cut our throats or even take little Carwyn in revenge. He came into the chantry without us hearing, remember.'

'Zophiel only thought he had,' I said without thinking.

Rodrigo flinched, and I wished I had bitten my tongue off, for if the Bishop's wolf hadn't taken the chalice, then in all probability Jofre had.

I had no choice. Osmond was close to breaking himself. I knew he'd take the relic by force if I didn't agree and I was no match for him. At least if the relic was still there in the morning, it might finally convince him that what was stalking us was not human. I held up my hands in a gesture of surrender. 'You're right, of course you are. I'll do it now.' I struggled to my feet.

'The wolf does not want the relic.'

I glanced round. Narigorm was crouching on the ground studying the runes spread out before her. There was a moment's silence as we digested this.

'Then ... then why is he still following us?' Osmond asked.

'The wolf wants death,' Narigorm said without emotion.

Adela buried her face in her hands and moaned.

'That's enough, Narigorm,' I said sharply. My bowels felt as if they had been turned to icy water, but I tried not to show it. 'If it's my death he wants, the wolf needn't trouble himself. At my great age he only has to wait a while and he'll get his wish without lifting a finger.'

Narigorm held up a rune shaped like a V on its side.

'*Kaunaz*, some say means a blazing torch, others say it means a boil, a place of death.'

Adela looked horrified. 'A boil! You mean the pestilence?'

Narigorm shook her head. 'If it is alone, it foretells that a gift is going to be given, a new life. But it is not alone.' She held up a rune with a single straight line on it. '*Isa* means ice. You don't see ice form on water until it's too late, but it's strong enough to destroy everything in its path. *Isa* stands for nine and the nine belong to Hati, the wolf that swallows up the moon. But now see?' She held the two runes up together. 'See the shape of the space between them.'

We stared at the space where her finger repeatedly traced the shape made by the two letters together, a line with a triangle half-way down.

'*Thurisaz*, the thorn, the troll rune, the curse rune. It changes the meaning of the other two. Now *Kaunaz* is filth and *Isa* is treachery. It means a gift will not be given, it will be taken. A life will not be given, it will be taken for his betrayal of those he loved.'

I suddenly remembered where I had heard her speak of troll runes before; it was the day we were trapped in the town while they searched for the fugitive Cygnus. Narigorm had watched Rodrigo, Osmond and Jofre walk off together, then she sang a snatch of song. 'Troll runes I cut . . . something, something . . . frenzy, filth and lust.' Then she'd said, 'I didn't know who the troll runes were for, but now I do.'

We hadn't realized it then, but that was the first day we numbered nine. Did she mean that the troll runes were for one of those three – Jofre, Osmond and Rodrigo? But Jofre was dead and now she was speaking of troll runes again; that left Osmond and Rodrigo. I looked across at Rodrigo, whose face was pale and hag-ridden, his eyes wide, staring at Narigorm in fear.

I turned furiously to Narigorm. 'Stop this, stop it at once. This has gone far enough.'

'Leave her!' Rodrigo shouted, then added more softly, 'Let her finish. I want to know what else she reads.'

The sun hung low in the sky. Narigorm raised her hand, palm out so that her hand covered the sun, then she closed her fist, sweeping her hand down slowly as if drawing the sun's rays down on to the runes. She picked up the third and last of the runes that lay in front of her. It was shaped like an arrow.

'*Teiwaz*, the rune of Tyr who put his hand into the mouth of the wolf Fenrir and swore a false oath. His hand was bitten off. He surrendered himself to the wolf to save his friends. This seals the others, for its troll rune is defeat. The person who this prophecy is for cannot win against the wolf. It will destroy him.'

Adela was clutching Osmond's hand so hard that I could see her nails cutting into his skin. 'But Narigorm, I don't understand, who *is* this for? If Camelot gives the reliquary back, surely the wolf won't kill him? He didn't steal it. He's not betrayed anyone he loved.'

'But I have,' Rodrigo whispered. He rose and walked rapidly away up the spur towards the heights.

Osmond prised himself from Adela's grip and hurried after him. He tried to grab him, but Rodrigo pushed him violently away. Osmond was not fool enough to try to touch him again. He turned back to the rest of us and shrugged helplessly. There was nothing we could do but watch Rodrigo go until he disappeared among the trees.

Osmond and I set out the reliquary on the far side of the night fires. We marked the place with a strip of linen round a tree trunk and a ring of white stones round the reliquary which would show up in the moonlight, if there was a moon. Osmond debated whether or not to set a torch up near it, but decided against it, thinking the wolf might take it for a trap. The sun was already setting and the air was turning sharp and damp. Rodrigo had not returned to the spur.

Osmond glanced uneasily towards the dark trees. 'You don't think he plans to stay on the heights and tackle the wolf after what Narigorm said, do you?'

'I'm afraid that's exactly what he might do. You start the fires and take first watch. I'll go and look for him.'

'But what if you're out there alone after dark and the wolf does come? You're no match . . . I should come too.'

'And leave Adela and Carwyn unprotected? You stay here. If the wolf wants blood, better it takes an old dotard like me.' I thought of Jofre and felt suddenly sick.

Rodrigo was sitting on an outcrop of rock, staring out over the marsh as the skies darkened and the sun began to slip blood-red behind the heights. He didn't move as I sat down beside him. Below us we could see the yellow dots multiplying in the distant fen cottages, as the villagers lit lanterns and rushes to keep the darkness at bay. There was a lantern too in a little coracle, a man fishing for eel in the gathering gloom. Overhead the birds filled the pink sky with their cries as they flew towards the marsh or departed for their roosting grounds. Thousands of starlings soared as one across the sky, twisting and turning until they resembled huge pillars of spiralling smoke, the sound of their wings like waves breaking on a shingled beach. Rodrigo gazed around him as if he was seeing it for the first time, or the last. Finally he spoke, his voice barely above a whisper.

'Go back to the spur, Camelot. The runes are meant for me, not you. It is me the wolf will come for. I will be the next to die and I deserve it. I will not run away from it.'

'Don't listen to Narigorm, Rodrigo. She's a child. She likes to frighten people. She's been worse since Carwyn arrived and Adela no longer fusses over her. You're not going to die and you most certainly do not deserve it. You are the gentlest and kindest man I've ever known.'

Even as I reassured Rodrigo, a voice inside me was hissing, 'Narigorm has never yet been wrong.' But if that was so, the prophecy was meant for me, not Rodrigo. It must not be for Rodrigo.

Rodrigo turned and looked at me, coldness in his eyes. 'Have you not understood, Camelot? I murdered a man and I cut off his arms and destroyed them so that he would enter the next life as one of the cripples he despised. But I am not ashamed of that even now. It was not the worst thing I have done. I let two innocent young men die, one of them the person I loved most in the world. I should have protected them and I failed. The fault is mine that they are dead. Narigorm spoke the truth; I betrayed them.'

'Rodrigo, listen to me. You can't blame yourself for their deaths. Jofre was killed by Ralph's father's henchmen. It was not your fault.'

'He would never have gone back to the town if I had stood up for him against Zophiel. When Zophiel threatened to flog him, he begged me for help and I turned away. He knew I did not believe him.'

'He wouldn't blame you for that.' I hesitated. I'd never asked him this before, but now it seemed important to keep him talking even if it made him angry.

'Rodrigo, when we first met, you told me your master had grown too old to manage his estate and his son had

496

taken over, bringing with him his own musicians. Was that really the reason you left your master's employ?'

Rodrigo grimaced. 'You were a stranger and . . .'

'And honesty doesn't oil the wheels of conversation,' I finished.

He nodded. 'Who really wants to hear the truth except a priest at confession? And he is paid to bear the burden of it.'

'I've never taken holy orders, but as the peat-cutter said, we're all priests now.'

Rodrigo sat in silence. He slowly opened his clenched fist and stared at the object which lay in his palm. It was the little glass tear which Michelotto had given Jofre. He rolled it around in his hand, watching colours slip from blue to purple. Then he held it up so that the flecks of gold glittered in the dying rays of the sun.

'Jofre was the son of a cousin of mine, but I did not meet him until his father sent him to England to be my pupil when he was just a boy. His father already suspected that Jofre would grow up to be a lover of men, and it revolted and shamed him and Jofre knew it. That is why he sent Jofre to me. The man had no love of music himself, but I was in England and that was far enough away for his father never to have to lay eyes on him again. Jofre was heartbroken to leave his mother. He despised himself because his father despised him. Maybe he thought also that his mother was ashamed of him, but I knew her and I do not believe she had anything in her heart except love for her son.

'Jofre soon showed his rare talent for music. He learned easily, maybe too easily. There were many distractions in my lord's court, but knowing how homesick Jofre was, I could not bring myself to be as strict with him as a master should be. Then my lord's heir, his grandson, arrived to be trained in the running of the estate. He was a year or two older than Jofre, but the two seemed instantly attracted to each other. At first the old lord saw no harm in it. His grandson was quiet and studious, more suited to the Church than to court. He had not mixed much with boys his own age, and the old man seemed pleased by their friendship, encouraged it even, the two young men riding off together hawking and hunting. He thought it would do his grandson good. But then rumours began to reach the old man's ear, rumours that what was going on between the young men was more than friendship. As you saw in the town, rumours of that sort disturb men greatly when they concern their heirs.'

I smiled wryly. 'If you have several sons, the predilections of the younger ones hardly matter; they can be sent into the Church or to war. In both professions it's an advantage if they don't pine for the company of women. But heirs must marry.'

Rodrigo nodded. 'Even so, I do not think the old man would have been worried by that alone. It is likely that in his youth he had taken comely young men as lovers before climbing into the marriage bed. With the virtue of high-born maids guarded like jewels, where else is a young lord to take his pleasure, except among beautiful young men, or pox-ridden girls in the manor kitchens or town stews? But discretion is everything and that is what Jofre and the young man lacked. When the old lord tried to caution his grandson to spend less time with Jofre, Jofre drowned his resentment in gambling and drinking, as he always did, and the studious grandson followed his example.'

I could see where this was leading. Only one thing alarms a wealthy man more than the fear that his heir will not produce sons, and that is the fear that his heir will gamble away his money and lands.

'My lord summoned me and told me that I must dismiss my pupil. But I had come to love Jofre. I do not mean in the way that Jofre loved men. My love for Jofre was deeper than that. It was the pure love of an older man for a younger. He was beautiful. He had so much life and vitality, so much talent, so much youth. He had everything before him. I was growing older, my body aging. I knew that my talent, which had never been as great as his, would depart as my fingers stiffened and my voice cracked. I could help him to be a great musician. I wanted to protect him, to take away the pain and self-loathing and teach him how beautiful he was.'

He looked at me, a desperate pleading in his face.

'Camelot, understand I could not dismiss him any more than I could cut off my own hand. I begged my lord for a second chance for Jofre. I promised I would control him, keep him far away from his grandson, but the old man knew as well as I did that it was like trying to keep a wave from breaking on the shore. The two had to be separated and since the grandson could not be sent away, Jofre must. He gave me a choice: either I dismissed him or he would dismiss me.'

'So you left and took Jofre with you.'

'In my lord's employ there were too many idle men with nothing to do but waste their time gambling and drinking. Away from them I thought it would stop. But as you know, it did not. He was miserable and that was his cure for misery. I did not know how to stop him. I tried everything. I even . . . I beat him, that night in the widow's inn, as you guessed.'

I nodded grimly; even now I couldn't tell him I had witnessed it and all that followed. I knew that would only add to his pain.

'You had no choice and it did seem to bring him to his senses for a while.'

'Until Zophiel started to taunt him.'

'Is that really why you killed Zophiel?'

For a long time he stared out over the darkening marshes. I thought he wasn't going to answer, then finally he said, 'I spoke the truth when I said I wanted to make him stop before he did to Cygnus what he had done to Jofre, but you are right, Camelot, I would not have murdered him to stop him. I would not even have killed him for what he did to Jofre when I thought he was just a man. But when I learned he was a priest . . .'

Rodrigo's voice took on a hard, bitter tone. 'I killed him because he was a priest, because it is priests and pardoners and their kind who destroy the young and the beautiful, the innocent and the helpless. Christ showed us compassion. He showed us God's mercy, but they use his name to torment those they should care for. They make them ashamed of what is beautiful. They make them despise their nature and their own body.

'There are many cruel men in this world, Camelot. Men who rob and kill and prey on the weak, but at least they are honest. They do not claim it is God's will. They do not drive a man to despair and say they are doing it out of love for him. If they torture someone it is only in this world; they do not condemn him to hell to be tortured for all eternity. Only the priests and bishops do that.'

The expression on Rodrigo's face was savage. 'The priests tell us that a man is born as he is because God wills it so, then they punish him for being that man. They tell us we are made in God's image, then what is God's image? You think God is like Jofre, with the voice of an angel, a man who loves men. You think God is like Cygnus, who once had love and faith enough to grow the beautiful wing of a swan. Or is Zophiel, the priest, the image of God? Zophiel

– it means God's spy, is that not so? I know about Zophiel. The Jews told me about him. He was the angel who told God that Adam and Eve had eaten the forbidden fruit. He is the one who guards the Tree of Life with a sword of fire to drive out anyone who tries to enter Eden. If Zophiel is the image of God, then I do not choose heaven; I choose hell.'

I had seen that terrible look on a man's face before, on the faces of those being dragged to the gallows. Some scream and plead, some swear and curse, some go serenely, convinced that the open gates of paradise await them. But the worst, the most chilling, are those who neither fight nor embrace it, but just accept it, their faces fixed in a look of sheer hopelessness and despair. The eyes stare out at you as if they are already the eyes of a dead man, and not a dead man in paradise, but one who is in purgatory or worse, far worse.

As Rodrigo rose from the rock and walked away, I knew he was not coming back. He knew that he was going to die and nothing I could say would change that. My art was the creation of hope. That was the greatest of all the arts, the noblest of all the lies, and yet I couldn't conjure it for him. His belief in Narigorm's runes and his own fate was stronger than any hope I could create for him, because, like those men who surrender themselves to despair on the gallows, he believed he deserved to die.

I couldn't let him go alone. I had no idea what he intended or what awaited him. I didn't know what I could do to prevent it, but I had to be there. If the wolf was out there waiting for him, I would see it, and if I could not kill it, at least I would finally know what it was.

It was dark by this time. The clouds lay heavy in the sky, obscuring moon and stars. But even without light it was not hard to follow Rodrigo. He blundered forward, crashing into bushes and stumbling over tree roots, as if being pulled along on an invisible rope. At least he was heading away from the marsh, that was something. Then the noise stopped. I thought I'd lost him, but as I reached the edge of the trees, I saw his dark shape walking across a clearing towards the biggest of the hollows.

The moon slid out from behind the clouds and in the moonlight I saw what I had never seen in daylight. A pearly-white mist lay in the bottom of the hollow. It only rose to the height of a man's knee and as Rodrigo walked into it, it swirled about his legs, but his body and head rose above it as if he was wading in shallow, luminescent water. I glanced about at the other hollows. They too had the same shallow pool of mist swirling in them and yet there was no mist between the trees.

Then I heard it, faint and distant, the sound I most feared – the howls of a wolf. The hairs on the back of my neck prickled and I gripped my stave so tightly it hurt. The howls were moving closer, but too quickly, too fast even for a running wolf. I stared about me, but the howls seemed to be coming from every direction as they had done that night in the gully. I searched desperately in the darkness for a pair of eyes, the shadow of a movement, but there was nothing. Rodrigo too was frantically turning this way and that, but he seemed chained to the spot in the centre of the hollow, like a goat tethered as living bait. He held out his arm protectively as if he was waiting for it to spring on him as he turned, trying to see from which direction it would come.

Then the sound changed; now it was a singing of wings as if a thousand swans were bearing down on us. But there was nothing to be seen in the moonlit sky. Rodrigo had sunk to his knees, covering his head with his arms and crouching so low in the mist that I could see only his clenched fists over his head. The noise grew louder and louder. I could stand it no longer. I ran towards the hollow, trying to reach Rodrigo, but as I broke free of the trees something white caught my eye just a few yards away. I hadn't seen it before because the trunks and scrub around me had blocked my view. Narigorm was crouching on the ground among the trees, her white hair gleaming in the moonlight. One hand was stretched over the runes in front of her, the other extended, palm outwards, towards the hollow. Her eyes were closed and there was a look of intense concentration on her face.

I took a pace towards her. The sound of the wings seemed to be coming from her, but that was impossible. The sound changed again, back to the howling of a wolf, and this time I knew beyond a shadow of doubt the howls were coming from her. She was the centre of it. She was the creator of it. But she was not howling.

Her lips were moving. 'Morrigan, Morrigan, Morrigan.'

The faster she muttered, the louder the sound which seemed to emanate from her outstretched hand. She must have sensed me coming towards her, for she opened her eyes just as I raised my staff and sent the runes flying in all directions. The howling stopped instantly as if it had been severed with an axe.

Narigorm leaped to her feet, her fingers clawing towards my face in fury, but I knocked them aside with my stave. I was too angry to temper the blow and she yelped in pain and surprise, stumbling backwards on to the ground, where she crouched like a cat, her bruised hands clenched tightly under her armpits. Any other child would have cried at such a blow, but Narigorm's eyes were filled with malice, not tears.

'It was you,' I screamed at her. 'All this time, you made us think we were being followed by a wolf, but there never was a wolf, was there, human or animal?'

'You heard a wolf.'

'You made us hear it.'

'Morrigan made you hear it.'

'Who is Morrigan?'

'The shapeshifter, the wolf, the swan, the bringer of chaos and death, the destroyer of liars. You only heard the wolf because you lied. You all lied.'

I suddenly remembered where I had first heard her use that name. It was Midsummer's Day, the day we first met. 'If you lie you lose the gift,' she told me. 'Morrigan destroys liars.'

'But you heard the wolf too, Narigorm.'

'I made it. I control it.'

'And you controlled it to drive half our company to suicide and murder. You evil, malicious little brat. How could you do that to us when all we've done is feed you and take care of you? You accuse us of treachery and betrayal, but it's you who have betrayed us.'

'You did it. You lied. I never lie. I only read what is there in the runes. I only tell the truth.'

'When I first saw you, your master was thrashing you for telling *your* truth, but if you think that was punishment, you wait until the others find out what you've done. You'll wish you'd never been born, my girl. Your vicious little game is over. You tried to kill Rodrigo, but you failed.'

'But you're wrong, Camelot. I haven't failed. All the time you've been talking, Rodrigo has been dying. Morrigan has destroyed him too.'

I spun round. Rodrigo was nowhere to be seen.

Narigorm smiled triumphantly. 'The mist that rises from

the ground in the hollows is poison. Didn't you see all the dead animals? Didn't you guess? Now Rodrigo is dead too. And you loved him, didn't you?'

I stared at her aghast, then, without stopping to think, I turned and ran into the hollow. I desperately tried to remember where I had last seen him. But my feet sent the white mist swirling around my legs, so it was like looking down into a mill race. My heart was pounding and my chest felt so tight I thought it was being crushed. Now that I was in it, the hollow seemed vast. The moon slipped behind the clouds again and all at once I was plunged into darkness. Only the mist still glimmered white. I bent down, trying to grope under it for his body. My senses were reeling. My head ached. I couldn't think what I was doing there. I was exhausted. All those nights without proper sleep were crowding in on me; my limbs felt stiff and numb as if I had been walking for hours. All I wanted to do was to lie down in the soft white mist and sleep, just for a few minutes, surrender to it and sleep. A few minutes wouldn't matter, then I'd be able to think, I'd know what to do. I could feel myself sinking to my knees and I was powerless to stop it.

27. The Sending

I heard Narigorm laughing. The sound was like a stinging slap. I pushed hard on my stave and forced myself to stand upright again. I took a big gulp of air. My head was still splitting, but my thoughts suddenly cleared. The mist hung close to the ground, that was why we had been able to walk through it during the day without harm. Only if your head was below it could it work its poison. If you stood above it, you could survive. I began to walk forward, sweeping my stave rapidly, and then it connected with something. I prodded, feeling my stave trace the shape of a human body. I held my breath, sank to my knees, hauled his arm round my neck and pulled down on the wrist as I struggled to my feet again, levering him to his feet.

I didn't know if he was dead or alive; all I knew was that I had to cross those few yards to the trees before I could let him go. I hauled, but he was taller and heavier than I was and even in my youth I'd have had trouble moving him. It was all I could do to keep his limp body upright without trying to move forward. I dared not lay him down and drag him for I knew I had to keep his head above the pool of poison. I pulled him forward step by painful step. My lungs felt as if they were on fire and my head was throbbing. Only another few yards, but I knew I was never going to make it. I had breathed in too much of the mist and now my legs were beginning to give way, I couldn't take another step. I stood there in the darkness, the weight of Rodrigo's body crushing me, the white mist swirling round me. I was so dizzy that I was forced to close my eyes to keep myself from falling. I could feel the world spinning round, the ground slipping sideways, shifting beneath my feet. I was pitching forward into the darkness.

Then I felt Rodrigo's weight lifting.

'Let go, Camelot, I've got him.'

Osmond was heaving Rodrigo's body over his shoulder.

'Mist . . . poisonous . . . get him out,' I murmured, but he was already striding away. I sank to my knees, but almost at once felt myself being hauled up again as Osmond propelled me forward to the trees. I slid down, leaning against a trunk for support, as the trees spun around me.

I could hear Osmond slapping Rodrigo hard. 'Come on, Rodrigo. Come on, wake up. Holy Mary, Mother of God, let him wake.'

I felt something roll against my leg. My fingers closed over it and I knew what it was without opening my eyes. I grasped the cold, smooth glass of Michelotto's tear and prayed.

I took several deep breaths and opened my eyes. The ground was still slipping and twisting, but not as badly as before. Osmond held Rodrigo by the shoulders and was trying to flap air over his face. Rodrigo's face was pale in the moonlight and his eyes were closed. I knew if I attempted to stand upright I would fall. I slipped the flask into my shirt and crawled over on my hands and knees.

Osmond shook his head. 'It's no good. I think he's gone. I came as soon as Narigorm came running for help, but if I'd got to him sooner . . .'

'Narigorm?'

'Yes, she said he tried to cross the hollow, but had fallen. She said the mist in the hollow was poisonous. I didn't believe her at first, until she said about the animals, then it made sense. Poor little thing, she was terrified.'

That wasn't right, but my head was swimming too much to think straight. 'No, no, it was Narigorm who –'

There was a cough. We looked down and saw Rodrigo's chest give a little flutter. Osmond pulled him up into a sitting position, supporting him against his chest, I pushed his head back to open his mouth and we frantically fanned the air near his face. Then to our relief we saw his chest beginning to heave rapidly, and finally his eyelids fluttered. He rolled over and began to cough violently, then lay back in Osmond's arms exhausted, his chest heaving painfully. He was alive. Rodrigo was alive.

It took a long time before he had recovered enough to stand and even then he needed both of us to support him on the short walk back to the camp. Adela came running to meet us and half-crushed the breath out of Rodrigo again as she tried to hug both him and Osmond together. We propped Rodrigo up in a half-sitting position on a pile of our packs and he lay coughing and wheezing, too weak to move.

None of us slept that night, though we were all exhausted. Adela and Osmond decided it would be too dangerous to let us sleep in case the poison claimed us again. So they spent all night helping us to sit upright and forcing us to drink hot broth whenever we looked as if we would doze off. My limbs were aching as if I had a fever. I could tell from his groans that Rodrigo felt no better than I did. But we were alive.

While Adela and Osmond watched us anxiously, someone else was watching us carefully too, but her face was expressionless. Flashes of the night's events kept bursting in my mind, but my head was aching so much, I couldn't make sense of them. I didn't want to think about it. I only wanted to sleep.

Never had a dawn been so welcome. The slow pale stain crept over the distant edge of the marsh, bringing with it the cries of gulls and plovers as the night slipped back like an ebbing tide. With the coming of daylight, Adela finally decided it was safe to let us sleep and we needed no persuasion.

When I woke again the sun was already sinking over the heights. I sat up clutching my cloak around me. The wind was sharpening and it was bitterly cold. Rodrigo was already up, though I guessed he had not been awake long, for he sat by the fire rubbing his swollen eyes as Adela handed him a bowl of something hot and steamy.

He smiled ruefully at me as I struggled over to join them.

'How are you feeling, Camelot?' Adela asked anxiously.

'Worst hangover I've ever had, except that I've not been drinking. What about you, Rodrigo?'

'Thrown by a horse and then kicked in the head by it, except I have not been riding. Osmond tells me that you risked your life trying to pull me out last night, Camelot. I am once more in your debt, old friend.'

'We both owe our lives to Osmond – it was he who got us out.'

'And Narigorm too,' Rodrigo added. 'If she had not realized the nature of the hollow and gone for help . . . I am so stupid. I did not see the danger.'

At the mention of Narigorm, I frowned. 'Where is she?'

Adela answered. 'She's gone fowling with Osmond. The

poor child was so worried about you both, Osmond thought it would cheer her up.'

I glanced up at the sky; they'd be back soon. 'Rodrigo,' I said urgently, 'what do you remember about last night?'

He massaged his temples. 'Not much. Talking to you, I think, but I cannot remember what we spoke about . . . Then walking through the trees, it was dark, but I do not know where I was going. Back to the camp, I suppose. Then . . . then I was lying down and Osmond was slapping me.' He rubbed his cheek and smiled ruefully. 'He has a hard hand, that husband of yours, Adela. Remind me not to offend him.'

'Don't you remember anything else?' I asked. 'How you came to be in the hollow? Try, it's important. Did you hear the wolf?'

He winced and clutched his head. 'I do remember that. When I was in the trees I heard him. I could not tell where the sound was coming from. I wanted to see him coming so I went out into the hollow where there were no trees. Then . . . then the swans, a huge flock of swans was flying down towards me. I tried to protect myself. The noise was deafening. I could not breathe.' He covered his face with his hands, trembling violently as the memory seized him.

'That's because you crouched down in the mist, to protect yourself from the swans. But there were no swans and no wolf. It was Narigorm who was conjuring those sounds. I saw her. She was in the trees watching you. The sounds were coming from her. It's been her all along making the wolf howls.'

They both stared at me as if I had grown two heads.

Adela said gently, 'How could a little girl make those sounds? When we've heard the wolf before, she's been with us. She hasn't been howling. It's the poison of the white mist. It made you imagine things.'

'No, it's not the mist. There never has been a wolf. Narigorm has been conjuring a Sending, the power of the runes sent out in the form of a wolf and sometimes a swan. I watched her do it last night. She's been using the Sending to drive us all to our deaths and she nearly succeeded again with you last night, Rodrigo, and me too. That wasn't a prophecy that Narigorm read in the runes yesterday, it was a curse, a curse she sent out. She traced the outline of the troll rune with her finger and brought its power to life.'

Rodrigo stared at me. 'This is madness. Adela is right, the white mist poisoned you, made you see devils and demons. Narigorm came to fetch help, is that not so, Adela? She saved our lives.'

'No, listen. I scattered her runes, I broke her spell. She delayed me until she was certain you were dead, then she sent me into the hollow. She was watching me, waiting until I collapsed. I could hear her laughing. Only then did she go for Osmond. She thought by the time Osmond found us, I too would be dead. She's spent hours there watching animals die in the mist. She knew it didn't take long. Perhaps she even thought Osmond too would succumb to the mist if he started to search for us.'

Rodrigo's frown deepened. 'You are imagining this. Maybe you are right, maybe there were no swans and the white mist made this illusion for me, but the wolf is real. Narigorm does not make this sound.'

He rose painfully to his feet and walked back towards the mainland, making it clear he wanted to hear no more.

I turned to Adela. 'If the wolf is real, did he claim his reliquary last night?'

She hesitated, then shook her head. 'But that proves

nothing, Camelot. With all the commotion, he was hardly likely to risk coming, was he?'

I glanced carefully around to make quite sure we were alone before I spoke. 'Adela, even if you do not believe me about Narigorm, promise me that you will not let her find out that Osmond is your brother. She must never know.'

'He's not! He's not! He's my husband.'

I took her hand gently. 'I think he is your brother and Carwyn is his child.'

She looked away, unable to meet my gaze. 'How . . . how long have you known?'

'I suspected from the first night in the cave, but I became certain the night you gave birth. He took you away from the convent, didn't he? Did they send you there because of the baby?'

She nodded, staring at the ground, her veil falling across her scarlet cheeks. 'I was betrothed to a merchant, a friend of my father's, but he had to travel on business, so the marriage date was set for the month after he returned. But before he returned my cousin told my mother that my linen had not been stained for two months and my mother called the physician. When they learned I was . . . was with child, they were enraged. They knew the merchant would not marry a woman who was pregnant by another, who would? They demanded to know who the father was, but even though they beat me, I wouldn't tell them. I couldn't. They were angry enough that I had slept with a man, but if they had discovered that man was my own brother . . . So my parents had me taken to a convent in disgrace.

'The nuns treated me as if I was a whore who should have been made to walk barefoot in a sheet through the town. They kept me locked in a cold, dark penitent's cell with little food for days at a time. Perhaps they hoped I'd lose the child. "The fruit of sin", they called him. If they'd really known the nature of that sin . . . But I wanted Carwyn. Even though I knew he was my shame, I wanted him so much because he was Osmond's son. As long as I could feel his child growing inside me, I knew they could not separate me from Osmond.

'But the nuns told me that when the baby was born, he would be sent away to be raised and I would become a nun, spending my life learning to subdue my lusts and atone for my wickedness. I would be a bride of Christ. He would be my husband. I would surrender every part of me to him and if I refused him, his vengeance would be terrible.'

'But Osmond rescued you?'

She turned and stared out over the desolate marshes, darkening now as the sun began to slip behind the trees. For a few moments she said nothing, then quietly resumed her story, speaking so softly I had to draw closer to hear her.

'Osmond was away. He was working as journeyman to a master painter. He didn't know that he had got me with child. When he returned on a visit, he discovered where I had been sent and why. He knew at once that the child must be his and he was appalled at what he had done, but he could tell no one. He came to see me, though our parents had forbidden it. He told the sisters he had come with a message from my father. He could see at once how wretched and thin I had become. He could not bear it, so he bribed one of the laywomen to help me escape. He couldn't return to his work, because he knew our father would come looking for us there. So we were forced to go on the road. His master still held his papers; he couldn't go back for them.'

'And without them, he can't work as a painter.'

She nodded miserably.

'Osmond must love you very much,' I said gently.

'And I love him. You cannot know how much. Without him, I feel I've been cut in two and as if part of my very being has been taken from me. Maybe Zophiel was right and I have damned his soul to hell, and he mine. But we cannot exist without each other. Can you understand that, Camelot?'

I squeezed her hand and nodded. 'But, Adela, at all costs you must keep this from Narigorm; she must not find out.'

'But she adores Osmond. Even if she discovered the truth, she would do nothing to hurt him. She would not report us to the Justices or the Church.'

I did not want to hurt her, but I had to make her understand. 'Come with me, Adela. I want to show you something.'

I led her into the dark interior of the hermit's shelter and scrabbled around under some empty sacks until I found what I was looking for.

'You remember the doll Osmond carved for Narigorm? Look at it, Adela, look at the face, she has destroyed it.' I thrust the doll into her hands.

She turned and held it towards the doorway. The light outside was fading fast.

'You're mistaken, Camelot, she's hasn't destroyed her. She's just painted a new face on her, white like her own. It was stupid of us, we should have realized that the child would want a doll which looked like her.'

I took the doll from her and stepped outside. I held it up so that the last rays of the sun would illuminate its face. Adela was right. Narigorm had given the doll a new face, but it wasn't painted. Its mouth was formed from the bleached white bones of a mouse, with sharp shrew's teeth set between the bone lips. The eyes and ears were fashioned from the bones of a frog and the nose was the blanched beak of a little dead bird. It had taken patience to do this, patience and skill far beyond that of a normal child.

Behind me I heard shouts as Osmond and Narigorm returned, swinging several birds by their necks. I just had time to slip back inside the hut to push the doll back under the sacks again.

'Just promise me, Adela, promise me you will never let her find out.'

But Adela had already gone to greet them.

All talk of last night was pushed aside as we plucked and drew and boiled the birds for supper. But every time I glanced up I saw Adela and Rodrigo watching me warily as if they thought I was about to run round the camp tearing off my clothes and babbling about demons. They clearly thought that the white mist had robbed me of what few wits my ancient body still commanded. I knew if the wolf howled again that night from the heights, it would only serve to prove my insanity.

I thought about it carefully. Narigorm could only control the Sending when she was awake. If Narigorm was seen to sleep and the wolf was silent, perhaps then they would finally listen to me. I remembered the poppy syrup in Pleasance's pack. I waited until the others were occupied, then I searched for it. Just a few drops would be enough and getting her to swallow them wasn't difficult; Narigorm always wanted more. Adela filled her first bowl, but I filled her second and Narigorm, as Adela herself remarked, slept the sleep of the innocent from dusk until dawn and, that night, so did the wolf.

28. The Game

Narigorm was still drowsy the following day and unsteady on her feet, something about which I had no qualms, given how I had felt after the white mist. At Adela's urging, she stayed in the camp while Osmond and Rodrigo went to see what they could catch. I followed on the pretext of searching for wood and hurried to catch up with them as soon as we were out of sight of the others. The black despair that had settled on Rodrigo since Cygnus's suicide had lifted a little, as if coming so close to death himself had temporarily jolted him back to life. The long sleep too had helped to recover his spirits a little, but I knew this recovery was as fragile as glass and would shatter in an instant if Narigorm resumed her tricks.

Rodrigo and Osmond glanced at each other as I called out to them. Clearly I had been the topic of conversation and they eyed me warily as if they thought that I might have to be restrained at any moment. I couldn't afford to waste time building up to the topic.

'Osmond, I take it Rodrigo has told you what I said yesterday afternoon about Narigorm?'

He nodded, saying hastily, 'But no one blames you,

Camelot. Rodrigo was saying that the poisoned mist made you both imagine things.'

I ignored this. 'Last night we neither heard the wolf nor did he take the reliquary. That's because Narigorm slept all night; you saw her. When she's awake, she controls the Sending; when she sleeps, the wolf is silent.'

I thought it wisest not to mention I had drugged her. They really would think I was mad.

'But that proves nothing,' Osmond said. 'Some nights the wolf howls, sometimes he doesn't. Look, I've been thinking about what you told Rodrigo, but I realized we first heard the wolf that night in the cave, the night Zophiel, Adela and I joined you. Narigorm wasn't with us then.'

'That night in the cave, it probably was a real wolf. There are wolves still remaining in that wilderness of caves and gorges. Or, as Zophiel said, it could have been one of the outlaws who hide up in those places, but human or animal, whatever we heard that night didn't follow us. We never heard a wolf again until Narigorm joined us, and then only when there were nine of us, which was weeks later. Remember what Narigorm said yesterday: "Nine belong to the wolf"? The day we first saw Cygnus telling stories in the market place, I saw her read the runes and she said, "There is one to come before it can begin," and only after Cygnus joined us, making the nine, did we start to hear the wolf and think it was following us. I know it doesn't seem possible, but the more I think about it, the more convinced I am that she has somehow been behind every death in our company.'

Rodrigo put his hand on my shoulder. 'This is not like you. You should rest. These deaths and the long journey have exhausted you. Go back to the camp. We will talk later.'

'No, you have to listen to me now. When you were in the hollow, Narigorm told me that each of us had heard the wolf because we had each lied. She's used the runes and the wolf howls to play on our fears and guilt to get us to expose our secrets and our lies, and then she drove us to destroy ourselves, just as she tried to do to you the other night, Rodrigo. Narigorm brought out Zophiel's knife deliberately to make you betray the fact that you'd killed Zophiel. Then with her runes she tried to play on your guilt to drive you to your death, just as she had Cygnus. Narigorm failed to kill you, but it won't stop her trying again, and when she has destroyed you she'll turn her attention to Adela and Osmond, even baby Carwyn.'

'A baby can't lie,' Osmond said.

'What if the baby is the lie?'

His eyes widened and he stared at me. Then he flushed and looked away.

Rodrigo was too wrapped up in his own thoughts to register Osmond's discomfort. 'But why should she want to kill us, Camelot?' he burst out, then, realizing he was talking to the old and mad, spoke slowly and patiently. 'Pleasance – she was not driven to her death by hearing the wolf.'

'But she was driven to betraying herself by him. Why did Pleasance tell us the tale about being midwife to the wolf when she had always wisely kept silent before? Because when we heard the wolf that night, it gave Narigorm the excuse to make her tell the tale of being the wolf's midwife. What if she knew the telling of it would trap Pleasance into revealing she was a Jew? You told me yourself that Pleasance knew she had given herself away by using that word *sheidim*.'

Rodrigo shook his head, 'How could a child know the danger that lay in a word? Pleasance cared for the child when she was abandoned. If Narigorm begged for the tale again, it was in innocence. It is Zophiel that you should blame for the death of Pleasance. It was his bitter words against the Jews that drove her into such fear.'

'But if they were companions, Rodrigo, it is even more likely that Narigorm had already discovered she was a Jew and was just looking for a way to trick her into revealing it to us. But it was not just Pleasance. Narigorm used the wolf's howl to convince Zophiel he was being hunted by the Bishop's wolf. She could have easily taken the chalice from the chantry herself to frighten Zophiel or make him turn on Jofre. She had as much opportunity as Jofre to take it. Don't forget, Zophiel said he didn't know it was missing until Narigorm read in the runes that something had been taken from him. Zophiel accusing Jofre of theft was what drove Jofre back to that town and to his death at the hands of Ralph's father's henchmen. And think back to why Jofre went to the town in the first place – because Narigorm insisted on seeing the face of the Madonna, knowing that Jofre would be upset enough to betray his feelings for Osmond. And in case that wasn't enough, she told us Jofre had feelings for Osmond in front of Zophiel, knowing full well that Zophiel would torment Jofre with it.

'And,' I rushed on desperately, seeing the disbelieving looks in their faces, 'why did Zophiel confess to us about the stolen church treasures? Because Narigorm had convinced him he was being pursued by the Bishop's wolf and she told us she had read in the runes that someone would soon get their just deserts for a dark secret they had been hiding. She produced that black marble ball, claiming the runes were meant for Zophiel, knowing that if he had anything to hide, it would terrify him into a confession. You told me yourself, Rodrigo, if you hadn't discovered he was a priest, you would not have killed him. She manipulated you into that just as she had manipulated Zophiel into accusing Jofre. And even if you hadn't killed him, she was driving Zophiel to such fear and aggression with her wolf howls that sooner or later Osmond would probably have been driven to attack him – that's if he hadn't knifed you or Osmond first.'

'You think I am so stupid I could be tricked into committing murder by a child?' Rodrigo said furiously. 'I killed Zophiel. Narigorm had nothing to do with it.'

Osmond laid a hand on his arm and shook his head as if trying to remind him they were dealing with a lunatic who didn't know what he was saying. 'Camelot, even if you're right about the others, Narigorm did not force Cygnus to reveal a lie.'

'But she did. Cygnus told us his stump had grown into a real wing because that is what he honestly believed, but I've been thinking about that. Do you remember the night we found Cygnus hiding in the wagon and brought him into the cottage with old Walter and his son?'

'Yes,' Osmond said, 'and I also remember it was Zophiel who forced him to tell his story.'

'But think about what happened afterwards. Narigorm pulled a feather out of Cygnus's wing. She said if the wing was real, the feather would grow back. But it didn't, and once that feather had been pulled out, the rest started to fall out. Pulling out the feather exposed a lie, even though it was one Cygnus believed in. And again she used Zophiel to torment him, that and the sound of the swans' wings she made him hear, night after night in his dreams.'

Osmond shook his head. 'I can see that Narigorm may have caused some trouble between us, but she couldn't have known what would happen. It was all done innocently. It would make more sense if you said it was the Bishop's wolf who was behind all of these deaths, except that not even a man of his cunning could have planned these things.'

'That's exactly what I've been trying to tell you; there never was a Bishop's wolf,' I snapped in exasperation. I took a deep breath. 'I believe somehow Narigorm used the runes to draw us to her, somehow she assembled us, because she needed us, nine of us, to play her game. But I don't believe she planned the details of the game itself. She has a child's instinct for discovering the fears and weaknesses in others and using them. She plays her game just to see what will happen. Have you never watched children play a game of chess? Adults plan their moves, but children just experiment to see the effect if they move this piece or that, and when they find a weakness they show no mercy, but drive it to checkmate. She has been deliberately pitting us against one another, using us as her chess pieces.'

'Camelot, what are you saying?' Osmond ran his fingers through his hair in exasperation.

'I'm saying that Narigorm will go on playing her game. She will find a way to destroy each one of us if we don't get away from her. We have to leave her here and go on without her.'

'Abandon a child?'

'Not a child, a ruthless and powerful killer. Osmond, you have Adela and Carwyn to think of. You can't risk her turning on them and, believe me, she will if she has the chance. Let's leave her here. She has shelter and she knows how to hunt and fish. She won't starve.'

Osmond backed away. 'Camelot, you can't mean this. Narigorm is an innocent child. She saved both your lives, remember? Rodrigo is right, if anyone of us is to blame for the deaths of the others, it was Zophiel with his vicious tongue. Rodrigo did us all a favour by killing him.'

'But, Osmond, can't you see –'

'No, Camelot, no, I won't listen to any more of this. Rodrigo, are you coming?'

'Rodrigo?' I pleaded.

He regarded me sadly. 'I am sorry, Camelot, sorry that you should believe such things.'

I watched him walk away and I shivered in the cold, knowing I had offended the one man whose good opinion mattered to me more than anything else. He'd forgive me in time, put it down to the madness of the poison, but only if I never spoke of it again, and I had to. The image of the doll's face flashed into my mind. What if Narigorm already knew about Adela and Osmond? I had to convince them all of the danger they were in.

Above the bare branches of the trees, birds were being punched back and forth by the strengthening wind. I picked up my stave and turned towards the heights.

'They'll never believe you.'

I wheeled round. Narigorm was standing in the shadow of a tree, a pail in each hand. How long had she been there?

'You're old and you're mad, that's what they think. They know you make up stories about your relics. They think this is just another one. You can't stop me. Morrigan is too strong for you.'

29. The Last Lie

It took me over three hours to reach the village on the heights. It would have been quicker by boat, but I didn't have one. There was no path and I just kept heading north through the trees, frequently having to cut inland to find ways across the tongues of the marsh which licked into the heights and the streams which flowed down from it. Finally, I saw the smoke from the cottages climbing into the sky.

The village ran round a small harbour on the side of a wide river that cut through the marsh and eventually emptied into the sea. Before the pestilence it must have been a bustling port, but there were no merchants' ships in the harbour now, only a couple of small boats big enough for two or three men to fish from. There was a small, squat church, no bigger than a chapel, dwarfed by its round, flat-topped tower that had a fire beacon set ready on top of it to guide the boats home in bad weather. Many of the cottages were boarded up and marked with the dreaded black crosses, but smoke was rising from some hearths and here and there I saw people busy about their work, mending a net, fetching water or washing clothes. As I descended from the woods I saw the raw bare mounds of earth on the far side of the village and the blackened circles where fires had burned around mass graves.

There were only four or five customers in the inn on the quayside. The innkeeper's wife was thumping down a steaming bowl in front of one them. She glanced up curiously as I entered, but did not recoil from the sight of me, as many do. An innkeeper's wife who keeps house on the quayside sees worse mutilations than my face among the sailors and fishermen she serves.

'Fish soup and bread. It's all I've got and there's some who should be thankful to get anything,' she announced, giving a sour look at the man she'd just served.

'Take my advice, stay away from the bread. She makes it with sawdust. It's that hard I'm thinking of using it to shoe the horses.'

He was a big man, with a backside as broad as a bear's, but he knew enough to cover his head and duck smartly as she aimed a slap at him.

'You watch your tongue, William. I'd like to see you make decent bread when all you've got is roots to grind.'

'You couldn't make decent bread when you'd best wheat,' chimed in another customer, but he was not as quick at dodging her hand and his friends laughed as he ruefully rubbed the back of his head. The potboy stood grinning inanely, but swiftly wiped the smile off his face as the innkeeper's wife turned on him.

'You seen to those pigs yet and I don't mean this lot? Get on with it, boy, or Master Alan here won't be the only one with a sore head.'

He hastily backed out again, while the men grinned broadly.

'What brings you from the old hermit's island? It's a fair step by land.'

I glanced around and saw, sitting on a bench in the corner, the man who had brought us the eels.

'Heard the fish soup was worth the walk,' I said, and the innkeeper's wife smiled in spite of herself.

'Not brought that white-haired girl, have you?'

I was aware of a murmur of interest among the other men. One spat on the back of his fingers. Clearly the eel-man had told them all about her. I took a deep breath. I had no idea if this was going to work. If it didn't, I could be making matters worse for all of us, but it was the only hope I had. 'It's about her I've come,' I said, and the men edged a little closer.

I've spun many stories in my time for food and for shelter, but never before for our lives. There was silence in the inn as I finished my tale.

'So you see, she has destroyed many villages just like yours. If you don't act now, then she'll destroy you too. The others in my company are under her spell and I'm an old man. I can't act alone, but I can help you deal with her.'

Finally, the eel-man spoke. 'Camelot's right about the girl. You all know I've not caught a thing since she gave me the evil eye, and my little'un fell and broke her leg in that very hour she looked at me. With that hair of hers she could whip up such a storm as to destroy all the villages on this coast. I remember my father telling of the great storm fifty years back that took whole villages. Not a soul left alive. Cottages, churches, fields, all still out there under the sea. That witch'll destroy us all if we give her half a chance. We've got to get rid of her.'

'That's all very well,' said the innkeeper's wife, 'but if she's as powerful as you say, how are we to do that?'

All eyes turned expectantly to me.

I'd had plenty of time to think this through during my long walk. 'Tonight, after dark, come by boat to the spur. I'll make sure my companions are asleep, the child too. You seize her, cover her head and tie her up, so she can't look at you. But you must stuff your ears before you reach the spur. She can conjure up sounds that can make you run mad. Whatever you think you hear – wolves, swans, a storm – take no notice. They're just sounds and can't hurt you, but don't unplug your ears till her hands are tightly bound. She uses her hands for the Sending.'

They nodded.

'Wax ought to do it,' the eel-man said. 'That'll stop our ears, but what do we do with her when we've taken her?'

I hesitated. I wanted to say, just lock her up, keep her away from us, until I've got Rodrigo and the others so far away she can never find us. But I knew that would not be enough to protect us.

The blacksmith shifted his massive backside on the bench. 'Seems plain enough to me: "Thou shalt not suffer a witch to live". Can't see as we have a choice. We have to kill her. It'll be the only way to lift the evil eye from Gunter here and stop her from harming the rest of us.'

There was silence as they digested this, but not even the innkeeper's wife protested.

'We'll have to do it so she can't curse us as she dies,' the innkeeper said.

Gunter nodded. 'And so her spirit can't rise to wreak vengeance.'

'First catch your fish before you argue about how to cook it,' the innkeeper's wife said tartly.

The innkeeper adopted the brisk tone of one who considers it his duty to take charge. 'Bring her trussed and gagged and lock her in the church tower. The church is holy ground and will keep her spirit bound. Then we'll hold a meeting to decide how the killing's to be done.'

I didn't want to know how they would do it. I thought if I did, my nerve would fail me. I rose. 'I have to get back before they become suspicious. You'll come tonight then?'

They looked at each other, then one by one they nodded.

Gunter said, 'You'll see to it your companions don't interfere? Those men you've got with you look as if they'd be handy with a quarterstaff and I've got enough troubles without getting my head cracked.'

'I'll set a light at the foot of the cross at the end of the spur when it's safe,' I promised.

'We'll wait for the light, then.'

It wasn't so easy to use the poppy juice a second time. I knew I would have to be seen to eat, so I couldn't risk putting it in the pottage itself, which would have been simple in the dark. It would have to go into the bowls, all of them except mine, but Adela usually ladled out the pottage. However, a surreptitious pinch on Carwyn's thigh made him cry and brought Adela running to comfort him, grateful for my offer to ladle out the pottage. I handed the bowls to Osmond and Rodrigo, who tucked in straight away, ravenous after a day's hunting, but as Narigorm carried her bowl back to her place she appeared to trip and the contents of the bowl landed upside down on the grass.

'Never mind, I'll get you some more,' I said, as calmly as I could.

She smiled sweetly. 'Oh no, you rest, Camelot. I'll get it.'

There was nothing I could do. Did she know I had drugged her the night before? She was clever enough to have worked that out.

Adela took a long time settling Carwyn and by the time

she came to eat, the bowl I had placed in front of her was cold. Before I could stop her, she tipped it back into the steaming pot, stirred it and ladled out a fresh bowl. No matter, I told myself, as long as Rodrigo and Osmond were asleep, I could deal with Adela, and maybe she had taken enough for she seemed sleepy anyway, which was more than could be said for Narigorm.

Osmond and Rodrigo quickly became drowsy and Osmond was happy to accept that I took first watch, in fact he could scarcely keep his eyes open long enough to murmur his agreement. I hoped that I hadn't administered too much. One by one I watched them curl up, until only Narigorm remained awake. She sat on the other side of the fire, her back to the marsh, her pale eyes glittering in the firelight and her hair turned to a mass of dancing flame as it blew in the wind.

As casually as I could, I went to the cross and set a lantern beneath it, so that the cross was lit up against the dark sky. It was bitterly cold and the wind was gathering strength. Was Gunter right? Was Narigorm capable of raising a storm with the shaking of her hair? I'd encouraged them to believe it. I prayed it was a lie that would not turn out to be the truth. I crossed back to the fire.

Narigorm was watching me. 'Why have you set a lantern there? Do you think the cross will protect you from the wolf?'

I nodded. I didn't trust myself to speak. My ears were straining to hear the sound of oars over the roar of the wind. The flames in the fire pit blew this way and that. I moved a stone to shelter the top a little more.

'You put something in my food last night to make me sleep.'

I didn't answer.

'You think if I sleep the wolf won't come. But you know she will come tonight, don't you?' There was a note of pleasure in her voice. 'That's why you made the others sleep. You think that if they sleep they can't hear the wolf. But they can. Cygnus heard the swans in his sleep. It is worse if you hear the wolf in your sleep, because then you have to face her alone. In your dreams she can do anything.'

'Why do you do this, Narigorm?'

'Because I can.'

There was no moon tonight, thick, heavy clouds blotted out the stars. The pale light reflecting from the cross seemed to penetrate no more than a hand's breadth into the darkness. Would they even see it?

'You spoke before of Morrigan. She's an ancient goddess, a savage goddess. Do you do this to serve her?'

I wanted to keep her talking, keep her occupied, but she wasn't listening.

She had taken the runes out of her bag and scattered them in front her. Then I saw her place something else in the centre of them. It was a clipping of coarse hair. I recognized it by the white bindings around it. I had tied it. It was hair I used to sell as the beard of St Uncumber. I'd given a piece of it to the bride at the Cripples' Wedding. My stomach tightened. I knew what Narigorm was doing, she wanted to use something of mine, but why had she chosen that? She could not know the significance of it to me. I prayed she did not.

She turned over one rune. '*Othel* reversed. *Othel*, the home. You think of your home long ago, but reversed means you are alone. You will be alone.'

Did that mean they wouldn't come? I tried not to think about the villagers, afraid that if I let my thoughts turn to them, somehow she'd see them in the runes.

'Now I'll ask them what you fear.' She picked up a second rune. 'This isn't a wolf rune. You don't fear a wolf. This is *Hagall* – hail. Threat and destruction. A battle.' She looked up at me. 'That's it, isn't it, a battle? Now what is the lie?'

I wanted her to stop. I knew if I scattered the runes I could stop her for tonight, but that would not finish it. There'd be other nights. Only if I let her continue did I stand any chance of ending this for good.

'*Beorc* reversed – the birch tree. The mother, but reversed. Your family dead, is that it? No . . . no, that's not the lie.'

She stared at me, her eyes widening in surprise, then she threw back her head and laughed. She picked up the tiny lock of beard and, pulling the binding loose, she held the hairs up in the wind, her other hand covering the runes.

She lifted her head and closed her eyes. '*Hagall*, Morrigan. *Hagall, Hagall, Hagall*.'

I heard the screams of women and children, the sounds of swords clashing, shouting and cursing. And above all the noise, I heard my own children crying out, begging me to help them. I turned this way and that looking for them. The night was too dark to see anything. I thrust a branch into the fire and pulled it out, but the wind immediately snuffed out the flame. The wind was roaring, but above its shrieking I could hear my little sons screaming from beyond the cross. They were crying for me, calling out to me over and over again, fear and desperation in every sob. They were out there on the marsh. They were in danger and they needed me. I had to get to them. I ran past the cross, towards the end of the spur. I could see their dark shapes in the marsh, their arms held out to me. They were sinking before my eyes. If I could stretch out to them, grab an arm, a hand, anything. I began to scramble down the edge of the island, slipping and sliding on the wet grass towards the marsh. My foot sank into the cold, dark, oily water. I felt myself falling. I tried to grab a tussock to stop myself, but the wet grass slid through my hands. I was sinking.

30. Truth

My leg had slipped up to the thigh into the cold, muddy water, before something heavy collided with me. Hands caught hold of me, yanked me upwards and thrust me aside and by the light of the lantern on the cross I saw two shapes dart past me. I turned just in time to see one of the figures slide up behind Narigorm and thrust a sack over her head. At once the sound of battle and screaming ceased. I could hear only Narigorm's muffled cries as she struggled. William – I could see it was him from his massive outline – was trying to stuff something under the sack into her mouth and cursing loudly as she bit him. Gunter was trying to bind her hands behind her. But before he could secure her another figure leaped at him.

'Leave her, leave her alone.'

It was Adela. She had woken. She was beating Gunter with her stave. He dropped Narigorm's rope and tried to protect his head, cowering under the blows that Adela rained down on his back. I moved swiftly, grabbing Adela's up-raised arm and jerking her backwards. She fell awkwardly, crying out in pain. I pinned her to the ground from behind.

Narigorm was fighting for her life. She had thrown off the ropes and it was all William could do to hold her. Two other men came running up the spur from beyond the cross. They grabbed Narigorm and held her as William and Gunter struggled to tie the ropes round the thrashing girl.

Behind the men, I saw Rodrigo stirring. He tried to roll to his knees, still drugged by the poppy juice.

'Get the girl out of here,' I shouted to William, then realized none of them could hear me. They had taken me at my word and stuffed their ears. If Rodrigo found his feet and his stave ... I took a gamble. I let Adela go and, snatching up her stave, covered the few yards to Rodrigo. I brought the end of her stave down hard across his shoulders; he groaned and slumped back down into the grass.

William slung Narigorm over his shoulder and all four men hurried down the spur and disappeared below the cross. In the darkness I heard the splashing of the oars before the sound was borne away on the wind.

I walked to the cross and crouched down with my back to it, staring out into the impenetrable darkness of the marsh beyond. Behind me I could hear Adela sobbing, trying to rouse Osmond and Rodrigo. Little Carwyn was wailing, but even the sounds of the wind tearing at the rushes seemed muffled as if my ears too were stuffed with wax.

What had I become? Was I that demon which stared out at me from the mirror? Had I truly become that foul thing? I thought of a child lying bound and gagged in the icy water at the bottom of a boat, being tossed up and down, unable to see where she was going or who had taken her. I imagined her terror, wondering what these strangers were going to do to her. And I knew they were going to kill her. I didn't know how, but I knew it would not be gentle. They had to do it thoroughly. What would they choose? Drowning? Hanging? Burning? I shuddered. What had Rodrigo said? 'You should not take the name of death in vain.'

She'd asked the runes, 'What was the lie?' There were so many and I had meant them well. My lies had brought hope where there was none. I'd believed mine was the greatest of all the arts, the noblest of all the lies, the creation of hope. I thought hope could overcome everything, but I was wrong. Hope cannot overcome truth. They cannot coexist. Truth destroys hope. The most savage cruelties man inflicts on man are committed in the pursuit of truth. My last lie had been the most honest, the most honourable of them all, for there is an art greater even than the creation of hope. The greatest art of all is the destruction of truth.

The clouds opened before morning. An icy-cold rain beat down with a savage ferocity in the wind. I welcomed the stinging of my face and hands; it felt like a penance, a cleansing. I sat there in front of the cross accepting the rain's whipping, until the candle in the lantern died and the pale grey dawn drenched the marshes in light. Behind me, the others stirred. Adela, unable to rouse either Osmond or Rodrigo, had taken Carwyn in her arms and cried herself to sleep. Now they were awake, I would have to face them. I only prayed I could make them understand that I had done it to save them.

Adela sat inside the hermit's hut and Rodrigo and Osmond huddled at the doorway. Adela had clearly recounted the events of the night before, for as I approached Osmond leaped up and seized my arm. His brow furrowed with anxiety.

'Who were they who came last night and where have they taken Narigorm?'

I thought about telling him I didn't know, inventing some tale of having dragged Adela away from Gunter to keep her from being hurt, even my hitting Rodrigo to keep him from harm. They would have believed me. They wanted to believe that. They did not want the truth; as Rodrigo had said, who but a priest does? But I was too weary to create a lie for them, too tired to make it well again for them. I needed to confess. I had no strength left to do otherwise.

'Villagers took Narigorm.'

Adela's eyes were red and swollen. 'But why did you pull me off them? I could have stopped them. I tried –'

'You were no match for four big men. There was nothing you could have done. It wasn't your fault.'

'We'll have to go after them and rescue her,' Osmond said. 'Where's their village? I can't understand why I slept through all that commotion, Rodrigo too. Adela said she couldn't wake us.'

Rivulets of silver water began to trickle around the stones in the grass. I wondered if this rain would go on falling until the next Midsummer's Day.

'I drugged you so you wouldn't wake. They would have hurt you if you'd fought them. They were determined to take her.'

All three of them stared at me, shock on every face.

Osmond rubbed his forehead. 'But I don't understand. If you knew they were coming, why didn't you warn us? We could have hidden her. We could have beaten them if we'd been prepared. And anyway, how did you know they were going to come?'

I was exhausted, couldn't they see that? Why were they asking me these questions? What did it matter? They were safe now, didn't they understand that?

Rodrigo winced as he moved his back. 'Why have they taken her, Camelot?'

'They were afraid of her white hair. They thought if she combed it, it would stir up the white waves of a storm.' I was sorry I'd hurt him. I must have hit him hard.

'Then we must tell them we'll take her away from here,' Osmond said quickly. 'They needn't be –'

'I think that is not the only reason,' Rodrigo broke in. 'You knew they were coming. Why did they take her, Camelot?' he repeated. There was a cold anger in his eyes as if he already knew the answer.

I took a deep breath and met his gaze steadily. 'You wouldn't believe the danger you were in from her, so I went to them. They were already afraid of her. It was easy to persuade them that she was dangerous. I believe she would have turned on them, once she'd finished with us, so that much of what I told them was not a lie. I convinced them they had to get rid of her.'

'And what will they do with her?'

This time I couldn't meet his gaze. 'They will . . . kill her. They have to. It's the only way to stop her.'

Adela clapped her hands to her mouth, her eyes wide with horror.

Osmond, already pale, was swaying as if he was about to be sick. 'No, Camelot, you wouldn't do such a thing, a kind old man like you, to trick a group of villagers into murdering an innocent child. You couldn't.'

Rodrigo was on his feet. He came unsteadily towards me. For a moment I thought he was going to hit me and I almost wanted him to. If he had beaten me half to death, I would have welcomed the pain of it, the punishment of it. But instead he stared at me as if he didn't know who I was.

'You have murdered a child and you did not even have the courage to kill her with your own hands. *Il sangue di Dio!* I have killed men, but at least I thrust in the knife myself, I did not get others to do it for me.'

He raised his fist as if he was going to punch me. I braced myself, but the blow didn't fall. He shook his head.

'I cannot bring myself to touch you,' he said in disgust. 'You are a coward, Camelot, a filthy coward.'

He spat into my face. I did not wipe it away.

'Go. Go now and get as far away from us as you can, for if I ever see your monstrous face again I shall kill you with my bare hands. And make no mistake; unlike you, I am man enough to do it.'

I picked up my pack and walked away without looking back. As I passed her, Xanthus pricked up her ears and gave a little whinny, but I could not trust myself even to pat her. I walked until I was far enough away from the camp for them not to hear and then I wept uncontrollably, like a child.

31. St Uncumber

I was finally going home, returning at last to the wild, lonely hills they call the Cheviots. There was no other place left for me to go, no other place on the face of the land where I could take refuge. I ached for it. I needed to touch it, to smell it, to bury myself deep in its earth. Only that instinct kept me walking, one step, then another and another. Like an animal hunted beyond exhaustion, even dying I would have crawled to reach my home.

But what is home? I had asked myself that question on the day it all began, a day that seemed like a lifetime ago. And I asked it again, tumbling it over and over in my mind as I trudged northwards. Is home the place where you were born? To the old that has become a foreign country. Is it the place where you lay your head each night? If that were so, then every ditch, barn and forest in the land I should name as home, for I've slept in most of them. Is it the place which has soaked up the blood of your ancestors? That's the home of the dead, not the living. Is home then the place that holds your loved ones? Not when the one you love is absent.

It has taken me months, years perhaps, to fathom the answer. Home is the place you return to when you have finally lost your soul. Home is the place where life is born, not the place of your birth, but the place where you seek rebirth. When you no longer remember which tale of your own past is true and which is an invention, when you know that *you* are an invention, then is the time to seek out your home. Perhaps only when you have come to understand that, can you finally reach home.

I had travelled through a devastated landscape, skirting deserted villages and empty barns. Crops, beaten down into the mud, lay unharvested, rotting to the colour of the dirt from which they sprang. Pastures were eerily silent, sheep and cattle dead or wandered off to fend for themselves. No smoke rose from the hearths of houses. No hammer blows echoed from the blacksmith's forge.

Once, children's voices had shrieked through windows; now weeds scrambled out through the empty casements. Thatch slumped to the ground and doors swung back and forth in the wind with the hollow banging of a leper's clapper. The churches still stood proudly, but they were hollow and empty. The market crosses rose in silence and no hands touched them to swear or seal a bargain. Little children and feeble old men wandered among the silent cottages, waiting for someone to return for them, but no one ever came. Once, among the black-crossed houses, I saw a man hang himself. He had survived and that was too much for him to bear.

The roads were full of people on the move, some travelling alone, their families dead or abandoned, some in groups making for the towns where there might be a hope of food or work. Some were mad with horror and grief; others were hardened to the point where they would cut a man's throat for a handful of dry beans. And if they did, no one lifted a finger to stop them, for there were no courts left to try a man and no executioners to hang him. Sometimes I wondered if God too had died up there in His heaven, if heaven stood silent and boarded up, the angels left rotting on pavements of gold.

Every village and town had its pits and, between them, smoking piles of leaves and rags. Once, on common land outside a village, I drew near a small knot of people silently watching at a distance as masked men swung the bodies of adults and children by arms and legs and tossed them into the mass grave. One child seemed to cry out and a mother in the group tried to run towards the pit, but others caught her and held her back.

'Gas escaping from the body is all,' one man muttered and the child was tossed in with the rest. 'You think you see an arm move or a chest expand,' he said, 'but it's only putrefaction. Doesn't do to look at them. Just swing and throw.' His voice was dead, without emotion, as if he described the harrowing of the fields.

One of the women in the little group turned away and as she did so she glanced briefly in my direction. Then she stopped and stared.

'I remember you.'

She looked vaguely familiar, but I couldn't place her. Me, with my scar, no one ever forgets me. I smiled faintly by way of acknowledgement and walked away, but she came hurrying after me.

'Wait, you were with the two musicians who played at our village once, for the Cripples' Wedding. Good-looking lads they were, especially the young one.'

'And you wore a yellow kirtle.'

She smiled. 'Fancy you remembering that.'

'There was a fight over you if I recall.'

She grimaced. 'Those two musician friends of yours, are they here?' She glanced around hopefully.

Tears welled up in my eye and, furious with myself, I dashed them away. I shook my head.

She turned her face away. No one asks any more what has happened to those who have disappeared. I was grateful for that.

'The wedding, did it keep the village safe?'

She shrugged. 'Is anywhere safe? But in any case I left soon after the wedding. Edward was the jealous type, used his fists too often, like his father. I'd seen what I was in for after we were wed. I ran off with another lad, but that didn't last. I get by; there are still men who'll pay for a good time, more so now when they think it might be their last chance.' She jerked her head in the direction of the pit. 'Reckon it's best if you don't have anyone you care about, then it can't hurt you. Don't have to be afraid of losing someone, if you've no one to lose.' A shadow passed across her face. 'I'm sorry about the musicians though,' she added. 'He was handsome, that boy.'

I turned to go, then stopped and reached into my pack. 'Wait. Take this. It's valuable. It's a relic of St Benedict. You can sell it. It'll buy you food and shelter for a long time.'

Once I would have told her it would keep her safe from the pestilence, but I knew that neither she nor I could believe that any more.

She drew back her hands. 'Why are you giving it to me?'

'A penance for a crime I've committed.'

'I can't pray for you. I don't pray for anything any more. What's the point?'

'That's why I am giving it you. I don't want to trade it

for prayers. I am beyond prayers. I want you to have it because you remember.'

'Thank you, master.'

'Master,' she called me. She was the last one to call me that.

I had travelled as fast as I could, certain that I would arrive too late. But when I reached the gates of the manor I saw with relief that there were no boards on the windows, no cross on the door. Then I stopped, afraid to go in. I don't know what I feared most, that I would see that look of loathing in their eyes that I had seen in Rodrigo's or that they would not even know who I was. I waited outside the gates for hours. People passing in and out no doubt took me for a beggar, but then I heard a voice at my elbow. A face I didn't recognize, yet I knew the eyes.

'It is you. I've been watching you all day to be sure. My mother always said you'd come back.'

'You know me?'

'I'd not have done, but for your scar. You'll not remember me. Cicely, Marion's daughter. She was dairymaid in your day. She often talked of you, of that day when you got your scar. I was too young to remember that, but I remember the day you left.'

'Marion . . . yes, I remember her. Is she well?'

Cicely's face clouded. 'She died, years ago. You've been away a long time.'

'And my sons?'

She hesitated. 'Nicholas is lord now.'

'The youngest. Then Philip and Oliver are dead.'

She pressed her lips together. 'But Nicholas'll be right pleased to see you. I've often heard him tell his children about you. Mind you, I dare say the tale has grown big enough over the years to wag itself, but then you'll be able to set him right.'

'I have grandchildren?'

She beamed. 'You have, and a great-grandchild too.'

Those steps into the manor were the longest and hardest I've taken for years, harder even than the steps I trod in leaving it. I couldn't believe that anyone I knew was still alive and I was more afraid to meet them than I would have been to see their ghosts. I knew ghosts. I'd travelled with them for a long time. I was no longer afraid of the dead, only of the living.

Every time I closed my eyes I saw her face and heard her cries for help. What had Cygnus said? 'No one who brings harm to a child can ever be forgiven.' And I had murdered her. No, not murdered, Rodrigo was right, for what I had done had been far worse than that. I was the most despicable of all cowards, for I had persuaded others to kill for me. How could Rodrigo know the pain and self-loathing which comes from that? I thought of the little girl the cordwainer had killed. He had done it himself with his bare hands, stared her terror and pain straight in the face. Was that less cowardly than what I had done?

But when I closed my eyes I would also remember the expression of triumph on Narigorm's face as she forced Rodrigo to his knees in the pool of poison and then I was not sorry. Not sorry when I thought of Pleasance and Cygnus and Jofre and yes, even poor Zophiel. Narigorm is dead and Rodrigo, Adela, Osmond and Carwyn are alive. She cannot hurt them now. She cannot hurt any one any more with her game of truth. And I would do it again, if by killing I could keep those I love safe.

The truth? Yes, I think it is time for that now, long past

time. Narigorm discovered the truth about me that last night when she held St Uncumber's beard to the wind. St Uncumber had to pray for her disfigurement; I was given mine.

I was, as I think you have already guessed, a woman once, a long time ago, and now I am again. My maid dresses me in kirtle and wimple. My grandchildren call me grandam, but still I forget. I forget how to sit and how to stitch tapestries and how to do all those things which make us women. But they forgive me because I'm old, a curiosity with strange tales to tell that they like to hear, but do not quite believe. They even forgive my scar now for when you're old you are sexless. Men's beards fall out and women's chins sprout hairs. Men grow plump dugs while women's breasts shrink to flaps and the skin on your belly hangs so loose who can tell what it covers, when what it covers no longer stirs despite your daydreams. And when the worms strip our corpses to the bone, who can name the mistress or the master, the beauty or the beast? And I've been all those in my time. Daughter, wife, mother – those too. Now I learn I am a widow, but I might as well have been a widow then for all the husband he was.

The crusades to the Holy Land were long over, but the Pope declared that fighting the Turks was still a holy war, a sacred duty, a noble cause, and gave his blessing to looting, murdering and raping round half the world in search of stolen wealth and glory. I gave my husband three healthy sons. They slithered out as regularly as lambs from a ewe and my husband stayed long enough to be sure he had spawned an heir and a spare, then he was off, away for years fighting the Turks, leaving me to mind his lands at home, raise his children and protect his property. But we got by well enough without him. To tell the truth, none of us could remember what he had done when he was at home, so it hardly seemed to matter if he came back or not, until the Scots decided to pay us a visit.

It was not an army, you understand, more a drunken rabble who'd scarcely been bothered to polish their weapons, not expecting any resistance with half the able-bodied men away. I heard the shouts of the men, the over-turning furniture and smashing of pots. Then I heard the screams of my children crying out in fear. I knew the servants would simply scatter in terror without someone to urge them to resist. But I would not let them hurt my children, not as long as I had breath enough to stop them. I was sick with fear, but I heard my father's voice ringing in my ears, 'Better he come home on a shield than as a coward.' So I put on a helmet and picked up a sword.

Anger can give you the strength of a man. Fear can make you far stronger. I managed to get in half a dozen creditable strokes before the blow fell on me. The servants were shamed into staying to fight and, ill prepared for any kind of resistance, the Scots fled with the job only half done. I was wounded, yes, but not quite dead. A glancing blow, the servants told me later, else it would have hewn my skull in two. They said St Michael himself must have been watching over me. If he was, his attention wandered, for the wound was deep, cutting right down to the gleaming white bone beneath. It took my eye and split my nose. Not that I knew or cared at the time.

For several weeks I lay in my husband's bed, drifting in and out of a drugged sleep and raging fever. Finally the fever broke and I got up, shaky as a newborn lamb, but what else could I do? There was still a manor to run. My wound healed well enough in time, but it left a vivid purple scar. My nose was spread half across my cheek and I had one empty eye socket, but I was alive and we carried on much as we had before.

My brave husband came back from fighting the Turks and brought me a robe of silk and a necklace of human teeth. He sat up night after night by his hearth telling tales of battle. Apparently the Turks are ten times more ferocious and fearless than the Scots. 'Perhaps we should invite them here to drive the Scots back,' I suggested, and he laughed, but he didn't kiss me. That's when I learned the truth about scars. A man with a battle-scar is a veteran, a hero, given an honoured place at the fire. Small boys gaze up fascinated, dreaming of winning such badges of courage. Maids caress his thighs with their buttocks as they bend over to mull his ale. Women cluck and cosset, and if in time the other men grow a little weary of that tale of honour, then they call for his cup to be filled again and again till he is fuddled and dozes quietly in the warmth of the embers.

But a scarred woman is not encouraged to tell her story. Boys jeer and mothers cross themselves. Pregnant women will not come close for fear that if they look upon such a sight, the infant in their belly will be marked. You've heard the tales of Beauty and the Beast no doubt. How a fair maid falls in love with a monster and sees the beauty of his soul beneath the hideous visage. But you've never heard the tale of the handsome man falling for the monstrous woman and finding joy in her love, because it doesn't happen, not even in fairytales. The truth is that the scarred woman's husband buys her a good thick veil and enquires about nunneries for the good of her health. He spends his days with his falcons and his nights instructing pageboys in their duties. For if nothing else, the wars taught him how to be a diligent master to such pretty lads.

So I handed my name to my niece, a flawless, whey-faced

virgin. Told her she could use it how she pleased. My only regret was leaving my little sons. But I had seen them shudder as they looked at me and watched them stare at the floor when they were forced to speak with me, and I knew they were ashamed to own me as their mother. So I put on a man's garb and set off to see where the road would take me. And there I found a use for my scar; it was the provenance of my relics and for this they paid me well.

If I had told Rodrigo the truth about myself, would he have forgiven me? Would it have made a difference that I was a woman? Would he still have called me coward? Probably he'd have called me worse, for the world thinks that for a man to kill a child is cowardice, for a woman it is crime beyond punishment. But it matters to me what he thinks, for Narigorm was right. I loved Rodrigo. I still do. I think he was the only man I ever loved. Would he have loved me, if he'd known? No, I'd have seen him recoil in revulsion; he is a man after all and I am a scarred woman, an old woman. Better he should hate me for being a coward than loathe me for being what I am.

Sometimes I take out the tear of Venice and hold it up to the light and remember those nights in the rain and the nights under the stars; the way the sunlight turned Xanthus's coat to fire and firelight reflected in Jofre's eyes as he sang and the way Rodrigo looked at him. I would have liked to have seen that city of light and the streets where Rodrigo played as a boy. I would have liked to have heard the music of the Jews as they danced at their weddings. But who knows if there are any Jews left in Venice now or even children to play in the streets?

In any case I am glad my travelling days are over. Here I sit surrounded by my son and my grandchildren and great-grandchild in the warmth and comfort of a solid house.

I sleep in a soft bed and sit in a comfortable chair. I only have to raise my little finger for maids to coming running with possets and mulled wine. I'm content to end my days here. What more could anyone ask?

Cicely comes into the solar now. She drops a curtsy.

'If you please, mistress, there's a child at the door begs leave to speak with you.'

'A child from the village?' I smile. There've been a lot of those. Some sent by their mothers with a small gift to welcome me home, some just curious to see if my face is really as terrible as their brothers and sisters have whispered.

'Oh no, mistress, she's not from round here. I've never seen this one before and she's not a child you'd be likely to forget if you had.'

'Why?' I ask, though I am too warm and drowsy to care.

'A strange-looking little thing she is, hair like my old mother's before she died. White, I don't mean blonde, white like skimmed milk and her skin's so pale, it's not natural, if you know what I mean. Still she can't help that, can she? She's such an innocent little smile, you can't help but be drawn to her.'

Suddenly, I am wide awake. An icy chill runs down my spine. The room seems to sway. It can't be. It's not possible.

Cicely puts out her hand. 'Are you ill, mistress? You've gone quite pale.'

'You're sure she asked for me?'

'Oh yes, mistress, she was very particular. It's you she wants. She seems to know all about you. Shall I let her in?'

Historical Notes

Eyewitness accounts differ as to exactly when the Black Death entered Britain; dates range from June 1348 to as late as the autumn of that year. Several towns and villages have claimed the unhappy title of being the site of the first outbreak, from Melcombe in Dorset, now part of Weymouth, to Southampton and Bristol. There probably was no single point of entry and a number of ships from the Channel Islands and Europe may have carried the plague to various ports in England within weeks of one another.

Although we now refer to the terrible epidemic which devastated Europe in the Middle Ages as the Plague or the Black Death, in fact neither of these terms was used until centuries later. At the time it was known as the Pestilence, the Great Mortality or, in France, *morte bleue*, from the bruises on the skin resulting from subdural haemorrhaging. Contemporary accounts suggest that the plague did not just affect humans; sheep, cattle, horses and pigs also died from it.

We now believe that not one but three plagues raged across Europe in 1348 – Bubonic Plague, spread by rat fleas, characterized by buboes or swellings in groins and armpits, which brings about death in two to six days; Pneumonic

Plague, attacking the lungs, which is spread through coughing and breathing; and Septicaemic Plague, where the bacteria enter the bloodstream, causing death within the day.

It is now thought that many of the victims in Britain in the 1348/1349 outbreak died from the more infectious Pneumonic Plague, spreading directly from human to human, although later outbreaks may well have been Bubonic Plague.

The 1348 plague was only the latest in a series of disasters to hit Britain. The period between 1290 and 1348 had seen a rapid and drastic climate change which was so noticeable that the Pope ordered special prayers to be said daily in every church. Eyewitness accounts claimed that 1348 was a particularly bad year, for it rained every day from Midsummer's Day to Christmas Day. Climate change brought about crop failure, liver fluke in sheep and murrain in cattle, as well as causing widespread flooding which virtually wiped out the salt industry on the east coast. This, combined with a population explosion, meant that as many people died from starvation as from the plague itself.

Many different causes for the plague were proposed by the Church and others, including divine punishment, bad air, imbalance of humours, overeating and vampires. At that time it was considered heresy by the Church not to acknowledge the existence of vampires and werewolves. Jews were also accused of causing the plague by poisoning the wells and were attacked and murdered right across Europe. Despite the Pope declaring that the Jews were not to blame for the pestilence and forbidding anyone to harm them, in Strasbourg on St Valentine's Day 1349, two thousand Jews were offered the choice between forced baptism and death. Many, including babies and children, were burned alive on a wooden platform in the cemetery. Even in

England, anti-Jewish hysteria was widespread, despite all Jews having been expelled from Britain in 1290.

In desperation people tried anything to stop the plague spreading, including the curious custom of the 'Cripples' Wedding'. This practice was widespread across Britain and Europe in the Middle Ages and continued for many centuries as a means of warding off the spread of deadly epidemics. The last known recorded case I have found was in Krakow in Poland in the late nineteenth century.

During the Middle Ages, there was a lively, though illegal, trade in second-hand monks' robes which were used to dress the corpses of the wealthy in order to fool the devil. Sometimes this was taken as far as depicting the deceased in a monk's habit on the brasses on top of the tombs. This practice may also have been to deter grave robbers, who might draw the line at disturbing the resting place of a holy man, especially if they believed that a poor monk would be buried with nothing of value.

The depiction of the Virgin as Mary *Misericordia* became popular as a protective icon against the plague. The earliest surviving example was painted in 1372 by the artist Barnaba of Modena for the Cathedral in Genoa, but I have taken a fiction writer's liberty of assuming that, since even the most insignificant medieval churches and chapels in England and Europe were covered in frescoes, there may have been earlier depictions of the *misericordia* by unknown artists which did not survive the ravages of time or the Reformation. Around this time, too, artists in Europe were beginning to experiment with the use of oil to bind the paint on walls. Most of these early experiments were not successful and the paintings decayed rapidly after a few years.

*

All the places named in the novel are real. St John Shorne's shrine became one of the main pilgrimage sites in England, attracting pilgrims from all over Europe, even though John Shorne was never canonized. The shrine of this people's saint attracted so much wealth that his remains were eventually taken to St George's Chapel in Windsor in 1478, when the chapel was rebuilt by Edward IV, where they were interred in the south choir aisle. The saint's boot was also put on display there. Income from pilgrims visiting John's remains was said to be worth £500 a year to the chapel at Windsor at the time of the Reformation. John Shorne's well at North Marston continued to be visited by the sick up to the late 1800s, and in such numbers that houses for invalids had to be built to accommodate them. The entrance to the well can still be seen in the village today, though sadly it is now kept locked.

Since the draining of the fens, the poison hollows have disappeared from the east coast of England. However, transient hollows, where marsh gas seeps up from rotting vegetation beneath the ground, still appear and disappear from time to time on Dartmoor and in Scotland, Ireland and Scandinavia. In areas where such hollows have existed, you also frequently find a local legend about a Sending.

In the Middle Ages, runes were used for divination and casting spells. As is shown in the Anglo-Saxon poem, the *Hávamál* of the Elder Edda, it was a basic requirement of a rune master to know how to perform 'the Sending'. Rune casting was fiercely condemned by the medieval Church as witchcraft and was poorly documented. So we have little knowledge about which futhark (or alphabet) was used by medieval rune readers in Britain or the interpretation they put upon the castings.

Whilst there is broad agreement on the meaning of the

runic symbols, each rune reader interprets the castings in different ways, since they regard runes as a tool to help them connect with the subconscious rather than as a fixed language. Modern rune readers would interpret the castings made by Narigorm in a different and, one hopes, kinder way. As history continues to show us, any system of belief or religion can be used to help or harm depending on the knowledge and intent of the individual.

Glossary

Avering   A medieval con-trick performed by beggars to obtain money. Some beggars would strip themselves, hide their clothes and pretend to have been robbed. Others would fake illnesses by sticking on fake boils made of wax, or tumours made from raw offal, to get alms from townspeople or the Church.

Barbette   A cloth band that went round the face of the wearer under the chin, which together with a band, known as a **fillet**, around the forehead, was the structure to which the veil, wimple or headdress was pinned. The barbette was worn by women throughout the thirteenth century, but by 1348 it was disappearing, to be replaced by a band that went round the back of the head instead of under the chin. The barbette was still retained by various orders of nuns well into the twentieth century.

Bastles and **Peles**   Unique features of the Border counties, especially Northumberland, where the constant raids and wars between the Scots and the English meant that people on both sides of the shifting border lived in fear of attack. **Peles** were oblong towers, built to withstand a siege, with stone walls about three to four feet thick, in which people could take refuge. Livestock and food were kept in the basement and people occupied the two or three storeys above. **Bastles** were fortified farmhouses where people would live all year round. They can still be seen today.

Boggart A mischievous imp or poltergeist inhabiting country areas. It caused destruction in cottages and farms, making things go bump in the night, causing weeds to spring up in fields and the cows' milk to dry up. It also played malicious tricks on travellers. It usually became attached to a particular place or family and would not leave.

Brawn and Sharp Sauce Fried brawn, known as *Braun Feyez*, was made from trimmings of the pig's head, trotters, tail and tongue boiled for hours with onions, spices and herbs. Once the liquid was reduced, the thick mass was left in a cold dish until the meats were set in jelly. The block of brawn was turned out, sliced and fried in lard or butter. It was served with a sour vinegar sauce, *Gruant Tartez*, to offset the rich, greasy meat.

Camelot A medieval peddler or hawker who also sold or carried news. Camelots had a reputation for trading in goods that were not always genuine or might have fallen off the back of a cart. The name is still used today in France for a street peddler or newspaper seller.

Cordwainer A shoemaker who worked in cordwain or cordovan leather, which was a fine red leather imported from Spain and used to make the best-quality shoes and boots. Eventually, *cordwainer* became the name for all shoe-makers.

Corpse Road Only parish churches were licensed to bury corpses, so villagers in outlying areas would often be obliged to carry their dead many miles across moors, hills or forests to bury them. These ways were marked by a series of stone or wooden crosses to guide the mourners. The last known use of a corpse road was in 1736 in Cumbria, between the village of Mardale Green and Shap parish church, a distance of around 6 miles (10 km) over steep hills.

Cote-hardie   An open-sleeved supertunic. For men, this was worn over a gipon (q.v.) and shirt. Tight-fitting across the chest, it flared into a skirt below the waist, open in front and reaching to the knees. Old and poorer men wore a looser and longer cote-hardie reaching to the calves. As the century progressed, fashionable men wore the cote-hardie shorter and shorter until it barely covered the hips.

Deodand   From *deo dandum*, 'given to God'. Any object or animal which caused the death of a person was declared *deodand* and it or its value was forfeit to the Crown. This might include a horse that trampled someone, a tree that the deceased had fallen from, a chimney that had collapsed on them, or a hoe that had accidentally hit them.

Faith Cakes   St Faith, third-century virgin and martyr, was patron saint of pilgrims and prisoners. She was martyred by being roasted alive on a brazen bed. When that failed to kill her, she was beheaded. On her feast, 6 October, people ate cakes griddled on hot irons, ensuring safe and successful pilgrimages.

Fret   An open-weave ornamental net which covered the hair. Wealthy women might have frets fashioned from silver or gold thread, or even studded with semi-precious stones.

Gipon   An under-tunic worn over a shirt and under the cote-hardie (q.v.). Close-fitting and slightly waisted, a man's gipon reached to the knees, with tightly fitting sleeves. The bodice was often padded for warmth and protection.

Golem   From the Hebrew, meaning *unformed*. In kabbalistic magic, soil or clay was made into the statue of a man and brought to life by placing a slip of paper under its tongue on which was written the tetragrammaton (the four-letter name of God). The resulting zombie-like being would only obey the master who had made him and was immensely strong and destructive, but very stupid. Christians came to believe that any book or paper with Hebrew lettering could be used to animate a golem.

Hue and Cry   The first person to discover a robbery or a body was legally obliged to raise the hue and cry, in other words sound the alarm and rouse his neighbours. On hearing this, all able-bodied men had to start hunting down the perpetrator. Failure to comply with this law meant heavy fines for the individual and often the whole community.

Kirtle   A gown worn by women. By the first half of the fourteenth century, the kirtle was cut to reveal the body shape, and moulded to the figure as far as the hips where it widened into folds which swept to the ground.

Livery   The aim of most minstrels was to obtain a livery, that is, gain a permanent position in a wealthy household. They would then wear the colours or emblems of the lord who employed them. This not only ensured a comfortable and secure employment, but meant they could charge their expenses to the lord's account if they had to travel. The penalties for wearing a lord's livery when you were not employed by him were severe.

Marzapane   The sweet which came to be called march-pane and then marzipan in England. Although some cities in Europe claim to have invented it when there was a drought and almonds were the only crop to survive, most researchers believe it was actually invented in the Middle East around the eighth century and was brought to Venice by returning crusaders. Since sugar was a key ingredient it was expensive. It only became widely used in England in the fifteenth century.

Midden   The place in a garden or courtyard used to dump kitchen waste, the contents of chamber pots, soiled rushes and manure from cleaning byres and yards.

Mutton Olives   A mixture of suet, onion, herbs and spices was spread on thin, beaten slices of mutton. The stuffed mutton slices were rolled up, skewered and baked in butter. The mutton olives were served sprinkled with crumbled hardboiled egg yolks and yet more spices.

Nixie   A beautiful, but evil, female water sprite. Their skins were said to be white or translucent like water.

Palfrey   A small, docile horse or pony, most commonly used by ladies or clerics who, hampered by their long robes or inexperienced at riding, found larger mounts hard to handle.

Pinfold   A stone or wooden enclosure, usually circular, used to corral animals at night. Often to be found on drovers' roads, so that herdsmen and drovers could safely contain the flocks while they slept. The term was also used for a pound where stray or confiscated animals could be held until the owner paid his fine.

Posset   Unlike the rich dish of eggs and cream which it was later to become, the medieval posset was a warming drink simply made from hot milk slightly curdled with ale or wine. It was sweetened with honey and flavoured with spices such as ginger, cloves and cinnamon. It was thought particularly effective at warding off chills.

Pottage   The main staple dish eaten at least once a day by everyone, rich or poor. Varying between a thin broth and a very thick stew, its base would be a herb, vegetable or meat stock, to which cereals, peas, beans, vegetables, meat or fish would be added depending on the wealth of the person and the season of the year

Scots and Tithes   As well each household having to give tithes, a percentage of livestock, grain, candles, etc., to the

Church on pain of minor excommunication, the Church also demanded scots, or sums of money, to perform certain rites such as christenings and marriages, including a soul-scot for burials.

Scrip   A leather bag used by pilgrims and travellers to carry small items.

Sending   People believed that warlocks and witches had the power to conjure a Sending, in the form of an animal or insect which could travel hundreds of miles to kill the victim. Often these were sent against wrongdoers who had fled or those from the community who had broken a promise to return home. Victims would feel its approach for several hours or days before it reached them and begin to feel sleepy, ill and terrified.

Trencher   A stale loaf of bread, usually four days old, cut into thick, slightly hollow slices, which would act as a plate on which the meal would be served. After the meal the trenchers which had soaked up the juices and gravies of the meal would be given to the poor or the dogs or pigs to eat.

Widdershins   To circle anticlockwise or against the sun, hence against nature, strengthening the forces of darkness. Going widdershins was often a feature of dark spells and conjuring the dead, therefore people were careful not to do it by accident for it would bring bad luck. But it could also be used to reverse the current state of affairs by turning a run of bad fortune into good.

Welcome to the Penguin and *newbooks* magazine reading group guide to *Company of Liars*. *newbooks* readers put forward the discussion points and posed the questions to Karen Maitland for the Q&A section.

This is the first jointly produced reading guide and we hope it will be particularly useful – a reading group guide determined by active members of reading groups across the country – and that Penguin and *newbooks* will go on to produce many more together.

Penguin would like to thank the following *newbooks* readers for their contribution to this reading group guide.

Miriam Bennett
Sue Corbett
Rebecca Gawith
Cheryl Kellaway
Mary Knight
Nicola Leedham
Hilary Letch
Beverley McWilliam
Chantel Sankey
Susan Sibson
Christine Yip
Andrew Yip
Sally Zigmond

Themes for further discussion

Character and Story
- We only have Camelot's voice telling us the story. How far do we trust this voice?
- Why did Narigorm do what she did? How would she have told the story?
- How old do you think the younger characters are? Why?
- Is Jofre a typical teenager in his concerns and behaviour?
- The story is very filmic – who would you cast in the principal roles and why?

Secrets and Lies
- Everyone in the book lies through expediency or fear of punishment. How many of those lies would be necessary today and why?
- Have our values changed in the centuries since medieval times? Do we still look for basic human goodness in people and expect wrongdoing to be punished?
- Have you told a lie and regretted it – or been found out?
- What if, one by one, your travelling companions are brutally murdered after telling the truth and you know that if you do likewise, you will be killed too. Would you lie then?
- Can a lie, however well intentioned, ever be harmless?
- Was everyone in the group a liar? Why did some survive but not others?

History and Context
- Is our society moving back towards superstitions and more basic beliefs, with more interest nowadays in herbal remedies, Reiki and courses on reading runes, for example?
- Who would be the modern-day equivalent of Narigorm?
- Is historical accuracy important in an historical novel? Or can too much accuracy kill a narrative?
- How important is the backdrop of the plague? Could the novel have been set in a different historical period and had the same impact?

Karen Maitland answers *newbooks* readers' questions below:

Have you ever told a necessary lie and did this influence your choice of theme for this group of travellers?

I was working in a hospital in Belfast at the height of 'the troubles'. A man was admitted to a side ward for treatment. Later, a young couple approached me saying they were trying to find a friend of theirs and naming this man. But I had an uneasy feeling they weren't intending to give him a get well card, so I lied about who was in the room. I later discovered they were armed and planning to shoot him. Incidents like that did influence the theme of the novel.

Another major influence was a rash of stories in the press about famous people headlined, '*The real truth behind…*' I wondered if you could ever have an unreal truth. People may pride themselves on telling the truth, and nothing but the truth, about themselves, but does anyone ever really tell the whole truth about themselves? Do you confess your darkest fantasies to your bank manager, your mother or even your lover?

'I had an uneasy feeling they weren't intending to give him a get well card, so I lied about who was in the room.'

The tales the individual travellers told have echoes of fairy tales, legends and myths swirling around them. As you grew up did this type of story influence you and perhaps lead to your ideas for the novel?

When I was a child a teacher read us the ancient story of The Six Swans. When the story ended, I asked what happened to the boy who was left with one wing. The teacher told me angrily that wasn't the point of the story, but I worried about him and spent weeks trying to do things with one hand to see how he'd manage.

I always read the myths and folk tales of any town or country I visit, because they tell you so much about the character of the place and people. Traditional myths and fairy tales contain great truths, more so than 'real-life' stories, so I wanted to use that style of storytelling in the novel, because a deep truth can be concealed in a fantasy story, even though the story itself is a lie.

'I worried about him and spent weeks trying to do things with one hand to see how he'd manage.'

4

I can't decide who is my favourite character; they are all so vivid in their own ways. Do you have a favourite?

My favorite character is the conjurer, Zophiel. Nasty people are always more fun to write. It's very cathartic, which is probably why crime and thriller writers seldom commit murder; we get it all out of our system on paper. But as a writer you also have to spend a lot of time thinking about what might have happened to the nasty characters earlier in their lives to make them so bitter and mean. Even if you don't include much of that back-story in the novel itself, as the author you have to know the 'why' of your character. I imagined the painful incidents in Zophiel's childhood, so I ended up feeling a great affection and compassion for him.

'It's very cathartic, which is probably why crime and thriller writers seldom commit murder.'

Which do you feel is more important in the novel? History or myth?

Both. One of the things that fascinate me about the medieval period is that people then didn't divide things into 'real' and 'unreal' in the way we do. They made no distinction between religion and science. Angels and demons, basilisks and witches were all part of everyday life. The Church believed in werewolves as much as it did in God. The great men of science and engineering also practiced alchemy and divination. Warriors would plan battles based equally on sound military tactics and on good omens. What we now call myth is as much part of the history of the Middle Ages as bad sanitation or great cathedrals.

'They made no distinction between religion and science. Angels and demons, basilisks and witches were all part of everyday life.'

With such a large cast of characters, all with their own story to tell, how difficult was it keeping to the first person narration and yet giving everyone a voice?

A first person narrator is regarded as the unreliable narrator, so since the novel is about lies, it seemed natural to use a first person narrative style. But before I began the novel I wrote detailed plots and back-stories separately for each character, trying to imagine I was telling only that character's story, then wove them together. Whilst writing the novel, I would often hot-seat a character and get them to tell me about themselves in their own words to ensure I was listening to their voice. But of course, everything then must be filtered through Camelot's perception, so the other characters might have told the story of the journey itself very differently.

'I would often hot-seat a character and get them to tell me about themselves in their own words to ensure I was listening to their voice.'

7

As an author you have the ability to create people and situations, does this make you an expert liar?

As a child you get punished for making up stories, as an adult you get rewarded for it. Storytellers are probably the better liars since they have to convincingly speak the lies in front of an audience. I think poets and romance writers must be the most expert liars of the literary world. But any story or poem is only half written by the author; the other half is created by the individual reader from their own unique imagination and experiences. A novel is a joint collaboration between writer and reader. So if authors are good liars, then I think readers must be too.

'I think poets and romance writers must be the most expert liars of the literary world.'

Are you superstitious? If so, are there any rituals you perform before putting pen to paper?

I read my horoscope in the papers, but if I don't like my own that day, I pick one of the others, which I think may be cheating.

I don't know if it's a superstition, but I never talk about a story, except to mention the basic subject, until the first draft is fully written. I don't worry the idea will be stolen; rather it's that I fear if I speak it, I won't be able to write it.

Before beginning a new story, I always spend time trying, and failing, to tidy my office, but that may not be so much a superstition as a pathetic excuse to put off starting work.

'I don't worry the idea will be stolen; rather it's that I fear if I speak it, I won't be able to write it.'